ROME'S CAPTIVE

AN ETERNAL GUARDIAN NOVEL

TASHA M TAYLOR

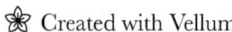

CHAPTER
ONE

God, it was so beautiful. She couldn't help but stare out the window and admire how the snow blanketed the forest around her. It was a regular sight to the rest of the world, but this was Alara's first time witnessing the beauty of actual snow. With her gloved hands and her bare face pressed firmly against the cool glass, she continued to stare in wonder as the Humvee drove swiftly through the snow and the hidden trail they seemed to be on. A harsh chuckle came from the driver's seat where her single guard sat with a cigarette perched between his lips.

When he spoke, his voice was thick with smoke and laughter. "I keep forgetting your ass ain't never been outside those damn walls." He took another pull from his smoke and smiled as he glanced back at her from the rearview mirror. "I'm sure there's a lot of firsts you've yet to experience, huh, doll?"

Alara cringed at the use of the nickname he insisted on calling her. He was right, though. She had yet to experience so many firsts and feared what he had in mind. For months, there had been talk around the facility about what they would expect of her within the coming days. The big boss was tired of waiting for her to be ready. Alara knew she never would be. She would never give Titan what they wanted. She had been a part of the facility for as long as she could remember and stuck within the walls for just as long. She was a captive—a prisoner. There was no other word for it, and tonight had been her first time outside those walls, although she had tried to escape several times before.

Something big had happened only hours ago. What sounded like a bomb had gone off before Titan had executed an evacuation protocol. She'd been rushed outside and into a waiting vehicle with only the clothing on her back. Every question she asked went unanswered, and of course, she'd gotten stuck with Blaine. He was one of the worst guards she had ever encountered within her twenty-eight years of life, and she had faced many of them. Blaine scared her simply because he had no moral compass. The man was a psychopath to the highest order. And although she had lived a sheltered life, she at least knew the signs of an unhinged man, and Blaine was one of those men. Lukas, the head of Titan Corp, insisted on him living as her guard 24/7, maybe because he was the most ruthless and would protect her at all costs. For the money, of course. Or maybe because of her fear of him because as long as he was around, she refused to test his limited patience. She knew just how cruel he could be when somebody tested that patience.

They hit a slight bump in the road that jostled the vehicle before Blaine swore violently and swerved to avoid a downed tree. They jerked to a sudden stop.

"What the fuck!" He cursed in annoyance. "Stay put, doll."

Alara watched as he climbed from the vehicle and slammed the door behind him. She jerked as far as the gold chain and collar around her neck would allow her to and stared out the front window as Blaine approached the downed tree in the middle of their path. With his attention elsewhere, she focused on the interior of the Humvee as she frantically searched for the keys that would release her from her chains. Alara wouldn't go so far as to remove the enhanced collar around her throat, but the chain had to go for her to get the hell away from Titan and what they wanted from her. She shivered slightly when a cold breeze blew in from the cracked window, and with it came the sound of someone trying to reach

Blaine through the communication device he always kept clipped to his hip. She quickly picked up on their conversation even as she searched for the damn keys to free herself.

"Come in, Team 1. It's home base; why have you stopped?" She didn't recognize the voice that spoke.

Blaine responded quickly and quietly as he circled the downed tree and drew his gun slowly from its holster. "There's a tree down in the middle of our route. It appears somebody cut it. Send back-up to my location immediately. I believe an escape attempt is imminent."

"Negative Team 1, there are no other heat signatures within a 5-mile radius of your stopped vehicle. Report the package is safe and find a way around your obstacle."

"I'm telling you something isn't right," Blaine snarled into the receiver after unclipping it from his belt.

Alara focused on him through the windshield as his gaze searched the forest around them, and he backtracked to the car. His gun was held loosely at his side in preparation for an attack, yet nothing could have prepared him for the dark shadow that dropped from the trees above and slammed the butt of a gun against his head. Blaine was instantly knocked unconscious. Alara froze for only a second before gripping the chain attached to her collar and yanking with all her might. She turned, shoved her feet against the back seat cushions, and used her legs to push her body as far away from the bars as possible. It refused to budge, and her fear increased. She wasn't sure what enemies Titan had precisely, but she knew they weren't normal, just like her. She refused to sit around and wait for those enemies to kidnap her, though. Or worse, kill her.

She was yanking at her chain uselessly when the back door swung open, and a behemoth of a man popped his head in and quickly unlocked the chain that kept her in place with the keys he had dangling from his fingertips. He did it in less than two minutes.

"Who are you?" She questioned hesitantly. She didn't sense danger from him; instead, she felt a kinship towards him that gave her pause.

He stepped back quickly as he spoke. His voice was smooth and refined with a hint of aggression. "Alara, we don't have much time, and I can't explain everything right now, but I need to get you out of here. You aren't safe; you haven't been for the entirety of your life. I haven't been able to help until now." He held his hand out, hoping she would grab it and follow.

She didn't. "I'm not going with you anywhere until I get answers. Better the enemy you know than the one you don't. Now, who are you?"

"God dammit, we don't have time for this!" He snatched the hood and mask from his face, and time stood still.

The biting cold sank into her as she scanned his face and forced herself to memorize everything about him. She knew him from somewhere, and yet Alara knew in her heart that she had never met him until this very moment. He was at least six foot three with a muscular build she could make out beneath his thick clothing. His hair was black and curly, falling to his shoulders and emphasizing the bronze of his skin. His features were harsh: a pointed nose, a rounded face that sported a 5 o'clock shadow, and a thin top lip with a thicker bottom that matched hers. She was starstruck. With thick, evenly plucked eyebrows that accentuated the misty gray of his eyes and brought out the light green, she could easily see within his pupils. She could see herself within the passive expression that clouded his face and recognized it, but what stood out the most was the crescent moon mark on the left side of his face, right in front of his ear. Alara had seen one before, on her own body. She recognized the man, and yet she couldn't place him. She didn't know him.

"How do I know you?" She inched forward to get a better look at him. He didn't just look familiar; he felt at home.

"Long story short, I'm the brother you've never met. Name's Alaric," He reached in and pulled her from the Humvee before removing his coat and placing it around her shoulders. "Like I said before, you aren't safe, and I need to get you out of here and as far away from Titan as possible. They'll send reinforcements as soon as they notice you guys have stopped. I need to remove the tracker in your hip and the collar, or your escape will be for nothing. Do you understand me?" He pulled a small controller from his pocket and removed a wicked-looking knife from his left boot before frowning. "I don't want to do this, but it's the only way."

Alara tried to focus on what she had just heard. She had a brother, a brother she'd never met until today. Sure, he could be lying, but that feeling in her gut that never steered her wrong said he was telling the truth. His face was also a dead giveaway since their features were so similar. On top of that new knowledge was the realization that Titan had put a tracker in her months ago after her last failed escape. She'd suspected as much. They'd told her that she had suffered an injury that needed immediate surgery, and yet Alara had no recollection of hurting herself or being hurt when the guards had finally caught up to her, but she'd felt a lump. They'd lied to her, and she wasn't surprised, but dammit, she'd been praying she was wrong. They'd tagged her like an animal.

She pulled the coat tighter to her body and frowned when she realized something else he'd said. "Wait, why do you have to remove the collar? It protects me and everyone around me."

He stared back. "Do you not want the ability to protect yourself?"

"I can't control it." She reached up and caressed the smooth gold band that encircled her throat and prevented her from using the powers she had been born with.

"Alara, there's a tracker in and on your body. That band doesn't just keep your powers in check. It also monitors your vitals and tracks your whereabouts. It must come off, but let me remove the tracker from your hip first. What do you say?"

It unsettled her, but did he expect her to say no? She'd been trying to escape for several months now. She'd failed at every turn. Here he was, giving her the freedom she'd been searching for. She was taking it, and hopefully, she wouldn't look back and regret her decision. Without overthinking the pain she was about to experience, Alara pulled up the jacket and undershirt and tugged down the hem of her jeans to bare her hip where a wicked-looking scar sat.

"This is going to hurt," he murmured seconds before he dug the tip of the blade right into her scar.

Her first instinct was to jerk back or punch him in the throat since he'd leaned down to get a better look at what he was doing, but she resisted. She'd experienced worse numerous times before, so she forced herself to stay as still as possible as he cut out the offending material within her body. It was like a burning sensation without the smell of burnt flesh or cauterized nerves, and it hurt just as bad. She watched as he removed the tracker before sliding it into his pocket. Before she could ask him what would happen next, he pressed a button on the small controller within his hand and felt her collar loosen before dropping into the snow at her feet.

Her powers flared up immediately. It wasn't slow or gradual in its pursuit for vengeance at being restrained and cut off from life. Alara didn't simply have one power; no, it would never be that easy for her. She had a few, but her primary ability was just too powerful. Sometimes, it was all-consuming and too much for her to control. She could siphon energy; whether that be someone's life force or another person's power, she could take it and make it her own. The collar protected humanity from the gift she couldn't seem to get a hold of. It had saved her from doing things she shouldn't be capable of doing. Her gloves gave her piece of mind, but they weren't something she always wore or even kept track of. As soon as Titan figured out what she could do, they'd created the collar and given her gloves that kept her powers concealed or nonexistent. She wore them now, yet her hands still felt like icicles. It saved many lives, but now she was free in every sense of the word, yet she didn't think this was the freedom she'd wanted.

Alara bent down to retrieve the collar and hopefully put it back on, but Alaric got to it first and quickly locked it around Blaine's throat after checking his pulse.

"I'm doing this to save your life." He moved towards a large pine tree covered in a blanket of snow and pulled a camouflage tarp back to reveal a small bookbag that he carried back to her. "A few things inside will help with your journey to where you're going. I can't go into detail, and I can't go with you. I need to cover your tracks and get rid of good ole Blaine before the cavalry arrives."

"And by getting rid of him, do you mean to kill him?" Her

stomach went queasy at the thought as distant memories she thought she'd suppressed years earlier pounded through her thoughts. She shoved them back.

"I can't very well leave him to tell them what truly happened here. They must believe he kidnapped you and turned his back on the company." He forced the backpack onto her shoulders and pulled her into his arms before she could compute what was happening.

He was hugging her tightly. So much warmth radiated from his body even without his jacket on, yet she was losing feeling in her fingers and toes. Alara felt that familiarity and pulled her arms around his waist to hug him back. Yet she made sure not to touch his skin with her own.

"This is surreal," she whispered, "I have so many questions. I need to know what's happening." She leaned back to stare up into his pensive expression just as the crackle of Blaine's walkie-talkie pierced through the air.

"Come in Team 1, why have you stopped?"

Alaric sighed heavily and pulled back. "Time to go angel." He smiled, but it didn't brighten his face. "Inside the bag I provided you, there's a map with your destination circled in bright red. Don't veer from the path. There's also a burner phone with my number saved. Only use it for emergencies. I need to go back to Titan and finish what I started, but they can't know I had anything to do with your release, at least not until all is said and done. Do you understand?"

She nodded as she watched Alaric lift Blaine into the back seat of the Humvee before he placed a set of handcuffs around his wrists and hooked him up to the chain. He moved fast and efficiently as he checked every inch of Blaine's body for any hidden keys or anything that could aid him in escape before he removed all pieces of communication equipment from his body and tossed them into the snow beneath the vehicle. He slammed the door and turned back to her with a more relaxed expression.

He pulled her in for another hug as he spoke again. "Head north, Alara, and don't look back. You'll know you've reached your destination when you have more questions than answers, but hope-fully, they can help you until I reach you in a few weeks."

"A few weeks?" She frowned, "Why so long?"

"Get moving, sis. I'm sure Titan will be coming soon, and I need to cover your tracks and get moving myself. If I'm not at my post within the hour, my cover will be blown to hell. Go north, now." He forced himself to release her and pushed her in the direction she needed to go, urgency spilling from his tone of voice.

Alara heard the concern within his voice and forced herself to trudge through the snow even as she glanced over her shoulder to watch him erase all traces of her presence. She stared until she lost sight of him through the trees, and darkness surrounded her. She removed the backpack and rifled through it until she touched some-thing that suspiciously felt like a large flashlight. Flicking it on, she searched for the map that was supposed to lead her in her direction and opened it up before returning the bag securely to her back. Small symbols within the corner of the map told her which mark-ings on the tree to follow, but when she shined her light on the surrounding trees, there were no markings to speak of. She kept walking, hoping that she had overlooked it or hadn't reached the markings yet, but still, she saw nothing. Shining the light higher up, she searched the bark for a telltale star—the marking Alaric had left behind—as the sound of rushing water reached her ears.

She frowned and moved the light back towards the map even as the ground fell from beneath her and sent her tumbling into a freezing river. Her scream pierced the eerie silence of the forest as water filled her lungs and dragged her beneath the surface. The water churned and tossed her every which way as the cold sank into her skin, numbing her already freezing body and dropping her core temperature to dangerous levels.

She screamed within her mind, hoping but knowing that no one could hear her cries for help. The darkness of the water pulled her deeper beneath the rushing liquid as she drifted unconscious.

CHAPTER
TWO

Miles away, within the more profound and denser part of the mountains of Van Scive, New Jersey, sat a single-story home that someone had built into the side of a mountain. Rome stood in front of one of the many floor-to-ceiling windows as he stared out into the darkness of the night. Several of his warriors sat behind him in the family room. He could hear them breathing and moving around as they tried to figure out who would address him first. They couldn't whisper for shit, and he didn't understand why they would even try considering they all had above average hearing. Usually, Erick, his second in command, would be the first to speak, but he was unusually quiet tonight, which meant something was bothering him on a deeper level.

Rome sighed heavily and turned to speak, gaining their attention instantly. "We need to address the influx of rogues that have been swarming the streets as of late."

"What is there to discuss?" Maverick growled from his lounged position on the couch. "They've been out slaughtering people like usual with us right on their asses to clean up the mess. I don't even know why we protect these weak humans."

Rome sighed heavily. "We protect them because that is our

purpose. Would you like me to petition the Gods for you and ask that we discontinue the fight for humanity's sake?"

Maverick's caramel features paled at the thought. Complaining about what they did for humanity was one thing, but none would ever wish to voice it to the Gods themselves. They were benevolent beings with a mean streak a mile wide if wronged or disrespected. Or at least that's what everyone who knew of them had heard over the centuries. Rome knew them intimately, and not all was what it seemed.

Maverick shifted his six-foot-six frame until he sat up with his larger-than-average feet planted firmly on the ground. Unusual gold eyes stared through thick eyelashes as he waited for Rome to say he was joking. With his strong cheekbones, square jawline, and broad nose, many found him to be an intimidating man to look at, and with dark brown hair that cut into a clean cut, it completed his look. With a body built like a linebacker, he was agile but had a massive chest and broad shoulders that could contradict that. He was Rome's fiercest warrior and usually the first man ready for battle. Now, he looked about ready to shit his pants at the mere mention of the Gods.

Rome chuckled at his fearful expression. "Don't worry Mav, I'll protect you from their wrath."

The five other warriors within the room outright laughed or snickered quietly in amusement. Maverick wasn't one to scare easily, but everyone but Rome feared the Gods. They had the potential to eradicate them from the world. The only reason they hadn't was because of the humans and the supposed Kindred—supposed to be the operative word, considering none of the Guardians had encountered a Kindred in many years. Humans needed protection from the vampire rogues that roamed the streets and gorged on their blood, ultimately killing or turning them.

Silas, a guardian with unique features that made him stand out anywhere he went, spoke over the laughter. "I believe the Vamps are starting to nest and work together in packs rather than going out alone. They're becoming more coordinated as if someone controls their moves and actions." He stroked the five-o'clock shadow along his angular jawline and leaned more casually into the wall that supported his weight. "The other night, Akio and I cornered seven rogues after disturbing their midnight snack. They fought differently as well. Way more disciplined and controlled. I think Titan's responsible."

"But they have no control. They're animals." Amirishka, the only female in the group, interceded from her perch atop the kitchen island.

The home layout wasn't ideal for Rome with its wide-open concept, but it worked in Maverick's favor. After all, it was one of his many homes. They all owned a few different properties world-wide, but Maverick's cabin residence was their current base of operation. Every room with a window was floor to ceiling with specialty-made bulletproof glass reflecting the sun and protecting them from the dangerous rays that would kill them. The home wasn't notice-able to the naked eye from the outside unless you knew what to look for. With seven bedrooms, eight bathrooms, and an underground tunnel that allowed them to escape a threat at their earliest convenience, they were pretty secure in their position within the mountains. He'd done good.

Rome's gaze lingered on Amirishka's iridescent gaze before he smiled softly. Amirishka was one of his longest and closest friends, and being the only female in their group, he was always inclined to treat her gentler than he treated his men, yet she was one of the most bloodthirsty guardians he had. With a mean streak as long as his life-line and the ability to eviscerate a man with only a few softly spoken words, she was a threat most didn't see coming. She was by far the shortest in the group at five foot five, with light brown hair cut into a pixie cut with hot pink tips on the end of each strand. Medium brown skin covered in a fair smattering of freckles gave her an inno-cence that had tricked many of their enemies over the years. Large iridescent eyes sat above a small nose, and full bow-shaped lips that most men couldn't tear their eyes away from, and a sharp chin with a cute little dimple and rounded cheeks made her face look even softer. She was the epitome of sinful nights and wicked fantasies. Not just because she could seduce anyone with just the sound of her voice but because she brought men and women alike to their knees with black skin-tight leather that enclosed a Coke bottle body.

"Need something, sir?" She practically purred when she spoke and ran her small hand over firm double d breasts that pressed enticingly against her bodice before they came to rest on her flared hips.

Rome wasn't swayed by her power of persuasion; her ability didn't work on him in the slightest. Maybe when they'd first met all those centuries ago, and his will hadn't been as strong, he'd been tempted to sample what she wanted to give, yet he'd never even kissed her. She was like the little sister he'd never had. The thought of bedding her just didn't sit right with him. In fact, it made him nauseous.

"You know that doesn't work on me, Amirishka. Now behave and tell me what you noticed on your last hunt." He glanced at his other men, whose eyes were glazed over with pleasure. His expression turned fierce in an instant. "Release them now."

Amirishka's powers are similar to those of a mythical siren. With the voice of an angel wrapped in sultry heat, it was easy to fall under her spell and do whatever she deemed to ask. Sometimes, she didn't have to ask a thing; she would just speak, and you were instantly pulled under her spell. She was alluring.

She sighed heavily. "Fine." She glanced at the rest of the warriors when she spoke. "You're immune to my voice, so act like you've got some sense."

They instantly snapped out of it. Some had faces of disgust because they, too, looked at Amirishka like a sister, while a few were unbothered. Rome needed to find a way to make them as immune to her charms as he was, or he'd constantly be corralling her until she finally learned to control it. He was under the impression that she could and just chose not to. He wasn't too sure.

"I didn't stop to watch and wait for them to attack someone, so I didn't notice anything new. I just acted." She shrugged and pulled out one of her blades to pick at her nails.

Rome nodded in understanding before zeroing in on Erick. He

sat in an oversized wingback chair with a solemn expression. With a height of six foot eight and a defined and muscular body, he looked like a giant to most people, although he wasn't as tall as Rome's seven-foot stature. With snow-white hair that fell to his waist in braids, skin just as pale due to his albinism, and deep red eyes that most people feared, Erick was considered their most closed-off warrior. His features could have been on the cover of Vogue with his thinly plucked eyebrows, sharp nose, and full lips. He was beautiful in a sort of ethereal way.

"What's bothering you?" Rome questioned as he moved to his friend's side and touched his shoulder in silent support.

"I don't have Silas' sight, but I feel like something is coming. Something big." Erick responded, his voice soft yet full of conviction.

Cairo spoke from his position in the corner of the room beside the blazing large fireplace. "I'm going to have to agree with Erick. The winds have stirred a warning to me on several occasions while out on the hunt. Things are changing, and I'm unsure if it is in our favor or our enemies."

Cairo stood at six foot two, decked out in his signature three-piece black-on-black suit with turquoise eyes that held pinpricks of violet beneath thick lashes. His alabaster skin stood out against the blackness of his suit, and his black hair was trimmed into the signature cut of anyone who had once served in the military. With serene, elegant features, an aristocratic nose, and a sculpted jawline, he gave the impression of a man who wasn't easily swayed. Yet, his dimples said something altogether different. As an elemental, he was significantly in tune with the elements, and occasionally, those elements 'spoke' to him, giving him an insight that had saved their lives on many occasions.

Rome frowned and tried to summon his inner power of foresight, but that was a power he hardly ever used, and so he lacked greatly in it, but that's why Silas was such an essential member of his group of Guardians. With Silas' ability to glance into the future, they were much more capable of preventing tragedies before they began and knowing what or who would be the tipping point in their current war between two factions.

"Have you seen anything, brother?" He questioned Silas as he glanced over his shoulder to meet his gaze.

Silas's gaze brightened as he donned a far-off look and zoned out. His right eye glowed an eerie dark green, while his left eye glowed a dark blue like the deep sea. Several moments passed in silence before he spoke. "It isn't clear. Something is definitely coming." He stared at Rome with a frown, pulling at the lines of his mouth. "It'll affect you on a deep enough level that it pulls each of us beneath layers of shadows I can't see past."

The room settled into an eerie silence as the ramifications of what he said clicked into place. Rome paced back to the window and stared out into the dark of the night once more. This wasn't good. Silas could always see at least something to indicate what was coming for them next; it's how they stayed one step ahead at all times. Now he was telling them he couldn't see shit. Not what was coming or what could possibly affect Rome enough to shake the foundation of everything they had built. With his hand pressed against the coolness of the glass, he released the breath he hadn't known he'd been holding and gasped in pain when a telepathic blast slammed through the barriers of his mind and sent him to his knee. He heard the rest of his guardians gasp in pain before he forced a mental shield around their minds. They weren't accustomed to shielding their minds from attacks like he and Silas. With them both being the only ones capable of telepathy, he didn't have to protect Silas; he already knew how to shield someone from his mind. Instead, Rome focused on the scream raging in his head and tried to zero in on the source as he regained his footing. That yell for help had been filled with pure agony and fear.

"What the fuck was that?" Akio, the youngest member of the group, snapped.

With a Japanese descent, he carried pronounced cheekbones, plush lips, a pointed nose, and a thin yet athletic build. He stood at six foot five with black eyes and jet black hair shaved at the sides while the tresses at the top were pulled into a tight bun. With a black trench coat that always covered his body, no one could make out the weapons surrounding him, including the two katanas strapped to his back.

"That was someone screaming for help," Silas responded with a groan as he pressed his hands against his temple, where a headache raged. He wasn't used to someone slamming through his mental barriers and taking up residence in his mind.

"Everyone stay put," Rome stated before focusing on the last tendrils of the voice that had slammed through his mind.

It had faded off into a soft plea for help before it disappeared completely, but not before he got a lock on their location and forced his body to dematerialize and reappear in an area that sent him miles from Maverick's home. The chilling cold instantly bit into his exposed face and hands as his eyes wandered over the expanse of forest in search of his target. The trees blocked out the moon's light, yet his superior eyesight allowed him to see perfectly in the dark as he zeroed in on the river's edge, where a still body lay in a bank of snow and shallow water. They were face down and caught on some driftwood with an oversized coat and backpack covering them entirely as he cautiously approached. He allowed his senses to flare outwards as he listened to the silence of the night. The body was so still, yet he could hear a faint heartbeat that assured Rome they were alive. A million questions ran through his mind, but what was most pressing was how this human had ended up in the middle of the Van Scive mountains when nothing but Mavericks' home and a dilapidated shack stretched for miles. Maverick had purposely picked his home so that no one could possibly stumble upon them, as well as the fact that he avoided humans. He actually hated them and everything they stood for. All they were good for was being blood donors, in his opinion.

Kneeling beside the prone body, Rome examined them visually before hefting them into his arms. The smell of fresh water, lilacs, and fear tickled his nose as he looked the small figure over. It was a woman. From what he could make of her face, she was absolutely breathtaking, with bronzed skin that had been chilled. Her features were angelic, with a pointed nose above a thin top lip with a plush bottom he itched to suck into his mouth. He needed to see if she tasted as good as she smelled. His dick jumped beneath his leathers when he pushed the hood from her head, and thick curly brown and burgundy hair tumbled to her shoulders in wet waves. Her face was rounded perfectly with thickly plucked brows. He was dying to know what her eyes looked like. Honey Brown was his best guess; they would put her beauty over the top if they were.

Rome teleported back to Maverick's home and straight to his private bathroom, where he could help her warm up. Hesitation pulled at him because he'd have to undress her to get her warm, and he wasn't sure if that was the best idea. The temptation to see all of her pulled at him, but he wanted to be respectful.

He pushed a telepathic command to Ami. *Meet me in my bathroom. I need you.*

He didn't wait for her response before he pulled from her mind and glanced around his bathroom, hoping to find somewhere to place her while he figured out what to do. The room was spacious, with a large jetted bathtub that could fit at least three people. A four-person shower sat in the corner with black and white marbled tiles that complimented the black and white marble double sink. A floor-to-ceiling window sat behind the tub, and thoughts of spreading her out on the lip of that tub as he devoured her entered his mind abruptly and sent his heart rate spiking dangerously. The lights flickered as his telekinetic power flared, sending tingles licking against his spine. He thought of the chaise that sat at the foot of his massive bed, and seconds later, it appeared before him before he laid her down and took several steps back. The bathroom door cracked open as Amirishka walked in and paused.

Her eyes were wide like saucers. "Rome, what's going on? Who is she?"

"Give her a bath and call for me as soon as you're done. I'm sure you can handle a mere human." Once again, Rome didn't give Ami a chance to respond before he teleported from the room. He needed peace to get his mind together and a game plan for what had to happen next. Because what he wanted to do, he couldn't. He now had a new mystery to solve. Who was she?

CHAPTER
THREE

Alara woke slowly to the feel of a plush bed and covers surrounding her like a lover's hold. The smell of food filled the room, and a masculine scent caused her toes to curl involuntarily as her core tightened as if in anticipation. The sensation was new. She sat up slowly, letting the sheet drop to her waist to reveal the oversized T-shirt that dwarfed her frame as she glanced around the large room with a frown screwing up her face. She was atop a massive bed that was covered in deep red sheets. A large chaise lounge sat at the foot of the bed, a black dresser sat against a plain white wall to her right, while a floor-to-ceiling window sat to her left overlooking a mountainside she could hardly make out due to the fog and torrential rain that splattered against the glass. Besides the pitter-patter of the rain, no other sound reached her ears as she continued to survey her surroundings. The bedroom was lavish and beautiful. Any woman's dreams, really. Alara climbed from the bed, pulled at the shirt that brushed her knees, and headed for the door she assumed would lead her to whoever had saved her from dying.

A sense of caution made her pause. She wasn't sure where she was, and she couldn't risk the chance that Titan had somehow found her and was now trying to lull her into a sense of false safety. She felt safe, especially with the sweet, woodsy smell of whatever men's fragrance lingered within the cotton of her shirt. It smelled like coming home, whatever home meant, but to her, that meant feeling safe, and yet that could simply be an illusion that would make her drop her guard. She reached up to touch her throat. The gold collar was still missing. That had been real, too. Knowing Titan, they would never be so reckless as to leave her free use of her powers. She tested them now and instantly felt something new sparking to life inside her. There was a pull. Something calling to her and filling her with so much untapped power it made her blood sing. Alara had never felt anything quite like it before. The energy was different, unique in a way that caused her hand to pause on the knob of the door as she tried to place why it was slightly familiar. Granted, she'd never encountered this unique energy, but she'd experienced something like it years before Titan started to keep her shackled and unfeeling.

With the collar on, she wasn't just unable to use her powers; she was subdued and forced to yield to whoever had control over the remote that could release her. Thank God for small miracles because, without Alaric's help earlier, she would have been subjected to whatever brutality Lukas would have rained down on her if she'd been recaptured by Titan. Her abilities were a question mark even to her. She couldn't explain it, but the life force of another human being pulled her in. She could feel their strengths and weaknesses, and with a simple touch, she could take it all away and temporarily leave them a husk of themselves. She was capable of killing with a touch. Alara froze as the ramifications of what she was seeing settled in. Too much skin was bare, her gloves were missing, and maybe that explained why no one was around. Had she touched someone? Killed them? Were they even now withering away to nothing? Was that the new energy she felt within her? It was weak but there.

Her heart started pounding within her chest, nerves getting the better of her as she moved around the room frantically in search of more clothing. Shit, anything to cover her hands and keep her skin from possibly coming into contact with another human being. She threw open doors that were slightly cracked and walked into a massive closet with all-black clothing and weapons lining the walls and drawers. She couldn't keep the fear she felt now from rising. She'd never forgive herself if she had killed someone while unconscious.

She frowned, wondering where the hell she was and why anyone needed this much weaponry? It had to be Titan. Altogether, avoiding the wall that housed every weapon imaginable, Alara grabbed a pair of oversized sweatpants to go with her equally large shirt before pulling them on and double-tying them around her waist. Whoever owned the clothing was massive. She grabbed a pair of socks, slid those on, and smiled like a kid in a candy store when she found a pair of gloves shoved into the back of the sock drawer. Everything dwarfed her, but she needed this layer of protection. Once she was as covered as possible, Alara left the closet, searching for whoever had saved her life. She had to thank them and find the bag Alaric had given her. She needed to contact him. She needed answers.

When she opened the bedroom door, the smell of spicy sausage gumbo tickled her nose and caused her stomach to growl loudly. Other doors lined what seemed to be a long hallway as she followed her sense of smell into an open living room that was separated by a kitchen island. It was absolutely breathtaking. From floor to ceiling, everything screamed luxurious yet homey. Someone with money clearly lived here. She moved further into the kitchen until she stood before a large pot filled with steaming gumbo. Alara bit at her lip nervously as her stomach growled louder. It wouldn't hurt to make herself a small bowl. Clearly, whoever lived here had taken excellent care of her. She was freshly showered and clothed, so it wouldn't hurt them if she helped herself to some food. Would it? She found a bowl and soup spoon in a cabinet before grabbing a hefty amount before her nerves could get the better of her.

Alara sat at a long rustic table just off the kitchen and stared out into the mountains, where she could see the sun reaching its highest peak in the sky. It was the afternoon; that much she could tell. The floor-to-ceiling windows allowed her to see just how much forest and snow surrounded her. It was beautiful. Untouched by society, and yet somehow Titan had been heading out this way, and she was now in someone else's residence. Someone who had created a home where there shouldn't be one.

She ate the food in record time, made sure to rinse the bowl, and placed it in the dishwasher before moving around the house. Curiosity sang through her as she took in every little detail. By the front door lay a shoe rack that held several different sizes and styles of footwear. It clearly indicated that multiple people lived here. Her curiosity grew broader, yet no one came to greet her, and she refused to go snooping where she shouldn't, so with a grumbling sigh, she headed back to the bedroom, locked the door behind her, and climbed back beneath the covers. Most people would probably snoop and look for answers to find out where they were, but Alara was different. She refused to be intrusive and hoped whoever had rescued her would soon show their face. Rolling to her side, she tucked the sheets beneath her chin and closed her eyes before she allowed herself to drift to sleep with a full belly and a sense of rightness. For now, she was safe.

SEVERAL HOURS PASSED before Alara awoke again, just as the sun set. Damn, she hadn't meant to sleep for so long; she had only intended to nap. She frowned as she sat up but abruptly froze when she spotted a man standing at the foot of the bed. He was taller than any man she'd ever seen at seven feet, even with black-on-black clothing covering almost every inch of his dark chocolate skin. Thick dreadlocks fell to the middle of his back and blended with his attire while eyes so blue and clear it was like looking into a reflective surface stared back at her. He had strong, high cheekbones with a defined jawline, perfectly shaped lips, an aristocratic nose, and a body that looked larger than life beneath his clothing. He was mesmerizing, and for the first time, Alara was experiencing what she assumed was lust. She was utterly speechless.

Her heart beat a little faster than usual. Not because a stranger was staring at her with a questioning gaze but because this stranger looked like sex on a stick, and her most feminine parts tingled with awareness for the first time in her life. It thrilled and unnerved her all in the same breath because, for the longest, she had assumed something was wrong with her sex drive, and in turn, something was wrong with her.

She moved onto her knees into a kneeling position and removed the gloves just in case things went south with this stranger. She allowed the sheet to fall around her so she'd have an easy escape. "Are you the one who saved me?"

"I did…" He paused as his gaze sharpened on her and seemed to slide over every inch of her body before he finished his thought. "Your psychic scream reached me from miles away. That shouldn't be possible, considering you're human." His voice was smooth and deep, sending tingles down her spine. "Now explain to me what you did to my warrior once I left you alone with her."

Alara froze as a thousand emotions and thoughts ran through her body and mind. So she'd been right. She must have hurt someone when they'd cleaned her up, and now he was trying to gauge how she had killed this warrior of his. Wait, warrior? And why had he mentioned being human? What else could she be if not human? Alara had never had to explain herself before. She'd never had to explain her powers and how she was capable of doing the things she could do. They had just known at Titan after the rigorous testing they had put her through. Here, she was flying blind.

"W-what do you mean?" She stuttered, afraid that the wrong answer would seal her fate.

The energy seemed to swell within the room, lights flickered, and a slight chill ghosted over her when his eyes narrowed in annoyance. "By nature, I'm not a patient man when I want answers, especially when I feel as though the livelihood of my brethren is threatened." He moved closer to the bed and smiled menacingly, "I want to know your name, how you got to be within the mountains, and how you incapacitated one of my fiercest fighters. You have five minutes, so you'd best get talking, little flower."

———

He'd been utterly and completely wrong. Her eyes weren't a honey brown but a misty gray smattered with streaks of light blue that seemed to brighten if the light hit them just right. Rome wasn't sure how to feel about the mysterious beauty before him, but he knew that she was dangerous on some level. It was leaking from her pores like lava.

After leaving Amirishka in the bathroom with his slumbering bounty, he'd gone on the hunt for his enemies, and for hours, he'd teleported from one side of the world to the other in his bid to help other warriors in their fight against death. For centuries, he and his warriors had fought for humanity's sake against the force that threatened to wipe humans from the face of the earth. Humans had no knowledge that their very lives were protected by Eternal Guardians night after night in a bid to eradicate vampires from the face of the planet. After slaughtering every vamp Rome had encountered, he'd checked his phone and returned home just as the sun peeked over the horizon. After finding out she'd been incapacitated, he'd slept below within the infirmary alongside Amirishka. Hours later, he'd awakened to check on his guest but found that Amirishka was still unconscious, and no one could get her to wake. He'd tried to reach her telepathically to read her thoughts, but he'd been overwhelmed. Silas had tried as well. Shit, he'd tried to heal her and had failed. Now, he was here for answers. She had to be the cause.

This beautiful, enchanting creature had to be the reason his guardian wouldn't awaken, and he wanted...no, he needed answers, and he needed them now because he wasn't the only one foaming at the mouth to get to those answers. The rest of his men were lying in wait, hoping he'd give the okay to kill her outright for harming one of their own. She'd been the last one to interact with Amirishka. It had to be her.

Alara continued to stare even after five minutes had passed, and his patience wasn't what it once was centuries ago. He moved faster

26

than any human's eyes could possibly track and hauled her up until her face was only several breaths away from his own.

She yelped but didn't try to escape his hold. Instead, she went still as a deer caught in headlights and spoke softly, her voice threaded with fear. "Don't touch my skin. I can't control it."

Rome's curiosity was piqued. "Can't control what?"

"I have powers," she murmured, "I can do things other people can't, and I don't know why or how. I was born this way. I can't answer any questions. I just know I steal energy."

He frowned. "Energy?"

"I told you, I can't explain it, but when I touch a person skin to skin, something happens where I sort of drain the person of energy and life." Her gaze flitted away from him before returning when his hold tightened a fraction in warning. "In some cases, they die, but not always!"

Surprise filled him. "So you're saying you took Ami's energy?"

"Yes…I mean, I don't know. I was unconscious, so if she touched me while I slept, then yes, I suppose I did."

Rome slowly released her and stepped back even as his body screamed at him to stay put. She had to be a Kindred with powers exhibiting those of a siphon. That was the only thing that would make enough sense to his rattled brain. It had been too many years since his last encounter with a Kindred. They were rare and unique humans with powers that defied all logic. Long ago, he'd been one of those humans until the Gods had literally and figuratively rained down upon him.

Before his mind could wander too far into the past, he spoke, all the while his eyes focused on every little twitch and movement in her body. "I am Romulus, but you will call me Rome. What's your name?"

"Alara, My name's Alara."

Even her name was beautiful.

"How did you end up in the middle of the mountains, nearly dead, Alara?"

Her eyes drifted to the window to stare out into the darkness of the night as a sheltered expression fell across her face. It was clear she wouldn't be answering that question any time soon. Maybe she had something to hide, and he should press for answers, yet something cautioned him against that. She might have been a plant put here by his enemies, but how would they know of his location? Only his Guardians knew of every stronghold owned and operated by every Immortal under his command. Being in charge of hundreds of warriors who would swear they didn't need an overseer wasn't easy. Just the thought of recent events with several of his men overseas made his powers fluctuate around him.

Alara tensed beside him. "What just happened? Did you feel that?" She glanced around the room and wrapped her arms around herself, almost as if to protect herself from an unseen force.

She continued to surprise him. She wasn't just powered. She was sensitive to her surroundings, aware enough to realize something powerful filled the air around them. Something even more powerful than the power she wielded. And what a mighty power she did have. No one within his command, not even himself, could siphon another person's energy. She would be a great addition to his people if she wasn't working for the enemy.

"You felt that?"

"Of course, didn't you?"

Her hypnotic eyes latched onto him and held. The smell of lilac tickled his nose as he inhaled her fragrance and computed it to memory now that the smell of fear was no longer filling the air. His dick jumped, as well as his heart rate. Something was happening he couldn't begin to understand. There was a draw to her. A strong pull that made him want to close the tiny gap between them and invade her space once more, but this time, he wouldn't stop at simply holding her still. He'd need more. Rome would need to feel her full lips beneath his own and her petite body pressed against his. The dominant part of him that he kept securely locked away was throwing itself against the fortified walls of his mind, demanding an out. An out he would refuse to give into.

"You have no idea what you are, do you?" Rome dragged his eyes away and forced himself to move before he caved to the pressing need running rampant within his mind and body. He needed to get some control.

He could hear a few of his guardians standing just outside the door as they listened in on their conversation. He could smell Erick, Silas, and Maverick as they shifted restlessly in anticipation. He knew Cairo was watching over Ami's comatose state while Akio was out doing only God knew what. It hadn't been easy to keep them out while he spoke to her, but as their leader and king, they'd had no choice but to listen or suffer the consequences. He hadn't wanted to overwhelm her. It would be hard enough to explain what they were without her noticing the abnormalities some of them presented with.

"What do you mean what I am? I'm human." She frowned, her delicate face screwed up in a way that would make anyone else appear less appealing than they were, but not her.

"You're human, but you're also more than that. You're what we call a Kindred."

CHAPTER
FOUR

Alara stared at the expanse of Rome's broad back when he paced away before striding back to her. Her mind slowly wrapped around his statement. It was bad enough her girly parts were throwing a fit that she didn't understand, and her heart rate had yet to settle down and find a decent rhythm, but now he was telling her she wasn't entirely human. As badly as she wanted to remain standing in a stranger's face, she also knew that exhaustion somehow still pulled at her resolve and made her retake a seat on the bed. Sure, she could feel some residual energy left over from whomever she'd come into contact with, but the energy signature was like nothing she'd ever encountered. It was more. It was foreign and scratching at her inner core, almost as if there was more attached to her than just another person's life force. She wanted to explore that sensation and figure out why she felt so different, but Rome spoke before she could.

"Kindred are humans that are blessed with extraordinary abilities that vary based on the individual. It makes them that much more special than the average human. You each carry a 1% marker within your DNA that gives you the ability to have these powers. Some say the Gods had a hand in who got that 1%. Blessed and highly favored is sometimes tossed around, yet it's been years since I've encountered a Kindred. I was under the impression there were none of you left." He watched her silently and ran his hand through his thick dreads.

Shock held her immobile for several moments. She couldn't have heard that correctly. Clearly, she was in the presence of a lunatic and had to tread carefully. "Are you trying to tell me there are more people like me?" She questioned with a frown.

Alara had never encountered another with abilities in all her years within Titan. Shit, she'd never known she'd had a brother either, but maybe Titan had hidden the simple truth from her, that Alara wasn't as unique and alone as she'd thought, or maybe Titan really didn't know of another with powers. Knowing them, she believed they would hide the truth.

"I don't think anyone is quite like you." His eyes seemed to blaze several shades brighter like the high beams on a car as they trailed her from head to toe in a slow perusal, "You're the first siphon I've ever encountered, and even I do not harness that power."

Okay, the eyes were a little freaky, and yet her pulse jumped beneath his gaze with excitement.

"So let me get this straight. As a siphon, that's why I can kill someone with a touch? These gods of yours gave me the shit end of the stick that makes it physically impossible to get close to anyone, and I can't control it." She paused and frowned. "Are you a Kindred as well?"

"I used to be, but now I'm more, and as for your inability to touch…I just think you haven't had an opportunity to practice the lengths to which your power can be controlled." He entered her space, causing her to shrink back farther on the bed. "We can test your power on me. I'm the eldest and strongest of my kind; hardly anything fazes me."

"For someone so good-looking, it's a shame you're certifiable. You must be if you're asking to be a test dummy for a power I just told you I couldn't control. How is your friend currently doing? You know, the one you were just grilling me about because apparently I incapacitated her? What if I don't simply knock you out? What if you die?" She snapped in irritation. "And what the fuck are you? Because your eyes keep doing that freaky glowing shit, and it's freaking me out."

Why would he want to subject himself to her power? She had just explained that she couldn't control it. She'd never learned how to harness it, thanks to Titan and their protective measures. They had never allowed her to work on it or even come close to mastering it, and because of that hindrance, she had hurt people a lot more than just simply putting them to sleep. Alara had killed without meaning to, and euphoria had filled her in the process. She was rewarded with a more significant energy boost, especially if they died. These powers made her an executioner who couldn't control the flow of the sword or the pressure behind it, and Alara refused to kill accidentally or otherwise ever again.

He pulled her from her thoughts when he spoke, shocking her further. "I'm an Eternal Guardian tasked with protecting humans from the knowledge and threat of the monsters that hunt them. As for your powers, I can help you learn to control them. As I've said, I'm the eldest and strongest of my kind at almost a millennium, and nothing can truly hurt me." He knelt, and they still weren't eye to eye, "I wasn't just tasked to protect humans. As a Kindred, you fall under my protection even more so, and with that comes guidance. Let me help you."

Alara pulled her bottom lip between her teeth and bit down out of nervous habit before watching a change overtake Rome's face. His eyes blazed brighter as his nose flared and his lips parted to reveal teeth that were way too sharp to be human. They were fangs. She should have experienced fear and uncertainty, yet a different feeling and emotion filled her. Adrenaline and excitement rushed through her at the thought of those fangs sinking into her skin. The image was vivid within her mind, and a small part of her knew that that wasn't okay. Actually, nothing about this was okay. She should have been figuring out how to get back in touch with Alaric. She paused when she remembered what he'd said about reaching a place where she'd have more answers than questions. Was this the place he'd been referring to? Was she at the destination she needed to be where they could help her?

"How can you help me?" Alara looked away from his intense gaze and focused on her hands clutched around the hem of her shirt. It was the safer option to look at because looking at him was causing reactions in her body that had never happened until now.

"I can show you what you're capable of and teach you how to harness it, but you need to trust me."

God, was his voice getting deeper? Shivers ran up her spine, her eyes latching back onto his own as a snarl passed through his slightly parted lips. Shit, he probably couldn't close his mouth over those daggers even if he wanted to. Before she could process what was happening, Rome moved faster than her eyes could track and pinned her beneath him on the bed. His body was flush against her own, his heat soaked through their clothing as his mouth descended upon her in a searing kiss that sent a shot of energy straight to her core. The power flowing from him and into her was like lightning repeatedly striking the same place. She gasped into his mouth and felt his tongue touch her own as more sparks flew and something shattered in the distance.

Pressure built inside her as her power flared and sucked his energy in like a starving beast. Rome fell victim to the pull. His hands threaded into her hair, pulling slightly and dragging another moan from her lips as his hips drove up and into her, begging to get closer. She felt the hard press of his dick against her stomach as her core clenched repeatedly around nothing. Alara wanted more. Whatever this was, she wanted more, and damn the consequences. He said he could handle it. God, she needed him to be able to because the power coursing through her now was like a drug she never wanted to give up.

ROME FELT as if his head would explode at any moment, not just the head above his shoulders but the one below his belt. She tasted of ambrosia laced with sex. With her pressed beneath him, he could gauge her need. She was like a live wire, causing his thoughts to fracture until he could only focus on her. He felt her powers pulling at him; shit, he could feel himself weakening even as his need amplified and his abilities flared outwards in another release of energy. When his lips had first touched her own, he'd felt his powers leave him in a rush as light bulbs burst, windows cracked, and any object teeming with glass shattered. She wasn't just taking his energy; she was affecting his powers on a level that surprised him, and for once, in as long as he could remember...he had no control.

He sucked at her bottom lip and snarled when he moved closer still, and her legs wrapped around his waist. Fuck, why did she taste so good? Her moan vibrated within his mouth as he dove back in for another meeting of their tongues just as Silas breached his thoughts. That wouldn't have been possible if he'd retained control.

What the fuck is happening? Do you need help? Is she hurting you?

He attempted to set his thoughts right and respond when her smooth tongue slid along one of his fangs, sending his body into an overdrive he never thought possible. The release of energy that left him was on a cataclysmic level that sent thunder and lightning tearing through the sky as glass shattered throughout the house. The sound of the bedroom door slamming against the wall registered even as an involuntary orgasm took him by surprise, and his eyes rolled into the back of his head as he lost consciousness.

THE SOUND of the bedroom door opening and slamming against the wall shocked Alara, but it wasn't as shocking as the man above her groaning in pleasure seconds before his full weight fell upon her and forced the breath from her lungs in a rush. Her chest instantly tightened as she fought to push him from above her to gasp in the air she desperately needed. Her pulse still raced from the kiss. God, and what a kiss that had been. Her whole body still tingled in remembrance from the feel of his skin pressed against her own. She wanted more with a desperation she didn't understand, and he'd been right. He'd lasted longer than anyone she'd ever encountered, and still, he lived. She could see he still breathed by the rise and fall of his chest.

"Romulus!" A brusque voice spoke from beside her seconds before Rome was rolled off of her and onto his back.

Alara scrambled to put space between her and the five prominent men who now crowded around the bed. Strangers, all of them. Each sported eyes that glowed eerily and fangs that were bared in aggression, but the one that scared her the most carried an air of menace around him she could feel to her soul. She could taste his energy within the air like a live wire that had been exposed, and of course, her need to protect herself took precedence. Upon awakening earlier, that foreign presence she'd felt flared its head and grew like a flower in the center of a thunderstorm, yet it felt different this time. This time, she could tell that this new feeling within her had come from Rome. It wasn't just his life force she carried but a touch of his abilities, and damn were they something else. She felt his energy surround her body entirely and stretch outwards in a protective bubble as a male with golden eyes launched at her with murderous intent shining within his gaze.

She flinched even as his body slammed against the barrier she had erected. His snarl sent chills down her spine as her eyes flew from one man to the next as she tried to think of a way out of her predicament. Silas tried desperately to wake Rome by shaking him and attempting to probe his thoughts while the rest of the men simply stared at her with contempt, anger, and curiosity.

"What the fuck did you do to him?" Maverick snapped and launched once more against the barrier.

With his calm demeanor, Erick moved around the bed until he stood to her left, his eyes watching her observantly. "Hello Alara, my name is Erick. We know you didn't kill him, so that's a good sign, but we need to know what you've done and if you can reverse the effects. We won't hurt you."

"Yeah?" She snapped, "Tell that to the dick that keeps jumping at me like a rabid dog! And how do you know my name?"

Akio and Cairo chuckled before Erick spoke again. "You have to excuse Mav. None of us are used to this, and Rome informed us as you two spoke privately, as well as us hearing for ourselves. However, his gifts occasionally interfered with our ability to hear the conversation."

"Used to what? Holding women hostage and trying to kill them for things beyond their control? I didn't hurt him. Shit, I hardly touched him, but he wanted more." She glared at Maverick. "He kissed me even when I told him I couldn't control it."

Cairo frowned and moved to her right until she was practically blocked in on the bed with her back to the headboard. "Couldn't control what? What are you?"

"According to him," she glanced down at Rome before focusing on Erick, since he seemed to be the group's ringleader, "I'm a Kindred. A siphon."

"Is that how you're creating the barrier? Did you take in some of Rome's power? Are you controlling that?" Erick reached forward and hesitantly brushed against the energy field that matched the one that encircled Rome whenever he needed it.

Wonder filled his gaze. Shit, wonder-filled her own. She couldn't fathom how she was capable of wielding such power. She was capable of many things, capable of things Titan wasn't even aware of because she hid the rest of her powers well, but this…this was something altogether different. This was true power, and she couldn't help but like it and want more.

"I don't know how I'm doing this," she whispered, "I'm just scared and in a place I don't recognize with men that aren't human, and I just found out I'm not as human as I thought I was. I just want to get my things and go."

"Out of the question!" Maverick snarled with his enlarged fangs bared. "He brought you back here to my home for a reason, so you stay."

Silas focused on her face, his mismatched eyes glowing brighter by the second before his face screwed up into a frown. "Why can't I read you?"

Alara shook her head and avoided his gaze entirely. She couldn't tell him that. She had two more powers that she could control. She could heal another as well as herself and read someone's thoughts as well as block her own. It was evident that Silas was capable of the former, and she couldn't risk him or anyone else knowing what else she could do. It might not be safe. This might have been a trick somehow.

"I don't know what you mean." She lied.

Silas still monitored Rome with his thoughts, yet focused on her. She felt him attempting to breach the walls within her mind. The force he used caused her resolve to weaken as the energy field around her began to flicker. She gasped in pain when he pressed on. Sweat beaded her brow and upper lip as her eyes frantically looked from one man to the next in a bid for help. Invisible claws were digging into her mind, attempting to remove her secrets and take whatever was worth taking. She didn't know how to fight back against this intrusion, and the pain started getting to her. It began to weaken her. Her eyesight blurred as fire ripped through her mind when the first wall of security around her thoughts fractured.

"P-please," she cried, "you have to stop!" She needed to protect her thoughts. Protect her secrets.

He spoke calmly as if hurting her was nothing to him. "Then lower your shields."

Alara shook her head in a futile attempt to remove him from her mind, but Silas was one of the strongest telepaths to ever walk the earth after Rome. She stood no chance against his advance and screamed when another crack spread within her mind. She was seconds from crying out again when an unholy snarl filled the air, and Rome launched himself from the bed before snaring Silas around the throat and slamming him against the reinforced wall.

"Release her!" Rome's voice was pure, unadulterated menace.

CHAPTER
FIVE

The last thing Rome remembered was tasting sex and sin on his tongue as he orgasmed from the pleasure of Alara's tongue against his fang before he heard the slam of his bedroom door just as he passed out from pure pleasure. He could still feel the mess in his pants from his involuntary release as he held Silas in the air by his throat. He'd heard her cries as he'd fought for consciousness and had wondered who would dare hurt her while under his protection. To know it was Silas was like a slap in the face. He expected Maverick or even Akio to act out, but Silas? Never in the years they'd known each other had Silas gone against him. It was unheard of, and yet here they were. He could hardly contain his anger as he tightened his grip around Silas's throat after glancing back to see how Alara was doing.

She was clutching her head in pain, her body curled into the most heart-wrenching position he knew: the fetal position. He could make out the energy field that surrounded her and knew that that little trick was something she'd siphoned from him. It made him proud. He wondered what other powers she'd taken in but instead zeroed in on one of his closest friends.

"What is the meaning of this!?" Rome snarled through bared fangs that pulsed along with his thumping heartbeat.

Silas attempted to speak, but it was hard to do so when his windpipe was being crushed by the strongest immortal to ever live, so Cairo answered for him in the hopes of de-escalating the situation. "He was attempting to read her mind. Silas couldn't read her easily and tried to breach her barriers. There might have been a mental power struggle within the process."

Erick moved within his peripheral vision and raised his hands in silent surrender. "Sir, you're crushing his windpipe."

Wow, excellent observational skills, Rome thought to himself snarkily. He released Silas after applying pressure once more in a silent warning. Even before the kiss Rome had shared with Alara, he had been protective of her, but now, after tasting her and feeling her beneath him, his every instinct was screaming at him. He felt she was his to watch over, protect, and shelter from everybody. Even one of his closest friends.

He looked down his nose at Silas and spoke loudly and clearly to make sure each of his warriors heard him because if they didn't, then it would be their funeral. "Alara is to be protected at all times. The next person to threaten her in any way will suffer the consequences. Is that clear?"

Erick and Cairo spoke at once. "Of course, sir."

"I'd prefer not to end up with a crushed larynx," Akio chuckled as he made his way to the bedroom door, "Hear you loud and clear, boss. I'm going to check on Ami and pass the message along."

He was wise to leave while anger still simmered within Rome's blood. He was still waiting for Maverick and Silas to acknowledge his statement when Alara groaned weakly and sent him moving to her side as he ushered them from the room with just a look. He'd hear their acquiescence once she was feeling better. He still needed answers and to tell her what he had learned from their kiss alone. Maverick helped Silas stand as he rubbed at his throat while Cairo and Erick followed behind them in silence. As soon as the bedroom door closed behind them, he spoke.

"I apologize for his mistreatment of you. I'm sure he was just

42

concerned for me, but that doesn't absolve him of what he did to you." He crouched down near the side of the bed and held out his hand, "If you allow me to, I can heal you."

"I just want my things so I can go," she whispered, her voice full of pain.

That pain pulled at him. He didn't like hearing it. He wanted to banish that feeling and ensure she never felt it again, but he wouldn't touch her without permission even as badly as he wanted to. Her kiss wasn't just breathtaking. It robbed him of all sense of self, and he could only imagine what more intimacy would do to him. He'd cum in his jeans like a preteen just from her kiss, and to make matters worse, he'd passed out, and his men had witnessed his weakness. Granted, they didn't know everything, yet they knew enough to realize she had gotten the upper hand. For once in his nine hundred and ninety-nine years of life, someone had bested and knocked him out. Her method was different, although the result had been the same. None of his warriors could best him, yet she had, and he would gladly allow her to do it again.

"Alara," he sighed heavily, "I can't just let you leave."

Her eyes narrowed at him in instant anger. "Am I to be your prisoner now?"

"No," he snapped in annoyance and stood, "but I need answers, and you need help controlling this power of yours. Who better to teach you than me?"

"And what did kissing you teach me? That you're powerful as fuck; sure, but it didn't teach me how to stop taking in energy. It didn't stop me from wanting more." She clenched her hands into fists and rose from the bed, causing him to retreat slightly, yet she kept her distance. Alara wanted a repeat of the kiss they'd shared, but she wasn't willing to risk her train of thought being derailed by a man who seemed to control everything around him. She felt the pull to him like a magnet and was sure he felt the same. The life force and power she'd garnered from him still strummed through her veins, and she was nearly drunk from this new power, but the headache that raged on caused her eyes to squint from the pain as her teeth clenched involuntarily.

"You're in pain," he stepped closer, his voice a soothing allure, "Let me heal you, and then we can talk. I need to heal you, Alara. Something is pressing at me to take care of you. This isn't a want; it's a need. If I don't heal you with your permission, I'll heal you without it."

The pain she was experiencing was enough to convince her that it was something she needed to let him do. She had never had someone nearly invade her mind with the force of a wrecking ball. Usually, she could heal herself, but something about this psychic attack hindered her ability to heal herself from the mental assault. She reluctantly nodded before a look of relief took hold of his features. The moment his fingertips gently caressed the sides of her head, that crushing pain evaporated as if it had never been there. A small gasp of surprise passed through her partially parted lips as he dropped his hands and stepped back. Alara smiled softly, glad to feel no pain and surprised that his touch hadn't awoken her siphoning ability.

"You look shocked," He frowned and tilted his head to analyze her more thoroughly, "Why is that?"

"Because my healing powers-" She cut herself off mid-sentence and frowned. "I mean because I didn't feel my powers pulling at your energy."

He made her forget herself. No one else knew what else she could do, and she wanted to keep it that way. Here he was, giving her a look that sent her stomach fluttering, and all she wanted to do was bear her soul to him. She had never found herself to be attracted to anyone before, especially to this magnitude. She literally itched for another taste of his lips. Staring into his intense gaze, Alara yearned for someone she hardly knew. He was powerful, though. Capable of withstanding her touch far longer than anyone else she'd ever encountered. She hadn't killed him, and that was enough to convince her that it was possible that more could happen. Especially if she learned to control it. Could he actually teach her that control? She wasn't sure, and staying to figure that out wasn't high on her list of things to do. She needed to contact her brother.

Rome smiled slowly, his pearly white teeth bringing attention to the fullness of his lips while his fangs remained absent. "So you have more powers? You aren't as singular as I assumed."

"What is that supposed to mean? Singular how?"

"A Kindred that only houses one power is considered singular. So, how many do you have, and how is your control? Will you need help with them as well?"

"I don't have any other powers." She replied stubbornly and lied through her teeth.

Rome narrowed his gaze, his eyes flashing a brighter blue as the lights flickered slightly before he pulled on the reins to his abilities. "Lying gets you nothing, Alara. I only wish to help you, yet you distrust me and force more barriers between us. Did I not save you? Help you? Have I hurt you in any way or made you feel unsafe? I thought I was getting through to you, but I'm not, am I?" He shook his head ruefully.

Getting someone to do as he bid was usually so much easier than this. He simply wanted the truth. No. Want wasn't the right word. He expected and needed her to be open and honest with him, allowing all shields to dissolve as every part of her opened to him. She was his. Rome could feel it in such a visceral way that it didn't quite make sense to him. That pull he experienced while being in her presence got stronger the longer he stood before her and inhaled the fragrance that seemed to radiate from her pores. Lilacs.

Did she need to fight him at every turn? It was tedious yet thrilling, making his blood pound as he imagined her running from him. If she did, she would bring out that need to claim. To sink his fangs into her and mark her so that every Eternal alive would know who she belonged to even if she didn't was a strong compulsion. One he had never felt before. He felt his eyes glowing again and forced them back to their standard shade of blue.

"How can I trust anything when you're trying to make me a prisoner? You told me I couldn't leave." She snapped and stabbed a finger into his chest with each word, "As a matter of fact, where are my things? I'm leaving Romulus. With or without your approval."

He glanced down at the finger still touching his chest before looking into her furious gaze. This wasn't exactly how he'd hoped to garner her touch, but he'd take it and more as long as she didn't stop his following action. He pressed her hand firmly into his pectoral muscle before yanking her into his arms and wrapping his other hand around the base of her neck. Her curly brown and burgundy hair caressed his skin, causing his dick to harden and his fangs to sharpen with lust as his gaze brightened again. The smell of her fear tickled his nose, and he snarled. He didn't want her fear. He wanted her passion. He wanted all the fire he could see that blazed within her gaze. He wanted her defiance, resilience, and even her refusal to bend to his will. He wanted it all with a passion, yet that slight hint of fear he tasted in the air forced him to release her. He took a step back before focusing on the bag he'd locked up within his safe as soon as he removed it from her. It appeared in his hand seconds later, earning a gasp from her before she reached for it with greedy hands. He would try a new method.

He held it just out of her reach as he spoke softly and forced his body back under control. "Not so fast, my little flower. From here on out, you'll tell me no more lies and make no move to escape me. I want to help you learn control as well as protect you from those who would do you harm if they were to ever learn of your abilities. Trust me, some in power would harm you and easily bend you to their will simply to harness your gifts. We wouldn't want that."

"You're just saying that to scare me into staying, but I can't." She ran her fingers through her hair in evident frustration. "I have to be somewhere, and the longer you hold me here, the longer it'll take me to get there. I have people waiting to help me, so if you could just give me my bag, I'll be out of your hair."

Now Alara didn't know whether that was true, considering Alaric had hardly given her any information to go off of, and she was sure her map was long gone, but she knew she couldn't stay with Rome. She needed to contact her brother. Sure, a part of her wanted to see how far things could go with him sexually, but not at the expense of her freedom. She'd been locked up all her life, and now that she was free, she refused to be locked up again. If she couldn't come and go as she pleased, what type of life would she have but one of entrapment? She wouldn't be trapped again.

He frowned, "What people do you have that will help you, and where are they? There's no one else around for miles on end, Alara. No one else but my Guardians and I. So, who are you searching for, and how did you end up on our mountainside?"

"You're supposed to be helping me out, remember? Now, please, if you will, hand me my bag."

He chuckled softly. "You can't have it both ways, Alara. Do you want my help or not? Because the only help I'll provide is what I've already stated."

Alara glared. Why was he so intent on keeping her there, and why did he even care to help her? He spoke about being a protector for humans and Kindreds, but that didn't mean she needed protecting. In fact, Alara didn't want it. She could defend herself now that the collar had been removed. All she needed was control. She was sure she could teach herself what she needed to know. She didn't need him or the others. She was sure of it, yet her voice lacked conviction when speaking.

"I don't need you...I just need my bag to contact my people and leave."

Rome's expression hardened. "And if you're somehow located and captured, how do you plan to free yourself from the clutches of Titan once they have a hold of you?"

That name froze her to her very core. How did he know about Titan? He said the name with such animosity and contempt. Was this the enemy he'd been speaking of before? She couldn't admit to knowing of their existence. What if he assumed she was a spy sent to infiltrate their stronghold? If she were him, that's what she would believe, so she played dumb. She played dumber than a stack of bricks and prayed harder than ever so he wouldn't see through her lies.

"Whose Titan?"

"Titan isn't a who but a what." He growled and stalked across the room to distance themselves as he spoke. "Titan is a corrupt institution founded by Theolonius Titan, the first man to come into contact with Eternals and learn of our true nature. We were created by the Gods to protect humanity, yet Theo wanted super soldiers to

47

sell to the highest bidder when he discovered us. He was backed by this corrupt government of yours to make it happen. We've been hunted and killed, while some of my men have even been captured and tortured before meeting the sun's rays. They want to learn our secrets and create more of us." He glanced over his shoulder and pinned her with an unmoving stare, "There is no creating more. In their attempt to do so, they've created worse beings that walk the earth and stalk the human population. It is because of Titan that Rogue vampires exist. Because of them, humanity needs us to hunt within the darkness of night to eradicate both of our enemies."

"I'm sorry, did you just say vampires? Isn't that what you and your friends are?" Alara crossed her arms over her chest and frowned. "I've seen the fangs and the freaky eyes on multiple occasions from you guys. I've watched TV before, so wouldn't that put you directly within that category, considering your vampiristic qualities?"

Disgust filled his face. "Vampires are savages. They are nothing compared to Eternals. We are their executioners. We are what keeps them from eradicating every human that walks this earth. Without us, humanity itself would be nothing but a distant memory. Everything reduced to ash!" He slashed his hand through the air and released a burst of energy that rippled across her skin.

"So you fight Titan as well as these vampires? Is that why you have all of those weapons in your closet? You're a warrior who fights for humanity's sake, and I've somehow stumbled into a war?"

"Correct. Now, if you'd stop being so stubborn, you would realize that this is the safest place for you to be because out there," Rome turned to stare out the window and into the darkness as he spoke with a much softer tone than usual, "Out there you're exposed. There's no telling who your true enemy is until it's too late."

CHAPTER
SIX

The tightness and pressure within his chest was unbearable. The feeling of drowning surrounded him as water sluiced over him, filling his mouth, nose, and lungs. This was the moment he would die. Alaric could feel it coming even as he struggled against the zip ties that held his head, wrists, and ankles immobile. He fought viciously and opened his mouth with a breathless scream just as the water stopped and the rag over his face was removed. He was pushed forward, where he hacked up half his lung and took in the bright lights around him. Two men stood within the room; one was the lackey, while the other was Lukas Titan. His boss.

At six foot three with a thin athletic build, Lukas Titan was dressed immaculately in a gray pinstripe suit with emerald eyes and golden blonde hair that, if not for the fact that it was slicked back by a copious amount of gel, would have fallen around his ears and nearly covered his entire face. His forehead was broad, his lips were thin, and a scar ran across the whole left side of his face. If you knew him, you'd know to fear him, but if you didn't and noticed the slight limp he walked with, you would assume he was an easy target. Alaric knew better.

"I want an answer, Alaric. Without it, this could be an all-day process, and that last session nearly killed you." He chuckled menacingly, "Where were you when Blaine escaped with Alara?"

Alaric continued to cough uncontrollably as he squinted against the brightness of the lights and clenched his hands over and over again in an attempt to return some feeling to them. They had been torturing him for several hours now—longer than he was used to. Lukas asked the questions while his man waterboarded him continually. Soon, the electric shocks would come into play. He wasn't sure if he'd be able to survive that form of torture, but Alaric damn sure had to try if he had any hopes of getting out of there and completing his mission.

Once he could speak, he replied through the pain of his lungs burning from oxygen deprivation. "I was at the market grabbing a few things for dinner when I got the alert and rushed back to base."

"Why were you off base to begin with? No one can come or go without my say-so during a transfer, so what gave you the right to leave? I know I didn't authorize it."

"Check my room," Alaric snarled through clenched teeth, "There's a bottle of rum with your name on it and your favorite brand of cigars. There should still be the receipt in the bag. I bought them with you in mind for the joining between you and Alara. It was meant to be a surprise. It's stashed under my bunk."

Lukas moved toward the only door within the room and opened it to yell out into the hall, where several guards stood at attention. "Someone check Alaric's bunk and bring me whatever's underneath it!" He slammed the door and came to kneel awkwardly before him, "Until then…put him under again."

"I told you what you wanted to know!" Alaric exclaimed and fought against his restraints as his chair was jerked back at an unnatural angle, and a wet rag was slapped over his face before water was poured, obstructing his airways once more.

Lukas watched on with glee. Torture was high on his list of things he loved, right next to Alara. At the thought of her, he returned to the first time he'd seen her.

. . .

Ten Years ago

Lukas trailed behind his mother and several staff members in charge of Project Romulus. He'd never been this far down in the facility before, but today was the day he would learn all about the family business. He knew things weren't at all what they seemed. To the outside world, Titan Corp was a research facility centered around gene therapy study and research, but Lukas knew there was more to it. He would hear the screams through the vents on late nights when he should have been sleeping, but he wasn't a child anymore who had to listen to the squabblings of his mother. Lukas was now thirty-three years old. He was old enough to know how the family business made money thanks to his father's will and last testament. If it had been up to his devious mother, he would never have been allowed within the restricted part of the facility.

Everywhere he looked, white walls stared back at him. They'd been walking for several moments now, passing door after door with no end, it seemed. He wasn't sure where he was heading or how far this tunnel seemed to lead, but the screaming he usually heard late at night could be heard now, along with vicious snarls that sent every hair on his body to attention. Fear spread through his veins like quickly melting ice as his eyes scanned ahead and focused on the single door at the end of the hallway. His mother, Alma Titan, spoke softly to the doctor who walked to the left of her.

"Is she awake, or shall we first show him to the beasts?"

Alma Titan was a beautiful woman in her sixties with silver hair that fell to her shoulders in waves, yet she kept it in a tightly controlled bun that pinched up her face and gave her severely tight features. The botox helped keep the wrinkles away and gave her smoother skin to hide her age. A bright blue mid-dress covered her body while a pair of black Louboutin heels pinched her feet with every stride.

Dr. Salazar grinned happily and clasped his hands repeatedly as he spoke. "We have one of them in a room where we intended to bring her shortly. We're testing her power. We need to see if she can take one of them down. I waited for your arrival before we put her to the test."

"And she's secure?" Alma questioned, surprise evident in her voice.

"Of course, ma'am. We've created a device that connects to the collar around her throat and forces electrical charges through it to control her and keep her docile. At the same time, we temporarily disable the power dampening within the collar."

"Show me."

The moment they entered an observation room, Lukas focused on the one-way mirror that looked into what appeared to be a vacant room, but upon closer inspection, it wasn't as empty as he'd assumed. Against the far wall, something straight out of a nightmare was chained by the wrists and ankles with no give in its restraints. Large fangs filled its jaw as piercing red eyes stared directly at him through the glass. An inhuman growl rattled from the very depths of its chest as he fought against the restraints. It was clear that this creature had once been a man in its past life. Lukas opened his mouth to ask what was happening but abruptly closed it when a door opened, and a girl wearing a blindfold was shoved into the room. A gold collar encircled her throat, and her arms hung loosely in front of her, although her wrists were locked within specially crafted handcuffs. An oversized white tee and baggy gray sweatpants covered her form, yet Lukas was captivated. There was something about her that just drew him in. He placed his hands against the cool one-way glass as Dr. Salazar spoke into the intercom.

"Subject 1, move forward with your arms outstretched and place them on the subject before you."

Her voice was hardly a whisper when she spoke, yet they heard her. "But I'll hurt them. I d-d-don't want to h-hurt anyone, p-please."

"Do it now! This is your only warning."

She shook her head defiantly and screamed abruptly when the doctor pressed a button on a small remote he clasped within the palm of his hand. She dropped to her knees in agony and clawed frantically at the collar as an electrical current passed through her small frame. Lukas wanted to object. Honestly, he wished to stab the knife that was stashed away in his jacket pocket and slide it into the good doctor's eye, but he knew any sympathy would make her pain ten times worse, so he remained silent and watchful as she climbed to her feet once the electrical surges stopped. Her arms were outstretched as she carefully walked across the room to the figure that remained chained and snarling.

"What is that thing?" Lukas questioned as the creature thrashed harder against its restraints.

Alma spoke from directly behind him. "This is what we've been perfecting: the T-virus. What you see is a failed project that we need to eliminate. That's what subject 1, also known as Alara, is for, or at least we hope she can be of some use in that area. She has the ability to take a life when she makes skin-to-skin contact, but we've never placed her with one of the experiments. Their life expectancy differs from ours, so we'll all witness now to see if she can accomplish such a feat."

They each watched in silent fascination as young Alara's hands finally came into contact with the bare chest of the male before her. For a moment, nothing happened. Seconds later, the body beneath her palms jerked in shock, his red eyes nearly bugged from his sockets in obvious pain before they rolled into the back of his head, and he became dead weight within his chains.

"She did it!" Dr. Salazar exclaimed. "She really did it!" He clapped ecstatically as he looked on with wonder.

Lukas simply stared as Alara slowly dropped to her knees and cried silently while everyone else around him cheered with glee over what they had just witnessed. He was just as surprised, if not more so. He never knew something like this was possible. He never knew someone like her could exist, but now Lukas had a new obsession and wanted her as his own.

HE WAS PULLED from his memories when the sound of Alaric's choking and the slight knock at the door reached his ears.

"Let him up," Lukas snapped and moved to open the door to find one of his men standing on the other side, holding up a large bottle of his favorite rum and pack of cigars. "Was there a receipt with it?"

His man nodded and held out a slip of paper that clearly showed the date and time of the transaction. At the time of purchase, Blaine was running away with his most prized possession, which revealed that Alaric had been clear across town.

He closed the door and returned to stand before Alaric as he gasped for air. Now, he could continue with the torture just for the fun of it, although the proof of his words had been shown, and to be quite honest, Alaric was one of his best men. He didn't want to lose him. Not just because he fought better than any other soldier beneath his command or even because of his higher intelligence. No. He simply possessed something no other man within his ranks had. He had an ability the same as Alara, although his ability differed. It was not as powerful, but definitely helpful in many ways. He could read minds and pull any information he desired in the process. He could wreak havoc without the gold collar that encircled his throat. He could topple the Titan empire in moments. He threatened everything Titan Corp stood for, and Lukas couldn't have that. Maybe if he knew that Alaric was utterly loyal to the cause, he wouldn't even need the device, but to remove it indefinitely, tests needed to be passed, and he knew of the perfect one.

"Untie him and get him some dry clothing," His smile was nothing if not devious.

Alaric watched them from beneath lowered lashes as the lackey who had nearly killed him released him from his zip ties before he left the room with his head held high and his shoulders back. He promised himself he would be the first Alaric killed the second he had the opportunity. There were no ifs ands or buts about it.

He rubbed at his raw wrists and focused on the man in charge. After clearing his throat and forcing himself to ignore the pain within his chest and lungs, he spoke with a nonchalance he didn't feel. "Does this mean I'm free to return to my post?"

"Not quite," Lukas replied, wiping non-existent lint from his shoulder, "I have an assignment for you, something that shouldn't be a problem if your allegiance truly lies with Titan."

"And what assignment might that be, sir?"

"I need you to interrogate the remaining members who knew of Alara's transfer, and when I say interrogate, that means I need you to use your power and dive deep. No holds barred. You'll be placed within observation room 1, where your power will be confined to that space, and I expect results. I must know which members must die and how to reacquire my beloved. He couldn't have pulled this off on his own." He shook his head as he paced, "Blaine doesn't have the mental capacity to put such an escape into place and execute it to this degree. He must have had help, and I want to know who helped him."

Alaric's gut clenched at thinking about what he had to do now. Using his power wasn't as simple as going into someone's mind and extracting information. Some people had natural barriers that were hard to remove, and sometimes, he would have to dig deep. Deeper than recommended because the results could be catastrophic to the person's mind that he was infiltrating. He could cause permanent brain damage. In rare cases, he could kill them. The thought of using his power after weeks of dampening it was slightly unsettling. Always with the release of his collar, his power actively searched for a mind to invade and obliterate. Without proper training, Titan had never allowed him to reach the level of control that would let him go into a mind without detection. Without that control, anyone with half a mind to understand what was happening to them would know that someone else was privy to every thought or memory they might try to cover up. It would feel almost like the tentacle of an octopus wrapping around your thoughts.

His boss was asking him to interrogate the minds of the men and women he worked with. Some of those men and women were oblivious to the true nature of Titan Corp. True; they knew of Alara and what she was to Lukas, but that was just the icing on the proverbial cake. Most were oblivious to the true nature of what went on here. Most had no knowledge of the beings they kept locked up on the lower levels, but Alaric wasn't oblivious. He'd been moving up in ranks for years, hoping to learn everything about the corporation. He'd needed to know their weaknesses and strengths, so he'd needed to gain Lukas's trust.

Alaric came to his feet once the guard returned and handed him a dry change of clothes. He dressed quickly and reacted before anyone could intercede or stop him from getting a little retribution on his own behalf. Alaric's hand whipped out, his fist connecting with the man's nose before he heard a satisfying crunch that sent the man sprawling to the floor unconscious.

"Are you done?" Lukas questioned with a bored tone. "If so, follow me."

Alaric adjusted the long sleeves of his shirt and followed him from the room. He didn't want to question anyone using his methods, but the faster he got this over with, the faster he could continue with his own mission. "Who am I interrogating first?"

"It's a surprise." He chuckled.

That sick feeling he got whenever he carried out a mission for Titan settled within him now. Something was happening that Lukas would find sick pleasure in, and he was one sick, twisted bastard. Years of witnessing and partaking in the actions of a madman had opened Alaric's mind to the depravity of some people, and Lukas Titan was at the top of that list.

His boss led him down several hallways before approaching a non-descript door he knew intimately. The room beyond had been specifically built to keep Alaric's powers in check. Once his collar was deactivated, anyone within the room with him would have their mind laid bare in the most painful way possible. A one-way mirror was directly beside the door with a light switch and an intercom that would allow communication with anyone inside. The light inside was turned off, but with a flick of his wrist, Lukas flipped the switch, and Alaric's objective came into view. His stomach dropped. The need to kill the bastard beside him rose with a vengeance because sitting strapped to a chair—similar to how he had been only moments ago—was the second person he was meant to protect and save.

She was the spitting image of Alara in every way, with misty gray eyes sprinkled with light blue streaks and dark brown and burgundy hair that fell in curly waves to her bare shoulders. They'd left her dressed in a skimpy bra and panty set that nearly exposed the parts that made her a woman. Tears slid down her cheeks as she struggled against the zip ties that held her in place. The need to protect her almost shattered his resolve, but to truly free her from this fucked up place, he would have to play his part. He would have to infiltrate his baby sister's mind and pray that, in the end, Alondra would forgive him for the role he had to play in her pain.

CHAPTER

SEVEN

S even days.

Seven fucking days of having this woman in their home. Within their space. Or, more accurately put….within Rome's space. A week of having her smell on everything he owned, hearing her voice, and seeing her smile whenever Akio said a corny joke was slowly driving him insane. He snarled softly from his position in the kitchen as he watched Alara walk across the room from his bedroom to sit beside Maverick on the couch where the rest of them sat watching a movie. The only one who hadn't warmed up to her was Amirishka, and with good reason. After waking up from her three-day coma, Amiriska had been spitting mad with a need for vengeance. To be knocked on her ass by a human was a blow to her pride as an Eternal, but with the threat of dealing with him, she kept the peace with the woman that currently had him in a perpetual state of arousal.

She was adjusting well to the reality of what her world had become. Rome had educated her on the truth of what he and his fellow brethren were and everything they stood for. Every night before they went out for a hunt, she helped him and his men prepare their weapons and lay out their desired clothing. It was almost as if Alara had become like their personal squire overnight. She anticipated everyone's needs before they had time to ask or think of anything. She wasn't just observant; she was patient, kind, and sickly sweet when ensuring his people were well-fed and cared for. Her need to please was in everything she did. From her cooking to her cleaning, she made their lives a little easier, and she carried in a wealth of warmth he hadn't known they'd needed. The only thing she seemed to avoid was being alone with him. She avoided him as if he carried the plague, unless it was for their early morning training but today that was ending. His main objective was to get her alone, taste her once more, and maybe learn more about where she had come from. So far, their lessons were progressing well. She quickly picked up hand-to-hand combat yet still struggled with controlling her siphoning ability. He planned to help with that.

"Give us the room." He spoke softly.

Every head in the room turned to look at him questioningly. Everyone but her. Akio went so far as to open his mouth to, no doubt, ask why but thought better of it when Rome shot him a withering look.

"I suppose we can start the hunt early tonight," Erick stated and moved for the back of the house to enter his bedroom as each warrior stood to follow after him.

Maverick lagged behind and paused just as he reached the hallway. "Listen, I know at first I wasn't too nice, but let's not scare her away, okay?"

"Leave us!" Rome snapped and felt his fangs lengthening with aggression.

Maverick rushed from the room without a second thought, finally giving him a moment alone with the woman who was fracturing his control bit by bit. He inhaled, making sure to take in her unique lilac scent. Smelling her calmed the aggression within him, but now his arousal was a constant pressure that seemed to build by the second.

"I can literally feel your eyes drilling into the back of my head. Have I done something to earn your ire, Romulus?" Her voice washed over him and curled around his straining erection, her tone filled with curiosity.

"And who says I'm angry with you?"

She jerked her chin towards the large windows and chuckled. "The weather begs to differ, and the fact that Cairo has to continually clear the skies of your thunderclouds says a lot about your darkening mood."

She wasn't wrong about that. Being around her daily was causing Rome's powers to fluctuate in a way he didn't understand. He had minimal control over them and could not stop the constant ebb and flow. Every day, the weather changed with his emotions, and for the better part of the week, his mood had been dark and full of unfulfilled desire. With that came the thunder, lightning, snow storms, hail, and biting cold. Although it was the middle of winter, it wouldn't explain the erratic shifts in weather, so every now and then, Cairo used his ability to manipulate the elements to correct the issue that Rome would cause. They didn't need Titan getting a bead on them due to his lack of control.

He moved until he stood directly behind her on the couch. "Who says that the emotion I'm currently experiencing is anger?"

"Well, what else could it be?" She turned to glance over her shoulder as her cold stare met his gaze, "Ever since I got here, your mood has been incredibly sour, according to the rest of the group. The way you look at me, speak to me, and practically avoid me, you would think I did something to you personally. Maybe you hate me because I refuse to answer any more questions about where I came from, or you're just upset you gave up your room for me. I'm not sure what it is, but quite frankly, your attitude leaves a bad taste in my mouth, and I'd rather not be around it."

He loved her fire. Sure, she was sweet and comely when it suited her, but fire blazed in her eyes whenever she spoke to him, and a temper he itched to correct was evident within her tone. She challenged him. Made him want to push her into submission. She didn't know his need to dominate almost every part of his life, and he knew it would take time to bend her to his will. His warriors knew what it meant to challenge him. They knew even with their words, they needed to speak a certain way or face his wrath. The only one to constantly go against him was Akio, but that was to be expected, considering their history. Everyone else feared him, and with good reason. He wasn't an easy man. Maybe once upon a time, he had been.

Alara stood and moved to leave the family room, yet he cut off her exit by moving directly into her path. He crowded her personal space. Okay...maybe he'd had it wrong earlier. He was definitely the one who'd been avoiding her and not the other way around. He'd done it because her scent was more pungent now, and the need to touch her was so overwhelming he could hardly ignore it any longer. The sessions between them were going well enough that a simple touch wouldn't put him on his ass, but prolonged contact was something she refused to let happen. That was ending today as well. When Rome wanted something, he usually got what he wanted, and now he wanted her. He wanted her mouth yielding to his as he tangled a hand within her thick hair. He wanted her beneath, over, beside, and pressed against him in the most intimate ways. He wanted inside her, and he damn sure wanted a sip of her blood. Rome was dying for a taste.

"Romulus... you're scaring me." She whispered and inched back as his eyes brightened and fastened onto her lips.

He tried to bargain with her. "A kiss for your bag." Yes, he still held her bag hostage at an undisclosed location and refused to give it up for this reason. Maybe that made him a fucked up individual for holding her things as a bargaining chip, but sometimes a man had to do what he had to do to get what he wanted. Especially from a woman who refused to see the blatant sexual attraction between them. Was she really blind to his need for her and of hers for him? If so, he wouldn't allow her to hide any longer. She would face this with him. He refused to be the only one suffering.

"You can't bargain with something that isn't rightfully yours." She narrowed her gaze and crossed her arms, causing her breasts to rise higher beneath the v-neck of her shirt and allowing him a better view of her generous 32c breasts.

"If it is within my possession, then that makes it mine, so what do you say, my little flower? A kiss for the bag?"

"We've been over this. I'm not your anything."

"Yet." He smiled softly and reached out to twirl a strand of her hair between his fingers, "Now, what's your answer?"

"If I kiss you," she paused, her eyes taking in his form from the black shit kickers that enclosed his large feet to the dark dreadlocks that were tied back from his face, "If I kiss you, you'll return my things and stop treating me as if I have the plague?"

"I hadn't realized I was doing so, but in my defense, you're a temptation I should avoid. I already feel possessive of you, and the anger you think I'm feeling is, in fact, desire and arousal. I want you, Alara, and if you permit it, I intend to pursue you until I get what I want." He hadn't meant to reveal his intentions, but now that he had, it was too late to take back.

"What about what I want, Romulus?"

"I told you before," he cupped her cheek and groaned at the softness of her skin against his own, "call me Rome. And if I can provide it for you, then I shall. What do you desire?"

He waited with bated breath to see what she would say. He hoped she wanted him as he wanted her. If she did, then his plan would accelerate tenfold. He was seconds away from pulling her into his arms when his warriors reentered wearing black hunting attire. She put distance between them and forced his hands to drop as they each paused at the threshold. Amirishka continued towards the front door, twirling one of her blades in her hand as she blatantly ignored them.

"We're going hunting, sir. We'll be paired up; Ami will be with Mav, I'll assist Akio, and Silas and Cairo will work together tonight. Should we need you, we'll call." Erick stated before he headed out.

Silas waited until everyone else walked out before he spoke. "I had an obscure vision. A dark cloud hangs above us all, the Rogues surround us, and death is imminent. Be careful tonight. Silence isn't always your friend." He headed for the door and closed it softly behind him.

Silas's visions were always cryptic and sometimes confusing to understand. He would speak in riddles only he seemed to comprehend, and he wasn't very forthcoming when explaining his visions. Silas had explained to them before that giving them the details of what he saw could alter the future and cause negative ramifications for humanity. Obscurity was best.

"What did he mean?" Alara questioned with a frown that screwed up her perfect features, "And shouldn't you be going with them? I thought that's what you were created for to protect humanity."

"No one but Silas understands his own words, and you heard Erick. If anyone needs me, then they shall call." He pulled her into his arms until she was finally flush against him. "Now, about our bargain, what shall it be? Kiss or no kiss? Bag or no bag?"

God, she was such a temptation. He knew this was bad. He was willing to sit out of a hunt to taste her again. He was willing to anger the Gods just to hear her breathy moan. The need that ran through him was foreign. It made him question why this woman had him in knots. It made his mind once again ponder the idea of how she came to be here. Maybe she really was a plant put here by his enemies to distract him, but that wouldn't explain the need that tore through him at just the sight of her. They couldn't force those reactions within him, could they? Add in the smell and the sound of her voice, and he could feel himself slipping into the mindset of a madman. She had to be his fated mate. There was no other answer, yet mates were a myth to his people. No matings had ever occurred.

ALARA STARED at the feral expression that was plastered on Rome's face. His eyes blazed brighter than she'd ever seen, and his fangs sharpened beneath her gaze as the band of his arm tightened around her waist. She wished that it was fear coursing through her, but instead, it was desire. Her breasts felt heavier than usual, and the area between her thighs got wetter by the second. Their skin wasn't touching, yet she could feel his energy surrounding her, cocooning her, and with a glance out the window, she saw the clouds forming in the sky as droplets of rain started to fall.

After a week of being with the Eternals, Alara had learned much from them and had learned just as much about them. She'd learned about them as warriors and as the individuals that they were. Romulus was definitely the enigma of the group. She never knew what he was thinking or what his true motives were. Sure, he said he wanted her, but she'd heard that before from Lukas. She cringed at the thought of him. Words were words, and if there was one thing she learned growing up, it was to listen to a person's actions instead of what came out of their mouth.

"Alara," Rome pulled her from her thoughts, voice holding her captive as he gently cupped her cheek, "tell me what you want, but know that I'll be getting what I want as well."

She didn't believe for a second that he would give her what she truly desired, but Alara at least had to try, even if she no longer wanted it as badly as she should. "Listen, I know that control is high on your list of things, but I need to know I'm free to come and go as I please. I won't be a prisoner."

His gaze hardened, yet his eyes focused on her lips as if they were the most important thing to him. She thought he would speak when his lips slightly parted, but instead, a slight snarl filled the air before his head bent, and his plush lips captured her own. Her mouth opened with a gasp, and he wasted no time sliding his tongue between her lips as he took control of the kiss. He surrounded her. He pulled her closer and slid his hand into her hair before he tugged gently on the soft locs while his other hand gripped her hip in a brutal hold that was sure to leave marks. He was strong. His tongue dueling with her own in a fight for supremacy. Alara could hardly breathe. Surprise ran through her veins at the pure attraction that continued to ping-pong between them. She couldn't feel that pull, that siphoning of energy that usually filled her. All she felt was pleasure. Her core tightened, and her hands gripped the cotton of his shirt to pull him closer as the kiss deepened further. Her moan filled his mouth, and his growl followed until she felt a sharp pain in her lip.

She jerked back abruptly, licked at her lip, and tasted a hint of copper, followed by a slight stinging burn that surprised her until she glanced up to find clear blue eyes fastened on her lips. A drop of blood smeared his bottom lip, and the look on his face was positively alarming. Fear slammed into her, erasing the pleasure that had nearly consumed her as she readied herself to fight him off if he made a wrong move. If living with the Eternals had taught her anything within the past week, it was to never interrupt them when they fed. They weren't like the Rogue vampires, where they needed blood to survive. In fact, they hardly consumed it unless they were seriously injured or in the middle of sharing sex and blood with a partner. Good ole Maverick had let that detail slip one night when they spoke over ice cream and movies. She'd asked for more, but he'd shook his head and told her to let it go. Now, she wished he would have spoken on it more because the look in Rome's eyes scared her. Eternals didn't need blood to survive, but that didn't mean they didn't still crave it. As turned on as he made her feel, Alara feared his fangs and what they could do to her. She wasn't a fan of needles, and she damn sure wasn't a fan of losing blood. Sure, she thought of what it may feel like to have those babies embedded deep within her vein, but looking at them now, she wasn't convinced she should find out.

"Romulus," she whispered, her arms outstretched to fend him off.

He licked at the blood on his lip, and the strangest thing happened when his eyes went darker than usual, and his fangs lengthened even more. She didn't know what that meant, but a look of such longing filled his eyes before he disappeared right in front of her and reappeared several feet away in the kitchen with his back turned to her. She could see the tension in his shoulders as he visibly shuddered. Alara opened her mouth to speak but paused when he flicked his hand, and her bag appeared on the counter. His voice was like gravel when he spoke.

"Do not leave, or I will come after you. Just stay inside, little flower."

Before she could respond, Rome flashed away, and she was

alone for the first time since her arrival. Not sure how to feel yet confident she had almost been drained dry, she moved for her bag and rifled through it with only one thought in mind. She needed to contact her brother and figure out where she needed to go because staying here was no longer an option. That interaction had been too close for comfort. She didn't want to die. Maybe Rome had more control than she gave him credit for since he'd walked away before anything more could transpire.

She found her phone buried at the bottom of the bag within a ziplock bag and quickly pulled it out and turned it on. Sure enough, Alaric was the only number saved, and although he'd told her not to call unless it was an emergency, Alara deemed this an emergency and hit send. He picked up on the third ring.

"Alara, is everything alright?" His voice was like a soothing balm to her soul.

She wasn't sure what to tell him or how much, so she kept it short and sweet, hoping he would hear the urgency within her voice and do what needed to be done. "I need you to come get me or tell me where to go. I think I'm in danger."

CHAPTER

EIGHT

"F uck!" Rome exclaimed, sending his fist flying into a large pine tree the moment he teleported away from Alara and appeared within the forest's center, miles away from Maverick's home.

The force of his punch pulled the tree's roots from the earth and sent it flying into the darkness of the night before it smashed into the ground. He couldn't believe he'd nearly lost control. Seconds. He'd been mere seconds away from sinking his fangs into her delicate neck and taking what he knew she wasn't willing to give. Yet. The taste of her blood when he'd accidentally nicked her was forever etched into his mind. She was pure ambrosia. He wanted to get drunk off her blood. He knew if anyone's blood could do such a feat, it would be hers, and that was the problem. None of the women he'd been intimate with or taken blood from had given him such a visceral reaction. None of them had ever moved him or made him want more. She made him want more, and he knew she could quickly become an addiction.

Something made Alara different, and maybe, just maybe, it was her position as a Kindred. Every Eternal alive knew the myth of the Kindreds and the Eternal man or woman they were meant for. It was said that the Gods had touched the Kindred so they could partner with Eternals on an intimate level. Considering how long an Eternal lived, a partner to share that lifetime with would make being alive all the more promising to endure. Living for centuries wasn't all it was cracked up to be, at least not to Rome. Loneliness was a sure thing. Yes, he had his warriors, but they didn't know the pressures of being king over a race that was above the laws of men. In the end, he was the law.

With the presence of Alara and what she brought out in him, Rome was beginning to believe the myth. He was starting to hope that a Kindred was placed explicitly upon the earth for a specific guardian and that Alara was his. How else would he explain his need for her? It was becoming an obsession. When he should have been out hunting with his brethren, he was instead playing guard dog around the house to ensure her safety. Instead of protecting the millions in the world from the Rogues that wished to drain them dry, he was watching her…the woman that wanted to leave him.

He snarled and sent a burst of telekinetic energy from his body, sending snow billowing around as more trees toppled over and smacked into the ground. His phone rang persistently within his pocket; he could feel the vibrations, yet he ignored it and dropped to the ground with his legs crossed and his head bowed. It only took a thought to erect a protective bubble around him as he forced his mind to reach out to the Gods. He formed a bridge between his mind and theirs. The sun god Helios was the first to appear before Artemis, the goddess of chastity, hunting, and the moon, followed by Zeus, the god of the sky and king of gods, and Hera, the goddess of women, marriage, and childbirth. Typically, he encountered several other Gods, but they weren't present. He couldn't see them, but he could feel them as well as the individual power they wielded surrounded him.

Artemis spoke first, her voice filled with annoyance at being disturbed. "Warrior, why have you summoned us?"

"I need guidance," Rome stated, "the Kindreds…is it true?"

Helios sighed heavily. "Is what true?"

"Is it true that there's a perfect match meant for every Eternal? Do my people have mates?"

When Zeus spoke, Rome could feel his power echo before it settled within his bones. "Why do you ask Romulus? Have you found yours?"

"I'm not sure, my king. How would I know she's for me instead of one of my warriors? I feel a possessiveness towards her that goes beyond reason, and I hate to admit this, but I've failed you all in my pursuit of the Rogues. Since she arrived, I have been less inclined to do my duty for humanity. All I care about is protecting her and assuring myself and her that she is happy and whole."

Hera took the opportunity to speak. "We have picked the perfect individual meant to be your counterpart as well as those under you, and we have done so to ensure the longevity of your race so that you may continue to fight for the sake of humanity. This woman you speak of could, in fact, be your mate, but that is a mystery you must solve on your own. We cannot and will not assist you in this matter. As for your duty, you have not yet failed us, but if you continue down this path of neglect, we will be forced to react and take matters into our own hands, so I suggest you do as we have asked you to do and protect humanity. Those Kindred may not continue to live long enough to bond with any of you if you do not."

The link between him and the Gods evaporated before Rome could respond or ask any more questions. His eyes snapped open, and he stared into the darkened forest as he mulled over their words. He hadn't failed them yet, but he was well on his way to doing so if he didn't return to his duty. Hera wasn't known for empty threats. Her anger was legendary against women favored by Zeus, and although the Kindred had only been created partially by him, jealousy was still a living thing within her. She would slaughter the lot of them if given the chance. He couldn't allow that. He first needed to learn if the myths were true. Could they indeed mate?

Rome stood and wiped the snow from his jeans as his phone vibrated again. Without looking, he pulled the device from his pocket and answered.

"Yes?"

The sound of clashing swords, screams, and battle cries could be heard in the background as Kai, a warrior stationed in Alaska, spoke. "They have us surrounded. I've lost three men, and we could use some assistance. Linc and I are the only ones left. We've lost the others."

"I'll be right there."

He wanted to check on Alara first to ensure she remained at home, but instead, he focused on Kai and Lincoln's energy signatures and forced his body to dematerialize and reappear right on the fringes of an all-out battle. Two dozen Rogues surrounded the warriors, who fought back to back with blades dripping black blood. Rogues were known for their piercing red eyes and razor-sharp fangs and nails. They were vicious when they fought, almost like rabid dogs itching for a kill. Before anyone could take notice of his arrival, he used his ability to call forth his long sword just as he sent a telekinetic blast into the fray. Several rogues soared through the air, opening a hole between them that allowed Lincoln and Kai to move more freely. Four Rogues jumped at him with extended claws and sharpened fangs that held tell-tale signs of his warriors' blood on them. Anger surged through him at the sight. Rome grabbed the biggest Rogue by the throat and used him as a shield as he cut through the rest of them like butter. Their screams were music to his ears. Everyone who lunged at him was sliced open and left to bleed out. The man within his grip struggled fiercely, sharp claws digging into his arm as his growls filled the air. He was strong but not stronger than Rome.

Instead of killing the feral beast with his long sword, Rome decided to kill him slowly. He used his telepathic ability to dive between the barriers of the Rogue's mind and slowly tore it apart. Piece by piece, he severed neurological pathways and cut off all oxygen to the brain before he dropped the body to glance around the warehouse. Three of his Eternals lay dead with numerous cuts that ran deep. They were younger, no older than four hundred years of age. They hadn't yet possessed the ability to cauterize their bleeding internally. It took centuries of practice and patience, and not all succeeded.

Almost thirty dead Rogues littered the ground, but their bodies had already begun to dematerialize. No one was sure how or why it happened, but when a Rogue vampire died, their body would slowly eat away at itself until all that was left was a pile of clothing. Rome believed it was their tainted blood that caused the rapid decay. On the other hand, Eternals were given a proper burial deep beneath the earth, and a protective barrier was placed above it to ensure they would never be disturbed.

"Thank you for the assistance, my king." Kai bowed deeply, his dark brown wavy hair falling forward to conceal his face before he stood upright with a smirk on his lips. Kai was a formidable warrior with honey-brown eyes that sat above a crooked nose that had never set right after being broken one too many times throughout his life. With a square jawline and the sculpted cheekbones of a model with thick plush lips, Kai made women drool over his six-foot-two frame. He was muscular and lean beneath all-black leather attire, with a long trench coat that concealed most of his form and weapons.

"I've told you before, Kai, address me as Rome. Nothing else." He frowned as he wiped the blood from his sword before he sent it back home where it belonged.

"I seriously wish I could do that," Lincoln grumbled as he wiped his short swords off with a dead rogue's shirt. He was seven inches shorter than Rome's seven-foot stature at six foot five with light green eyes and auburn hair that fell to the middle of his back. Lincoln had narrow features with dimpled cheeks and full lips, but a multitude of scars lined his face and body from his years of being tortured by Titan. He was the only warrior who had been captured by Titan. He had escaped, yet he refused to talk about his time there. Even Rome chose to respect his need to keep the traumatic events in his past.

"It's not all it's cracked up to be, Linc," Rome smiled ruefully, "If I wasn't so old, my energy would be drained simply from using my telekinetic ability. It takes a lot from me, but years of practice have allowed me to harness it to the best of my ability."

"Says the most powerful Eternal alive." Lincoln scoffed, sheathed his swords, and quickly pulled Rome into a bear hug.

Rome smiled softly and hugged him back before he disentangled himself and clasped his forearms with Kai's. "Now that pleasantries are out of the way, tell me what happened? How did you come upon so many rogues? They don't usually hunt in such large packs."

Kai jerked his head toward one of the dead warriors and grimaced, "Tanner stumbled across a group of rogues several blocks away who appeared to be carrying four humans back to this warehouse. He called us in, and we interrupted their feeding," He snarled abruptly and shook his head in disgust, "Tanner was the first to fall, followed by Rick and Bartley. We tried everything to help them preserve their blood, but there were too many of them, and many Rogues continued to feed on them well after they had passed."

"And the humans," Rome glanced around the warehouse, "where are they?" He inhaled, hoping to catch their scent, but the smell of blood ran too heavily within the air for him to latch onto anything.

"I kept them safe." Lincoln waved his hand towards a pile of garbage bags stacked in the corner. The image instantly changed to show four humans passed out on top of each other.

While Kai had an eidetic memory that never allowed him to forget a thing, Lincoln had the power of illusion and psychometry. Each of his warriors was exceptionally gifted, and Rome occasionally failed to remember just how much. With their unique gifts, Rome had placed them within groups of five to six within multiple cities, towns, states, and countries worldwide. He didn't always see them all, but if any one of them called for assistance, he could be there within seconds.

His phone rang abruptly and disturbed the silence that had settled between them. He fished it out and glanced at the screen to see Maverick's name flashing across it. Maverick wasn't one to call him. In fact, if he could, he avoided reaching out to anyone for help, so to see his name caused Rome to freeze for only a second before he picked up.

"What's wrong, Mav?"

His voice was a growl when he responded, "I don't know. We encountered a group of Titan soldiers; there were eight of them, and one of them shot Ami with a dart filled with something that knocked her clean out. I fought the rest of them off and grabbed her before they could cart her off somewhere. We're returning home now, but she isn't looking too good. Her breathing is choppy, and she convulsed after the dart hit her."

"I'll meet you at home. How far out are you?"

"Five minutes."

"Then I'll see you in five." Rome snapped the phone closed. Worry filled him at the thought of anything happening to Amirishka. "Kai, give our warriors a proper burial and contact Azriel to erect the protective barrier, and Linc, you make sure the humans get home safely. If they need a stronger mind wipe than you can give, call me, and I'll return as soon as I handle this."

They both nodded in turn before he flashed himself home. He would now have to figure out what to do with Lincoln and Kai because they couldn't work alone for long. Silence stretched throughout the house and made him pause and listen closer. Usually, he could at least hear Alara's heartbeat even if she was in another room, yet he heard nothing. It was eerily silent. A sinking feeling filled him at the thought that she had left, but he had no time to check. The sound of Maverick running for the house from the cover of the trees reached his ears as he moved to meet him at the door. Maverick stormed inside with Amirishka's limp body hanging from his arms. He could hear the faint pitter-patter of her heart and smell whatever drug she'd been injected with seeping from her pores. The scent turned his stomach, yet somehow, it was vaguely familiar in an unsettling way. He couldn't place it.

"Bring her to her bedroom, and I'll take care of her there." Rome rolled up his sleeves and followed Maverick after him before he spoke again, "Mav, I need you to go find Alara. She isn't here."

"And how exactly did that happen? Weren't you here with her?"

He neglected to answer. He couldn't admit to the hothead of the group that he'd nearly lost control and taken Alara in any way he could have had her. To acknowledge that weakness would have his warriors questioning his stability. He never lost control. Ever.

"Just find her and bring her back. Kicking and screaming if you have to." Rome snapped as he placed his hands on either side of Amirishka's head and closed his eyes to focus.

He listened as Maverick left before the silence stretched once more. Rome pushed healing waves from his hands into Amirishka's body as he searched for the root of the problem. Whatever Titan had shot her with was like nothing he'd ever come into contact with before. It was a virus unlike any other, eating away at her very cells as he raced to heal them. The act of healing her completely would probably take hours and nearly drain him of energy if what he sensed was right, but he would do it to save her. He had to force his mind away from Alara to focus on the task. He had to believe Maverick would find her before anything could happen to her. He wasn't sure he would be stable enough to control his emotions if his warrior didn't find her and bring her back. He wouldn't care about the destruction he would wreak if he didn't have her back. She wasn't safe out there without him.

CHAPTER
NINE

The cold bit into her lungs as Alara sprinted through the snow in her haste to get away. Her breathing was raspy, and her hands, feet, and face were numb from the cold as she pulled on her energy to attempt to conserve the heat she desperately needed within her body. In her mind, running wasn't her only option, but it was just the best one. She had to get far away from Rome and his guardians. The fear that he would finish what he had started was enough for her to take off. Alara couldn't risk what she had felt for him at that moment. She couldn't risk losing herself to him. She knew it was possible. That kiss had been proof of that. If he hadn't nicked her with his fang, she would have thrown all caution to the wind just to feel the rest of him against her

"Shit!" She cried out when her foot slipped from under her, sending her face-first into the cold, unforgiving snow.

With the clothes she had pulled from the closet near the front door, she was sufficiently covered, and yet some of the items dwarfed her and caused a few pockets of snow to slide between the cracks. It numbed her skin even more and sent chills down her spine. She struggled to her feet just as a low growl filled the cool air around her. The hair on her body stood up for an entirely different reason as her eyes frantically searched the area to find the animal or beast that had made the sound. Alara glanced up when a few chunks of snow fell down around her and paused when large golden cat eyes stared back at her from the tree limb that hung just above her head.

She forced her body into a stillness she didn't feel even as every fiber within her told her that she should run, but this was a breed of cat that screamed danger. This cat watched her, hoping she would run so it could chase after her. According to the pattern of its fur and the way it blended into the area perfectly, it was clear to see she was dealing with a snow leopard. She didn't know much about them. Shit, she didn't know much of anything, but she did know that this leopard was nothing to play around with. Over the years, she'd watched enough Animal Planet to know that big cats occasionally played with their food. This wasn't some backyard kitten or cat she could play with and get to know; this was a dangerous animal she desperately needed to escape.

"Good kitty," Alara whispered, slowly backing herself into the tree to keep the animal within eyesight.

The moment she felt bark against her back, she glanced around, all the while wondering if it was traveling alone or if the species itself hunted within packs or pairs. From what she could tell, it was massive, with paws as big as her head. She was even sure the body itself was more prominent than her own. Her fear was a living, breathing entity as she stumbled over what to do to get away safely. It growled softly and dropped down from the tree before turning its back and disappearing behind the treeline as if she were insignificant. Alara didn't even attempt to move for fear that it was simply watching her from a different vantage point. Cool tears slid down her cheeks and froze to her skin as she attempted to slow her heart rate and control her breathing. The wind whistled through the air as time trickled on before she heard a familiar chuckle. Her gaze sharpened and focused on the tall male who stepped out from behind a tree decked out in black tactical gear that hugged his body and exposed a decent amount of skin. How he wasn't freezing his ass off was beyond her level of thinking. She was positively frozen solid and desperately wanted to get somewhere warm.

"You lost?" Maverick smiled as he leaned casually against a tree trunk with his ankles crossed and his arms folded as if he had all the time in the world.

She pulled her arms tighter around her body and searched the trees frantically as she spoke with a hushed tone. "A big snow leopard is prowling around. It could be back any second to finish us off. Can you…"

He cut her off before she could finish speaking. "The leopard was one of my forms," His eyes flashed brighter, reminding her of the leopard, "You're perfectly safe, but we must return before Rome finishes healing Ami. He isn't too happy about you leaving."

"Wait! Ami's hurt?"

"She was shot with a tranq. I believe something was laced on or within the dart. Normal tranquilizers don't affect us because our genes differ from humans. We are built differently, and our cells naturally kill anything that isn't a part of our physiological makeup. Rome is attempting to heal her now, but he's distracted by your disappearance, so he sent me to search for you. We need to return."

Alara shook her head softly and moved around the tree until it stood between them. She couldn't go back. Not after seeing that other side of Rome being directed at her. Not after witnessing how fast he or any of them could turn on her. Sure, he hadn't attacked her, but it had been too close for comfort, and an emotion she wasn't sure she wanted to deal with had presented itself. Rome was considered the strongest of his species, the man with the most power and control, and yet, for an instant, he had succumbed to his baser desire for blood. She wouldn't put herself in a position to become a victim even if she slightly wondered how his fangs would feel pressed against her skin.

"What do you mean no? Rome has asked me to bring you back, so let's go and stop this nonsense. Shit, you're practically frozen solid from the cold. You can't last much longer out here without catching hypothermia." He frowned and walked towards her, his stride full of determination.

She didn't think so. Alara turned and ran deeper into the woods in an effort to get away and find the run-down shack her brother had mentioned on the phone. Alaric said someone would be waiting for her. She had to trust in that. She yanked her phone from her jacket pocket as she ran and glanced at it. It was a burner phone like no other, clearly customized and fitted for a soldier, and she hardly knew how to work it. When she had spoken with Alaric earlier, he'd told her a button on the phone would pull up a map and direct her to the location he needed her to go. She didn't understand it and didn't even attempt to as she glanced at the screen to see a deep red dot that flickered several miles ahead of her. She forced herself to run faster. She just needed to get there. She fumbled with her phone to return it to her pocket just as Maverick grabbed the back of her hood and lifted her from the ground, nearly choking her. The phone tumbled from her hand and sank into the snow bank right before her eyes.

"Let me down, Mav!" She screamed and kicked.

The noise of her struggles echoed for several miles as he pulled her over his shoulder in a fireman's carry and turned back in the direction they had come from.

She beat against his back and screamed frantically as he clamped her legs down and snarled. "If you don't stop fighting me, I'll call Rome to come deal with you. Cut it out!" He snapped.

Alara froze. "You don't understand." Her voice was just a whisper when she spoke, "he nearly attacked me. He drew blood from my lip, and his eyes went feral. He could have killed me if he hadn't forced himself to gain control. Do you want him to kill me? Is that it? Let the king have the first taste, and then the rest of you will help drain me dry!? Mav, I remember you telling me that the urge to continue is hard for you guys the older you get... he's ancient; maybe his control is waning, but I won't stick around and be the crash test dummy."

Maverick stopped but didn't place her down when he spoke. "What are you rambling on about? He would never hurt a human, much less a woman. We protect humans, and you know, when we feed, it's never to the point of draining a human dry. Trust me, the temptation is there, but we protect human life, not take it. Control does slip with age, but that's only for those who start to not care for those we are sworn to protect. If you knew the truth of what happened to an Eternal when that control faltered indefinitely, you would not be so quick to accuse him."

"Well, you weren't there. You didn't see it. He was going to take from me whether I was willing or not."

Indecision filled him. Rome was their leader for a reason. He had taught them patience with the humans and trained them not to kill and instead protect those weaker than the Rogues and themselves. Rome was the epitome of strength and control. There was no way he'd nearly attacked her, right? Maverick ran over the possibilities within his mind. Rome had acted strangely since Alara arrived, but they all had. Life had changed for them since she had become a part of their lives. Her presence might have been affecting their king on a deeper level. That was very possible. Shit, Rome had gone so far as to threaten his very warriors' bodily harm if anything should happen to her. She was definitely the common denominator, but to harm the woman herself, that wasn't something that was computing for him. If Rome was indeed succumbing to a weakness for her blood, he would tell someone. Maverick had to believe that.

"We'll talk to Rome once we arrive. I'll be with you." Maverick stated firmly and took off at a faster pace than before.

Alara returned to pounding her fists into his back as she fought for her release. It wasn't just the fear of returning but that she had lost her only way of communicating with her brother. There was no way of telling him what was happening or where she had ended up. She'd attempted to tell him over the phone, yet his paranoia had reached through the line when he told her to save it for when they stood face to face. Although she had been trapped within the walls of Titan all her life, Alara had learned many things that could help her in the real world, so she had paid attention to the things that happened around her, and she'd listened in on conversations when no one noticed. TV helped, so she knew it was possible for a phone line to be tapped, and she knew the only likely person to be listening in would be Titan.

"Mav, I can't go back," she pleaded in a final attempt. "Just pretend you never found me."

His snort of humor could be heard over the crisp wind. "None of them would ever believe that. My ability to shift into animal forms gives me a keener sense of smell than most, which means that once I have the scent of whoever I'm hunting, I'm guaranteed to find them, and if I shift into any one of my animals, then the odds of anyone escaping me is nearly impossible. You were smart for wearing someone else's clothing, but it does nothing to hide your natural scent."

"I didn't even think to hide from your nose. You know I could get away if I wanted to, right? Romulus taught me enough control to take as little or as much energy as needed without putting you into a coma. I can knock you out. Don't make me do that. Just let me go."

"It's too late. We're here."

She didn't want to believe him, yet she had no choice but to when they stepped from the tree line and approached the hidden front door. Her escape attempt had failed miserably, and she was sure that with her return, Rome would keep a more watchful eye over her in case she attempted to leave once more. He had told her she wasn't a prisoner, yet here she was, slung over the shoulder of one of his men as he stepped back over the threshold and entered the warmth of the family room. The only thing to be heard was the roar of the fire as Maverick placed her on her feet and headed down the hallway toward the bedrooms. As badly as Alara wanted to run again, she knew that if she did, she would find herself right back over his shoulder...or worse, so instead, she followed behind him and entered Amirishka's room. Rome stood by the bed with his palms hovering over her still body. He was in a healing trance with his eyes clenched tightly closed, brows furrowed in concentration, and sweat trickling down his brows, and yet somehow, she could tell that he was getting nowhere with the healing process.

Alara didn't know how she knew it, but from her position near the door, she could sense that he was trying and failing at forcing whatever drugs coursed through Amirishka's veins to come out. She wasn't getting any better. In fact, Alara could sense the rapid decline that was happening right before their eyes. She didn't need to touch her to feel the wrongness that radiated from her smaller form. Her medium brown complexion was pale, black bags of exhaustion hung beneath her eyelids, and her chest's rise and fall slowed as her breathing turned choppier. They were losing her. Alara crossed the room with a frown when a familiar energy pressed against her as soon as she reached the side of the bed. Rome's eyes snapped open to stare at her, exhaustion etched within his features as sweat dotted his brows and upper lip. It was clear to see he was straining and forcing every ounce of healing power into her.

"Let me help," Alara whispered, placing her hands on Amirishka's forehead and chest.

The power to heal was the second ability that had manifested within her at a young age, and it was intense. She couldn't just heal, though. With one hand, she could sense what was causing an injury or where it originated; with the other hand, she could push healing cells to fix the problem. Alara could heal most wounds, but she had never tried to heal someone who looked to be on the brink of death. She knew attempting to heal Amirishka would most likely put her out of commission for hours, yet she still had to try. If she could help, then she had to try.

"Romulus, I need you to move back." She stared into his tortured gaze, hoping to instill trust that she would try everything she could to save his warrior, "I can't heal if someone else's energy is mixing. I might end up healing the wrong person."

His stare turned into a glare, and his voice was harsh when he spoke. "I knew you were lying about your powers, but how do I know that once I stop pushing my healing energy into her, you'll be able to do any better when I couldn't?"

"Just as you asked me to trust in you…I need you to trust in me."

For a moment, she thought he wouldn't budge, but reluctantly, he stepped back and dropped his hands to his sides to allow her to take over. She wasted no time and pulled on her ability as she searched for the problem with the hand resting above Amirishka's forehead. Alara's hand began to glow brighter as it hovered over Amirishka's chest seconds before a burst of healing energy left her in a rush and slammed into her still form. The force shocked Alara, but what was even more alarming was what she found eating away at Amirishka's DNA. She couldn't keep her small gasp of surprise inside. The energy signature had felt so familiar to her because mixed within the tranquilizer drug was Alara's own blood. Somehow, Titan had created a drug infused with her blood. It was draining the energy from Amirishka, eating away at her cells and slowly but surely killing her.

Rome's voice broke through her concentration. "What is it? Can you stop whatever virus this is?"

How did she tell him that the very thing that was killing his warrior was from the making of her own blood? How could she tell him she knew of Titan more intimately than most and that she'd played an involuntary part in creating this new drug? It was simple…she couldn't. None of them would ever trust that she wasn't a part of Titan. They could never learn the truth of where she'd come from.

She forced more healing energy into Amirishka until every last drop of the virus was gone before she dropped her hands and stepped back. Black dots filled her vision, her head swam, and her body swayed seconds before Rome lifted her into his arms and cradled her against his chest. His energy penetrated the thick clothing that covered her body, but without skin-to-skin contact, she couldn't take any of his power in to replace what she'd lost. Her head lolled to the side as nausea and dizziness pulled at her in an attempt to drag her into an unscheduled sleep, but Rome seemed to sense her problem and abruptly pressed his warm lips to her own. His power immediately flowed into her and filled her with strength as if he were directing it himself while his lips sucked and licked at her own. A recent memory tugged at her until Alara quickly pulled back. She couldn't get hypnotized by the scent and taste of him again.

She met his gaze and shook her head slowly. "We can't do this."

"We can and we will. Only when you're ready, but first, you'll tell me what else you can do and how you could heal my warrior." He murmured, pushing back the loose hair that partially covered her face from his watchful gaze.

CHAPTER
TEN

An hour had come and gone since Alara had healed Amirishka before promptly falling asleep in his arms. He'd placed her in his bed and walked away. Although he'd craved to join her, he needed to distance himself. What he and the Gods had discussed earlier still rang within his ears like an annoying bell that refused to cease. He couldn't keep putting her first. At least not for now. As the leader of his race, he needed to do his duty to society and ensure the humans were safe and his warriors were staying in line. Maverick and Amirishka were the only ones sitting out for the night while the rest of his Eternals were still hunting down Rogues. With less than six hours of darkness left before the sun rose in the sky, he had some time to get back out there and hunt down a few of his own. He needed to join them, yet he walked into the family room where Maverick sat with a pensive expression.

"Has Ami awoken?" He questioned as he approached the couch with a raised brow.

Maverick shook his head hesitantly as he spoke. "She still sleeps, but she's breathing easier, and her heart rate has regulated. I need to know how Alara did it? How did she heal her?"

"That's something we'd both love to know." He sighed heavily and ran a hand through his dreads in frustration, "In my effort to heal her, it was almost as if the virus was attacking me and killing her slowly. The pace of deterioration was slow, but it was evident and stronger than anything I'd ever encountered within a living being. We could have lost her if not for Alara."

"We need to know what they drugged her with. Do you think she figured out what it was? If it did that to Ami, it could do it to us. Maybe even you!" Maverick's eyes flew to Rome and narrowed, "We need to kill these bastards once and for all before they learn the drug is successful in taking us out."

"Did any of Titan's guards see Ami fall after she was shot? Because if they did, then they already know it affects us."

Maverick nodded grimly, "I didn't think of that. I couldn't successfully kill them all without one of them possibly grabbing her while my attention was divided, so I shifted into one of my forbidden forms to get her safely away."

Rome glared and snarled through his slowly lengthening fangs. "Which form, and did they see it!?"

"Apologies, sir, but I used the one you strictly told me not to use in the presence of others." He winced when Rome's snarl turned into a thunderous growl that made him momentarily cease breathing.

Maverick had the ability to shift into any animal form, including animals of mythology. There were forms he was strictly forbidden to show to any human for apparent reasons, and one of those was his most lethal and dangerous form. His golden dragon. In that form, he was impossible to kill and more vicious and cunning than most would think, and for some inexplicable reason, he was no longer alone within his mind. Another presence would shadow his thoughts and sometimes control his actions. For years, Rome had forced a mental barrier between him and his ability to shift into the beast until he'd gained more control and promised to never change within the presence of another, especially in front of a human. Their minds wouldn't be able to process what they were seeing, and it could lead to hysteria and fear that could and would incite riots and events that could upset the balance of society.

"If you were going to do something so reckless, the least you could have done was burn them all to a crisp before you got her out of there." Rome paced the space between the fireplace and the coffee table as he tried to rein in his temper. "Now they know what you can do. They probably have files on each of us, and I'm sure they've been collecting information since we first encountered Titan. You've probably reached the top of their list right after me."

Silence descended between them, allowing Rome to open his mind and contact each of his warriors telepathically. *"I need each of you to be extra vigilant from here on out. Titan has created a drug that can incapacitate and kill you if you aren't healed in time. If it happens, notify me immediately, and I will come to you."* He could feel the shock coursing through his mind from each of his warriors across the globe. The message was received, and they were aware, so he promptly closed all telepathic communication and reinforced his mental blocks before focusing once more on Maverick. They had another pressing matter to discuss.

"How far away did she get when you found her?"

Maverick smirked. "Not as far as she'd hoped, I'm sure. I found her almost 10 miles from here, towards the west, near that dilapidated shack we keep forgetting to get rid of. It looked like she knew where she was heading, but that's impossible, right?" That smirk of his transformed into a frown quickly. "She also told me you nearly lost control from a sip of her blood. Is this true?"

So she'd told one of his men. Rome wasn't surprised by the information in the slightest, but it did beg the question of whether his warrior now thought less of him for almost losing control. "It won't happen again." He responded almost stiffly and quickly changed the subject to their current problem. "It's possible that these friends she mentioned before were helping her somehow, but I'm unsure what form of communication she could have used to keep in contact. Did she have a cell phone with her when you found her?"

"I didn't see anything in her hands when I approached her, and I damn sure didn't pat her down in search of one. You never checked that bag of hers?"

Rome knew no one would ever touch her in any way if he had a say on the matter. She was his. Whether she knew it or not, she belonged to him. Was he living in the medieval days? Acting a bit barbaric? Possibly a caveman? Sure, but he never said he was perfect, and he'd never had such a visceral reaction concerning a woman. In fact, he couldn't remember the last time he'd had the pleasure of being with a woman. It had been several years since he'd been intimate in any way. His mind almost dragged him back to a time when he'd slept with most of the women who threw themselves at him, but instead, he focused on the woman who was now taking up residence within his mind at all opportunities.

"I wasn't going to take away her right to privacy along with everything else. Now, will you allow me to see where you caught up with her? I'd like to check the area for anything she may have dropped or attempted to rid herself of." Usually, he wouldn't ask permission to probe someone's mind, but at times, a person deserved to know when their mind was being searched for information, and if anyone was due that courtesy, it was Maverick.

Maverick gave a tight nod, tension radiating from him in waves. Pushing a thought into someone's mind and actively searching through those thoughts and memories were two different actions with entirely different outcomes. With the volatile nature that accompanied Maverick's changes, Rome had spent quite a bit of time checking his thoughts to ensure that the other side of him never had the chance to take over.

With his approval, Rome searched his memories, found what he was looking for, and drew back quickly before he spoke, "Watch over the girls. I'll return shortly." Rome teleported to the location he had spotted within Maverick's mind and found himself standing several miles away in the forest.

The air was crisp and cool as flurries continued to fall from the sky, and several inches of snow that had been absent before were now present. It covered the possible tracks Maverick and Alara left behind, yet he could smell their scents lingering in the air. He moved towards a tree that smelled strongly of Alara's scent before pressing his nose against the bark to inhale as he inhaled the smell of her fear. This must have been where she encountered Maverick in his snow leopard form. He moved on and paused when he stood several feet away from the tree before his ears picked up on the sound of a steady vibration that was somehow muffled. He searched the ground as he walked with slow, deliberate movements and focused his hearing until he located a sleek black phone buried in the snow.

The caller ID flashed brightly within the night and displayed the name Alaric. Unjustified anger burned through his veins at the sight of another man's name. Who the hell was this? He picked up before the call could end and simply waited for the other male to speak. His anger simmered the longer he waited. Call it stubbornness, but he needed to know who he was dealing with. He attempted to locate the other male's energy signature or thoughts through the line and got nothing. An impenetrable wall stood between them. Whoever this male was, he had mental blocks that rivaled his own as well as Silas's. Alara's were strong as well, yet nothing like this.

Finally, after several long minutes of silence, a deep voice filled Rome's ear, anger lashing through the phone with every word. "I know this isn't Alara, so who the fuck is this, and where the hell is she?"

"The better question is, who are you to her?" His question was a snarl.

"Give the phone to Alara. Now."

Rome chuckled. "When you can answer my question, you know how to reach me." He hung up and shoved the phone into his pocket before he teleported back home to appear in his bedroom.

He glanced out the window yet moved towards the bed where Alara continued to slumber. The sun wouldn't rise for several more hours. He should be out hunting, yet he was again by her side as he neglected his duties. He had to believe that the Gods wanted this for him, at least partially. How else would you explain his pressing need to be near her? Sure, he needed answers from her, but there was more that urged him to stay by her side. There was protectiveness. Shit, there was definitely possessiveness. He rubbed his hand down his face and sighed heavily. His eyes took in her more diminutive form beneath the sheets as he allowed his gaze to eat up every inch of her that wasn't covered. The color of his eyes brightened, his fangs lengthened, and his mind slipped back into thoughts about his near slip-up. His dick hardened as he recalled the feel of her in his arms and the sounds she made when he touched, kissed, and caressed her. God and the taste of her blood still sang within his veins.

He'd never tasted blood so sweet and filled with an innocence that should be impossible for her age. He wanted to ruin that innocence and take it for himself. He simply wanted to take, but he knew it was dangerous. She made him act irrationally. Stole his control. Turned him into someone he hardly recognized. She shifted beneath the cover, exposing her lower back and the elastic band of her bright purple panties to his view after her borrowed shirt had ridden up. He wanted to be a perv and push the rest of the sheet down to reveal the fullness of her ass, but he denied himself that pleasure and tugged her shirt down before pulling the covers up to her shoulders with his telekinesis. He knew if he reached for her, his resolve would weaken.

Rome moved across the room and sat on a chair he kept near the window. It was directly across from her and within full view of her face. The chair was there for days when he decided to read in the early mornings of the day or simply to watch the rising sun. Like all Eternals, the sun weakened him in ways that made him wish for slumber, yet at his age, he could force that need back and occasionally enjoy the sunrises that would slowly brighten the sky. Today wasn't a day for reading, though. He needed answers. Since returning home, the phone, currently burning a hole in his pocket, had vibrated several times before falling silent, only to start anew. This man, Alaric, was a persistent son-of-a-bitch.

He spoke softly but ensured she could hear him from where he sat. "Alara, I need you to wake up."

Her movements were slow as she came awake with a yawn, pulling her mouth wide before her gaze landed on him. Her eyes were tinged with fear, yet there was also an unidentified emotion he didn't quite recognize on her face. "Romulus?" Her voice was sleep-filled and seductive.

"Who is Alaric?" His voice was calm when he spoke. His anger was slowly boiling in his veins as he felt the phone start vibrating once more.

Saying his name made her freeze. The fear he'd glimpsed only moments ago rose like a tidal wave and filled the room with its pungent scent. It wasn't a smell he wanted to associate with her. He wanted her to fear nothing, yet he knew without a doubt that some of her fear was because of him. She didn't trust him, not after their last encounter. He couldn't say he blamed her. She knew their true nature, knew what he desired, but if she were to learn just how deeply his need went, then there'd be no telling what she would do or how fast she would run from him again.

Alara shook her head as she spoke and sat up straighter, her eyes dropping to the ground quickly before returning to his own. "I-I don't understand. How do you know that name?"

"Answer the question, little flower, who is Alaric, and who is he to you? I need answers. You're hiding something. Something you clearly don't want me to know, but sweetheart…lies and deceit can only get you so far in this world, and I told you once before that lying to me was unacceptable. I'm cautioning myself with you, willing patience and understanding, but you seem undeserving of it, quite frankly. Especially if you're just going to keep playing your little head games."

"I'm not playing any games with you," her voice quivered, "I don't have all the answers. I can't tell you what I don't know."

"But you know him!" His restraint on his powers weakened as he sent a telekinetic wave lashing through the air and sent things toppling to the floor within the room.

The phone continued to vibrate within his pocket, annoying him on a deeper level before he pulled it out and placed the receiver to his ear. Before he could get a single word in, Alaric's voice was filtering through, full of malice and contempt. "I don't give a fuck who you think you are, but you've never met a bastard quite like me. If you don't put Alara on this phone right now, I'll find you and kill you where you stand. Give it to her. Now, you stupid fuck!"

Rome paused. He wasn't sure whether to commend the man on

his bravery or get angrier. He definitely had a pair of steel balls to marvel his own. It wasn't as if he knew who he was talking to. How could he? Rome couldn't deny that he was tempted to test this man's strength, see how far he could drive him up a wall before he told him where to meet to settle their differences. Alaric wanted to get to Alara. That was never going to happen…but a phone call? He could do that. Besides, he had every intention of listening in and getting his desired answers.

He stood and crossed the room to hand Alara the phone, but he covered the speaker and spoke softly before he did. "Put it on speaker, or I take it back and snap it in half."

She nodded. He handed over the phone and watched her press the speaker button before she spoke. "A-Alaric?"

An audible sigh filled the air. The tone of Alaric's voice when he spoke was softer and filled with a tenderness that made the hair on Rome's body stand at attention as his lips pulled back from his lengthening fangs.

"He told you to put me on speaker, didn't he, angel?"

Rome didn't even try to refrain from snarling loud enough to allow the bastard to hear him. No, he wanted him to hear it. Rome needed him to hear the threat within the sound and know that the moment they met, he would die in the most brutal way possible. Especially for thinking he could give his woman any type of cute pet name. Alara was his and his alone. He had no intention of ever sharing her with another soul.

Alara replied with an equally-sounding sigh, "Yes, he wants to know who you are and what you are to me."

"And who is this he? What's his name, angel?"

The concern that filled Alaric's voice rankled Rome's nerves, still with the pet name. It unsettled him. Was this her boyfriend? Husband? Is that why she was so quick to try and get away from him? Was she trying to run back to this man because they were together? Hell no! He refused to believe they could be anything more than friends. He hadn't scented another male on her when they'd met, but that could have been due to the river and how he'd found her. Maybe this male was trying desperately to get out of the friend zone. Yeah, that had to be it. No other answer was acceptable.

"Call her angel again, and this phone conversation is over. Got me?" Rome snapped and stared directly into Alara's eyes, willing her to understand his side. He needed her to realize that anyone who felt comfortable enough to soothe her and call her names of endearment was a threat to his position. A threat to what he considered his.

ELEVEN

Alara looked into furious blue eyes that continued to brighten the longer she met his stare. She could hear her brother's voice calling to her from the other end of the line, but she couldn't reply just yet. She was entranced by Rome's gaze, trapped within eyes filled with such heat and anger that it held her immobile. She couldn't understand why he was being like this. Acting like she was his property, like he owned her somehow. As if she had no say in the matter. He was a possessive, sexy asshole making her question everything about him. The situation from earlier became a distant memory the longer she was around him, yet she remembered the look in his eyes when he'd tasted her blood. He had no intention to ever let her go. She knew by his possessiveness that she might never be free of this larger-than-life male. Running to Alaric was out of the question. If Rome were to ever learn just how deep their ties went and where those ties connected them, she was sure he would kill her where she stood. Or, in this case, sat.

She clutched the phone tighter as the situation dawned on her. Rome or one of his warriors would have the pleasure of sinking fangs into her and draining her dry if they ever learned the truth. They were deader than dead if they even suspected that she and

Alaric came from Titan. The way the Eternals spoke about killing every Titan operative and Rogue that walked the earth sent chills down her spine whenever Alara heard them discussing their hunts. It didn't matter that she thought of Titan as the enemy; they would surely kill her because she'd spent her entire life beneath Titan's thumb. She wasn't a plant or a mole, but she knew that's what she would look like if anyone ever found out the truth. She could never let them know.

Somehow, she needed to explain to Alaric where she was without truly giving anything away. Shit, all her life secrets had been her shield and friend, yet now it was a hindrance that put her life and her brother's in jeopardy with a powerful race of immortals.

"I swear to God, Alara, if you don't say something, I will assume the worst. What the hell is that bastard doing with you? I didn't rescue you from-"

She cut him off abruptly. "He isn't hurting me. I'm safe. I promise." She didn't need him mentioning anything about Titan. Not in front of Rome.

"You told me you were in danger. I moved up my plans and executed them faster than I wished because I assumed things hadn't worked out for you and I needed to come to your aid. Are you saying it was all for nothing? That I sacrificed weeks of planning when I didn't need to? That I could have waited a little longer before I made my way to you? Is that what you're saying?" Alaric's voice steadily rose with each word until he practically yelled through the receiver.

She didn't know Alaric's plans other than rescuing someone he claimed was vital to him. It sounded like he might have succeeded in the rescue, but his anger gave her pause. She didn't know her brother well. In fact, she didn't know him at all, but this level of anger was alarming. Had he maybe failed, and it was her fault? A thousand questions filled her.

Alara spoke softly, her muster evaporating beneath the sound of evident disappointment in his voice. "I truly thought I needed help and to get away," she glanced up to stare into Rome's furious gaze, "but I don't think he intends to hurt me. He's been teaching me control and keeping me safe, and his uhh…family is also watching out for me. I'm okay, Alaric. I'm sorry if I made you believe otherwise with my frantic call, but I promise you, I'm safe."

It wasn't a lie. Being with Rome was smart. He had taught her more than she ever thought possible in just a week. He was safe, even if a small part of her knew that staying with him would ensure she lost something of herself along the way. Whether that was a good or a bad thing remained to be seen.

"Alara, who is he? Who is this man you trust with your life? Is he truly safe?"

Rome shook his head and spoke through sharp fangs that refused to shorten. "Don't answer that."

"Well, what can I tell him?" She snapped, annoyed that he even needed to participate in the conversation.

It would be much easier if he was nowhere near her while she spoke to her brother. The possibility of a slip-up was at an all-time high. The fact that Alaric was oblivious to who she was genuinely dealing with and that Rome was just as much in the dark about their background and just as clueless wasn't lost on her. She knew just how dangerous this all was for her and everyone involved. Someone could die. Someone possibly would if she didn't play her cards right.

"You tell him nothing until I meet the man who seems to be so important to you. I need to make sure he's cleared."

His eyes blazed with that anger and passion she was so used to seeing, but the flaring nostrils and constant clenching of his fists were another matter entirely. He was strung up tighter than a violin string, with his chest rising and falling with every harsh breath he took. Something was seriously wrong with him, and she couldn't help but worry. Sure, they didn't see eye to eye on some things, but his emotions concerned her. Rome was naturally a volatile male used to getting his way in all things according to his people, yet he was lost the moment she entered his life. His control was frayed, his needs were intense, and his powers fluctuated in ways that could be dangerous to anyone around him. Anyone but her.

She wanted to tell him the truth about Alaric and where she grew up, but the fear of retaliation was like a voice within her mind that screamed she'd be making the wrong choice. Trust wasn't easy for her after everything Titan had put her through. Trusting Rome was a hurdle within itself. He'd trusted her enough to educate her about the real world and what he and his people stood for, yet she knew there was more to the story. Maybe it was her turn to trust him, or perhaps that's just what he wanted her to do; after all, he treated her as a prisoner. A comfortable prisoner for sure, but a prisoner nonetheless.

Alaric spoke once more. "You want to clear me…fine, where shall I meet you? I can come now."

Rome chuckled, but there was no humor in it. "Eager, aren't you?"

Alara glared at him but abruptly froze, reinforcing her mental barriers when it felt like someone was attempting to penetrate her thoughts. The blank look that transformed Rome's features told her that she wasn't the only one. His gaze snapped to the window and narrowed as the energy around him seemed to sizzle within the air and caress her skin with the barest touch. Something wasn't right. His power was off. Wrong.

"Romulus, What's happening?"

Rome grabbed her by the arm and pulled her up gently as he spoke, "Mav just told me we have company incoming," he pushed her towards the closet yet moved for the window, his gaze steady on the outside world, "I need you to get dressed, grab one of my guns for protection and then head for Ami's room." He glanced over his shoulder and met her gaze with a penetrating look that spoke volumes. "I need you safe. I hear about three dozen soldiers making their way to us; they'll be here any moment. Go into the closet out of view and shoot anyone that isn't one of my people."

"Alara, what's happening?" Alaric questioned, urgency laced his voice.

She didn't pause to ask or answer questions. Alara headed into the closet, pulled on a pair of Rome's sweatpants, and cinched the waistline so they wouldn't fall off. She took Alaric off the speaker and pressed the phone to her ear. "Soldiers are coming," she whispered, hoping Rome couldn't hear her, yet she wouldn't be surprised if he could.

"Get out of there! Now, Alara!" Alaric screamed as a concussive blast came from the bedroom, sending her flying into the wall.

The impact pushed the breath from her lungs as her head connected with the hardwood of a shelf. Stars filled her vision as she crumpled to the ground. The sound of Rome's inhuman growl filtered in from the bedroom as Alaric's voice droned on in the background, but she could hardly make out his words. Shit, she could scarcely function, and yet she felt a familiar energy approaching them.

Had Titan finally found her?

Was this it for her?

The pain in her head was debilitating. She had yet to catch her breath as nausea turned her stomach, and fear nearly consumed her. Alara lifted her hand and tenderly touched the back of her head, where a large gash leaked blood. Dizziness swarmed her as she attempted to stand but found it nearly impossible.

"Romulus," she whispered as darkness filled her vision, and she promptly passed out.

ROME LOWERED the energy shield that had protected him from the blast and prayed that Alara was okay. He could hear her steady breathing, yet she wasn't moving. He'd heard it the moment her body was thrown into the wall. It shouldn't have been possible for the blast to reach her from where she'd been. It seemed Titan was coming out with bigger and better weapons to fight against them. Maybe now they might stand a chance in battle.

One of the disadvantages of having a sizable single-story home was the ability to grant the enemy entrance from several different openings. He could hear several other devices going off in another part of the home where Maverick and Amirishka were. Their defense was weak. Proof of that was the seven soldiers wearing black tactical gear with the Titan insignia embroidered on their sleeves as they stepped through the glass that now littered the floor. Following them were two Rogue vampires that were obviously juiced up on blood. Their eyes were bloodshot, fangs elongated, and nails sharpened to deliver severe damage. It looked to be an unfair fight on their behalf.

Rome smiled ruefully and looked each man in the eye before he spoke. "I regret to inform you that Titan has officially sent you to your deaths. Any last words before you cease to exist?"

The one who appeared to be in charge stepped forward and removed the ski mask that covered his face, revealing a bald head with dark, empty eyes. "You're him, aren't you? The Eternal our boss wants? Romulus, right?"

Rome didn't recognize him, not even when he spoke, and he knew a lot of Titan's operatives. He must have been new. He inclined his head in silent acknowledgment and frowned at the slight sound that filled the air. It was like a puff of air that came from his right. Something had pierced the skin of his neck. He reached up to pull out the small dart protruding from his skin. As he sniffed at the tip of the minuscule needle, Rome knew he'd been drugged with the same tranq that had taken Amirishka out. He allowed the dart to roll from his fingertips and hit the floor before he launched into action and jerked forward to grab one of the bastards by the throat. Rome lifted him clean off the floor before snapping his neck and moving to the next soldier, who stood only a few inches away. Gunfire erupted as he moved around the room, snapping the neck of every human present until all that remained were the Rogues. They were harder to kill, and he could feel the silver within the bullets beginning to weaken him from where they were lodged inside his body. He needed to kill them quickly because that wasn't all he felt. The drug was starting to wear on him. He attempted to pull on any of his abilities and came up with nothing. He couldn't feel his powers at all. He tried to teleport across the room to attack one of the Rogues from behind and realized he couldn't. Whatever this new virus was, it was malignant. He could feel it feeding off of him.

A Rogue with harsh features and red hair launched at him with bared fangs as he swiped sharpened claws across his chest. The scent of Rome's blood filled the air around him as he attempted to right his blurring vision. The drug was hitting him a lot harder than he thought was possible. Is this what Amirishka had experienced? As the oldest and strongest of his kind, he didn't think a drug could have the capability of taking him out. Rome snarled ruthlessly and forced his healing cells to work overtime as they fought whatever foreign drug was swimming within his bloodstream.

Before he could right his footing or focus, a fist slammed into the side of his face. The hit took him airborne before he hit the wall. Rome quickly righted himself and swung out at the following blurry form that stepped within arm's length. His fist connected with flesh, and a crash followed shortly behind it along with a pain-filled groan. Nails raked across his stomach and rib cage, sending a searing sensation through his nerve endings. It gave his healing cells something else to mend as he swung out again. This time, he successfully grabbed whichever Rogue had stood too close. Rogue vampires were fast, but Eternals were faster, even Rome, with his slowly depleting power.

As soon as his vision cleared completely, he focused on the Rogue he held within his grip as claws dug into his arm and wrist. More blood seeped from him, but he refused to tire. He needed to get to Alara and make sure she was okay. The sound of her breathing was much more shallow now, which worried him. The vampire before him had dirty blonde hair and red eyes. He was locked so profoundly within the trance of bloodlust that all he did was snarl and growl as he attempted to free himself.

The red-headed Rogue spoke from his position across the room as he wiped blood from the now leaking wound on his forehead. "We just want the woman."

"What woman?" Rome snarled and tightened his grip until the man before him barely gasped for air, and his struggles slowly ceased.

"We were sent here after tracing a call. We came for subject one. We didn't come for you," he pulled a curved blade from his boot and smiled, revealing fangs covered in dried blood, "but you could be an added bonus that'll boost my ranking if I bring you in for the boss."

Rome would never be a trophy for anyone who worked or associated with Titan. He snapped the bastard's neck within his grip and attempted to pull on all of his power. He felt the soft tendrils of his telekinetic gift. God, he'd thought he'd lost it all. Without stopping to think or rationalize his actions, he used his ability to yank the bastard off his feet and pulled him in until he floated before his face. Rome sent his fist slamming straight into his chest, breaking through skin, sinew, and bone before his hand wrapped around the precious artery that was his heart and squeezed until life left his eyes and death took its place.

Most humans assumed that vampires stopped breathing and no longer had a pulse, but that wasn't true, and it was the same for the Eternals. Rogues survived on only blood, but Eternals were different. They breathed air like humans, ate food, felt pain and pleasure. The only real difference was their occasional need for blood, heightened abilities, longer lifespans, and slight physical differences.

Rome swayed on his feet and pressed his hand against the wall when he thought he would topple over. God, this was so unlike him. Weakness pulled at him and tempted him in ways that made him want to falter. Secretly, he wanted to let it consume him. He wanted to fall into a deep slumber and forget the world's worries. He wanted it so badly he could practically taste oblivion on his tongue.

Yeah, that didn't sound right. Rome inhaled and froze when the scent of Alara's blood teased his nose and filled his mouth. Fuck... she was hurt. He made his way over to the closet as he listened for more approaching soldiers, yet the second he saw her body unmoving and still amongst the wreckage of his things, he could focus on nothing but her.

"Alara," he whispered and dropped to his knees beside her before gathering her in his arms, "Wake up, little flower." He shook her gently, "I don't say this much, but...I need you. This new drug they've got is taking me for a spin, and I need you to get us all out of here before reinforcements come. I can't do it. I need to heal you."

He tapped at her cheeks lightly and frowned when she didn't

respond. He could feel the small puffs of air that passed through her lips and hear her heart pumping within her chest. She was definitely alive. He stared into her lovely face and smiled as an unfamiliar warmth filled him. She was so damn breathtaking. The smell of her blood was more potent now that he held her in his arms. He looked her over frantically and growled when his fingers encountered the open wound on the back of her head. Was that why she wasn't responding? Did she have a concussion? A possible brain bleed?

Fear started to fill him, but he ignored it and instead forced his body to create more healing cells before he attempted to heal her. He knew he shouldn't. He didn't have enough energy or power to heal and protect her in case more soldiers arrived, but he also couldn't leave her like this. He needed her to be okay, so with the last of his energy, he pushed a single thought into Maverick's mind. *"I'm going to lose consciousness any second now, and I need you to watch over us until the rest of our people return."* He struggled with the rest of his thoughts, afraid to show weakness yet knowing he had no choice. *"I can't protect us, Mav. Do whatever you need to protect us until the others arrive, and as soon as she awakens, you have Silas help Alara. She needs to teleport us. If she needs more power, you force her to take it from me. Force her because I'll heal."* He didn't know if he would, but that didn't matter as long as she awakened, and they all got away before more of Titan's operatives appeared.

He felt it the moment his power depleted and his energy left him. He slumped against the wall with Alara tucked onto his lap as his eyes slid closed and darkness crashed into his mind.

CHAPTER

TWELVE

Alara snuggled into the warmth that surrounded her and smiled softly. She felt safe and protected as a familiar masculine scent filled her nose and warmed her insides. Her core clenched with a need she was still getting used to, her nipples throbbed, and she moaned softly when she inhaled and took in that fragrance again. Rome. She knew it was him. Only he could smell that good, but she refused to open her eyes to make sure. What if it was simply a dream? She would hate for it to be a dream. The last thing she remembered was Rome's disapproving look as she spoke to Alaric before they were attacked. A sick feeling told her it had been Titan. They'd found her and intended to drag her back, kicking and screaming.

She was curling further into his warmth when pain lanced through her skull. She remembered that pain. Her eyes shot wide open as the barriers within her mind strengthened, and her energy flared outward to protect herself. Everyone she'd gotten to know over the past week stood before her inside Rome's bedroom closet, each wearing equally strained expressions and blood that coated their clothing and skin. Silas moved closer when he realized her eyes were open before he held his palm up towards her as a look of pure concentration masked his face. The pressure that had dissipated within her mind before returned full force.

"W-what are you doing, Silas?" She gritted through clenched teeth and pushed against his mental probing as she moved into a sitting position. She also wanted to attack his mind but feared the probability of him finding out that she could do a lot more than simply keep people out of her head.

"I need you to let me in," he stated plainly, "Rome tasked me with helping you get us out of here since he decided to use his last bit of strength to heal you, but I can't do that if I can't get into your mind. Lower your shields and allow me to guide you. It's not as easy as you may think it is. He's had centuries to learn and adjust. I don't need you cutting off important body parts when we make this jump."

"We've been over this before! No one goes into my mind but me! Now get out!"

Amirishka moved from her position guarding the door alongside Cairo and removed one of her sleek knives from its holster on her thigh. "I say we cut her just a little and feed him her blood so he can wake up and do this shit himself," she twirled the blade restlessly between her fingertips, "I'm still convinced we can't trust the bitch, and she's hiding something."

"Or it could be your jealousy," Akio chuckled. "Besides, the boss man will kill you if you hurt a precious hair on her head. She'd got him whipped."

Amirishka snarled and threw her knife faster than anyone could blink, but with a wave of his hand, Akio used his telekinesis and forced the blade to turn and embed within the wall several inches from her face.

"Next time you throw something, I'll make sure it hits the spot and damn the consequences." He glowered.

"Enough!" Erick snapped in annoyance, "We need to get out of here and head to another safe house before a third wave of reinforcements arrives. I've killed enough already for one night. Besides, the sun will be up soon, and we'll all be sitting ducks if they attack again."

"Fuck that!" Maverick exclaimed and turned on Amirishka, "She saved your life when she wasn't obligated to do so. She's allowed the benefit of the doubt, even from you." he paused, his expression turning sheepish, "I trust her."

Alara was more than grateful for having Maverick stick up for her, especially after their rocky start. He was the surliest within the group and least likely to trust an outsider, but he trusted her. Change wasn't easy for any of them. After centuries of doing the same day-to-day fighting with nothing mixing it up in between, they'd all gotten used to living a certain way. With Alara now a part of that equation, it wasn't unusual for them to be uncertain about the future. They were even more unsure of what role she would play in their lives and what that would mean for Rome, their king. They could see his attachment to her and feared the retaliation he would mete out if anything should happen to her.

Alara glanced over her shoulder to stare at Rome. His features were soft, eyes resting closed as his chest rose and fell steadily. "Romulus," she smiled softly and turned to press her hands against his chest.

She no longer experienced fear when she looked at him. The only thing she feared now was Titan finding her and taking her back or Rome finding out the truth of who she was. Erick and Silas were right. They needed to get the hell out of there before more of Titan's men found their way up there.

"Silas, Tell me what I need to do. How do I use his teleportation, and how will I know where I'm going?" She questioned but kept her gaze firmly on the unconscious man before her.

As badly as she wanted to get away for her own sake, Alara quickly realized that with Rome unconscious and unable to protect himself, he might be easy pickings for Titan. If they ever got their hands on him, she feared to think of what they could do to him and what would happen to the Eternals. Even if she couldn't save herself, she would at least save their king. After all, he had saved her when she thought no one had heard her cry for help.

"You need to allow me access to your mind so I can project my thoughts into yours and let you see where we need you to take us."

Silas folded his arms across his chest after pushing his blood-streaked hair away from his face.

Alara shook her head and shuddered at the sight. The fact that they were so comfortable with blood covering almost every inch of them was nauseating, yet she understood it. Blood was a healthy part of their lives. It was something they occasionally consumed and shed nightly when they fought their enemies, but it still turned her stomach to see so much of it.

"There has to be another way." She frowned.

"Unless you can also read minds, then I don't see how any other way would be possible." Silas crouched in front of her. "Listen, we can't sit here and debate this; just let me push the thoughts into your mind and allow me to show you what I see in Rome's mind when he teleports. I can't breach your shields, so let me in so that I may teach you. Maverick assures me you're plenty juiced up from the boost our king gave you."

It was true. Alara could feel Rome's power coursing through her like a live wire, and with her palms touching him, she could also feel the pressing need to heal him. Her own powers screamed at her. They told her he was suffering from the same drug that had incapacitated Amirishka. It was killing him but at a slower pace. She could attempt to heal him now, but there was no guarantee she would be successful in waking him from his catatonic state, and if she wasn't successful, then they would truly be sitting ducks for the next wave of operatives, and she would be just as useless if not more so. She knew healing him would take a toll on her powers and energy. She had to be wise about this and get them to safety before she could focus on healing him. The possibility of him recovering on his own was slim. With the drug fashioned as it was, it was highly probable that only she could fix the damaged cells because only she seemed to recognize what was happening with it.

Alara wondered if it would be so bad if they knew she possessed another gift besides those they already knew of? But of course, it would. The downfall would be another secret revealed, and they'd have even more cause to not trust her. She didn't want that. She needed them to trust her. The lies were becoming increasingly tedious, but they were for the better. She had to believe that, not just for her safety but for theirs as well.

"Rome healed me. His energy and his powers are flowing through me. If he wants me to teleport, then we all know I can use his other powers as well, so how about you allow me to probe your mind instead, and then we can get the hell out of here before more come." It wasn't entirely a lie. For the moment, she did possess many of his powers, but to probe Silas's mind, she meant only to use her own. Besides, she needed to be more vigilant with him, especially since he was constantly attempting to examine her thoughts.

At first, he didn't look convinced, but he reluctantly nodded. Alara wasted no time diving into his mind. His thoughts were chaotic. Occasional barriers were in place to most likely keep her out of areas better left undisturbed. She saw memories from his past as they attempted to hold her attention, but she avoided them. She wasn't there to snoop. She was there only for the information she needed.

Silas's voice penetrated her singular thought process with his own. *"I'm sure Rome wants us to head into town. Here's a visual of the home."*

Alara wasn't sure what to expect, but a clear visual of a large Victorian home with wrought iron fencing and a wraparound porch wasn't it. The home was positively beautiful, with light blue accents that made the white of the house pop with color. Large bay windows and two large towers made the home look much more prominent, along with the 4 car garage attached via an enclosed breezeway. The view changed abruptly, a large bedroom coming into view with a California king bed covered in black satin sheets and an abundance of pillows. She could practically smell the cleanliness in the air as she looked over the ornate dresser and large decorative fireplace several feet away from the end of the bed.

She thought of the warmth that would emanate from that hearth if she ever used it and the comfortability of the bed that looked more inviting by the minute. She felt a soft pressure build inside of her. It was a foreign feeling but not an unwelcome one. It kept building until it felt as if a bubble surrounded her before that pressure popped. Exclamations came from the warriors that stood around her. Alara opened her eyes. She hadn't realized she'd closed them and was equally surprised to find that they were all within the bedroom from Silas's memory. She couldn't comprehend how she'd made it happen before everyone was talking at once.

"How the fuck did she do that?" Akio snapped from his position at the foot of the bed alongside Cairo and Amirishka.

"We weren't even touching." Maverick chuckled, "That's fucking amazing."

"I didn't even have a chance to explain to you how to use his power," Silas frowned, "How did you know what to do?" His voice was filled with suspicion.

Alara shrugged, "I'm not sure. I just thought about it. I thought about getting us all to safety and how this is where we needed to go, and it just happened. I didn't realize what was happening. I just felt a pressure around me that seemed to expand and expand until it popped. Then we were here." She glanced down at Rome's still form and realized a pretty large amount of his energy still filled her. "I should probably try to heal him now that we're safe."

"We'll leave you to do that, but I believe a meeting should take place as soon as he awakens," Erick stated, his face a mask of indifference, "You'll be sure to call us the moment he wakes?"

She nodded, but she wasn't sure how accurate that would be. Usually, when she healed someone with multiple wounds, it took a lot out of her. She'd occasionally lose consciousness. Looking down at Rome, she could barely make out the numerous cuts criss crossed across his chest thanks to the shirt plastered to his body. It was soaked in blood. She thought about asking one of the guys to help her undress him but decided against it. Rome wouldn't be too happy about that. They had already been witnesses to his weakened state. They didn't need to see him in an even more vulnerable position. Alara listened as everyone left the bedroom before the door softly shut behind them. How she would get him naked was a question for the books. She pushed a few of his dreads back from his face after they'd come undone from his ponytail and simply stared down at him as she wondered what he could look like beneath his clothes. It would be much easier to clean and heal him if his clothing wasn't in the way. Frowning, she thought of him naked and what that could possibly look like and jumped in surprise when his clothing did, in fact, vanish.

She knew Rome's residual energy was the only reason she could achieve such a feat. God the man was powerful, and it was a heady feeling she was quickly becoming addicted to. She could hardly breathe, and yet her eyes took everything in. This was her first time seeing a naked male, and the sight before her was shocking, yet it turned her on. He turned her on. With the herculean build of his body holding her captive, she scanned him from head to toe, taking in the broadness of his chest and shoulders that were covered in deep scratches, as well as the prominent 12-pack that dominated his midsection with just as many open wounds. Her gaze traveled farther south. She couldn't control her need to look, and if she was being honest with herself, she didn't want to. Alara was curious, dying to know what the rest of him looked like. Her gaze landed on the thatch of hair between his legs, her eyes widening. His manhood was nearly the width of her wrist and at least five inches in length sat atop his balls, flaccid and unresponsive. She could only imagine what he would look like, hard and turned on. How much would he grow?

The videos she'd been forced to watch while with Titan were ingrained within her mind. The sight of the lewd and dirty acts she'd been forced to review was imprinted in her mind, but he was nothing like that. This wasn't what she'd been expecting when or if she ever came face to face with an actual penis. She thought she'd be just as disgusted with the real thing as Alara was with the numerous photos and videos she'd encountered. Instead, a curiosity filled her, along with a warmth that steadily grew within the pit of her stomach. That feeling spread outward until her whole body felt like a tingling live wire. She grabbed the end of the comforter and threw it over his lower body before curiosity could get the better of her and she touched him without permission. She needed to stop ogling him and get started on healing him. Alara placed her hands above his chest and forehead and closed her eyes to focus, but she couldn't erase his body image from her mind as she worked on him. She couldn't help but wonder how he would feel within her palm if she ever managed to touch him intimately. Would he let her?

The same drug that had coursed through Amirishka's veins was running through his, and she knew that, but something was different. It wasn't as volatile. Sure, it was attempting to eat away at his cells, but it wasn't very successful. In fact, it started eating away at itself little by little the longer she examined it. She couldn't tell how or why it was working against itself, but it was. She used little to no healing on her part. It seemed Rome's healing cells were doing precisely what they were intended to do. Alara pulled her hands away when she sensed he was more than on the mend. Lethargy didn't pull at her, and the need to sleep wasn't present. The only thing she could feel was excitement. A sensual thrill was running through her. Confusing her. The energy humming through her veins was an abnormality she wasn't used to.

Alara ran the tips of her fingers across his chest and watched as his flesh knit back together. It was fascinating. Not just the healing process but Rome in general was utterly fascinating. She continued to run her fingertips along the expanse of his dark chocolate skin and marveled at the tingle that continued to flow and ebb through her. Her breasts became heavy, nipples tightening to unbearable points of sensitivity as her inner core clenched repeatedly in need. She wasn't sure what that need was, but she knew she felt empty. There was something she was missing. Something that would change her life entirely if only she were educated enough in the matter of man to know what that something was. The videos had never convinced her to try or learn, but the man before her was making her wish she had. He made her want what she had never had.

She lowered her hand when Rome's growly voice spoke up, forcing her gaze to his face. "If you travel any lower, you'll get more than you bargained for, little flower."

He sat up slowly, pulling the comforter as he went to ensure it stayed perfectly placed along the lower half of his body. He leaned back against the pillows, lying against the headboard as his eyes devoured her. That was the only correct term for the look on his face. Desire was etched into every one of his features as he pushed those long dreads of his away from his face and watched her.

"I see we got away. Good job; I knew you could make it happen with guidance."

"No one helped me," she pulled at the length of the t-shirt on her body and frowned, "I just saw what Silas wanted me to see and brought us here. I didn't even realize what I was doing."

"That makes me even prouder. Where are the others? I can't yet access my powers to telepathically communicate with them. I'm still feeling the effects of this damned drug."

That was a weakness he wouldn't usually admit to having, but since meeting her, he'd admitted to many drawbacks he'd encountered. She commended him for that. He wanted her to see every side of him, even if he wasn't sure if she truly deserved it. Though not that far down, Rome knew she was still lying to him. She was still keeping secrets that could possibly reshape their lives. He knew it with an eighty percent probability rate, yet he couldn't resist wanting her. Couldn't resist confiding in her and bearing himself to the woman he knew to be his.

"I'm sure they went to clean up," Alara smiled softly, "just as you should."

He glanced down and chuckled and saw the blood that had dried on his arms, chest, and torso. "I suppose you're right. Maybe you should avert your eyes while I get up?"

"I've already seen all of you...but if you insist." She closed her eyes to grant him privacy as a small smile tugged at the corners of her lips.

CHAPTER

THIRTEEN

Rome stood beneath the spray of warm water as he showered off the grime and blood from the last few hours. A million thoughts were racing through his mind, but what stood out the most was that sweet, innocent look Alara had donned when her eyes closed. He'd wanted her to look at him and see him, but he didn't think he could walk away if she had. The need that had been building since he'd encountered her was steadily rising. It was a carnal need, and he wasn't sure how much longer he could keep his hands to himself. He smacked his palms into the cool tile in frustration and groaned at the painful erection that protruded from his body. His eyes blazed brighter at the thought of kissing her again as his fangs sharpened and nicked his bottom lip. He ignored the sting and simply licked the blood from his lip, sealing the cut effectively as he allowed the water to rinse off the heavy layer of soap from his body.

A soft knock came from the bathroom door, followed by Alara's soothing voice. "Silas and Erick are asking for you. What should I tell them?"

"Tell them I'm deciding to rest."

"I'm sure they can hear you." She chuckled, the sound going straight to his balls. "They feel like a meeting is in order."

"Like you said, they heard what I said...Besides, I can feel the sun rising from the east. They'll be sleeping soon whether they want to or not. We'll meet later tonight when everyone has rested."

He needed to talk to them about the attack and figure out how or why Titan had been tracing Alara's call. The only answer that seemed to fit the bill was that Alaric was responsible. He'd sent men for her. If that was the case, her so-called 'friend' worked for his enemy. That now made him enemy number two. He smiled with glee. He couldn't wait to rip the fuckers throat out now that he knew he could.

He listened as Alara walked away from the door before he glanced down and wrapped his hand around his thick erection. He really shouldn't be doing this. God, he couldn't remember the last time he'd masturbated or had any sexual gratification, but he needed this. It was either this or go after her and impale her on his throbbing cock. He didn't think she would be up for that. Maybe she'd let him bury his face between her legs to lap up her cream, or perhaps she'd allow him to slide his dick between her plush lips to see how deep her throat could take him. He groaned at the thought as his hand slid up and down the straining mass, precum leaking from the tip as the visuals ran through his mind. The idea of her taking him in hand and licking him from root to base was enough to send his load jetting out to splatter along the tiled wall. He'd finished much sooner than anticipated.

"Fuck," he snarled, disgust filling him at what he had just done. That was way too quick. If he ever got close to having Alara, he'd probably cum before his dick ever touched her pretty little lips with the way he was starving for her.

He shut the water off, pulled a towel around his waist, and headed back into the bedroom as the sun's pull started to take hold of him. In his younger years, the sun would have affected him more, but now, at nearly a thousand years old, he could withstand being awake for several hours. No one was sure why the sun affected them so profoundly or why it made them sleep until the dawning hours of the night, but it was something he planned on looking into and hopefully fixing. Every day, the threat of Titan finding them as they slept grew larger and larger. The only saving grace was that Rogue's had even more of an aversion to the sun then they did. But, he needed a solution. He needed a way that would allow each of his warriors to walk beneath the sun's rays once more. Maybe a few trusted humans could serve them, but they each had learned early on that humans were the most untrusting people alive. They'd sell him and his people out for a quick buck if Titan got to them. He shook his head at the absurd thought, even if it did have some merit. It could potentially benefit them if they trained and trusted the right people to protect them as they slept. Maybe he'd look into it. Or maybe the Kindred could help if he located more.

He sighed heavily as his eyes drifted to land on the woman sitting atop his bed with one of his large shirts cloaking her body and a pair of his sweatpants. His dick immediately jumped right back to attention. He turned to face the wall in an attempt to gain a semblance of control. He didn't need this. Shit, he didn't want to have such a loss of control over something he'd never struggled with before. Being near her was becoming a struggle in patience and restraint. He was currently losing the fight for restraint. He wanted her with a desperation that was lost to him. She had to be his fated mate, his better half, the woman who would complete his heart and soul. She was his. She had to be. It was the only thing that could explain this unnatural need he had for her.

"Romulus," Alara spoke up and knelt on the bed, "Are you okay?"

She moved as if she planned to come to him; he heard it and growled words that were barely discernible through clenched teeth. "Don't come to me. I need control."

"Just tell me what's wrong." She climbed from the bed and stood, hands pulling nervously at the hem of the shirt with no intentions of getting any closer than necessary.

Rome swallowed harshly before glancing over his shoulder to

stare into her eyes; all the while, he burned with the need for her. "You tempt me. Tempt me beyond reason or control, and right now, I'm losing this fight," his eyes trailed down her body, and he sighed, "I need you to go. Find Erick and tell him I sent you. Have him set you up in another room."

"B-but I don't want to sleep somewhere else."

"You need to. It's for your own good as well as for my sanity, little flower, just go."

"Tell me what would happen if I stay."

Fear wasn't necessarily starting to take root in her blood; it was excitement. The look in his eyes was feral and hungry, those beautiful fangs of his barely peeking from behind his lips as his expressive gaze told her she might have been biting off more than she could chew, just as he'd warned her. Yet, she stayed. The need to know was slowly consuming her thoughts. How deep did this need of his go, and what would she discover if he acted on those impulses?

Rome narrowed his gaze and turned, hands clenched at his sides, dick straining against the towel. "How much experience do you have with men? How far have they gotten in the past with that tight little body? How many have had you?" He snarled the last question, afraid to know the answer. He didn't want to know. He feared what he would do if he did. The simple answer was murder. Every man that had ever tasted her lips or any other part of her would die. The complex solution would be unending torture before he sliced their dicks and heads from their body after hunting them down. The anger festering through him at just the thought of her with someone else alarmed him so profoundly that it took him a moment to realize she now stood before him. Unafraid.

"Your powers are returning, Romulus; I feel your energy building. Please, tell me what's wrong?"

Concern filled her voice, her expression showing no offense had been taken from his line of questioning. She hadn't answered him, though, and he needed an answer. Maybe he shouldn't be reaching for her and curving his hand around her neck to drag her closer, but he couldn't stop now that he was in motion. Her skin against his, her natural scent clogging his nose so he could only smell her. It was weakening him by the second.

"How many men, Alara?" He tightened his grip and pulled her closer, her small hands pressing against his chest as her lips parted in surprise when only a breath of air separated them.

She shook her head as much as she could within his grip. "I h-haven't...I don't know what you mean."

Confusion practically radiated from her skin. Rome could hear the tremor within her voice. He wanted to reassure her that everything was okay, but the primal side of him that he kept buried deep within emerged with a vengeance at her non-admission. Confusion and innocence poured from her like a flame and he was a moth. Inexplicably drawn to her. He knew he should pull away. He knew it, and still, he stayed.

"You tell me no at any point, and I stop," he whispered as he dragged his fingers into her hair before closing those last few inches that separated their lips.

The kiss was soft yet intense. Rome sucked at her lips, attempting to coax them apart for a deeper kiss as he turned and pressed her more diminutive form against the wall. The moment his erection pressed into her, Alara moaned into his mouth, giving him that small admission that made a world of difference. He took complete control, his tongue diving between her lips to duel with her own as he tightened his grip on her hair and moved his other hand beneath the hem of her shirt until his palm connected with smooth, warm skin. He hissed through sharpened fangs and pulled back to lick along the nape of her neck. She froze for only a second but quickly moaned into his ear the second his hand came into contact with the weight and fullness of her breast.

"Oh god," her voice was breathy, filled with a need she didn't recognize.

"God's not here, little flower." Rome snarled.

He clamped the tip of her nipple between his thumb and pointer finger and tugged gently as he slid his thigh between her legs and applied pressure. His fangs itched to sink into her skin, but he ignored the urge and instead paid attention to every moan and groan that passed through her lips. It was like music to his ears with every soft tug to her engorged nipple. The scent of her arousal grew stronger with every nip and lick he applied to her flesh. He refused to untangle his grip on her hair, fearing she would move away. He needed her to stay. God, he needed to taste her.

He whispered against her ear lobe as his hand moved from her breasts to trail down into her pants. "Has anyone ever tasted this pretty pussy?"

Maybe he was moving too fast. Or maybe he wasn't moving fast enough. Whatever the case, the moment his fingers came into contact with the small patch of hair nestled between Alara's thighs, his entire body jerked, and energy like nothing he'd ever felt before charged through him. His powers were back, and with his needs raging the way they were, he attempted to erect a protective bubble around them to protect the world from his inability to control himself. Their continued contact assured him that Alara was siphoning his energy without her realizing it. It was little by little, but he felt the pull. Shit, he felt the pull deep in his soul where she seemed to be making herself right at home.

He encountered warmth and wetness, the pads of his fingers sliding along the lips of her pussy yet going nowhere near her center. She didn't seem to like that. Her moans were now mewling cries and whispered pleas that pulled at his balls. Her head was thrown as far back against the wall as she could get it. Her body was pliant yet tense against the weight of his own as he continued to suck at her throat and massage the edges of her cunt. Her tiny clit hid just beneath the hood as he continued to tease her. Her little nails dug little grooves into his arms as if to pull him closer while her body dilated against him. He could taste the excitement on her skin and knew that these sensations were all new to her, but he still needed to hear the words. He needed to know she was present. He needed to know she was with him and not somewhere else within her mind.

He tapped the pad of his finger against her now engorged clit and smiled when her moan went deeper with need. "Will my tongue be the first to taste this little pussy?" She nodded, but that wasn't good enough for him. "I need the words Alara. Will I be the first?" Fuck, he was a greedy bastard.

Her whispered yes was precisely what he needed to hear to make his next move. He could have used his telekinetic ability to undress her, but he wanted to unwrap her like a present. He dropped to his knees quickly and removed the sweats from her body as he forced one of his claws to lengthen and slice down the center of the shirt, leaving her bare to his onlooking gaze.

"God, you're fucking beautiful," he groaned and took in the sight of her large breasts, narrowed waist, flared hips and muscular legs. "Put a leg over my shoulder, little flower."

Uncertainty filled her expression, but he gave her no time to let fear of the unknown change their trajectory. He didn't just need this for him; he needed it for them. He wanted to ease her into it. That had been the objective, but now he was battling his mind and her mind, and he didn't need that. She didn't need that. They just needed to feel. Without pause, his mouth latched onto her moistening core and he groaned in absolute pleasure. His fangs lengthened to the point of pain, his eyes brightened and ecstasy washed over him like a rainfall. His hands tightened around the thigh over his shoulder as well as her hip. Her fingers frantically dug into his dreads and grasped at them as his tongue and lips devoured her. Fire raced down his spine at the feel of her dainty nails digging into his scalp. If she'd been an Eternal, it would have hurt like a bitch, but luckily, she didn't have claws.

"Please," Alara moaned when his tongue slid lazily through the lips of her pussy as if he had all the time in the world, "Romulus, please."

She clung to him, her toes curling with every lick he delivered to her core. Her body was tightening, tensing in preparation for the cataclysmic orgasm that would take her under. Rome marveled at the taste of her. The earthy womanly fragrance surrounding him and her thighs around his head quickly became his newest obsession. The deeper he licked her, the more honey seemed to flow from her, and still, he wanted more. He wanted her pleasure. Rome wanted everything now that he had her where he needed her.

The windows were explicitly built to reflect the sun's rays, yet Rome could feel the heat along his back, and although it didn't burn him, he felt the heat crawling over and through him. Felt it flowing deep into his bones as he continued to devour her. The leg thrown over his shoulder was rubbing against his shoulder blade, igniting his blood in ways that had his mind conjuring images of them tangled up together as he brought her to orgasm repeatedly. Rome attempted to do that now, tongue licking, mouth sucking at her as her cries continued to turn into pleas. He could feel her right on the edge, her nails digging deep into his scalp, causing a snarl to push past his lips as he sucked at her clit with an eagerness that shocked even him. Alara jerked beneath him. Just as he thought her orgasm would crash over and into her, he was shoved away so abruptly that he landed on his ass.

He couldn't help it. He laughed. It appeared that she was indeed strong when she wanted to be. "Why did you stop me, little flower? You were right on the edge."

She placed an arm over her breasts to shield herself as one of her small hands hid her pussy from his hungry gaze. Her expression was embarrassed and ashamed, while her voice was barely a whisper when she spoke. "I don't know what I felt, but it was intense. I don't know if I wanted that…that intensity."

"How will you know unless you try? Are you telling me you've never played with your sweet little cunt? Never took yourself to the edge and over? Never fallen into oblivion?"

He returned to his crouched position and moved back into her personal space, his hands gently cupping her hips as he pulled her closer. Her hands stayed where they were, obstructing his view of her beautiful center. He kissed her hand, smiled when she shuddered beneath his touch and moaned softly. She was so sensitive to him; her skin heightened to levels she wasn't familiar with.

"I've never…" she paused, bit her lip, and shifted uncomfortably beneath his penetrating gaze, "I've never…well you already know I've never done anything like this before."

"Then let me show you how it could be, and allow me to teach you that that feeling only gets a thousand times better."

"It won't hurt?"

Rome chuckled and pressed another kiss to her hand as he inhaled her fragrance once more. "Absolutely not. And if it does, that just means it's being done wrong. I won't do it wrong, little flower. I'll make you forget your own name and you'll thank me for it." He was a cocky son of a bitch and he knew it. He grinned wickedly and waited.

Alara stood there staring momentarily until she dropped her hands and hesitantly placed her left leg back over his shoulder. He thanked the heavens above for her acceptance and submission and quickly returned to worshiping her. He licked and sucked at her lips and clit. One hand helped to keep her balance while the other reached up and grasped one of her large breasts. Her moans were back, louder this time, as her nails found purchase and dug into his shoulder blades. She was already sensitive to the touch, so bringing her to the precipice didn't take much. Later, he might regret his next actions, but he basked in his choice for now. The second Alara was right on the edge of her orgasm, he struck, his mouth jerking to the innermost corner of her thigh as he sank his fangs into her femoral artery. The reaction was instant. Her scream rattled his eardrums as her nails scoured his shoulders. Her entire body tensed up, her cry of ecstasy was music to his ears as the aphrodisiac within his fangs hit her bloodstream. The taste of her blood coated his throat and warmed him, sending an orgasm rushing through him to dirty the inside of his towel, but he felt no shame, only satisfaction as he smiled wide against her skin. He couldn't wait to make her do it again.

Rome lifted her into his arms, climbed beneath the covers on the bed, and pulled Alara into his side before smiling softly. He was more content now that the driving urge to be inside of her as well as taste her blood was quenched. He ran his fingers through her hair and tugged on the strands until her head tilted back and her eyes met his. Her face was flushed, eyes sparkling with excitement as her hand trailed lovingly against his chest.

"Do you know how beautiful you are?" He dug his fingers into her scalp and massaged her head thoroughly.

Pleasure filled her expression with a soft moan to go along with it before she moved closer and spoke against his lips. "I'm sure you plan on telling me just how beautiful I am."

He nipped her bottom lip playfully and chuckled. "So orgasms make you saucy. Interesting. That gives me much to look forward to."

"What do you mean?"

"Just that I had you pegged wrong." As he continued to massage her head, Rome used his other hand to grab her thigh and pull her leg up and over his hip until they were practically entwined with one another. "There's a confidence within you that I thought was buried so deeply that you weren't even sure if you had it, so I simply mean that getting to know this other side of you should be interesting. For the both of us even."

Alara sighed before her hand paused against his chest. He watched her cautiously and stilled in his ministrations as he watched her expression morph from one of pleasure to sadness. He didn't enjoy that look on her face and wasn't sure what had even caused it, but he would be finding out. He would never stand to see that particular expression on her if he could help. It was almost like watching the life leave a person's body.

He gripped her small chin lightly between his thumb and forefinger. "What is it? Why have you grown sad?"

"I just realized I don't even fully know myself." She bit her lip nervously. "The way I grew up didn't really grant me a lot of access to explore much about myself."

"And how exactly did you grow up?"

He regretted the question as soon as it passed through his lips because he knew she wouldn't answer him. Being open with him wasn't something she seemed too keen on doing. She held her secrets close to the vest when really he wanted her to lay everything bare. He wanted to better know the woman he had within his arms.

Rome pulled her in for a light kiss against her forehead before he spoke again. "Forget I said anything. Rest." He kissed her again and pulled her even closer to his chest before resting his chin on the top of her head.

Alara was stiff for several moments before she relaxed fully into his side. He felt it the second her body went heavy with sleep. His mind instantly began to wander. What would he have to do to get her to trust him? It wasn't enough that he protected her because she still believed herself to be his captive, and in some ways, she was, but it was all for her safety. It was also for very selfish reasons. Alara was his, and he needed to make this something more permanent.

CHAPTER
FOURTEEN

An hour ago, the sun shone high in the sky with no clouds in sight until an abrupt rainstorm appeared as if from thin air. Alaric stood by the window inside a rundown motel, a Glock 19 in hand, as he peered out the dingy curtain in search of possible Titan operatives. Pain radiated throughout his entire body, but what hurt the most was the gunshot wound in his side. Blood seeped from the poorly gauze-packed bullet hole and soaked his clothing. With no enemy in sight, he slid the curtain back into place, double-checked the locks on the door, and turned to stare at Alondra. She was curled into a fetal position on top of one of the double beds, furious eyes staring back at him. She rubbed at her arms, a soft glow emanating from her palms as she healed herself from the wounds she had sustained during their escape. He wanted to ask her to heal him, but he already knew what her answer would be. She still hated him for his part in her torture, and he couldn't blame her. He still blamed himself for his actions"I need to head into the bathroom and clean myself up." He groaned softly when another piercing pain came from his side, "I'll need to stitch this hole closed. Can I trust you not to run off and to just stay and watch for incoming soldiers?"

After healing herself, she climbed from the bed and practically snarled her words. "Give me a weapon to protect myself. I'd rather get as far away from you as possible, but I don't know how to survive in the real world. I understand that I need you to stay hidden from Titan for the time being, but get this through your thick skull now. As soon as I can navigate this world myself, I'm leaving, and you aren't to follow me. In fact, you will swear to me here and now that you'll forget I ever existed because I don't care if our blood tells us we're related. You mean nothing to me."

She was asking for the impossible. As her older brother, it was his duty to protect and shield her from the world's dangers. Working for Titan had sometimes clouded his judgment, but he'd done it for them. He'd played a part in her torture, which had created a rift between them so wide that the possibility of them being a family was close to nil, but it had been necessary. He knew the atrocities Titan had performed upon her. Alaric knew her pain and what she'd had to endure, and he refused to abandon her again but he could make false promises for now. If lying to her would help her trust him, he would lie.

"As soon as I teach you all I can about the world, I promise to let you go and live your life without me as your shadow. Now, watch for trouble." He pulled another Glock 19 from the waistband of his pants and held it out to her. "Do you know how to use this?"

"Would you like me to show you how well I can use it?" She snatched the gun and waited until he headed for the bathroom before she took up a position near the window.

Alaric grabbed his first aid kit from the backpack he'd managed to snag before they escaped. With the door wide open to monitor Alondra, he turned on the faucet to cleanse his wound and quickly laid out a needle, thread, antiseptic spray, and gloves. He couldn't risk an infection. He needed to be alert and ready to fight if Titan managed to track them down. He hadn't gone all this way to gain their freedom just to throw in the towel now. They'd be running and looking over their shoulders for the rest of their lives, but it was better this way. It was better than being a captive or working for an organization that saw you as less than human. It hadn't been easy for them to get away. The years and months of planning not one but two successful escapes had nearly robbed Alaric of all sense, and he'd barely gotten out alive the second time.

After Alondra's escape, security had doubled, and he'd been partnered with a fucking Rogue of all things. He hated those sadistic bastards and everything they stood for. Getting away from him hadn't been easy; in fact, he'd had to kill the Rogue in order to successfully escape, and he damn sure didn't regret it. Alaric pulled the shirt from his body and turned to view his back, hoping that the bullet had made an exit wound, but unmarred skin stared back at him. It was still lodged inside. He sighed heavily. He had no choice but to leave it in place as he washed his hands, pulled on the gloves, and quickly cleansed the wound as best as he could. He groaned at the pain but forged on before he lost his nerve. His hands shook slightly from the pain as he stitched himself up. He could feel Alondra's eyes on him but ignored her and instead forced himself not to pass out from the agony of shoving a needle repeatedly through his skin. He thought of other things. Things like Alara and where she'd ended up. He was sure she hadn't meant to slip up on their phone call and speak her savior's name, but he was glad she did. Now he knew where she'd gone.

She was with Romulus, leader of the Eternals. Alaric smiled through his pain. When he'd helped her escape, he'd hoped that he'd been sending her in the right direction. He was glad to know she'd arrived unharmed and that they were, in fact, protecting her. After learning of the Eternals' possible base of operations, he acted fast when he heard of Alara's transfer. The Eternals were the only ones he could think of who could protect and teach her how to control her powerful abilities. As a top soldier within Titan, he'd been privy to even the most confidential information, Project Romulus being one of those confidential matters and where he and his people might be. Romulus was power personified and easily the strongest being in the world. Titan had been hunting him since before Alaric's time, and they had yet to capture or weaken him.

With the new drug in play, Titan could gain the upper hand and before they'd fled, Alaric had learned that it was, in fact, possible.

According to some, another Eternal by the name of Amirishka had been shot with a tranq, and she'd actually succumbed to the drug, but before they could grab her, another Eternal, Maverick, had shifted and flown off with her. After learning that he could change into a dragon, the entire site had buzzed with activity. That's when he'd been able to set his plan into motion for his second escape attempt. The files on each of Rome's warriors kept getting bigger and bigger, and capturing them was becoming a high priority. Still, Alaric doubted that anything was more important to Lukas Titan than re-acquiring his sisters and him.

He stitched the last thread and tied it off before he wrapped a compress around his sides. He cleaned up quickly, grabbed a shirt from his pack, and approached Alondra cautiously. Although her gaze was out the window, he noticed when she felt him beside her.

Her entire body tensed as she glanced over to meet his gaze. "I suppose you're done now?" She asked, venom no longer lacing her tone. Could it be out of concern for him? Doubtful.

"I'm as good as I can be considering the circumstances." He replied and shifted the curtains back from the window to peek outside, "You should try to rest before we get moving again."

"Moving where? Where could we possibly go where they couldn't find us? Sure, we removed all possible trackers, but that won't stop them from hunting us down and possibly killing the both of us."

"They won't kill us. They need us."

"Even if they don't, we'll wish we were dead. So where can we go? Who could protect us from them?"

"We're going to locate Romulus and his new possible base of operations and gain his help. I'm sure they've relocated after the attack that just took place the other night. He already protects our sister. I'm sure he'll protect us as well, and if not me, then they'll surely look after you. I may not survive the meeting once we find them, but as long as you both are safe, my job is done. Romulus will protect you both." He knew he wouldn't survive the encounter if Romulus had a say. Their shared words from their phone conversation were proof enough for him.

Alondra's expression morphed into a frown. "I'm sorry, what? We have a sister?"

"Dammit," he shook his head in annoyance, "I forgot you were kept in the dark about her. We're a triplet set; we have a younger sister who I helped to free a few weeks ago, and before you ask, the answer is no, she wasn't and isn't more important than you. She just happened to have fewer guards on her on the transfer day. It was then or never."

"I have a sister." She whispered as a vacant expression filled her face. She moved away and retook a position on the bed, the gun hanging limply from her hand as she looked to be processing the information. "Was she...is she okay? Did they hurt her like they hurt me?"

Alaric winced at the thought of what Alondra had endured at the hands of Titan. "No, they needed her for another purpose. Alara was sheltered for the most part."

"Good... that's good, and you say she's with this Romulus guy? Who is that? Another Titan soldier that decided to go AWOL?"

"He's an Eternal. The king, to be exact."

Her eyes jumped to his, recognition blazing within her gaze as she spoke. "You're right. She's safe where she is."

It was Alaric's turn to frown. "You know what an Eternal is?"

"I was a prisoner but I paid attention and did it well. I may not have tried to escape, but I wanted to be aware of everything happening around me. I listened and learned, but I never tried to run."

"Never?" He found that hard to believe. He would have left years ago if he hadn't had to worry about his sisters in the earlier years of their captivity when he'd learned the truth about Titan. Even Alara had tried to escape a few times over the years but they always caught her before she could reach the outside world.

"For what? Where could I have gone? I had no one and nothing Alaric. I only knew those four walls inside my room and the occasional interrogation room. You remember that room, don't you?" She paused, her eyes staring directly into his soul as she spoke, "Well, it wasn't just for torture. Sometimes, I was sent there to heal people…monsters I wish I'd never encountered. I'm sure you know all about those monsters too, but there was one that… never mind."

He did. He knew precisely what monsters Alondra spoke of. Titan was full of them, men and women who had created a virus that could twist the very fabric of human DNA and turn someone into a creature of darkness and savagery. The virus turned people who were once human into brutal and effective killers who followed every order that was given, and if they didn't, they were executed. The creation of the Rogues had given Titan more of a fighting chance against the Eternals before the new tranquilizer drug had been created. Weeks ago, the head scientists had created the virus as if from thin air. Alaric was convinced that everyone who worked for that vile place was evil through and through. They were all monsters. Sometimes, he even felt like one himself after working for them since his early teenage years.

They were free now and he had no intention of ever returning or allowing Titan to get ahold of them again.

"You really should get some rest." He peered through the curtains again to see that the storm still raged on, yet no new cars had pulled into the lot, "We'll get moving again sometime around one or two o'clock. It's better to move when the Rogues cannot follow during the day."

"I don't think I could possibly sleep, besides…I have questions. Like, what the hell is a Rogue? Is it those fanged creatures that walk the halls at night? And what happened to our parents? How did we end up with Titan in the first place? As far back as I can remember, I've been a victim of them. Have we been prisoners all our lives?"

God, he wasn't ready for this line of questioning. There were so many things she was better off not knowing. He knew the answers only because he'd found the letters that had been left for them. He also had to do some vile things to convince the corporation that he was loyal to them so that he could learn more. He couldn't tell Alondra what he knew. He didn't want her to see the true darkness they'd finally freed themselves from.

"The only thing that matters now is that we're free, and we're never going back," he moved to the other bed she wasn't occupying and sat down, "now if you won't rest, then I will, but that means you need to keep watch and wake me the moment anything remotely suspicious happens."

"You can't shelter me from the things I have a right to know." Alondra snapped and moved to take a position near the window as she held the gun he'd given her loosely within her grip.

"Trust me, I know, but now isn't the time to rehash all of that. We need to stay focused and pay attention to the situation we've found ourselves in now. Knowing the events of the past won't change that. Once we figure out our situation and get somewhere safe, I'll tell you whatever you want to know. For now, we need to focus."

She nodded mutely before turning to stare at the world outside. Alaric sighed heavily as he forced himself to close his eyes and relax into a light sleep, but he kept his gun within reach and hoped that nothing would happen moving forward.

He would need his strength and his senses about him if he had any hope of staying under Titan's radar while he searched for Alara's location. He had every intention of telepathically scanning for her signature as soon as he reached the center city of Van Scive. Knowing that the Eternals would potentially kill him didn't deter him. Making sure his family was safe was all he cared about now. He needed to make up for failing them for the first twenty-seven years of their life. He cared about their freedom, and he intended to ensure they remained that way. Free.

Lukas Titan stood within his lab several floors beneath the surface of his newly located base of operations. His blood was boiling, anger running through him in waves at the clusterfuck that had become his life. Almost several weeks ago, his most prized possession had escaped with one of his most trusted soldiers, and now his lieutenant and his healer had run as well. He would have never thought Alaric could betray him. Maybe he'd put too much faith and trust in the man, but his actions for Titan were unquestionable. Alaric had turned into one of his greatest accomplishments. Alaric had killed without question, stole without thought, and lied with such ease that he'd been duped.

He launched another beaker into the sterile white wall and watched it shatter into a thousand pieces as three employees shied away from him in fear. Ethan, his personal guard, strode from the elevator with a grim expression fixed upon his face. He was six foot three with eyes as black as midnight and hair as black as sin cut low to his scalp with military precision. His body was lean, built like a tank around the shoulders, chest, and arms. He was a killing machine thanks to the rigorous training he'd been forced to undergo when first recruited by Titan.

"Sir, we believe we've located Subjects 2 and 3. They appear to be holed up in a motel close to town, but I have issued a stay-back order until night falls."

"And why the hell would you do that?" Lukas exclaimed as he yanked up his cane to stride forward without fear of losing his balance. He hardly ever used it. He hated to show weakness, but at times, it was necessary. Since his accident he'd never regained full use of the muscles within his injured leg. "I need them captured now, Ethan! I want that bastard Alaric tortured until he's close to death, and then I'll force his weak sister to nurse him back to life before I start all over again!"

"But he's without his collar." Ethan frowned, "Sir, he would know we were coming if we got any closer. They could escape again before we could make a grab for them. It's better to wait for the night when the Rogues are beside us. It's harder for him to enter their minds and read their intentions. We should wait."

Lukas moved fast as he struck out with his cane and pushed the hidden button beneath his thumb that allowed a blade to slide out the end, cutting across Ethan's face. "Do I pay you for your opinions, or do I pay you to follow orders?" He snarled.

Ethan staggered back and placed a hand over the dripping wound beneath his eye, yet he made no sound and avoided all eye contact as he spoke. "I'm paid to follow orders, sir."

"Then I suggest you follow them and get my possessions back

now." Lukas righted himself and moved to take a seat behind his desk. "The next time you return, I expect them to be with you, and if not, then we shall see just how red you can bleed." The smile on his face could only be described as sinister.

Ethan nodded with understanding and left the room without a word as the rest of the employees within the lab busied themselves. Lukas didn't have heightened senses like his family's creations, but he could see the fear on their faces. It was heady, almost drugging to his mind as he grinned with pure malice. Their fear ensured their loyalty, and if there was no loyalty to be had, they died beneath the slice of his blade or through more torturous, more exciting means.

Alara had betrayed him.

Alaric had betrayed him.

And Alondra had left with her brother. Although the video footage he'd recovered showed her struggling against him at first she had still betrayed him in the end. He had no intention of killing them for their betrayal, but he did intend to make them suffer. He did intend to make them wish for death, and being the sick, twisted bastard that he was, he would grant them no relief. Instead, he would get what he'd always wanted from them. He would get their submission, and he would finally have Alara.

Lukas smiled at the thought as he glanced at the framed picture of a thirteen-year-old Alara perched upon his desk.

Soon.

Soon, he would get what was owed to him.

CHAPTER

FIFTEEN

"Please, oh god, please, please…" Alara moaned as her legs tightened around the head nestled between her legs as Rome licked and sucked at the lips of her warm cunt.

Her back arched, her hands gripped the sheets, and her feet dug into the bed as pleasure whipped through her, stealing all her control and leaving her with nothing but the need to cum. Tears crept from the corners of her eyes as his hands tightened around her waist, pulling her closer to his talented tongue. She screamed in complete ecstasy as the fourth orgasm of the afternoon ripped through her and stole the very breath from her lungs. Rome slid up her body moments later, his naked form rubbing against her own as he captured her lips beneath his own and kissed her deeply. It only lasted a second before he pulled away and moved to her side to lay back against the headboard. A content smile lit his face, and lower down, his erection stood proud and heavy as if it was reaching for her, yet when she went for it, he simply grabbed her hand, kissed her palm, and laid it on his chest.

Alara frowned and sat up as all the pleasure that had swamped her before quickly evaporated. "It's been three days since we escaped that attack squad, three days since you've woken me up literally every afternoon with an amazing orgasm, and yet you won't let me touch you. Why? Do you not want my hands on you? I know I'm new to this, but I recognize the signs of a man desperately wanting to cum, so why are you stopping me? Is it my inexperience?"

Clear blue eyes watched her quietly before he lifted his hand to caress the side of her throat. Hunger shone brightly within his gaze as it fell to the vein that thrummed heavily beneath his fingertips. "My need for you is too strong. If you touch me, I may very well snap, and I need my control. I'll handle my problem a little later. For now, I'd like to lay with you before I prepare myself for tonight's hunt."

She smacked his hand away and glared. "Is that what you've been doing? Handling it on your own?" The expression on her face could only be described as hurt.

"Of course. When you head down to eat with the rest of them, I shower and relieve myself."

The need to hit him nearly overwhelmed her as she spoke through clenched teeth. "So it's okay for you to touch me, but I can't reciprocate?"

Rome watched her quizzically, not understanding her anger. "I just told you, Alara, my control will slip."

"Then no more touching for you!" She snapped and attempted to climb from the bed to put distance between them.

He snared her around the waist and yanked her into his lap, her legs falling into place around his hips as his dick brushed against the curves of her ass. She shuddered at the feel of him as she met his furious gaze. His fangs made an appearance, causing flashbacks of them sinking into her thigh to fill her mind. Her breathing became labored as a yearning she didn't fully understand began to pump through her. She thought she would have hated him for what he'd done without her consent, but instead, she ached for him to do it again. She wanted to feel his fangs sinking into her as she reached a powerful climax. Alara knew the injection of his essence had been the tipping point for her. She had been told that an Eternals essence held a potent aphrodisiac that heightened arousal.

Rome watched her steadily as his eyes flared brighter. "Are you telling me that if I don't allow you to touch me, you'll, in turn, deny me?"

"It seems only fair, doesn't it? You shouldn't be able to touch me while I'm constantly being denied."

He snarled, the sound sending chills down her spine as his eyes narrowed into slits. "Then I suggest you put those pretty little hands on me and weaken me before you touch my dick. And don't hold back, little flower."

Surprise filled her. She didn't think he'd agree, but now that he had, his hands had dropped from her waist to grip the covers tightly. She knew what he was trying to do. He wanted her to make it so that he couldn't overpower her and take whatever he wanted. She could make it happen. With the lessons she's been taking from him, Alara had gained more control over her power with each day. Siphoning from him had actually become something she looked forward to. His energy blazing through her was nearly as good as any orgasm. Sometimes, for hours after, it felt like she carried him with her until the power and energy finally evaporated, leaving her feeling slightly empty.

She placed her hands hesitantly against his chest, focused on her power, and started slowly sucking the energy from him through her palms. It was such a drugging feeling that she quickly became lightheaded and pulled back before she took too much and knocked him unconscious. His power and energy flared through her, igniting her in ways that had quickly become addicting.

"What now?" She whispered.

He licked at his bottom lip, those fangs of his warming her from the inside out as his body became pliant beneath hers. "Scoot back and touch me, little flower, but only with your hands. Be gentle at first; get used to the feeling of me within your grip."

Alara smiled softly and quickly moved between his legs, her eyes zeroing in on his cock before she gently grasped it at the base and marveled at how soft his skin felt within her hand. Rome hissed through clenched teeth as his eyes zeroed in on her. She slowly slid her hand from base to tip, watching as drops of precum sprouted from the slit. Alara licked at her bottom lip, her throat running dry at the thought of placing him in her mouth as he'd done with her several times. She moaned at the thought and rubbed the leaking fluid into his skin before gasping in shock when he abruptly grabbed her wrist in a tight hold to halt her movements.

"I don't think I can do this," he whispered, eyes blazing with need.

She smiled at the apparent vulnerability within his stare and tightened her grip. His weakened powers pulsed around them as if she hadn't drained most of his energy as a vicious snarl whispered through his quickly lengthening fangs. God, how were they getting longer? Objects shook within the room as his telekinetic power flared, and the sky outside began to gather clouds as a turbulent storm quickly approached them.

Whenever Rome experienced heightened emotions, his gifts took on a mind of their own, almost as if he couldn't control the very powers that made him the king of his people. Alara could feel all of his tightly wound power running through him as she attempted to siphon more of his energy before she used her other hand to delicately grab his balls. They were heavy and lightly sprinkled with hair, but they got his attention as she rubbed them gently between her fingers. Rome released his grip on her wrist, dropped his hand, and closed his eyes as his lust-filled groan filled the room. She wasted no time and continued her exploration of him as she slid her hand from base to tip continually, his precum making the glide that much easier as it added lube to her up-and-down motions and poured fire on her already raging desire.

She smiled with pride as Rome lost himself beneath her steady grip. His weakened abilities still called out to her as they continued to undulate around them the closer she inched him towards release. Her panting breaths matched his own. Excitement sang through the air, her nipples pebbling to dangerous proportions as her pussy clenched and dripped with a need to be filled. She was quickly beginning to recognize this new sensation, yet she wasn't sure if she was ready to feel his length and girth inside of her. The moistness between her thighs momentarily distracted her just as the sky

146

opened with a downpour of rain, lightning, and thunder. A thick jet of cum sprang from his tip to coat her hands with the sticky substance as his ecstasy-filled shout echoed through her ears. His body relaxed further into the bed as euphoria filled him.

"Fuck," he murmured softly.

He opened his eyes and watched as Alara hesitantly licked a drop of his cum from her hand. If her hum was any indication, she enjoyed the small taste. Rome snapped. There was no other word for it. He launched himself at her faster than human eyes could track as he pinned her beneath him, intending to slide his hardening dick into her dripping center. A light knock at his bedroom door gave him pause just as his tip rubbed against her moist core. God, he'd just cum, but his dick was hard as steel once more. He barely restrained himself from sliding into her as deeply as he could. He wanted to forget where she began or where he ended. Her legs tightened around his waist, tempting him beyond reason to ignore the rest of the world for several hours in favor of Alara. Yet he couldn't.

"Silas, what is it?" He could sense him on the other side of the door, his heartbeat slightly elevated, his thoughts a jumbled mess that confused even him.

Something was wrong.

He forced himself to extract from the warmth of Alara's body as Silas spoke through the door, his voice filled with confusion. "I sense someone searching for us. Someone strong, like us, yet not. They have their sights set upon us, closing in like the jaws of a gator. Also, you might want to control your powers; considering how centered this downpour seems, it's like a beacon to our enemies. It stretches for miles, but they could track us easily if they know what to look for."

Yeah, there he went with cryptic warnings that even Rome had trouble deciphering.

"I'll be right out." He donned a black tee before going full commando in one of his favorite pair of jeans. His eyes stayed glued to the beauty within his bed as he spoke. "I'll return shortly. We've got forty-five minutes before the sun completely sets, and I intend to gorge on your sweet nectar for another hour before heading out for my hunt." He leaned over, his lips brushing her forehead in a chaste kiss when he desperately wished it were her lips instead, but if they had been, he'd never leave.

"You should grab a bag before you come back to bed. You're starting to look extremely peckish."

He grimaced and left the room quickly, knowing she was right and hating that fact. For the past three days, his hunger had increased, his need for blood reaching levels that disturbed even him, yet no amount of packaged blood seemed to satisfy him. Eternals weren't meant for prepackaged blood, yet he couldn't bring himself to hunt the streets for a willing donor, and he refused to ask Alara to present her vein to him. He knew that what he had done days prior was a violation. He'd taken her blood without consent, sipped from her as if it was his very right to do so, and now the taste of any blood but hers just wasn't enough. He was essentially starving.

Eternals didn't need blood every day to survive like Rogues did. The strongest could survive from one feeding weekly, while younger immortals required at least two or three feedings within a week. Rome could usually go months without needing a drop of blood unless he was severely injured, but recently, he hungered for it in ways that terrified him. She had ruined him for any other blood source, and he needed to find a solution for his problem before his inability to eat became apparent to his warriors, or even Alara, but it seemed she might already be noticing.

He left the bedroom and went in search of Silas.

ALARA SMILED SOFTLY to herself as she stretched atop the bed, energy coursing through her in continuous waves that made her heart race. Every time she took in Rome's abilities, she analyzed them, hoping to figure out what powers she would possess for however long they seemed to linger within her. His telekinetic power seemed to be his most powerful ability. It was something she received with every siphon she performed, while his telepathy, teleportation, and ability to manipulate the air followed quickly after. Other powers were harder to decipher and understand, but soon, she hoped to learn every single one of them. She wanted to have access to his gifts at all times. Alara wanted to be as strong as him, if not stronger. She wanted to be able to protect him as he protected her.

She turned to her side to curl into a ball when a heavy yet familiar presence brushed against her mind. She froze. Her hair stood up on her arms as she tried to figure out who was attempting to reach out to her. Was she going to allow them access to her mind? Although the presence that brushed against her barriers felt familiar, it didn't mean they were friendly; they could be the enemy. She wasn't sure who all Titan had within their employ. They might have had other powered humans that had abilities like telepathy, but she knew she had never come across one. At least she didn't think she had. Her fear of this familiar yet clouded energy was heartstopping, but her gut told her to trust. It told her to lower her shields and allow whoever it was admittance into her mind. Hesitantly, she did so and stilled when Alaric's voice filled her head. It was filled with pain and a hint of fear that made her jackknife into a sitting position. Fear didn't sound right coming from him. Something was seriously wrong.

"Hey, sis, could really use some help right about now." She could sense his labored breathing as if he stood within the room with her. *"We're trapped in a hotel room on the outskirts of town with no way out. Maybe you could convince your protector to come save our asses."*

"Who's we? Are you hurt, Alaric?" Alara questioned as she hopped from the bed and quickly threw on clothes Rome had ordered for her recently.

The Eternals were obsessed with the color black. According to them, hiding the blood from wounds they could obtain within a battle and the blood they would shed from their enemies was easier. So she dressed in a black long-sleeved v-neck and black leggings that molded to her body, along with a leather jacket she absolutely loved, and black tactical boots with a hidden blade in the soles. She wasn't sure how to use it, but she was sure if shit really hit the fan, she'd quickly figure it out.

"Remember that other person I told you about who needed rescuing? Well, it's our sister. She's a healer but she can't do much for me right now. Something's wrong, Alara…"

He paused, the connection between them becoming hazy before it strengthened again. With that strength, a picture of where he was came into view, along with a woman utterly identical to her. Alara gasped at the image and forced herself to focus on their surroundings instead. She knew she should say something to Rome. She should have alerted him or, at the very least, let him know what she planned to do, but a sense of urgency filled her, and she was acting before she even realized it. The image became stronger within her mind as Rome's ability to teleport sizzled through her bloodstream, and allowed her to teleport until she was standing in the center of a rundown motel with her brother and sister standing vigilantly by a window with guns in their hands. Blood was oozing from a wound in Alaric's side, sweat was plastered to them both, and the stench of their fear filled the room.

Alara wasn't sure how she recognized the smell of fear from them, but it was evident within their eyes when they spun around, guns now trained on her before shock colored their expressions.

"How'd you get in here?" Alaric frowned and glanced behind her to look into the bathroom without a window before his eyes shot back to the window behind him.

Alondra stepped towards her, her hands going limp as she took her in. "God, you're beautiful." She whispered, her voice slightly deeper than Alara's own.

"We look so alike," Alara marveled back as she took several steps forward.

An all-consuming energy filled the room, and Alara froze in place while Alaric and Alondra tensed in preparation for a fight as Rome popped into the room with Silas and Maverick by his side. Alaric reacted, his gun firing as Rome quickly erected a bubble of pure telekinetic energy that melted the bullet into nothing before he shot across the room and jerked Alaric into the air by his throat. An unholy snarl filled the room as he bared his fangs, intending to strike. Alara's touch stilled him even as the aggression within him rose.

Her voice flowed into him, fear and concern dripping from her tone as her hands gripped his arm with a strength he hadn't known she possessed. "Stop! That's my brother, and she's my sister!"

CHAPTER

SIXTEEN

R ome could hardly contain his anger as he held Alaric up by the throat. Maverick stood with a woman who looked like the spitting image of his mate. The sister fought Maverick's hold like a hellcat to get free while Alara stood beside Rome, holding his arm tightly as she pleaded with him to release who he now knew was her brother. Shit, he could see their relation in his pointed nose, rounded face, and the fire within his gaze. Did that mean he let him go? Of course not; the bastard had shot at him, and the sense of danger still hung heavily in the air. Where was it coming from? He allowed his senses to spread out and determine what could be setting off his inner alarms when he sensed several soldiers heading for the building and a swarm of rogues. Hell, it was a trap.

"Fuck," he snarled, "all of you touch now, we need to leave! Right the fuck now!"

Silas and Maverick immediately jumped to do his bidding as he allowed his powers to flow through him and around them. A flash-bang grenade was tossed through the window the moment he erected a shield and teleported them from the room. Rome made sure to appear within the lower levels of their current base of operations, where their infirmary and cells were located, before he released the man he held and rounded on Alara.

"What the hell were you thinking?" He snapped, "You could have been killed, or worse, captured. Why would you just leave without saying anything? I would have helped you had I known you even had family to worry about! It was a fucking honeypot trap. They had the place surrounded."

She didn't shrink away from him like most would; in fact, she stood up straighter and glared. "I didn't think to grab you, okay!?" She snapped back and glared, "He asked for help, and I knew something was wrong. They're my family, Romulus, so I planned to act with or without your permission. You aren't my damn keeper. My jailer, maybe, but nothing more if you keep this shit up."

God, her spicy mouth was becoming one of his favorite things about her. To most men, it would antagonize, but for Rome, it was his own personal turn-on. No one spoke to him the way she did because everyone else feared his response, but she tempted him. Practically waved a red flag in front of his face like the bullish bastard he was. Alara was the only one who defied him without fear of repercussions, and the longer she was with them, the more she emerged from the shell of a woman who had seemed afraid to speak before. Her fire was a flame he couldn't resist.

Rome yanked her into his body and crushed his lips against hers. She practically melted within his arms as his tongue plundered her mouth and his hands tangled within her wavy hair. Her soft moan vibrated through him, hardening his entire being as his fangs itched to sink into her delicate skin. The thought alone caused his eyes to brighten like blue LED lights as he fought for a semblance of control. He lifted her into his arms and began to back her into the wall when the sound of a bullet falling into a chamber reached his ears and gave him pause. He took stock of the room. He could feel the nose of a gun pointing at him even from a distance, and he damn sure didn't like the feeling of being someone's idea of a target. Especially not with Alara in his arms.

The infirmary held three medical beds with every possible machine they might ever need, including cabinets along the walls with every drug a person could think to use to assist in life-saving feats. This was Erick's domain as the in-house doctor of the group, and although they hardly needed the infirmary, it was better to be prepared for the what-ifs. It wasn't completely unheard of for an Eternal to need medical assistance but it did rarely happen.

Maverick still had a hold of the female who looked so much like Alara that Rome would have thought it was her if not for the difference in their scent. She was no longer struggling; her eyes were wide and locked on him in shock. Maverick and Silas showed that same shock while that damn brother of hers once again pointed a weapon at him. He could smell the blood leaking from him, betraying his weakness, and yet his expression was full of aggression as his arm stood straight and true. The intention to shoot was within his stance, while his gaze and words were just another confirmation of that fact.

"If you don't back the hell away from my sister, I'll shoot you so full of silver you'll never recover. You may have stopped the bullet before, but I'm guessing you're a little weakened now after all that prolonged contact." His voice was guttural and filled with a pain that matched his scent.

Once again, Rome was mildly impressed with the man. Like his sister, Alaric didn't seem to fear him. He was either foolish, or he indeed did have balls of steel. He recognized the voice from their phone call as Rome placed Alara back on her feet before he stood between her and the gun pointing toward them. On any given day, a gun pointing at him wouldn't have caused him to react, but the possibility of Alara being hit in the crossfire was too much of a risk for his liking. And he was right; prolonged contact with Alara had weakened him, but not by much.

"Drop the gun, or I'll break your arm and ensure you're incapable of raising it again." He spoke calmly when all he really wanted to do was follow up with his statement. He didn't care if this was her brother. He was putting her in danger, and that was something he would never accept.

Silas stepped forward, eyes focused on Alaric's face before he frowned. "You were the one in my vision…the one searching for us."

Alaric's gaze snapped to him and sized him up. "You see the future or something?"

Silas moved to stand between Rome and the gun before he spoke again. "Or something. We need to stop that bleeding if you hope to remain on your feet. You're Alara's family, so I'll refrain from using forceful measures to remove the weapon from your hands, but if you don't lower it, I won't be responsible for how you'll be disarmed." He pointed with his chin towards the entrance to the upper levels where Erick and Cairo now stood.

Alaric spun around and swayed slightly on his feet before his eyes rolled into the back of his head, causing Silas to catch him before he could hit the floor. Alara reacted instantly, jerking forward to see what was wrong when he was placed on one of the beds. Rome came to stand behind her before he placed his hands on her hips. He looked her brother over as Erick came forward to see to his wound before his eyes shot to the silent sister standing behind Maverick. She was in the far corner of the room, away from the rest of them, as if she feared getting close to any one of them. Rome couldn't place it, but there was something off about her. He knew that she wasn't at all what she seemed though. He was curious, wondering how someone so similar to Alara could rub him the wrong way. She even smelled wrong, causing his nose to wrinkle in disgust.

"Damn, this is poor work," Erick commented when he pulled up Alaric's shirt and saw the stitches on his side. "Sir, could you scan him and tell me what you see? He shouldn't still be bleeding this much. The wound is closed, yet blood seeps through the thread."

"Watch out, little flower." He shifted Alara until she stood at his side before he placed his hands on either side of Alaric's head.

The connection was instant. Rome couldn't see into his mind… yet, but the pain running through his body was practically overflowing and all centered from the bullet hole in his side. He could feel his pain as if it were his own. He clenched his teeth, not knowing how her brother could withstand it as it tore through him.

That pain was rapidly spreading throughout. He wasn't sure what surprised him more: Alaric's ability to withstand what felt like razors scraping against raw nerves or the markers within his blood that revealed the virus.

"He's still bleeding because the bullet is still inside of him. I believe it was a hollow tip that fragmented upon impact, and he appears to be fighting off the same virus that attacked Ami and me when we were hit with those tranq darts." He frowned and focused harder when attempting to penetrate Alaric's mind but met a strong resistance he could not get past. "He seems to have the same barriers in place within his mind as Alara. Stronger even. I can't get a true reading on just how much pain he's in right now. What I do feel no human should be able to withstand."

"What's his ability? Clearly, he's a Kindred as well." Cairo questioned with a raised brow as he pointed at the apparent Kindred marking on Alaric's face. "Can he also heal himself or siphon?"

"Without a view into his mind, I have no idea."

"He's a telepath with strong mental shields, so if you're attempting to read him, you won't be able to," Alondra commented from her position in the corner, hands pulling nervously at the jacket that covered her body. It seemed the sisters had the same nervous tic.

"And what can you do?" Maverick grumbled and glanced over his shoulder to pin her with a stare.

Rome tried not to laugh at the curious expression on his warrior's face. Usually, Maverick was quiet and watchful, but it was clear to see the sheltered interest within his gaze. The fact that she was the spitting image of his fated mate didn't sit too well with Rome at first, but he quickly got over that fact when he realized that he could already see the differences between the two. One of those differences was how Alana seemed to always be on guard, her stance revealing that of a fighter. His little flower was no such thing. She was a spitfire at times but a fighter…not at all. She was sweet and innocent, while her sister carried an air of danger around her like a shield.

"I'm a healer. Nothing more and nothing less."

"Sure you are." Maverick smirked and addressed Rome, "Where would you like me to set them up, sir?"

Rome thought about it. His home was large enough to house an army, and he often did so whenever he got a large amount of his guardians together for some much-needed downtime. He had more than enough room for everyone to get their own, but he needed to keep the siblings apart. At least for the time being. Something wasn't adding up. Why had Alara never mentioned them, and why was Titan after them? They were Kindreds, that was obvious, but they were each hiding something. He couldn't say he trusted Alara completely. She had lied to him since the beginning and continued to do so but he damn sure trusted her siblings even less, especially her sister.

After pushing healing cells into Alaric's mind and body, he removed his hands and allowed Erick to take over and place an IV with fluids into his arm. With the virus coursing through him, there was no telling if his healing ability had worked, but with him still having cells similar to a regular human, Rome believed it was possible for modern medicine to help in ways he couldn't. There was no sense alarming Alara when there was no need to, and with her looking weak from using her gifts, he refused to cause her more harm. He turned to find his mate at his back and quickly pulled her into his arms until she was snug against his chest.

"Set Alaric and… what's your name, little one?" He speared the sister with a questioning look and waited for her response.

He didn't have to wait long. "Apparently, our parents wanted all A names. Alondra, my name is Alondra."

A few snickers filled the room. Even the woman huddled in his arms gave a breathy laugh before he spoke again, addressing Maverick and hoping his other warriors within the room received his underlying message. "Put them in the west wing of the house."

Maverick, Amirishka, and Akio inhabited that part of the house, while Cairo, Erick, and Silas took up the east wing. Rome lived along the entire top floor for maximum privacy. It wasn't often they came into the town and resided within his home, but among all of their residences combined, his was the most fortified with top-notch security that could rival Fort Knox. Here, they were safest. Especially Alara.

Alondra stepped around Maverick, keeping her gaze steady with Rome's as she spoke. "Is my sister on that side of the house as well? I think she and I should bunk together, and once Alaric is feeling better, it's only right that you put him in a room beside us."

"Not until I have my answers." He glanced down at the woman in his arms to find her staring back at him with a closed off expression. Yeah, his little flower was hiding something alright, and it was time to get to the bottom of it.

"What answers?" Alondra questioned.

He didn't respond and instead sent her a hard stare as he ushered Alara towards the hidden door in the back of the infirmary; it housed a secret elevator that would take him to his private floor. He needed to speak with her alone before the siblings could come together and figure out their story. He knew something wasn't right. He sensed it. There were too many inconsistencies within her story, too many things she didn't want to speak on, and too many coincidences in which Titan was involved. They were running from Titan; that was clear, but he needed to know why and how the corporation had even gotten wind of gifted humans. They were the most well kept secret within his society, even more so than Eternals. The Kindred are considered a myth to his people. Some believed them to even be stories of lore, and although he had met a few in the past, they had died shortly before ever meeting their other half. Kindred didn't have the lifespan of Eternals. Without the bond, they were just gifted humans with the same mortality rate as regular humans.

He spoke over his shoulder when the doors to the elevator opened, "Erick, we'll be upstairs discussing things. You let me know the moment he awakens. I believe big brother knows more than they do."

"Of course, sir," Erick replied as he gently cut out the stitch within Alaric's side.

The doors were closing on the elevator when Alara rounded on him with a glare. "I wanted to stay with my family. I need to make sure my brother is okay, and that my sister is good with all of this. I can help."

"And we need to talk." He glared back, his eyes shining an inhuman glow as his emotions began to riot within him, "You're still keeping secrets, secrets that could get any one of us killed, and I want to know why. Why is Titan hunting you and your siblings, and how do they even know you exist? You'll tell me the truth and you'll tell me now, or your little family reunion will continue to wait."

"There's nothing worth telling." She quickly avoided eye contact and backed herself straight into the wall.

He followed her, his eyes zeroing in on her throat as his thirst for her blood intensified. With the danger to her over and the fact that they were now within an enclosed space that was small enough to surround him with her mouth-watering scent, all he could think of was sinking into her in every way possible. He wanted to taste her blood as he pounded into her body and took her to peaks she had yet to discover. Rome wanted to devour, own, and bend her into a beautiful submission that they'd both be enraptured in with no way out. The thought of finally taking her in the most dominant way possible caused his blood to travel south until his dick pressed roughly against his zipper's teeth. Every thought process he owned zeroed in on the woman before him, causing his incisors to lengthen within his mouth as a snarl filled the small space. He placed his hands on either side of her head and leaned forward until his dreads hung around them like a curtain as he stared at her like the meal she was. God, she was just so damn beautiful.

"I need you to stop looking at me like that and back up," she whispered, "you're making me nervous."

"I'm making you nervous, am I?"

He chuckled softly and moved until his lips brushed her ear, causing shivers to run through her body just as the elevator dinged at the top floor. She scurried out and under his arm before he could stop her. The need to chase after her blazed through him like wildfire, but he refrained and slowly adjusted his pulsing member before he followed.

His elevator entrance opened into the back of his closet behind a flush panel wall that most would overlook. It had been convenient and practical in his earlier centuries when he'd first bought the property, primarily where his extracurricular activities were concerned. Now it was just there, hardly used yet convenient enough. His energy was depleted after bringing everyone back from the motel and touching Alara for prolonged periods. She hadn't even attempted to block her power from taking what he couldn't afford to lose. Losing that energy weakened his body and mind to a point that made his control slip into dangerous territories. Territories he needed to avoid.

His eyes trailed her, watching her beautiful heart-shaped ass shift beneath the tight black leggings that molded perfectly to her form. His hands clenched into fists as he followed her, hunting her and snarling without meaning to.

"God, would you stop with that sound?" She snapped in annoyance, "It's driving me crazy, Romulus!" She moved to stand in front of the roaring fireplace, making sure to keep a chair between them.

He lifted a brow at her attempt to put distance between them but didn't press her on it. It was probably for the best in any sense. His control wasn't what it should be, and he needed answers without the added distraction of her blood or body getting in the way of those answers.

"I need you to tell me why Titan is tracking your family." He would attempt to practice patience, and hopefully, she would come clean, although he knew there was no guarantee. She seemed intent on keeping her secrets.

CHAPTER
SEVENTEEN

Alara gripped the back of the chair beneath her hands as she stared into Rome's unnerving gaze. She knew it wouldn't prevent him from getting to her if he approached and took her in his arms or beneath those beautifully sharp fangs peeking at her from plush lips moistened by his tongue. He would take from her if he wanted to, and she'd have no objections against it. She wanted it to happen. Needed it in a way that she didn't quite understand, but the unnatural attraction and sexual chemistry that flared between them was breathtaking. She wasn't sure she wanted to live without it now that she'd experienced it with him, but there was more. The more is what terrified her.

She watched as the pulse within his throat thumped faster the longer she stared. Something was off about him. A new level of danger surrounded him, giving his aura a darker vibe leaving her breathless and curious. Alara didn't think he knew it, but she saw his struggle with blood. She saw how desperately he wanted it, yet he never made a move for her, and the times she would watch him covertly, she never saw him consume the bagged blood they had within the fridge. He wasn't eating as far as she could tell. When he left for his hunts, she hated the thought of him putting his lips and fangs on or into another willing woman, yet when he returned home, he was even more amped up than before. His other warriors probably didn't realize the balancing beam he was currently walking, but she knew. She saw how thirsty he was, and dammit to hell, she might have to use that against him to escape her mess because telling him the truth wasn't the answer.

"I can't tell you what I don't know."

She lied. She knew it might come back to bite her in the ass, yet she knew that Rome might retaliate in ways that would hurt her and her family if she didn't. Maybe even get them killed. Alara knew powerful men. She knew the lengths they would go to be on top and stay on top. Lukas had taught her so much in the years she'd dealt with him. He'd been gentle at first but had quickly turned harsh, wanting things from her that she couldn't and wouldn't give. At a younger age, his mother had been the tormentor, making her do things against her will or suffer the consequences. Alma Titan had made her kill for the company. She'd dirtied her soul in ways that left her haunted by demons of the past and now the present. Her influence had pushed Lukas into wanting her to bear his children. She had poured into his obsession, and now he was hunting her and her family in a way that left her feeling more vulnerable than ever before and the one person she wanted to tell she couldn't. If Rome knew all the facts, he'd have the means to protect them; she understood that he could, but would he? And trusting was hard for her. Trusting a man who killed his enemies for a living was hard for her to swallow because, in reality, she was an enemy. She'd worked for Titan. Unwilling, sure, but that wouldn't matter to him. Would it? She wouldn't matter to him, and she needed to matter. No, she wanted to matter because he was coming to mean everything to her and deep down she knew that maybe, just maybe, he would never hurt her or the people she loved.

Rome spoke softly, yet his eyes blazed with fury, or maybe that was desire. "Can't or won't Alara?"

"Both," she whispered back as she glanced towards her left and then her right.

With the fireplace at her back and Rome standing just on the other side of the chair between them, Alara didn't think it was possible to make a run for it. To her right, a mahogany desk and a leather wingback chair sat in front of a large bay window covered by white translucent curtains. His bedroom was larger than any she'd ever been in, with an armoire behind the bedroom door and a small seating area leading towards his walk-in closet and bathroom. She wanted to head to the bathroom to her left but knew he'd catch her. Maybe it was best to get this conversation over with and put his assumptions to rest. He couldn't know the truth and would just have to live with that for now. There would be no running for her.

Alara pushed her hair away from her face as she spoke with a calmness she didn't feel. "I simply can't tell you where I came from, how I ended up in the forest, and why I didn't tell you about my brother and sister. I just can't give you those answers right now, and I need you to be okay with that. We have more to worry about than the answers to those specific questions. What I can give you is my loyalty and promise that I have no intentions of harming you or your people. I wasn't sent here by anyone, and the fact that Titan is hunting us..." she sighed heavily, "they know we're special. They figured out what me and my siblings could do, and they want that power for themselves, same as they want from you and yours."

"This is the answer you're sticking with? You won't tell me how they learned this information to begin with?" He dragged his hand over his face and shook his head in disappointment. "I don't know what I can do to prove that I'll protect you and that I don't intend to harm you or your family."

"You already did, Romulus. You attacked my brother!"

"He fucking shot at me! You thought I would let that stand? Besides, the bastard had it coming. How was I to know the man you were so desperate to get back to was your brother? You seem intent on keeping secrets, but maybe that was one you should have just owned up to." He snapped and moved as if to walk around the chair, yet paused when he realized his anger was getting the best of him. He didn't want to scare or intimidate her; he just needed her to understand where he was coming from. "All of this is new to everyone involved but the longer you keep these secrets the more you allow a rift to remain between us."

"You need to feed. I can tell that something more is wrong than what's happening with me and my family. Whatever is going on with you should be the more pressing matter."

His eyes darkened even as he snarled his words at her. "You speak of what I need, and yet your lies constantly pass through those edible lips of yours as if I don't need the truth as well."

"I see what you hide from the others." She rounded the chair and approached him cautiously, "You're moody, irritable, and those damn high beams of yours keep zeroing in on my neck like a starving beast. If you need blood, I'll give it willingly." She bared her throat the moment she stood before him and simply waited, her eyes locked onto his own.

Shock spread across his features as he took a hesitant step back. "No."

He knew what would happen even as badly as he wanted to sink his fangs into her. His need to make her his entirely and utterly would soar through him, causing him to mark her in every way known to his kind. Sinking his fangs into her would only be the beginning of the mating. He would then need to sink his cock into her simultaneously to inject his essence and fill her with his cum as he sipped at her blood. Only then would she be marked wholly and utterly by him, and only then would others of his kind understand the significance of their bond.

"Listen, something is going on with you, and if my blood will help you, then take some. Make yourself better because your attitude is becoming unbearable. I can't deal with the mood swings, constant snarling, and growling that seem to be directed at me."

She held her breath, waiting for him to move, yet knowing it might not happen. She didn't have long to wait before he turned his back to her and quickly left the room. She sighed heavily and rolled her eyes at her growling stomach. Throughout the day's chaos, she'd hardly eaten, and her body was making that fact known and known loudly. She left the room shortly after Rome's abrupt departure and gasped when she ran straight into Amirishka at the top of the steps.

Amirishka glared and bared sharpened fangs in aggression before she spoke. "I realize that Rome has been attempting to keep us from ever being alone, with good reason, I might add." Her voice deepened, her power of persuasion flowing from her lips like a roaring river, "I don't like you, and I know you're keeping secrets that could get one of us killed, so do us all a favor and leave with your family once we're all asleep for the day. Leave so that my King can regain his control and lose this infatuation he has for you."

Her powers should have worked on Alara, yet they did not. Alara's mental barriers were too substantial for such an attempt on her willpower, but that didn't mean she hadn't felt her abilities creeping in. Oh no, she had felt Amirishka's power on the very edges of her mind, but it hadn't fazed her. Her persuasion had failed. If anything, her attempt to use her gift on Alara only angered her, sending her thoughts spiraling with ideas of much worse outcomes. The group's female guardian wanted to eliminate her without Rome's knowledge. She was going against orders Alara knew he had given to each of his Eternals. She was supposed to be protected and safe, yet she was attempting to remove her.

Anger and jealousy powered through Alara, and she was moving before she even realized it. She gripped Amirishka's arm tightly and called on her power until she was siphoning her energy and ability. Amirishka's energy felt different than Rome's. It was seductive, compelling, and feminine in nature as it flowed through her in continuous waves until she dropped her hand and stepped back. The power was familiar to her and yet not.

Amirishka swayed unsteadily on her feet as she grasped at the wall and slid to the ground. She struggled to speak. "W-what have y-you done, Alara?"

"Don't you mean what have you done? You caused this, Ami, not me." She snapped as the new powers she'd acquired flowed through her.

God, how did Amirishka deal with this daily? It was so sexually intoxicating that her body readied itself for sex. Her nipples tingled, and every hair on her body stood to attention as her center clenched with need and moistened at the thought of penetration. The idea of

Rome penetrating her in the most intimate way caused a cramp to start in her core as a breathy moan passed through suddenly dry lips. Her thoughts attempted to right themselves. Nothing close to this had happened when she'd taken Amirishka's power before. No, this hadn't occurred at all. Maybe because before she hadn't siphoned nearly as much from her. Now the feeling was painful but euphoric in nature. Her body was heightened to such levels of sensitivity that she felt everything. From the A/C blowing around her to the fabric that brushed her skin and sent shivers down her spine. She was completely enthralled by this new ability thrumming through her bloodstream.

"Do me a favor and leave me the hell alone if you don't like me. I see the way you look at Romulus," Alara snarled, realizing that she sounded just like Rome, "He is mine! So back off before I make you. He would have taken you up on your blatant offer if he wanted you." Her eyes looked her up and down in what could only be described as disgust.

Amirishka attempted to warn her, "You don't know how to control what I can do, Alara. Go back to the bedroom and avoid everyone," her expression was filled with concern as she steadily attempted to climb to her feet. "I'm sorry. I just want to protect him."

Alara ignored her and headed down the steps in search of Rome. Her heart beat wildly in her chest as she searched room after room until she found him alone, standing in the kitchen holding a blood bag. His eyes jumped to hers, a range of emotions flowing from him to her as she struggled to find her words. All she felt was this unbearable need as her womb repeatedly pulsed. She watched him, taking in his broad form as she moistened her lips with a swipe of her tongue.

He placed the bag on the counter and watched her warily as she approached, the sound of his voice causing a new wetness to dampen her panties. "What's happened?" He inhaled deeply, his chest rumbling with a satisfied growl. "You smell like sex. Why?"

He gripped her by her hips the moment she came within reach and watched her for a moment longer as he inhaled repeatedly, dragging more of her scent into his nose. The smell of her need was strong, amplified to heights that didn't make sense. Alara smiled at the feel of him and pressed her body closer until she could feel his hardness against her. He was like steel against her. Unmovable and unyielding. She wanted that hardness. No, want wasn't an accurate description of what she felt. She needed him. Alara wondered where her shyness had gone? That fear of the unknown was a thing of the past for her as she gripped Rome's neck and dragged him forward with the strength she'd received from Amirishka. This new ability had given her the strength to finally let go and test out whatever this budding need between them was. She kissed him deeply, for once controlling the kiss. She took and teased him relentlessly with her tongue along his lips as his hands tightened around her waist and dragged her that much closer. Her body was flush against his own before he seemed to pull at the reins of his control enough to step back.

"Little flower, what has happened? This isn't like you." He whispered and frowned as her body continually rubbed against his own, soft moans falling from plush lips that begged for another kiss. He ignored the temptation enough to focus. He shook her gently. "Tell me what happened!" He snapped.

"Amirishka...I siphoned her energy. A lot of it. It's strong. God, it's intoxicating," she moaned, her voice the embodiment of sex.

Rome shuddered at the sound. God, this was bad. She shouldn't sound like sin-filled nights. She was innocent in the ways of sex. He knew that. He trapped her hands at her sides the moment she attempted to grab his dick through his pants and held her back from him when all he really wanted to do was take what she was offering. He couldn't do that to her, though. She wasn't herself, and she wasn't ready for sex. She was experiencing the effects of Amirishka's powers. With the power to persuade nearly anyone it gave her a rare advantage in any fight, but wrapped within that power was the ability to tap into any woman or man's deepest pains, desires, needs, and wants. Amirishka's ability couldn't just make you do whatever she wished; she could also manipulate sexual energy and magnify it to degrees that generally couldn't be reached by regular means.

Thankfully, when his Guardian used her power, Rome wasn't affected, but this time, he could feel something within Alara's voice and he knew it would affect him.

He spoke calmly, "Let's take you back to the room so you can rest." He attempted to lead her from the kitchen but froze when she spoke.

"No, Romulus," her voice was breathy, filled with a sexual promise that called to him on every level he possessed, "I want you to let me go and take off your clothes. I want to feel you."

He tried to fight against the persuasive words that penetrated his eardrums but failed horribly as his hands peeled his clothing from his body just as she'd demanded. She smiled softly, stripping her clothing as she went, knowing that the energy that flowed through her was influencing her every action and word, yet she couldn't stop. In all actuality, she didn't want to stop. She wanted this like she needed her next breath. She wanted Rome, and she needed to know he wanted her too.

"Tell me the truth, Romulus." Her voice was whisper soft, her hands gliding slowly up her rib cage before she cupped her breasts.

His expression shifted. A glare appeared on his face as he growled low and revealed sharpening fangs when he spoke. "And what truth would that be?"

"Do you want me to walk away? I could attempt to handle this myself. I've never played with myself, but I could figure it out. I know I want you for this. I need you, but only if you want me to."

"You know what will happen if we continue down this path. You know what I'll take from you. Your innocence. That pretty little cherry no one has ever had before. Do you understand that? Tell me you do, and I promise we can go to the room right now, and I'll take what I've always wanted from the start." He approached her, pressing his body into hers until she leaned against the counter, her head falling back to meet his gaze as she continued to rub at the breasts he claimed as his own.

"You won't hurt me," she whispered, "and I need you right now. I'm empty, Romulus, please."

Rome didn't care anymore; he'd given her fair warning. Maybe she didn't truly understand what he was about to do, but he'd walk her through it, and God damn anyone who thought to interrupt them. He intended to take what he wanted. Fuck the control he cherished so much. She needed him. She was begging for release, and he intended to give it to her. Thoroughly.

He wrapped a gentle but steady hand around her throat and pulled her closer until their lips were a breath away. "I need to be in charge, do you understand? No persuading; in fact, no talking at all because with that little boost of power, Ami gave you, I seem unable to resist. Nod if you understand."

He loosened his hold on her throat as she bobbed her head up and down before he swooped in for a drugging kiss. Excitement sang through her veins as he sucked at her bottom lip, his fangs scratching lightly at the skin and sending sparks of need into her womb. She moaned into his mouth and gasped in shock when he abruptly pulled away and spun her around before he dropped to his knees behind her. He had her bent over, face pressed into the cool granite countertop with her hands held behind her back by telekinetic means as he gripped her lush cheeks and parted them to reveal her moist core and puckered rosebud. A chilling growl filled the air seconds before his tongue slid between her lips, sending fireworks booming throughout her body. Her orgasm was instantaneous, taking them both by surprise as she cried out ecstatically.

Rome chuckled softly as he licked her clit between each word, "If you don't stay quiet, the others will surely come to investigate. You can be quiet though, can't you, little flower?"

"I can be quiet," Alara moaned breathlessly as she fought against the invisible bonds that held her wrist at the small of her back, "Please, Romulus, fill me."

CHAPTER
EIGHTEEN

Her words were the sweetest plea, and yet he ignored them because they didn't quite sound like a demand and continued to lick her from pussy to ass, taking in every little sound she made and simply marveling at the taste of her. His balls and fangs ached insistently. The need to claim her screamed through his tightly strung body as her moans caressed his ears. They caressed his entire soul.

They were moving too fast. He knew that, and yet he couldn't stop. He licked at her cunt until he felt her body tensing for another orgasm. He pulled back at the last second and climbed to his feet as she snarled incoherently and thrashed against him. She was beginning to make the same sounds as him when frustration and annoyance ate at him. It simply hardened his dick further as his hands glided along her waist, and he smiled down at her restrained hands. He couldn't remember using his power to keep her in place, but he was glad he had because his control would shatter if she touched him now.

"Romulus, you bastard," she exclaimed, "do something right damn now, or I'll cut your godforsaken dick off!"

The need to listen to her command slammed into him, nearly doubling him over, but he held it back by a mere thread; maybe that power was wearing thin. He chuckled softly as he grabbed his dick and pumped it several times, precum leaking from the tip before he tapped it against her clit with severely sharp slaps. Her moan went deep, causing his balls to draw up further to his body as he stroked himself between the folds of her lips, ensuring that every last drop of her cream bathed him before he spoke.

"When I slide my godforsaken dick into this tight pussy all I want to hear from those pretty little lips is my name rolling off of your tongue since you just can't seem to stop talking."

She panted breathlessly as she pressed her lush ass back against him. God, he shouldn't be doing this. Taking her now would take away from the sweet seduction he'd had planned for her later. Much later. Shame filled him along with the insurmountable desire he felt for her as he placed his aching dick at her core and slowly pressed into her. The slickness of their combined fluid made it easy but not so easy that he didn't feel the untried tissues of her inner core.

"Fuck, you're so tight. You tell me if I hurt you. Promise me, little flower," Rome groaned as he sank deeper.

"I promise," she moaned and clenched around him like a vise, sucking him deeper than he'd meant to go.

"No, baby, relax. Don't tense, fuck don't tense." He cursed.

His control fractured marginally, sending wave after wave of telekinetic energy from his body that toppled objects within the kitchen and sent the chairs scrambling away from the island they occupied. He wouldn't last long. He knew it. God, he knew it like he knew nothing else. Rome gripped Alara by the hair and pulled her up until a beautiful arch happened with her back. It gave him a perfect view of her breasts and easy access to hold one of them in his hand. He glanced further down to see the birthmark of a crescent moon on her left ass cheek and grinned. Oh yeah, she was definitely a mate to a Guardian with that distinctive birthmark and he intended to solidify that bond now.

He growled low before his gaze zeroed in on her elegant throat. He shuddered at the thought of what he was about to do. Something instinctive now drove him, rendering his control a simple thing of the past. Once he did this, she would be his entirely and without question.

"Romulus," she pleaded and pushed back against him, sinking him that much further inside her.

"I know, baby. I know."

He licked at her sweaty throat and slowly pulled out of her before he slammed forward, sinking his fangs into her jugular and tearing through her virgin barrier in one thrust. Her body tightened like a violin string as she orgasmed and screamed his name, her cunt gripping him tighter than anything ever had before. He powered into her, taking her harder than he should have, but having no control as he sipped at her blood and clutched her tightly. He simply took. Moaning at the feel of her, the woman that had been destined for him. There was no doubt in his mind now as bonds seemed to wrap around them. He felt her essence digging so deeply within him that he'd never free himself from her again. His orgasm built until those telltale tingles raced up his spine, indicating he was close to his finish line. Fuck, she was so perfect. He fucked her harder, the sounds of their slapping skin ringing in his ears. He couldn't slow or stop and he was a bastard for not wanting to. Alara's cries went higher, her core clenching so tightly around him that stars burst behind eyelids he hadn't realized he'd closed.

He tried to hold out, tried to control his need to mark her with his cum, and ultimately failed. He'd wanted to draw this moment out, yet his orgasm tore through him along with a release of energy so strong that his ears rang, and his legs shook like those of a newborn calf. He released her throat and snarled like the beast that he was before he gently lapped at her puncture wounds and eased out of her warm center. The sight of her blood coating his dick sent a primal urge through him to retake her, yet he ignored it.

He turned her around to face him. "Did I hurt you, little flower?" He cupped her cheek and kissed her forehead before his gaze snapped to the hallway entrance where Cairo stood with his back turned to them.

Anger poured through his veins in the seconds it took to realize he'd never heard him approach. He'd been so wrapped up in Alara that protecting her hadn't been too high on his list of concerns, but he never thought one of his Eternals would come searching for him when he knew they could hear her cries of ecstasy. The idea of anyone seeing her in such a state sent a shaft of jealousy through him along with rage. These emotions were one's he hadn't been expecting. Rome gently pushed her to stand behind him, her entire body pressing into him from behind as her arms wrapped around his waist, and her soft lips kissed his back.

He tried not to let her actions affect him as he hid his growing erection behind the island. "Cairo, what is it?"

"Silas found Ami unconscious near the foot of the staircase leading to your level. We believe Alara siphoned from her, causing her to lose her footing before she took a fall down the steps. She's in the infirmary now. Erick is helping her cells speed up." He paused and cleared his throat, "Also, Maverick locked Alondra within her room and put Akio on guard while Alaric remains unconscious. I believe a meeting is needed to discuss our next course of action against Titan."

"Let Erick know that I'll be down to heal Ami and we shall meet in the chamber." He gripped Alara's hands within his own when she attempted to trail them down to his erection and squeezed lightly when her tongue licked along his back before she bit down softly. "Leave us, brother!"

Cairo walked away with a chuckle.

Rome spun around to pin Alara's roaming hands against his chest. He kissed her forehead again and smiled against her skin, her scent hitting him squarely in the gut. "Tell me what happened with you and Ami. I understand you siphoned from her. You explained that earlier, but why did you take so much and leave her vulnerable?"

She spoke softly, her voice heavy with satisfaction as her small nails dug into his chest. "I'd rather not talk about it; besides, is she really so vulnerable in a home filled with her people?"

She kissed his chest and hummed softly, the sound going straight to his balls. All he could imagine was sliding back into her heaven, but dammit, all to hell; he needed to focus. He flashed them to his bedroom and quickly realized that she had taken more energy from him than he realized when he stumbled.

"Are you okay?" Concern filled her voice as her misty eyes looked him over. "I was siphoning without realizing it. I took too much of your energy, didn't I?"

"Is that what you did to Amirishka? Did you take too much without realizing it?" He shook off the effects of her gift when he forced his healing cells to work overtime. Her power didn't hit him as hard as it used to, and his body was adjusting to the pull of her ability the more intimate they became.

She stalked away from him and headed into the closet to grab one of his shirts from a hanger before she slid it over her head and covered her body from his wandering gaze. A growl left his throat without provocation as he watched her. She grabbed a scrunchie from his nightstand and tied all of her glorious hair into a bun, and still, he just stood there with his dick standing at full mast as he watched her.

"I'd rather keep our conversation to myself if you don't mind." She crossed her arms and met his stare head-on, with no fear or uncertainty when before she used to at least falter.

He shrugged his shoulders and headed into the bathroom to grab a quick shower. "I'll just find out when I speak to Ami." He pushed the door closed behind him and released a heavy sigh.

Now that he'd mated her, the need to keep doing so was tearing through him more viciously than before. He needed a moment to himself. He needed to get his head screwed on right and he wondered when he would tell her what he had done.

After dressing in his usual all-black attire, Rome left his bedroom after checking to see that Alara had fallen fast asleep atop the large bed. The sheets had been wrapped around her like a lover's hold. He'd wanted desperately to join her but instead ignored that urge. He wasn't too happy with her at the moment. He thought that after the intimate moment they'd shared, she would have warmed to him more, but instead, her walls were stronger than ever. Even in sleep, he couldn't breach her mental shields. She was still hiding things.

Still forever lying to him. His eyes flashed with fire at the thought as he snarled at what truths she could be concealing. His incisors sharpened like they always seemed to do around her as his telekinetic energy built inside him until it felt like it would burst from his very flesh. His anger choked him as he stalked through his home, descending the steps until he reached the lower levels that couldn't be found on any blueprint. When he'd purchased the house and land, he hadn't just had the infirmary and cells built below. There was also a meeting chamber and a tunnel leading to a warehouse several miles away. It housed multiple vehicles in case they needed to escape if he wasn't present to teleport them.

When he entered the infirmary, he strode to Amirishka's side, where she lay unconscious in the third bed while Alaric occupied the first. Handcuffs connected his wrist to the guardrail, keeping him secure in case he awoke before they realized. He chuckled at the image and looked towards the corner where Erick's desk sat, yet the man himself was absent. He turned and placed his hands on either side of Amirishka's head before pushing healing energy into her body. Her iridescent eyes snapped open, and her tiny fist swung at his face. He caught her hand within his own and smiled proudly when it wasn't simply her fist he held. She'd moved faster than he thought and held a thin blade no bigger than her hand clenched within her grip. He wasn't sure where she'd pulled it from, considering the woman was a fanatic for sharp, pointy things and kept them well hidden amongst her body. He wouldn't be surprised if it was coated in silver nitrate. Her specialty.

"I apologize, sir," she stated, moving into a sitting position when he stepped back. "Your female packs a mean punch with that power of hers."

"About that," he slid his hands within the pockets of his jeans and looped his fingers through the belt loops, "why did she use her ability on you? Speak freely and give me the truth, or I shall dive into your mind and find out by my own means." He raised his brow and simply waited.

Amirishka squirmed beneath his gaze as she tucked the small knife back into a hidden slit on the side of her pants. It wasn't easy to disobey him. Rome knew this and saw the struggle take place within her as she debated on whether to tell him the truth or not. She'd done something wrong. He could tell by the expression on her face. It wasn't guilt but something else, an emotion he hadn't seen on her face in centuries. Shame.

She sighed heavily and came to her feet, her fingers tunneling through her hair as she pulled gently at the roots before she replied. "I tried to persuade her to leave, but my power didn't work on her, and she retaliated and siphoned from me. I was too weak to stand and follow her, but I still attempted to and fell down the stairs before passing out. That's the truth." Her gaze wouldn't meet his own but stayed locked on the floor. "I know I'm meant to protect her, but something isn't right, and you can't see straight because of her. I was only trying to protect you."

Rome barely controlled his anger as his fangs and claws descended with a vengeance. He wanted to retaliate. He wanted to hurt her for attempting to run off his mate, yet he didn't. He would never hurt Amirishka, not really. It wasn't because of her gender; there was more to it, something more profound. He pulled his anger in and took several steps back before turning his back on her. The betrayal that lanced through him was a powerful emotion he hadn't felt in so long that he'd forgotten what it felt like.

"I'm sorry, Romulus," her voice was barely a whisper.

"You'll stick to formalities from now on. I am simply King Rome to you." He turned back to her and glared. "Until you earn my trust, you'll be my mate's full-time guard. You'll no longer hunt. Your only duty is to protect the queen of our people. If you should veer from this path, then you will be no more. You'll be stripped of your rank and placed within a different group far enough away from here that the actions of your betrayal will shine bright enough for all to see. There's a meeting in the chamber, but you're now responsible for ensuring Alara and her family stay put. Is that clear?" He walked away knowing she would abide by his ruling. He was sure that he was doing the right thing.

If there was anything Amirishka hated more in this world, it was not being able to hunt every night and kill the Rogues that now gave her purpose. She was one of his best fighters, there was no doubt about that, but he was sure he was doing the right thing in this. Maybe spending time together would give Amirishka a new purpose. That new purpose was the protection of their new queen and the possible continuation of their species.

CHAPTER
NINETEEN

The meeting chamber was nothing more than a reinforced room with a large oval table, several chairs, and an old-fashioned globe that sat in the corner next to their high-definition surveillance system. A biometrically sealed weapons cabinet sat to the left of the door, while a miniature coffee bar sat to the right, courtesy of Cairo and his love for the beverage. Rome leaned back in his chair and looked his fellow warriors over. Silas sat to his left with a brooding expression while Erick sat to his right, looking over the labs and blood work he'd run on Alaric. Akio sat at the surveillance system, where he viewed pictures and videos of the last hunt they went on the night before. They should have been out hunting now, but with the new problems with Titan and Alara's family, Rome had put hunting on hold, at least for a few hours.

Hacking the surveillance cameras that covered their region was illegal but worth it. Humans weren't aware of their people and never would be if they could help it. As Eternal Guardians, they listened only to the rules of their King and what he deemed appropriate and or necessary for the survival of their race and the human faction they protected. Hacking into surveillance systems was the only thing that guaranteed their existence could be wiped from the records if they were spotted on camera. They couldn't deal with that type of exposure. Humans learning of their existence was like an open invitation for mass hysteria. Titan was proof of what happened when humans learned the presence of another species greater than their own, so keeping the rest of the world oblivious was for the better.

Maverick took his seat next to Silas after grabbing a large cup of tea as Cairo kicked up his feet across the way from him and raised his cup of coffee in silent cheers before he took a healthy gulp. Maverick glanced towards the door and back to Rome before he spoke. "Where's Ami? Shouldn't she be here for this too?"

"She's been placed on bodyguard duty." He didn't even attempt to sugarcoat his words. They needed to know he would accept nothing but the utmost loyalty to his woman and everyone she loved, even if she was keeping secrets from him. "She's now responsible for the well-being of my mate and her family."

"What did she do to earn that punishment?" Cairo chuckled before he took a sip of his coffee. "Will she be okay not hunting?"

Rome frowned and stared each one of them down. "She tried to get rid of my queen, your queen!"

"So she is your fated mate?" Silas questioned with a hushed tone. "I had a feeling she was."

"I thought fated mates were a myth...does that mean we each get one?" Akio glanced over his shoulder with a smirk, "Personally, I'd like to go without. I prefer sticking my dick in whoever I want whenever I want."

"Ami will adjust. As for the rest of you...Everything you ever believed in the Kindred is true, and although none have mated our kind until now, I believe there is still hope for our future. If you show signs of aggression, need, unbearable hunger, jealousy, and especially fluctuations in your unpredictable gifts, let me know immediately because you may have just met your match."

"If the Gods will it, then so shall it be," Silas stated. "We can talk about this at a later date. For now, let's talk about strategy and what we're doing about Titan and these new developments? How do we fight these bastards now that they've developed a weapon that can incapacitate us? They already know that long exposure to the sun and pure silver can hurt and possibly kill us, but this drug…shit, this drug is an entirely new beast we aren't sure how to fight against if another one of us is shot with one of those darts or bullets."

Erick shifted through the paperwork in front of him, his voice filled with an emotion that sounded too much like excitement. "I've been looking over the blood work I did on Ami and Alaric, and what I'm seeing is unusual, but if I'm being honest, it's simply fascinating. Ami's cells fought to survive. They kept the virus attempting to kill her at bay as her healing cells rapidly worked overtime to heal her, yet she couldn't successfully heal herself until Alara pushed her own healing energy into her. With Alaric, his cells merge and then separate from the virus with small trace amounts of the virus attached to each cell. It's moving like a cancer, growing throughout his body yet keeping him strong. He's not in a coma like Ami was; he's simply resting from the trauma of the gunshot wound. I've examined him five times, and the cells have grown, multiplied even with each glance. I give it at least a year for his entire being to be corrupted by this virus, but I'm not sure if he'll survive it. For now, he appears to be healthy. I'm not sure how long that will last. I'll attempt to closely monitor him to determine exactly when I see a major decline."

Rome thought it over. "Did you attempt to have the sister Alondra heal this virus?"

"Yes. It did nothing. It took some persuading on my end to get her to even try. It seems there's no love between the two. She healed the gunshot and artificial wounds sustained but had no leeway with the virus."

"Then we'll get Alara to try. She healed Ami; maybe she can heal him as well. We can't lose him. He holds an importance to my mate, and although I don't particularly like the bastard, he can't die."

Erick nodded, his mind already on the different variations that could happen within Alaric's body. "I'll have Ami bring her to the lab as soon as he awakens."

Cairo stood up to pace as he always did. His expression shel-

tered, his movements stiff. "How do we combat a drug that incapac-
itates us and nearly kills us if we aren't healed in time, and why does
Alara seem to be the only one capable of healing us? You're the
strongest Immortal alive, yet your healing properties do nothing
against this drug."

His words were accurate and disturbing, all in the same breath.
There was nothing he couldn't heal, and yet this virus eluded him.
Fighting it drained him on a level he couldn't comprehend. It
drained him to the point of needing sustenance to replenish his lost
energy and power. He remembered his fight with the Rogues, being
shot with the tranq, and experiencing dizziness and fatigue. He
remembered it coursing through him, slowing him to certain
degrees yet waning in strength within him, enough to allow him to
use his abilities once more. If Alara hadn't healed him, there was no
telling how the drug would have affected him or if he could have
recovered by himself. He knew it hadn't knocked him out cold as it
had done to Amirishka. That didn't mean it was any less deadly. Oh
no, this virus would be the catalyst to their downfall if they let it.
Finding a cure was the only answer. He couldn't let his people come
to more harm.

Rome leaned forward in his chair and shoved a loc from his face.
His expression was thoughtful as he tried to determine how they
could go up against this new problem. "We need the doctor that
created the virus." He decided. "Akio, I need you to get on that, and
once you do, I want you to go after him or her and bring them
to me."

"Of course, sir." Akio's fingers flew over his keyboard, instantly
attempting to do a deep dive into the Titan corporation and all of
its employees. He would find the answers they needed; he always
did. No matter how long it took he always found what they were
looking for.

"Isn't anyone else wondering how the brother and sister you
rescued know about Titan?" Silas frowned.

The room got quiet, the silence stretching for moments as they
thought about it before Maverick spoke up. "How are we so sure
they do know about them?"

"They were holed up in a motel, guns at the ready as if they were expecting a fight," Silas paused, making sure to glance at each of the men within the room, "they knew someone was coming after them, and they looked ready to fight to the very death. Only people who know what to fear react in such a way. Alaric is a warrior, someone who's fought battles. I think he knows exactly what Titan is. For God's sake, Titan had that motel surrounded when we got there."

"We can't just assume," Maverick interjected after sipping at his tea; his expression was calm and detached. "It's possible that with his ability to read people, he sensed the danger and acted accordingly."

Akio chuckled, although there was no humor within the sound. "You seem to have a hard-on for protecting this family, brother. What is it? Do you want the sister now that you know without a doubt that our new queen is no longer available to you?"

Silence descended before Maverick launched himself over the table to tackle Akio to the floor. Between the two, Maverick would be considered the better fighter with his animalistic aggression and heavy hits, but Akio was a master at his ability; after all, he had learned from the best. As an immortal capable of harnessing telekinesis like Rome, he applied pressure to Maverick's throat and constricted his airway. It made it possible to push him away to land a clean, solid punch to Maverick's jaw, sending him sprawling to his back as he clutched his throat. Akio came to his feet and brushed his clothing before releasing Maverick from the telekinetic chokehold he had him in.

Rome anticipated the moment Maverick intended to launch at Akio again by the brightening of his eyes and lengthening of his fangs and instantly moved to intercept. With his hand pressed into his chest to keep him still, Rome stared into Maverick's glowing eyes and growled low, his own fangs punching from his gums when he spoke.

"Calm yourself and have a seat so we can finish this meeting." He shoved him toward his chair and waited until he sat. "Akio was simply defending himself. I don't care what little hard-on you think you had for my mate. It ends now, and the sister isn't to be touched by any of you bastards. You got me?" He looked at each of them in turn and waited for their nods before he retook his own seat and forced his own aggression back.

The idea that any of his men desired his woman bothered him, and yet he understood why. Alara was beautiful. There was no denying that. She was sweet, attentive, and more caring than they were used to. When they left on a hunt, she worried about them and doted on them each morning they returned. She treated each of them fairly and justly, making sure to spend time with each of them in different ways, whether that be learning to play videogames with Akio, bantering over what coffee flavor was better with Cairo, or getting her ass whooped in chess by Maverick and Silas. At times, he'd seen her speak with Erick in an attempt to learn more about his interests. She even tried to win Amirishka over by cooking her favorite foods, yet their female guardian had never taken the bait. He supposed he should have realized the tension between the two before now, but he'd been blind. Blind to the fact that his mate was now within his reach, and now that he'd finally tasted her purity, he had no intentions of ever letting her go. He couldn't even if he wanted to.

"I don't need you to protect me, Rome," Akio commented with a snarl as he moved to his chair and crossed his arms over his chest like a petulant child.

"Noted."

"We don't have time for this!" The usually calm Erick snapped. "Titan's soldiers are literally out there right now wielding weapons that have the potential to kill us. Why are we worried about Alara and her family? If they intended to do us harm, it would have already happened. She's been with us for weeks now. It's safe to say they aren't the enemy."

"They? Are you forgetting that 'they' just got here? Alaric and Alondra are strangers, people we never knew existed until today, and I'm telling you right now that they know who Titan is. They're probably moles sent here to find a weakness in our defense so they can report back to our enemy. Romulus, we need to interrogate them." Silas argued.

Rome had heard enough. "No one is interrogating the family. I shall speak with them, see where their minds are, and go from there. There's nothing we can do about the virus until we learn the makeup of it. There's no way to determine Titan's next moves without surveillance, so how about we focus on that. We'll hunt tomorrow."

"Is that the wisest decision?" Silas frowned.

Everyone else remained silent as Rome sat still and unmoving. It wasn't easy being in charge of strong individuals who sometimes couldn't just let him lead, and it was beginning to wear on him. It had actually been wearing on him for quite some time. He wasn't always the best at knowing when to give an order or when to throw out a suggestion; sometimes, he failed them and failed himself in the process, but he never tried to steer them wrong. As Guardians over the survival of mankind, they became restless and stubborn when it seemed as if a battle would not be available to them. It was as if they had been made only to fight, but that couldn't be true, especially now that he'd learned the truth about fated mates. Knowing they were real and plausible, something within reach for his species, gave him hope that they could do more than just fight for humanity. Now, maybe they could fight and strive for someone to share eternity with on a deeper level than friendship or brotherhood. Perhaps not all the myths were simply myths, and they could procreate. Rome could only hope.

He came to his feet, his expression stern, his voice like granite. "Tonight, I want everyone to remain in-house. Sleep, spar, invite a blood donor over, but no one leaves." He met Silas's furious gaze, "I understand the need to bloody the streets with our enemies, but for now, I say we sit back and watch. We wait, and we learn what their next move will be. If you want, search surveillance with Akio, learn who the key players are within Titan, and watch their every move. Maybe they'll give something away, or maybe they won't, but maybe you'll feel better about not simply sitting on your ass."

"This sitting and waiting is an open invitation for the Rogues to slaughter as many people as they desire. How can we do our duty if we're stuck inside sitting on our blades when we could be out there fighting and rendering them to nothing but dust?"

"We know the Rogues are within Titan's employ, so what happens if you're shot, Silas? If they carry the same weapons to take us out, what then? What humans will you protect if you're knocked unconscious, and no one can get to you? There are so many ways a hunt can fail now that this virus exists. We don't know what the Rogues know or have access to. We can't keep running around blind in this war!" Rome thundered and sliced his hand through the air, his anger growing as his powers practically pulsed beneath his skin. "I refuse to lose warriors' I cannot spare! Is that understood?"

"And what will the Gods say, Romulus? Will we not neglect our very purpose of being now that we have one? You told us years ago that our purpose in this life was the protection of humanity. That we needed to fight to protect the weak from those created only for darkness and death. We were created within a war and then tasked with the continuation of a species that doesn't know we exist. Do we just go against our creators? Go against who and what we are?"

Rome sighed heavily. Silas always had good points. It's what made him such a strategic warrior. There was no doubt about it that the Gods would be furious. In fact, they might even strike him dead at any moment. They'd already warned him. "Hopefully, the Gods will see my hesitancy as a smart play, and if they do not, then I suppose I shall find out what they truly think of me when I am summoned." He left without another word but could hear the continuation of Maverick and Akio fighting as he headed into the infirmary.

The moment he entered the med bay, his entire focus narrowed to the bed Alaric was trying to escape from. He was sitting on the edge of the bed, pulling out the wires that connected him to the monitors, when his eyes landed on Rome and narrowed as he lifted his shackled wrist in silent question.

Rome felt him attempting to penetrate his thoughts and quickly erected several more barriers around his mind before he spoke.

Alara's brother was a stronger telepath than he had given him credit for. "I don't have a mind that's easy to breach. You're strong, I'll give you that; maybe even stronger than Silas, but don't attempt that again. Next time, I might not refrain myself from retaliating."

"Where are my sisters?" He snarled and climbed from the bed as he yanked at the cuff on his wrist.

"They are perfectly safe, Alaric. You can have a seat. You're still weak from the virus they shot you with."

He watched the telltale stiffening of his shoulders as if he knew exactly what he was referring to. Silas might have been right. Did Alaric understand who and what Titan really was? Was he aware of the virus on an intimate level, and if so, why had he been shot? Rome watched as a calculated expression crossed Alaric's face before he sat down with a grimace. He glanced at his healed side and spoke softly.

"Before you ask, I can already assume that you and your people believe my sisters and I work for your enemy. I can assure you that we do not."

Rome crossed the floor until he stood directly across from the man who meant so much to his woman and glared. "So you're aware of Titan?"

He nodded slowly, his eyes never straying from Rome's. "I'm not just aware of them. I'm the reason they're after us."

"Explain!"

"You have to understand," Alaric paused, his eyes becoming vulnerable orbs that Rome was sure he hadn't meant to expose. "There's no right or wrong in what I'm about to tell you, and the only reason I feel that it's pertinent that I do so is so that you'll protect my sisters no matter what I say. I did what I needed to do to save my family, so if you want to kill me, that's fine, but my family is to be protected. That bastard Lukas cannot get them back."

"What do you mean get them back?"

He snarled, his anger quickly rising at the ideas that filtered through his mind in an attempt to make sense of Alaric's words because, so far, nothing was. Rome attempted to leash his temper, but his fangs lengthened, and his eyes blazed brighter than fire as the need to cause someone pain began to take precedence within his mind. A sickening feeling took root in his gut and grew to insurmountable levels as he fought for a calm he didn't feel. He needed to hear what Alaric had to say, yet his ears wouldn't stop ringing, his heart wouldn't stop racing, and sweat was steadily gathering along his body at the thought of his mate with that sick bastard. God, he was having a panic attack, of all things. The almighty King of Eternal Guardians was having a fucking panic attack. He scoffed at this new weakness he'd never before experienced.

"Hey man, are you alright!?" Alaric frowned and reached out as if to help him.

"Stay," he murmured, "just tell me what I need to know." He attempted to gather his wits about him and still the racing of his heart.

"Promise me that my sisters will be safe with you even if I'm not."

Rome nodded and promised himself that he would protect them no matter what he heard. He had to for his mate.

"Titan raised us," Alaric stated, shattering Rome's entire thought process. "We were all separated at birth and kept that way for years. I didn't know my sisters existed until I was about sixteen, but I'd begun working for Titan when I was thirteen. From that day forward, I learned the truth about our parents and vowed to do whatever I needed to get us away from their clutches. It wasn't easy. I played the part I needed to play. I lied, I stole company secrets, and I killed for Titan. I did it all to get us free, and I'd do it again to save them." He looked away, his hand rubbing at his side as if the wound still remained, as his eyes gained a far-off look filled with pain. "Alara was treasured, but what they had in store for her was unthinkable, and Alondra had suffered enough. They need protection. They're worth more to Titan alive than you or I will ever be. They're women with abilities, women capable of birthing children who will be just as resilient and powerful as them, if not more. I'm sure I've been marked for death after my betrayal if you and your people don't kill me first."

The information was hard for Rome to process. His mate, the

woman who had him nearly wrapped around her finger, was the same woman who had lived for years with his enemy. She was a victim, yes, but she'd lied, kept the origins of her life a secret that shattered any lick of trust he thought he could have towards her. Sure, he'd known she was hiding something, but to this magnitude? No. He never would have thought this level of betrayal could be so utterly heart-wrenching. So devastating, in fact, that he wasn't sure where to go from here, but he knew he needed answers. Sheltered life indeed.

"What did Titan do to her?" Rome's voice was barely a whisper, hardly recognizable through the tremor.

"She was forced to kill. She was treated delicately for the most part as long as she behaved. She learned early on to do what was asked of her."

"What unthinkable thing did they have in store for her?"

Alaric shook his head. "I got her away. It's not worth mentioning now."

Rome jerked forward and gripped him by the throat as his anger took hold, and his powers flared and wrapped around them, shattering beakers and items in all directions. "I promised protection to them, not you. Now speak, or I'll shatter your larynx, and you'll never speak again. In fact, you'll cease to exist."

That was a lie; he'd never hurt him, but the bastard didn't need to know that.

"Lukas planned to impregnate her. He wanted her to bear his children so that he could start a new line of kids that harnessed abilities. Unbeknownst to him, I stopped him numerous times and got her out at the earliest opportunity." Alaric gasped out as he clutched at the hand around his throat.

Shock tore through Rome like a tornado as he released him and moved away before his anger could get the best of him. God, he needed to breathe. He teleported without a word. He didn't know where he was headed but he knew he couldn't be around anyone when the need to kill practically radiated from his pores.

CHAPTER
TWENTY

N ine Years Ago
Alara sat atop the firm mattress of the bed within her cell.
Yeah, the place may have looked like a typical bedroom with the lone
dresser in the corner and the en-suite bathroom, but she knew what it really was.
This was her prison. This place, with its white walls that held no pictures or
posters, was her doom. It contained no windows, trapping her in a solitude so
complete she didn't know if she would even know what freedom was if she had
it. She stroked at the golden collar around her throat and sighed heavily as she
stared at one of those white walls. Sure, her jailer came to visit along with his
unthinking soldiers, but she hated their visits, especially his.

Lukas.

He was the man that haunted her dreams and made it nearly impossible to
sleep. At first, Alara had believed him to be a friend, but wrapped in that sickly
sweet smile lurked a monster just like his mother. He hadn't hurt her. At least not
yet, but his eyes told another story. His eyes screamed evil, telling her without
words that he had something planned for her, and whatever it was, she wanted no
part in it. Every week for a year, he came to visit, his gaze intense, his hands
gentle yet cold while his voice sent tendrils of fear down her spine. She knew
Alma Titan didn't like the attention he gave her, yet she never stopped it. When
he left her for the night, she heard the yelling through her door, heard his mother's

disdain when she came for a visit shortly after and cried in agony when her collar was used to shock her into a submission she'd already granted them.

Alara nervously bit at her lip as she pulled at the hem of her thin shirt and peered at the clock atop her dresser next to an assortment of lotions and perfumes he insisted she use. He said she had to smell good for him, and the scents he gave her ensured that.

Ten minutes.

In ten minutes, he would appear, carrying a travel chess case along with their dinner for the evening. With every visit, he expected Alara to eat what he brought her and play chess with him when they sat for hours talking about whatever he desired. Slowly, he'd begun to ask for more of her. More of her time, her skin against his palm, and more of the taste of her flesh whenever he leaned in to skim his lips across her cheek. Every encounter was filled with a nervous energy that terrified her because she knew what was coming next. She knew because they'd unknowingly prepared her for this. They'd forced her to watch porn, of all things, and they'd educated her on what to expect regarding male advances. She knew what they wanted her to do. Knew what men wanted from women. Now, at nineteen, she knew precisely what Lukas wanted and how badly he wanted it, but she would never give him the satisfaction. His mother was the one saving grace that kept him from simply taking what he wanted. Alma disapproved. To his mother, she was an abomination meant to be controlled and studied, nothing more; for that, she was grateful.

The sound of her door unlocking and creaking open jarred her from her thoughts. Her eyes jerked up and paused, her breath stilling in her lungs as Lukas stepped over the threshold minus the chess board and food. He closed the door behind him, his movements fluid even with the cane he used to help him walk. She caught sight of the blood splattered on his clothing and tried not to let her fear win. It was clear that something had happened. He'd hurt someone. Possibly killed them. The look in his eyes told her he was still riding high off of inflicting that pain.

"Hello, my beautiful Alara." His voice was like gravel, grating over her skin and turning her stomach as he slowly approached the bed.

The closer he came, the more blood she could see seeped into the fabric of his light blue suit. It was clear to see this was something that had happened quite recently. Alara forced herself not to move backward. He didn't like it when she moved away from him.

"Hello, sir," she whispered as she averted her gaze, "Are you okay?" She didn't really care if he was or wasn't, but she knew he'd appreciate her concern even if it wasn't real.

Lukas grasped her by the chin the moment he was by her bedside and forced her eyes to meet his own. His touch was clammy, green eyes piercing as a harsh smile graced his face. If he wasn't literally evil incarnate, she might have found him to be handsome. "I took care of our problem, my love," he caressed the cleft of her chin with his thumb, his eyes turning lustful as the seconds ticked by, "I mean to have you tonight, Alara. I'm done waiting."

Her fear became a living thing as she kicked out before she even realized what she was doing. Her foot connected with his left thigh. He jerked back before he lost his balance and fell to his knees as she leapt up to run for the door. Before she could get too far, he gripped her by the hair and yanked her backward, a scream tearing from her lips as she fell onto her back atop the bed. Lukas wasted no time in crawling above her before he pinned her hands above her head. Tears were cascading down her face as she tried to regulate her breathing. His expression was hard, the look in his eyes telling her that he was done playing around.

"Sweetheart, do you really think I won't hurt you?" He snarled, his face inches away from hers as the smell of his spearmint gum filled her senses and brought more tears to her eyes. "Do you wanna know why I have blood all over me? Do you want to know who I tortured and killed because they wouldn't give me what I want?" His hold on her tightened until he transferred her wrists into one of his hands and grabbed her by the throat with the other. "My mother struggled the same as you, but that only made her pain that much sweeter for me. What makes you think your struggles will sway me?"

Alara stilled beneath him as her fear consumed her and swallowed her whole. She knew he wasn't lying. He'd talked about killing his mother for weeks now, so it wasn't surprising that he had actually done it. What was surprising was the fanatic gleam in his eyes, the pure pleasure of knowing she was dead and no longer stopping him from pursuing whatever he desired. That desire being her.

He squeezed her throat, cutting off what little breath she had left as he licked at the tears trailing down into her scalp. "I'm taking what I want, Alara, and no one can stop me this time."

Alara jerked awake with a scream, her shirt sticking to her sweat-drenched skin as she peeled the covers back. It was one of the more recurring nightmares that traumatized her on levels she refused to put too much thought into. Lukas hadn't gained access to what he'd truly desired that day, but he'd still taken away her free will in other ways. He'd still defiled her. She winced at the sound that passed through her parted lips and stilled when she felt another presence within the room. Rome sat before the fireplace, his back to her, posture stiff as a board as he stared steadily into the flames. She could feel his anger from where she sat. It poured from him, and she found she didn't like it; in fact, she hated it.

She climbed from the bed and approached him, her hand resting on his shoulder as soon as he was within reach. "Romulus, are you okay?" He tensed beneath her touch.

Minutes ticked by as she waited for a response, yet none came. Alara moved to stand before him and yelped when he grabbed her by the waist and yanked her down until she was straddling his lap. His expression was furious, eyes blazing like blue fire as he stared at her, snarls passing through lengthened fangs she hadn't noticed before. One of his hands curled around her throat as the other kept her hip hostage, his hold tight but non-threatening.

"Were you dreaming of him?" He grimaced as his hands tightened marginally, drawing a small gasp from her lips.

She shook her head gently. "Dreaming of who? It was just a nightmare." She cupped his cheek and cried out when he pulled her forward until his fangs were inches from her face. His expression was positively feral.

"Stop with your fucking lies, Alara." He nipped at her lip, causing a drop of blood to well up before he sat backward and watched her expectantly, "You'll tell me the truth. Not because I want you to but because you know it's the right thing to do. Especially considering everything I've done for you since we've known one another."

"What truth?" She whispered.

"Were you dreaming about that sadistic fuck? He's constantly on your mind, isn't he? Taking up residence in places where only I should be?"

Cold reality penetrated her thoughts. Rome knew. Oh god, he knew about Lukas. Who else could he be referring to? No one else could instill fear within her and take up the places she associated with pain within her mind. She struggled within his hold and froze when he snarled again, but instead of fear, excitement filled her. God, why did he make her react like this?

"Who told you?"

"The real question is, why didn't you?" He pulled her forward once more and licked that drop of blood away before groaning softly as he squeezed her tighter. "I had to hear it from that trigger happy brother of yours. Why didn't you tell me you were Lukas Titan's pet project? You're his deepest desire and the key to his downfall, aren't you? Dammit, Alara, why didn't you trust in me and believe that I'd protect and help you!?"

His anger bled into her, as well as his power. She wasn't trying to siphon from him, but still, she felt him filling her. His emotions were so potent and aggressive that her body became tingly and sensitive to the touch. The feeling of his hand gripping her throat and hip assured her that bruises would surely form, but a part of her wanted his touch to always remain. Her breathing went choppy, but not from fear. He wouldn't hurt her. She believed that even if his expression told her otherwise.

"I know how much you hate the company," she spoke softly, her hands clutching the hand around her throat as the feel of his body soaked into her. "If I had told you the truth, you would have assumed I was a spy. You're warriors would have killed me."

His glare was positively murderous before he dragged her close enough to speak into her ear, his lips brushing against her skin. "Do you know what you are to me, what you signify in my world?" His nose ran along the length of her throat before he licked her thumping pulse. "You're my mate, little flower, and I have no intention of allowing anyone to harm you, ever, but for your lies and deceit, I think it's time you paid your dues in the only way I think you'll understand."

"W-wait, what? Mate?"

"Yes, little flower, and we solidified that bond when you allowed me to take you. You are mine!"

Within seconds, Rome removed his hand from her throat and quickly ripped the shirt from her body, leaving her bare to his gaze. He tangled a hand within her hair and jerked her head backward. The pain was instantaneous, bringing a yelp from her lips before he quickly dumped her from his lap and deposited her onto the floor between his legs. Everything was happening fast. He was moving too quickly for her to process, and her heart was pounding within her ears. He had his pants opened and shoved down to his ankles in seconds as his massive erection protruded from his body like a waving flag.

"Romulus," she whimpered, unsure of what was happening but aware that the man before her was way past reasoning.

"Place your hands on my thighs, and don't move them." His words were guttural, filled with excitement and anger, all in the same breath. "Open your mouth, baby, tongue out."

She did as he asked, her nails digging into his thighs as he slapped his throbbing dick against the flat of her tongue several times. The brief taste of him had her clenching in need. Her nipples throbbed as the heat of the fire caressed her back, and that brutal grip on her hair tightened further, causing tingles to race up and down her spine.

"Anyone ever had this mouth?" He growled.

She shook her head as best as she could before he jerked her body upwards until she came to her knees with a yelp, fire coursing through her scalp at the sting. He leaned forward and whispered against her lips, "Use your words, little flower. From here on out, you'll open that devious little mouth of yours and speak nothing but the truth or so help me; I'll spank your ass until it's black and blue. Understood?"

"Yes." She moaned.

His lips captured hers, sucking and licking at them, drawing a deep moan from her as her body began to fidget restlessly in need.

His hand eased within her hair, allowing her body to return to a kneeling position.

"Now tell me, has anyone ever enjoyed using this pretty little mouth to stretch it wide?"

"No, Romulus."

He grinned. His face morphing into one of pure enjoyment as he released his death grip on her hair and gently rubbed at her scalp. "Get it nice and wet with your tongue, and then be a good girl and swallow it. This is your punishment, Alara. You'll suck me off until I cum down your tight throat."

Gray eyes with streaks of light blue stared back at him in mute surprise before she hesitantly leaned forward and swiped the underside of his erection with her tongue. Alara didn't think this would be much of a punishment for her. She'd wanted to taste him since they'd started sharing a bed. Laying next to him nearly every morning was a test of her control, considering Rome never allowed her to simply touch. Beneath her tongue, his skin was soft and smooth, yet she felt the hardness beneath as he pulsed against her, his groan fueling her actions. His hands gripped the arms of the seat when Alara chose to spit on the tip of his cock to watch as her saliva slid down to the base, coating him effectively and earning herself a snarl. She was beginning to love that sound more than anything. His lips peeled back to reveal his fangs as his power flowed over and through her.

"Don't play with it, flower. Put it in your mouth and suck; I'll be gentle." He promised through clenched teeth.

Yeah, this was a dangerous game he was playing, testing his control like this. Testing hers. He'd come to the room to talk, not use her mouth and throat, but now that he was here…now that he had her naked and kneeling before him, he had no intention of stopping. He wanted everything from her. Rome wanted her throat just as he'd had her pussy. He wanted her thoughts, her dreams, her hopes. He even wanted her lies when he knew he shouldn't, but most of all, he wanted her trust. Her love. Her devotion. He wanted everything she was and everything she'd grow to be, and he didn't care how he got it just as long as he did.

He growled deeply when her beautiful lips wrapped around the mushroom tip of him and swallowed him just as he'd asked. He barely kept his eyes from rolling into the back of his head at the feel of her inexperienced mouth and tongue. Her head bobbed gently, attempting to take all of him within her throat. It wasn't possible. No one had ever taken the entire length of him, and with this being her first time, there was no way in hell she'd be the first, but he silently commended her on her attempt. His vision went hazy.

Teeth grazed him, and he tensed, sweat beading on his forehead and upper lip. "Easy, sweetheart, watch the teeth," he whispered, "cover them with your lips and try again."

He watched as Alara pulled back, fitted her lips over her teeth, and sucked him back in. His hips jerked forward without meaning to, and he touched the back of her throat, eliciting a breathless gasp from her that had his balls drawing up in warning. Fuck, he shouldn't have been this close to coming. Anyone else, and they'd be down there for hours until he could finish, but with her, he was losing this fight. He didn't even know when it had become a fight, but he felt it in her shallow sucks, felt it in the small moans that vibrated through her body and into his, and he felt it when a delicate hand of hers gripped his balls without warning and tugged gently.

"Fuck, fuck, fuck!" He exclaimed and sat helplessly still as load after load of his cum shot down her throat.

Alara didn't shy away. She swallowed every drop and licked him several more times before she sat back on her heels and looked up at him adoringly.

"That wasn't much of a punishment for you was it?" He chuckled as tingles continued to run up and down his spine.

"No, Romulus, I've wanted you like this for quite some time now." She responded with a smile that disarmed him.

"We should be talking, getting to the bottom of how deeply your lies go so I can figure out our next move, but you drive me insane. Was that ok? Me taking control as I did?" He pulled her into his lap and groaned as her cunt slid along his slowly hardening length.

"It was good, actually, it was better than good." She whispered as she rocked against him and moaned softly while her hands tunneled through his dreadlocks. Her lips trailed along his throat, eliciting another groan from him before he stilled her hips and gently shifted her back. She smiled and gave him a reassuring nod.

Rome captured her lips and kissed her deeply before he spoke. "Now I've figured out your punishment," his chuckle was throaty, "no pleasure for you until you tell me everything. And when I mean everything, I mean that quite literally, little flower. I want to know everything about you and Titan, and you'll start from the beginning. Are we clear?"

Alara didn't want to agree to any of this. She didn't want to discuss Titan at all, yet she found herself nodding in agreement because as badly as she didn't want to discuss the events of her life, she wanted Rome more. She wanted whatever this mating thing was, and she wanted it more than the secrets of her past. Him taking control, forcing her mind into a state of such stillness she wasn't sure how to comprehend had lightened her in ways that made the smile on her face stretch wider. She could get used to this.

CHAPTER
TWENTY-ONE

Alara settled against him with the fire at her back, his hands caressing her from ass to shoulder as her head lay heavily against his chest. The position wasn't comfortable, yet she didn't find herself wanting to be anywhere else than right where she was. Maybe now she could come clean and finally feel what true freedom was. She needed that freedom in order to have the ability to walk beside this larger-than-life male without the shroud of secrets she carried with her.

Rome casually gripped her by the throat and met her gaze. It seemed to be his favorite way of holding her, but Alara didn't seem to mind. His expression was relaxed, yet she could feel the tension within his body. His fangs were no longer present, his eyes had lost their eerie glow, and his power no longer wrapped around her with its intensity, but she still felt that aggression.

"We can talk like this, or we can go to the bed where you'll be more comfortable," he commented as he caressed her throat, "I can feel the strain within your body. Your legs are uncomfortable, aren't they?"

"Yes," Alara responded with a moan and a downward shift of her hips.

He smacked her ass playfully, "Stay still, little flower." He chuckled deeply, "For someone so inexperienced, you're very eager for pleasure, but you'll get none until after we've talked." He stood carefully and headed for the bed, where he dropped her atop the sheets before undressing and settling beside her. They were comfortably lying side by side with her breasts firmly pressed against him when he spoke.

"Alaric tells me that Titan raised you. Is this true?" He cupped her cheek and forced her eyes to find his, although she itched to look away.

"Titan's all I've ever known until you," She conceded, "The night that Alaric freed me, I knew nothing else. It wasn't always bad being their prisoner, at least not until Lukas took over completely. His mother was bad, but he was worse. At first, I didn't think someone could treat me as horribly as she did, but it was like Lukas made it a mission to do worse than she ever did. He made it a mission to make me feel utterly alone and cut off. More so than I already was. I don't know exactly what my brother has told you, and I don't know how much he knows about my experience there, but it really wasn't all bad."

"But you have powers, Alara. How were they capable of controlling you and your siblings? You had the ability to take your own life into your own hands, and you're telling me you didn't take it?" He needed to understand how someone with her abilities ended up trapped and controlled by lesser beings.

"You don't understand," she sighed heavily and moved to sit, her expression shifting from lust-filled happiness to sorrow in seconds, "They don't just have a virus. The collar they made controlled me. It kept me docile and unable to feel my abilities." She glanced down into his eyes with a pleading expression that tugged at his heart. "I was powerless, Romulus, and at times, that's what I wanted to be. I wanted to be powerless, I wanted to be unable to please them, and I wanted to be normal. They made sure to remind me I never would be. With every act I was forced to do, they reminded me just how much of a freak I actually was."

"Wait, they kept you in a collar!?" He snarled.

She flinched at the sound of his voice as it resonated through her. His anger was palpable, filling the room and overwhelming her with its intensity. Alara watched him move into a seated position as he stared with eyes filled with shock and anger. A hint of pity could also be seen within his gaze, but she chose to ignore that. She didn't want his pity. She didn't deserve it. He'd hate her once he knew the truth about her and everything she'd ever done for Titan. She had no doubt he would.

"Their engineers and scientists worked together to create a collar that could suppress my powers once they learned what I could do. It was lightweight. So light, I'd forget I even had it on at times." She brushed at her neck in remembrance of her shackle and closed her eyes to block out the look on his face as she continued. "It didn't just keep me docile, though; it allowed them to hurt me without ever touching me. If I didn't listen, they'd send an electric current so strong into me that I'd be brought to my knees. Sometimes, I'd pass out from the pain. That was their line of defense in case the power dampener failed."

"Alara, what did they make you do?"

His question brought her eyes open. He'd moved closer, his knee brushing against hers as his eyes stared into the windows of her soul. It was like he could see into and through her, but in the best of ways. His posture was relaxed, but she knew that was a lie. He was amped up and ready for violence. His body said one thing while his eyes screamed another. It wasn't just his eyes, though. It could never be that simple when it came to Rome. His energy practically blanketed her. She could feel him within her, his power surrounding her, soaking into her skin as his anger steadily built. All of that magnificent power swelled around them and cocooned them in a bubble of pure energy. It caressed her and tempted her in ways that only he could. She wanted to wield that power. She just wanted more. Alara wanted to harness the abilities that seemed to radiate from him in waves the longer she sat there without responding to him.

Rome's patience seemed to wear thin as he swore violently and pulled her into his lap until she was once again straddling him, but this time, she was more comfortable, her core resting snugly against

TASHA M TAYLOR

him. "You seem to only listen more when I have my hands on you. Is this how I get you to listen and respond when spoken to?" He questioned, his hands pinned her hips still as he rubbed soothing circles into the plushness of her hips.

She nodded as she melted into his arms. She couldn't keep her body from doing anything else but relaxing beneath the onslaught of his tender touch. She didn't want to admit what his touch truly did to her. It didn't just make her listen; it calmed her and brought her a peace that robbed her of every sense she possessed. She didn't want to show her weakness, but staring into his clear blue gaze, she fell deeper beneath his spell as her mind scrambled to remember everything of importance so she could bear her soul to him and come clean about the monsters that plagued her nightmares.

"Before Lukas killed his mother to gain control of the company, she forced me to kill her failed experiments; that's what she called them. I could never see them, but I felt their energy. There was something different about them, and I felt that same energy the night we were attacked by those Rogues. I didn't know it then, but I know now she was making me kill Rogues, and with each kill, I was granted a reprieve from the pain they could cause me if I refused to do their bidding. I was their puppet, willing and ready to do anything they asked of me if only to avoid the debilitating pain that came if I refused an order."

"You did what you needed to do to survive. I don't blame you for your actions." He whispered softly as he cupped the back of her head and forced her to meet his gaze. "You had no choice."

Wetness coated her lashes as tears formed in her eyes, and her heart broke with her admission. "But I did have a choice: suffer or kill. I chose to kill."

"That's not a choice. The Rogues you were forced to kill were no longer human. They lost that humanity the moment the virus corrupted their cells, and they succumbed to the inevitable blood-lust. There's no coming back from that, Alara. That type of infection is incurable. Trust me, Erick has spent centuries trying to find a cure. You did the right thing."

She tried to allow those words to soothe her, but they didn't.

208

"What about the ones that weren't Rogues? What about the humans I was forced to kill? Did I do the right thing then, Romulus?"

He stiffened beneath her, his hand tightening slightly against her hips. "You were forced to kill humans?"

"I was forced to kill anyone they put before me."

"How do you know they were human?" He dragged her closer, his glowing eyes watching her closely as she shifted slightly to loosen his hold. He didn't budge an inch.

His grip didn't hurt, but she also didn't know if the anger she felt coming from him was directed at her or the atrocities she had been forced to commit.

"Their energy," she finally responded. Moments stretched by where they simply stared at one another before she spoke again. "I can feel the differences. It's hard to explain, but there's a darkness and a lightness in humans that Rogues don't possess. They just seem to have a void. It's like a black hole that sucks me in and under the closer I am, and once I touch them, there's a pause right before they die. With humans they have a balance of light and dark, there's a constant flow between us until they slowly fade away. It's like a slow drawl, but I don't believe they suffer, but if their energy is pure darkness, I think they do."

"If you can feel energy, what can you tell me about me and my Guardians? Are our energies different from the Rogues and humans?" He moved a hand into her hair and rubbed at her scalp.

The anger she'd witnessed in him before was now gone, and in its place was a look of understanding and acceptance. He still didn't blame her. He still didn't hate her for her role in Titan. She didn't deserve it, but the relief that ran through her was intoxicating. Maybe things would be okay between them now that he was learning the truth.

Alara placed her hands against his chest, and she felt the pull of her ability for the first time since he'd pulled her into his lap. She chose to ignore it and simply focused on the man beneath her. "It's intense." She smiled softly as his hands continued to massage her scalp, eliciting a moan that caught them both off guard before she chuckled. "There isn't a lightness or a darkness per se, and there isn't a void but an all-consuming feeling. The energy of a Guardian is incomparable. It's almost as good as sex with how it washes over me, molding and conforming to fit with me until only tingles of pleasure remain. There are different levels between you; obviously, your energy is the most overwhelming, but it's also comforting. I can feel the power within you all. It's simply intoxicating."

"So you don't feel that with humans or Rogues?"

She shook her head and groaned in pleasure when his hand dug into her scalp one final time before trailing down to the overly sensitive erogenous zone that was her neck. Alara leaned into the touch, her teeth biting delicately into her bottom lip as she watched his face morph from curiosity into pleasure. He dragged her forward until she was forced to place her hands on his chest before he nipped at her bottom lip. Thankfully, his fangs weren't present, but she knew that that could change at any moment. In fact, she probably wouldn't have minded if they did.

"Don't think you can tempt me, little flower...soon," he chuckled and kissed her thoroughly before forcing her to sit back, "we aren't yet finished with this conversation. Tell me about Lukas. What has he done to you or made you do? Why does he haunt your dreams?"

"I don't want to talk about him," she whispered.

"And I don't want your thoughts filled with another man; especially that bastard. He haunts your dreams and gives you night terrors that have you sweating and gasping in your sleep. I should be the only one in your mind. Me and only me. Besides, maybe telling me your traumas will alleviate you of them."

"It doesn't work that way, Romulus."

"How would you know unless you try? Just tell me. We agreed no more secrets or lies, Alara."

Contemplation filled her. She didn't mind telling Rome about the Titan corporation as a whole, but to talk specifically about the man who visited her frequently within her dreams was another matter entirely. Lukas was evil incarnate. He was her living, breathing nightmare come to life. She hated to think it, but when his mother had held the reins, he had been much nicer to her, almost brotherly with his affection. Now that she'd learned the truth of his intentions and had felt just a lick of his desire for her, she now knew what genuine fear was and how he would go to any lengths to simply have her.

Alara nervously plucked at the fabric of Rome's shirt and stilled the moment he clasped her hands within his own. His finger notched her chin up until she was staring back into eyes that spoke a thousand words yet nothing all at the same time. His voice was smooth and soft when he spoke. "I want to protect you, and I will, but I need to know what I'm up against. How deep does his obsession go, and what would he be willing to do to get you back?"

She froze up. She was sure she'd heard him wrong. It sounded a little like he meant to use her as bait. Her eyes narrowed, and she pulled away from him as best as she possibly could while remaining in his lap. "Do you mean to serve me up to him like a filet mignon on a silver platter? Romulus, I won't talk about him. I refuse to give him more places to live within my mind than he already does."

His eyes went cold and dark with that eerie glow that always seemed to rattle her nerves. His voice was deeper and edged with an anger that had never been directed at her before. "Serve you up? Do you think I would let anyone have what I consider mine? Did I not just tell you that you're my mate? That I would defend you from anything and everything?"

"You say that like I know what that means."

"It means you're mine to protect, mine to nourish, and mine to care for. You became a part of me the moment I sank my fangs and cock into you before I shot you full of my cum and essence. You're supposed to be a myth to my people," he cupped her cheek gently, "In all my years, I've never met an Eternal that forged the mate bond. It changes the couple on a fundamental level, and there's no going back once the bond is in place, at least not to my knowledge."

"I don't understand," she frowned.

It almost sounded as if he was speaking on a permanent level. Were they essentially married now? Is that what the word mate meant? That couldn't be true. They didn't even know one another deep enough for that, especially if their current predicament was any indication. She stared at the man before her, realizing she knew nothing about him. She didn't know how he'd become the man he was today or what he'd been through in his long life. All she knew was her inhuman attraction to him and how deeply she was already falling for him. She knew how he made her feel and how he made her want things she'd never truly desired before.

Rome continued to cup her cheek before deciding to run his finger delicately along the length of her jaw until his thumb trailed across her plush bottom lip. His eyes glowed softly as he watched her. A frown quickly formed on his face, "I won't be getting any true answers about my enemy, will I?"

She shifted restlessly against the bulge beneath her warm center and shook her head softly as she spoke. "I can't talk about him. I'll talk about anything but him." She pressed her hands into his chest to ground herself in the moment and felt the firmness of his body as the feminine parts of her melted at the contact. "Maybe you can explain this mate thing to me."

"I'm still trying to figure it out myself, but it's like I said, mates are believed to be a myth for my people," he shifted slightly and dragged her closer to his chest until she was inches from his lips, "Legend says you're a gift from the Gods." He trailed thick fingers through her hair and kissed her softly before pulling back with a groan. "Centuries ago, before war broke out in the heavens, each Eternal was once a Kindred. When the war started, blood spilled, and a few hundred of us were exposed. That exposure forever changed us, turning us into the beings we are today. It wasn't something the Gods had intended, but the damage had been done, and believe it or not, Eternals are what stopped the blood feud between the Gods. We became their entertainment of sorts—at least for a while. We had to teach ourselves not to kill humans indiscriminately. At the beginning of my change, I wasn't as careful as I'd assumed, and I was discovered by Theolonius Titan. Running and hiding became paramount, but when Rogues appeared in the 1970s, I was tasked with bringing the Eternals together to protect the humans."

"Wait, so rogues came after you? How? Were they born or created?" She interrupted, her curiosity now officially peaked.

"The very corporation you're running from created the virus that made Rogues possible. When Titan realized they couldn't capture us, they needed an edge. Rogues cannot procreate."

Alara paused, her thoughts running rampant with the new information. She had so many more questions but decided to hit the more complex topic of their discussion. "If Eternals were Kindred before their change, wouldn't that mean we were already here? Does this mean Eternals can procreate?"

Rome chuckled and kissed her once more before sucking her bottom lip into his mouth to tease it with his fangs and tongue. He forced himself to pull back the moment she began to squirm within his lap. "Kindred were touched by the Gods too many years back to count, but mates were not. Kindred with the ability to tie themselves to an immortal and live out the rest of their existence with them has never happened until you and I. We're the first mated couple in history. You are now our people's queen, and as far as pregnancies go…it is unclear if we can procreate."

"How is this possible? How do you know we've truly mated? What if you're just hoping, and this isn't actually a mating? What if our attraction is simply lust that's been magnified because of what we are?"

"Lust wouldn't explain how I can practically feel your entire being surrounding me as we sit here and talk, and lust couldn't hold a candle to the feelings that rise and fall within me whenever I look at you. Lust pales in comparison to what we have. I don't just feel you because we're touching Alara; you're inside me here." He emphasized his words by placing his hand right over his heart, "You've wormed your way inside of me, and I don't want to be free of this sensation. The moment I tied you to me, I felt a bond snap into place between us. We're locked together, you and I."

"Will I turn into an Eternal with this bond we now have?"

"I don't believe so. To my very little knowledge of matings, you'll live as long as I do as long as you take in small increments of my blood weekly, and if I die, I believe you'll live on, but you'll age a lot slower than humans do until eventually, you die by regular means."

"What if I die before you?"

"I don't think I could survive in a world where you don't exist."

"Did you know what I was to you when we met?"

"Not with one hundred percent certainty, but I had a feeling you were meant for me."

"You didn't think to let me know? I'm sure you were expecting more of a mate than me."

His relaxed expression quickly turned into a glare as his hands grabbed her hips and pulled her down onto his throbbing erection. "Do I seem displeased with you? And you would have run had I told you what I thought."

"I wouldn't have, and that could just be physical attraction," she gasped at the intimate contact that immediately made her core moisten in preparation.

"No, this isn't just physical attraction. I want you constantly and without fail. Now, the questions are over. You didn't answer everything I wished to know, but for patiently waiting for your pleasure, I believe you are due some."

Rome nipped at her lips and trailed his hand to her warm wet center, where he encountered the lips of her pussy. He groaned deeply and flicked at her clit as it peeked out from beneath its hood. He pulled her into a drugging kiss that robbed them both of breath as her nails dug into the grooves of his shoulders. She moved against the hand between her legs and moaned abruptly into his mouth when two thick fingers penetrated her and sent cream rushing from her center.

"Good girl," he whispered against her moist lips, "Now let's make you cream all over my cock."

TWENTY-TWO

Three days, seven hours, thirty-two minutes, and six seconds had come and gone, and yet Alaric still felt the pain of that bullet piercing into his side before it had made itself right at home within his body. For three days, he'd been a prisoner once again. At least this time, his jailers were more likable, and there was no killing or torture he had to partake in. The only thing he was forced to do was be present every night as he subjected himself to testing done by Erick. He grimaced at the thought of heading into the labs to be poked and prodded again, yet he had no choice. They were still trying to understand how or why the virus was affecting him the way it was, and he needed answers as well. Tonight, he was finally going to admit that he still felt the burn of the bullet entering his side. He needed to tell them that he could feel the tendrils of the poison coursing through him. They needed to know he felt it with every beat of his heart and every breath he took, and maybe they could find the answers to cure him.

When Erick explained the trouble they'd had in getting Alondra to heal him, he believed it, yet she'd done it before being brought to her room. He could hear her now within the room beside his own as she paced restlessly. Alaric thought he heard her whispering quietly for a moment, but the second he'd moved towards the wall that separated their rooms, silence had greeted him before her pacing had started anew. It was four in the morning, and he was usually up at this time every day like clockwork, thanks to the strict regimen Titan had kept him on. For him, old habits were now too hard to break. He didn't think anyone else would be up at this time, especially not Alondra, but she seemed to be wrapped in the same sleep pattern as him. Since their escape from Titan, she seemed to hardly sleep and yet functioned at a high level of intelligence when he could barely keep his eyes open.

He wasn't meeting with Erick until the sun began its descent from the sky, but the need to be checked out now ran through his blood with an urgency that unnerved him. Something was wrong. He couldn't put his finger on it, but Alaric knew something wasn't right. When Rome and even Alondra healed him, he should have been fine, but instead, he suffered. He was experiencing a phantom pain like a constant stabbing and burning sensation within his side. He needed a doctor, or maybe he just needed a better healer.

He headed for the door to test the knob and found it locked. Every morning when he woke up, it was to find a fresh tray of food on his dresser that someone had managed to place as he slept, as well as his bedroom being locked from the outside. They didn't want him roaming the halls of the house. That much was clear, but today was different for him. Today, he had no patience to wait hours until someone came to unlock the door. He needed answers right now, and he intended to get those answers. With the door locked, Alaric headed for the private bathroom, where he was sure he'd seen several bobby pins within a drawer and located them before he started the task of picking the lock but froze when another idea formed within his mind instead. Maybe using his powers was a better alternative because Rome might not be so understanding if he was caught outside his rooms without an escort.

He thought about Alondra as he pulled her into focus within his mind and made his way over to the dresser, where a hot serving of eggs, bacon, and toast sat on a warming tray. He was taking his first bite of the seasoned eggs and buttered toast when he felt himself breach the very edges of her mind. It was like parting the layers of a translucent shield that surrounded her thoughts and memories. Their relation to each other made it easier for him to get past the natural guards that most people had within their minds, but the walls she'd purposely built were a little harder to penetrate; somehow, he made it possible.

"Alo, I need your help."

He only felt her surprise for several moments before annoyance quickly shadowed it. Luckily, she didn't raise her shields higher, and she didn't kick him out, although she certainly had the power to do so. Her mind wasn't as weak as most humans. Shit, her mind was nearly as fortified as his own. He had to hope that maybe she was warming up to him.

"Why are you in my head, Alaric? And don't call me that." She snapped.

"I need your help, little sis-"

"You don't have the right to call me that either! I helped you enough when they asked me to heal you. I helped you when, in fact, you should have just died. I should have just let you die, especially for what you did to me!"

"I did what I needed to do for them to trust me. I did it to get us out, Alondra. You may not believe that, but it's the truth."

Her words were but a whisper in his mind when she responded. *"Please just get out of my head and leave me be."*

Alaric left her mind immediately as guilt filled him to nearly bursting. He could only imagine how she truly felt about him. If he could have played his cards differently before and still gotten them out from under the crushing thumb that Titan had had them under, then he would have done so. At the time, he had seen no other way. Pushed into a corner and forced to hurt someone he loved and adored had been his only choice. He'd be making things up to her for the rest of their lives if she had any say in the matter, but he'd gladly do so to get into her good graces.

He finished the rest of his breakfast without really tasting the food, just as another phantom pain pierced his side and caused him to groan as he pressed his hand against solid flesh. There was no doubt in his mind that something was very wrong. Erick had explained it to him days ago. The virus flowing through him had been created by Titan, and they couldn't figure out how to neutralize it. He'd told him that somehow, Alara was the only one able to heal someone once exposed to the virus, but he hadn't seen her yet. In fact, none of them had seen Rome or his sister for several days now. He reached out with his mind now, hoping to locate his Alara, and smiled just as he brushed against the edge of her mind. Like Alondra, Alara also had strong shields, but hers were softer and more open to allowing another into her mind. On the other hand, their sister was like a fortress, almost impenetrable if she truly made it so.

"Angel," he spoke gently, just outside the barriers she had around her mind, and smiled when they opened for him, *"I've tried to see you, but they haven't allowed it. Have they told you I'm still sick?"*

Maybe it was wrong of him to search so desperately for a cure after everything he'd done in his life, but he'd done it for the greater good of his siblings and their welfare. He'd done everything to protect them and get them free. He only regretted the hurt he'd inadvertently caused in the process. Now, he needed a miracle. He needed his sister to save him. There was no doubt in his mind that this virus was killing him. He wasn't sure when it would take him out, but he knew it was inevitable and hoped to avoid that at all costs. He needed more time to right his wrongs.

Alara's response was short and sweet but also filled with confusion. *"No, that can't be right. Rome told me Alondra healed you."*

"She did, but not all of me. The virus is still present and strong. I can feel it running through my blood."

"No. Rome told me you were healed. He wouldn't lie to me."

"Wouldn't he, though?"

She was silent for several moments before she spoke again. *"Where are you right now? I'll come to heal you while Rome sleeps."*

"I'm where I've been since they allowed me to leave the infirmary…locked in a bedroom next to Alondra's. I believe we're in the west wing of the house."

"Wait, you're locked in? You know what, never mind, I'll be there shortly."

Alara pulled from his mind before he could comment, leaving him to his thoughts as he questioned Rome's intentions. Had he honestly not told her that he was still hurt? Did no one else know he was dying slowly and painfully? If anyone knew the actual length of his health, it was Erick and Rome.

His mind was still racing with questions when the sound of the lock disengaging within his door reached his ears and caused him to turn, but it wasn't Alara who stood within the threshold.

"Rome."

———

ALARA PACED within the bedroom she shared with Rome, annoyance practically radiating from her skin. He'd been listening. That sneaky, sexy, annoying man had somehow slipped beneath the layers of her mind even as he'd slept and listened in on the conversation she'd had with her brother. He shouldn't have been able to slip beneath her shields unbeknownst to her, and he shouldn't have been capable of even waking as early as he had. From his explanation, the sun made his kind fall into a coma-like sleep. Apparently, it was not deep enough for Rome, but maybe that came with the territory of being the eldest of his kind.

Of course, when she'd opened her eyes to find his clear blue gaze on her, they'd argued. Alaric was still sick. No, he wasn't just sick; he was dying, and they'd neglected to tell her. Tears formed in her eyes at the thought. She could see it now. Rome had been keeping her separate from her siblings; in fact, he hardly, if ever, let her leave the room since they got here. The question was, why? Why did he want them separated? As she pondered on that thought, she tried to use her power of telepathy to reach out to Alaric but was met with a familiar block. Rome was even keeping her from speaking to him telepathically; that asshole. She grabbed the nearest thing she could find, a small glass ornament, and launched it into the wall, where it shattered on impact. The sound was like a concussive blast to her ears, yet it wasn't as loud as the thundering in her heart.

She grabbed another item from his dresser and threw that as well, but the clunk of the book hitting the wall didn't give her as much satisfaction. Alara wanted to destroy things and release the anger that steadily built within her. The life she'd gotten away from and the one she was currently living was almost like a mirror image with her being locked within a room as someone else dictated how she should live it, only there was no torture this time. Could she really blame him, though? Could she blame him for being cautious after the lies she'd told and the truths she'd circumvented? The answer to that was no. She should have been truthful and honest from the very beginning, yet the fear of him abandoning her had held her in a chokehold so strong she wasn't sure what maneuver she could have used to free herself.

Locking her up was one thing. It was one thing she could maybe accept because of how desensitized she had become, but keeping her from her siblings? From the only family she knew? Now, that was a form of torture she just couldn't get behind. This wasn't something Alara would ever be willing to accept. She tried to pull on the residual energy Rome had left behind as they'd slept but found it inaccessible to her. It had been over twenty-four hours since she'd had access to his abilities, yet she felt a constant pulse of his energy within her. Alara could sense tendrils of his life force flowing through her and wondered if this was part of the mate bond he'd referred to. Was this something she should expect from now on? Would she always feel him around her and inside of her without his actual presence? She didn't know if she would ever get used to that.

She headed for the bedroom door and yanked at the knob, yet felt no give before cursing Rome and repeatedly slamming her first against the wood. "Romulus, you open this fucking door and let me see my brother!" She screamed at the top of her lungs. She'd grown a steel spine since being with the Eternals and had no wish to return to her meeker self.

Silence greeted her for several moments before the room filled with his energy, and she spun around to find him and Alaric standing beside the bed.

"Alaric," she whispered as relief filled her, followed by a sense of overwhelming sadness.

"Hey, angel," he smiled and headed for her before he pulled her into his arms and hugged her with a grip much tighter than she'd been expecting.

His hold was solid and sure. The urge to cry pressed in on Alara, yet she ignored it and instead risked a glance around his taller form to find Rome watching them quietly. She tightened her arms around Alaric's waist and pulled back to meet his gaze.

"Tell me how bad you're feeling on a scale of 1 to 10, and where does it hurt?"

He chuckled without humor, the light green flecks within his gray eyes shining brighter than she remembered as his hand rubbed soothing circles into her back. "The pain is at a seven, but it comes and goes. It's not consistent, and it's where I was shot. It still feels like the wound is there."

"How long has this been going on?"

"It doesn't matter."

She frowned. "But it does matter. Alaric, tell me how bad it is? As a matter of fact, let me just try to heal you. I need you to lay down."

He glanced towards the bed and glared. "I'm definitely not laying down on that."

"We have a chaise," Rome chuckled as it appeared in front of the floor-to-ceiling window.

They headed for the window, where Alaric sat down and pulled his legs up to lay back as Alara knelt beside him and placed steady hands above his chest and forehead. She closed her eyes and focused; it didn't take long to realize that her brother's body was almost entirely consumed by the virus coursing through his veins. It was worse than she could have ever imagined. A small part of her knew there might not be enough healing in the world for him, but that didn't mean she wouldn't at least try. She tried until her body grew weak from overexertion and her mind grew foggy. Once she did stop, a small part of her was happy for the amount of cells she had healed within him. By no means was he healed completely, but she'd killed large trace amounts of the virus, enough to make her breathe a little bit easier and enough to give him a lot more time to live until they found a definitive solution because her brother was, in fact, dying.

Alaric's voice was a whisper when he spoke. "I don't feel the pain anymore." His eyes closed as a sigh of relief left him.

Alara swayed slightly before Rome scooped her into his arms and pulled her close to his chest as he watched her warily and pushed healing cells into her body. "Did you heal him completely?"

"No," she replied softly, "I tried, but there was too much damage to his healthy cells. I think they're corrupted now. I was only capable of stopping the virus from surrounding his major organs. He should be okay for now, and I'll try again later when I'm not feeling so weak."

Rome's chest shook slightly beneath her face as he snarled. "If it'll continue to weaken you this way, then the answer is no. I forbid it."

"You can't forbid me from healing my brother Romulus," she chuckled softly as he moved for the bed before he placed her atop the sheets.

Alaric spoke up from his position on the chaise. "Healing me wasn't good for you, was it?"

"That doesn't matter as long as we get that virus out of you. I'm convinced that once it reaches all of your major organs, you'll die, Alaric, and you can't die. I just got you. So if I need to heal you every day in order to rid us of this disgusting thing, then I will because I can't lose you."

"But is this hurting you, Alara?"

"It does." Rome interrupted, "The amount of healing cells I just pushed into her shows me how close she was to losing consciousness. She can't keep doing this. I won't lose her over you."

"Well, no one else is capable of healing him; it needs to be me." Alara snapped as she glared at them equally. "I'm helping with or without your approval. Just because my brother means less to you doesn't mean he does for me."

Rome paced the room as he spoke. "But why is that? What are you seeing that we aren't? How can you heal anyone who comes into contact with this thing when it seems no one else can? I can't even determine what this virus is…let alone how to neutralize it. Can you see what I'm missing? Are you keeping things from me yet again?"

She gazed into Rome's furious eyes and sighed heavily. She began plucking at the shirt fabric that dwarfed her body as her nerves got the better of her. "I'd like to sit with my brother alone if that's okay with you."

Rome stared for several moments before he glanced at Alaric and promptly left the room. He didn't fight to stay and get answers, and for once, she was happy about that, but it made her wonder just how far she was pushing this man who seemed to have more than enough patience for her. In fact, sometimes she felt that he might just have too much and one day that pushing would take him over the edge.

TWENTY-THREE

Alara breathed a sigh of relief the moment Rome left the bedroom. At first, she hadn't thought he would after throwing out that question. Sometimes, he was like a pit bull with a bone and wouldn't let things go. This was one situation where she needed him, too. She couldn't tell him the truth no matter how badly she wished she could. She wanted to be transparent. Sure, he'd been forgiving of her past, but this—the matter of her DNA being the virus slowly killing anyone that came into contact with it— was another level even she didn't understand. Guilt assailed her. Hadn't she promised no more lies? But was it really a lie? She was keeping something from him, withholding information, but did that make it a lie?

With her mind deep in thought, her words flowed unchecked for the first time in her life. "I don't understand why you won't heal completely. We share the same DNA, we carry the same blood cells... I've seen them, but I don't understand. Nothing makes sense."

"What are you going on about?" Alaric frowned as he sat atop the mattress and clasped her hands within his own to stop her fidgeting. "What does our DNA have to do with anything?"

Her eyes went as wide as saucers as she realized her slip-up and shook her head in denial. "I can't talk about it. I don't even know why I said that," she whispered, "I shouldn't have said that."

"Open your mind to me. We can talk freely there…trust me, little sister."

She wasn't sure if it was such a good idea, but what other choice did she have? He needed to know what was killing him. He deserved to know that she was the reason for this virus and that she was the disease slowly killing anyone who came into contact with it. She lowered her mental shields and was immediately greeted by Alaric's calm cognitive presence before his mind completely enveloped her own.

"What was that sensation?" She frowned softly as she watched him.

"Rome's telepathic as well. I assume you don't want him to overhear this conversation, so I blocked him from entering our minds while we spoke. I didn't think to do it earlier because I never thought he'd stoop so low and enter your mind as we spoke," he replied. *"For years, I've wanted this. To be this close to you without the guards and cameras between us. It is the most fulfilling experience I've ever had. To be free of Titan is all I've ever wanted for all of us. We're free, Alara."*

"But are you and Alondra really free?"

"What do you mean?"

"They're keeping you both trapped within your rooms; they constantly monitor you, and apparently, you need an escort just to come and see me. I can only imagine how they're treating Alondra. That isn't freedom, at least not by my standards, so I'll tell Rome to treat you fairly. I can't have them looking at you both as if you are the enemy. I won't stand for it."

Alaric chuckled softly. *"I can't really blame them. They're just being cautious. They don't know us, and the fact that they were forced to rescue us while a contingent of Titan soldiers surrounded us would make anyone suspicious. If they see us as the enemy, that is fine as long as they allow me to prove that I am not."*

"Alaric, that isn't good enough. You both are my family. I want you to be treated fairly."

"Life isn't about fair; let's forget about that for now, and you tell me what's really bothering you. What's going on that you don't want them to know?"

228

Alara pulled her hands from his hold and stood up to pace within the room, her thoughts now frantic while her chaotic emotions ran rampant. Although Alaric had access to her mind, she knew he couldn't see the thoughts that were currently running on repeat like a cinematic movie. If he knew, he wouldn't be asking what was bothering her. If he knew, then he'd be aware that she couldn't imagine telling the man she felt herself falling in love with that she was the reason Titan was capable of seriously injuring his people. They were her people now, too. Sure, it hadn't been long since she'd met the Guardians that Rome considered his family, but they were her family now, too. In her heart and mind, she cared for them just as much as she cared for Rome. She even cared for Amirishka.

She moved to stand in front of the window to watch as a fresh blanket of snow began to cover the ground. Her voice was soft and filled with hesitancy. *"I think I'm the cure for this virus because I'm why it even exists. Titan created it using my blood. I'm the reason why the Guardians can be weakened only to end up in critical condition. I'm the reason why you're dying, Alaric."*

Silence stretched between them as she waited for him to say or do anything. She needed him to say everything would be okay, but the look in his eyes didn't give her much hope that it would.

ROME STALKED AROUND HIS HOME, weariness pulling at his body as he cursed himself for caring about Alara's feelings. He didn't like secrets being kept from him, and obviously, that's what was happening. Again. Shit, she refused to even tell him about her tormentor, that bastard Lukas Titan. He should have pushed and pressed to know what she kept from him. She had to be too afraid to tell him; what other explanation would there be? She wasn't working for his enemy; he knew that, and yet she might have been simply trying to hide her involvement in previous things from her past. He couldn't and wouldn't fault her for what had occurred in her past, but he wouldn't accept a current involvement with his enemy. She couldn't be protecting Titan or anyone affiliated with them. That was something he would never tolerate, even from his mate.

He headed for the back door and stepped out into the midday sun. The exposure didn't affect him as it once had. The need to sleep no longer pulled at him like it should have, and even his eyes were unaffected by the rays of the white orb in the sky—not since consuming Alara's blood. Nothing started to burn or hurt; in fact, to feel the warmth truly against his skin without the protective UV film covering each of the windows within his home brought a small smile to his face that belied his true feelings. On the inside, he was unsettled and angry, confused even.

Rome stood out on the back deck until the very last sip of sunshine began its descent from the sky before he finally felt his warriors start to move around inside. All the while, he'd attempted to listen in on his woman and the brother he wasn't too sure was on their side, but they hadn't said a word to each other since he'd left the bedroom. He knew what that meant, and Rome had tried numerous times to breach the barriers of their minds to eavesdrop but learned quickly enough that Alaric's mental barriers were strong. There was no give and no way to access either of their minds, so he'd given up, but later tonight, after he ran a personal errand, he had every intention of getting answers from his woman. He needed to know what it was she was keeping from him. They couldn't keep going in circles like this. He needed the truth, and she needed to learn how to trust him.

The sliding glass door opened behind him moments before Maverick stepped out, his lips already moving a mile a minute as he spoke. "She refuses to leave her bedroom unless it is to see her sister. I'm unsure what to do, sir; she's refusing to eat or drink anything and hardly sleeps. I'm sure she thinks we're trying to poison her. The only saving grace is that she showers; thank the heavens for small favors. I know you said she isn't to speak with Alara, even with one of us within the room, but what would you have me do? If she keeps this up, she'll need medical assistance from lack of sustenance."

"They can talk tomorrow. Tell Alondra that as long as she eats and rests tonight, she can spend time with her sister tomorrow, but if she doesn't, all bets are off." Rome replied, "For all I care, she can stay in the room we've provided. As much as I dislike the brother, I trust Alondra even less. Something's off about her, and I can't place it, but tonight, I'll get my answers."

"Answers from whom?"

"I'll need you to stay home with Ami to watch over Alara and her family while the rest of them head out for the night. In the meantime…" he pulled a watch and a small bracelet from his pocket and held it up to his eyes to examine them closely, "In the meantime, I'll be seeing if my good friend Linc can get a read on these."

Maverick chuckled as he shook his head in amusement. "And when exactly did you get the opportunity to lift those off them?"

"While they slept, of course."

"Then what necklace was Alondra wearing when I saw her just before hunting you down?"

"A realistic illusion. As long as everyone believes they see it, it shall be."

"When did you acquire that power?"

Rome placed the watch and necklace back into his pocket and fixed the collar of his shirt before his vision focused on the people who began to mill about inside. They were shoving weapon after weapon into holsters on their bodies as they spoke quietly amongst themselves. "I've always had the ability," he finally responded as his gaze latched back onto Maverick, "It's hardly ever used because it takes an exorbitant amount of energy, but lately, my powers seem to have increased, and things that previously weakened me no longer do. There's a lot you don't know about me, Mav."

Maverick frowned as he pulled a silver-lined dagger from his ankle holster. "How's your aversion to silver?"

Rome reached out and fisted the sharp end of the blade, a slight sting spreading through his palm to travel up his arm before it dissipated completely. He released his hold and stared at the faint pink mark upon his flesh before pushing healing cells throughout his body. The mark quickly faded until perfect skin remained.

"You should have burned, and the pain should have been excruciating. How are you okay?" Maverick expressed shock, but alongside that was a little bit of awe.

"The only thing that's changed within my life is Alara." He moved for the banister and looked towards the vast backyard, focusing on the large fence that obstructed the world from his home. "From the moment she entered my life, it's been turned on its axis. She's changing everything, Mav, changing everything I ever thought I knew, and becoming everything to me. I must make changes for humanity's sake and our people's succession. Changes that can fracture the newfound relationship I've created with her. So after tonight, there will be no more nights off for us, and hopefully, I'll have my answers and know what I need to do regarding her family. Everything changes tonight."

"Alright, Ami and I shall watch over them. I pray you get the answers you're searching for." Maverick smacked him on the back and returned inside, leaving Rome alone once more.

As badly as he wanted to see Alara before he left, he decided against it and quickly teleported to Lincoln and Kai's home within the deep woods of the Alaskan forest. Considering they were best friends and practically inseparable, it only made it right that they would have a house together. It was a quaint two-bedroom cabin with large windows, a roaring fireplace, and plants that Kai insisted on raising. He had a true green thumb when it came to nature. When Rome had first found them centuries ago, they'd been grifters, never staying in one place for long, and with Lincoln's ability to erect illusions around anyone or thing, they'd been excellent thieves, but at Rome's behest, that had halted in its tracks. They couldn't be protectors of humanity if they were also robbing them blind, at least not according to Rome's thinking.

He knocked softly and smirked when Kai opened the door decked out in a red apron that read 'Kiss the Chef; he doesn't bite" with a pair of fangs etched into the fabric while a coat of flour covered the bottom half of the apron along with his cheeks. There was even a tiny smatter of it within his hair.

"My king, what brings you here?" Kai smiled, left the door wide open, and headed back into the kitchen as he spoke over his shoulder, "I'm just baking Linc his favorite oatmeal raisin cookies because he seems like he's still down about the warehouse slaughter."

"I'm fine, you idiot," Lincoln snapped as he made his way from the darkened hallway into the kitchen decked out in his black leather hunting attire. "You need to get dressed."

Rome wasted no time in telling them why he was there. "Linc, I need you to get a read on these two objects and tell me what you find. The darker the secret, the better." He handed over the watch and necklace and waited patiently as Lincoln grasped them within his palm and closed his eyes in concentration.

Not even a second passed before he frowned and opened light green eyes that sparked with annoyance as he stared at the objects that had been given to him. Several more seconds inched by before he finally spoke. "I'm not getting anything, sir. No secrets lie within."

CHAPTER
TWENTY-FOUR

Rome stood beneath the faucet of his shower after returning Alaric and Alondra's items while they slept. Cold water stung his skin as his eyes stared intently at the drain as blood mixed with water. The tangy metallic smell of Rogue blood differed significantly between humans and Eternals. He could smell the wrongness within it. He could tell that their sanity had long been lost to them, and all that was left was the madness and need to bleed someone dry. His fangs lengthened in aggression at the thought as he reached for his rag and bar of soap. He could hear the rest of his warriors settling in for the day after a long, successful night of hunting. With him no closer to answers about the true intentions of Alara's siblings, he hadn't been capable of relieving Maverick and Amirishka, but he'd made sure to make up for their absence. He winced when soap suds seeped into the many cuts that covered his skin.

He wasn't sure why he hadn't healed himself yet, but the sound of the bathroom door quietly creaking open brought his attention to the small female who slipped through the crack just before the door closed again. He closed his eyes against the sight that greeted him and turned his back to her. The image of one of his button-down shirts dwarfing her body as her curly dark brown and burgundy hair caressed one of her exposed shoulders, and her small teeth dug into the plushness that was her bottom lip severed into his mind. He heard it the second his shirt dropped to the tile flooring moments before she entered the shower and placed her small palms against his back. Rome groaned hoarsely as she pushed healing cells into his body to close his wounds and sent a burst of energy through him that he didn't need. If there was anything he did need, it was her beneath him or over him, with his fangs so deeply embedded in her skin that it would take centuries for them to be removed.

"You should be sleeping," he stated, hoping his harsh tone wouldn't hurt her but instead would urge her back to bed, "I'm not in a pleasant mood, little flower; besides, the water is freezing, and I don't need you getting sick. Go back to bed, and I'll be there soon."

He thought she'd leave, but it could never be that easy with her. No. Alara was like no one he'd ever encountered before. She didn't fear his anger. She didn't fear him at all, to his knowledge. Maybe at first, she had, but now she seemed to test the very reins of his control with her refusal to listen when advised to. Her naked form pressed flush against his back, causing him to groan again as his cock hardened in anticipation and his fangs began to ache with a familiar need. He could feel his eyes blazing like fire beneath his lids, his hands smacked against the tile, and his legs widened as her hand trailed lazily along his sides, chest, and stomach.

"Why are you trying to get rid of me, Romulus?" She whispered, her lips sliding languidly against the very center of his back.

His balls tightened, his breathing turned shallow, and he questioned why he needed her to leave in the first place. There was no actual answer. Sure, he was in a piss poor mood after receiving no real answer, but that didn't explain why he needed space from the one person that had the potential to calm him as no one else could.

"I'll take you. Hard." He responded and stilled the progress of her slowly descending hands as they moved to travel below his waistline.

"Have you fed?"

He snarled. She should know the answer to that. Since the

moment she'd entered his life, and he'd sampled her blood, he had no inclination to drink from any other source. She was all he wanted and needed. To take in the blood of another would sour his stomach faster than the bastards he murdered on a nightly basis.

Rome spun around and crowded her against the cold, unforgiving tile as the water beat against his back. His fist tangled within her hair as his other hand gripped her hip. "I'll feed when I'm inside you."

She chuckled softly, the sound sending tingles down his spine. "I'm all yours."

His lips slammed against hers, yet he was careful with his fangs. He couldn't taste Alara's blood yet, or he'd indeed lose himself to her. He licked and nipped at her lips, earning moans that sent his heart rate soaring and his cock lengthening to painful degrees. She tasted like sunshine and sex. Her scent enveloped him, pulled him deeper beneath her spell as his hands moved against the softness that was her skin. He could stay in this moment for eternity with nothing, but Alara pressed against him, taking whatever he had to give her, and he knew she'd give as good as she got. She may have been new to everything related to sex, but she was the most enthusiastic partner he'd ever encountered.

He licked along her nape, his fangs itching to sink into her jugular and quench the thirst he felt rising within him, but he held back and simply enjoyed her for now. He moved to her breast and sucked her taut nipple between the parting within his lips. His groan and her moan reverberated throughout the bathroom as her hand dug into the damp dreadlocks that hung loosely down his back, and his grip turned more possessive. Rome snarled when the scent of her sex deepened even further and sent his control fracturing inch by inch.

"Use your gift," he snarled around her breast as he used a mental push to turn the shower off.

She didn't question him. She knew he would only request such a thing if his control was on the precipice of shattering. It didn't take long for him to feel the pull of her power as he continued to suck at the tips of her breasts while his hands molded against her waist to pull her closer.

"Romulus!" She groaned as her legs trembled unsteadily beneath her.

"What do you need?"

"I need more. Please." She tugged at his hair before attempting to push his mouth further down her body to where her moist core awaited his touch.

He knew what she wanted, yet he wanted to tease her, to draw this out and grant her a stronger release, but when he glanced up to meet her heady gaze, he couldn't deny her. God, she weakened him and strengthened him all in the same breath, and that was without using her abilities; with them, he was pulled to his knees. He wanted to please her and give her whatever she desired whenever her expressive gaze turned to him. With his eyes steady upon her own, he found himself kneeling until her cunt was lined up perfectly with his mouth. The position he found himself in wasn't comfortable, but the second his eyes dropped to her warm center, he could have cared less.

"God, you're beautiful," he whispered and placed a kiss right above her clit.

Alara's back arched, and he felt the tremble within her legs worsen. He needed her steady. He couldn't have her falling on his watch. He grabbed her legs and forced them around his head as he slid his tongue between the valley of her dripping labia. The taste of her cream had stars bursting behind his eyelids as he kept her back pressed against the wall to maintain a perfect balance. The heels of her feet dug into his back as her thighs clenched around his head, and her moans went deeper. The longer he continued to tease her core with licks and sucks meant to ease yet torment her, the harder she tugged at his hair. He couldn't help but smile against her warm center.

Rome felt her need to cum; shit, he felt it himself with the pressure building within his balls. He desperately wanted to stroke at his erection as he licked at her center, but he denied himself. The feel of his own hand wouldn't satisfy him. The only thing that would benefit him now was her pussy wrapped around his shaft, with his fangs puncturing her throat as he sipped at her blood. With that thought in mind, he forced himself to move faster than her eyes or body could follow. The new position had him leaning against the cool tile with her legs wrapped around his waist as the tip of his cock barely touched the lips of her core.

"Open your eyes, little flower." His words were strained as he waited with bated breath for her eyes to find his.

He wasn't disappointed when they did. They were lust-filled and hazy as they latched onto him before abruptly widening as he sank inch after inch of his erection through her folds and into the very heat of her center. It was a struggle to keep his eyes open as her warmth surrounded him and pulled him in with every thrust he delivered, but he did. He managed it as his gaze bounced between her face filled with ecstasy and her luscious breasts that bounced with every sharp thrust.

"Oh god!" She screamed when he angled deeper until his tip was kissing the very opening of her womb. "Fuck! Too deep!"

"No, baby, you'll take it and reward me with a nice hard orgasm just as soon as I sink my fangs in." He grunted and pumped into her more vigorously.

Alara's nails dug into his shoulders, his hips strained and bucked against him as his balls slapped against her ass. The feel of her cream soaking his cock and balls brought another vicious snarl from his lips as his fangs lengthened and sharpened until he could wait no longer. He struck. His fangs sank deep into her jugular vein. Her core clenched around him tighter than a fist ever could the moment he sipped at her blood, and the orgasm that slammed through her sent her scream ricocheting around them as her ability to siphon sucked at him, nearly draining him dry.

He slowly slid to the floor of the shower as his mind grew heavy along with his eyes. The powerful draw of Alara's gift had been uncalled for, and yet that, mixed with the feel of her and the taste of her blood coating his tongue, had sent his orgasm rushing through him until his cum was coating her insides only to leak between them. He'd be getting a bench seat installed a lot sooner than later.

It would come in handy if they ever planned to do this again, and if he had his way, they would be participating in shower sex more often.

Rome kissed her forehead and smiled. "Good girl."

ALARA STRETCHED LANGUIDLY, felt the cool sheets of the bed against her naked flesh, and opened her eyes to the brightness of the sun shining through the windows. She didn't remember climbing into bed after the explosive orgasm Rome had granted them both, and when she turned to check the time on the clock, she found that hours had passed since their interaction. Four hours, exactly. Had they passed out? She couldn't remember anything after the intense orgasm he'd granted her. Alara stretched once more, felt the soreness within her core and thighs, and glanced over to find Rome passed out beneath the sheets. He was laying on his stomach looking every bit like the handsome warrior, his face serene, his lips bruised from her kisses, and his throat peppered with hickeys she didn't recall giving him. He was genuinely sleeping. Not that fake napping he attempted to get away with every morning, but a legit rest that eased her nerves like nothing else could. She wanted to stay there and watch him sleep all morning, but the pressure within her bladder wouldn't lessen. Her need to pee was much greater than her desire to watch him slumber. She vaulted from the bed and barely reached the toilet before her urge to go became unbearable. She sighed in relief for making it on time, knowing she wouldn't have lived that down if she'd had an accident.

Running her fingers through her hair, she smiled softly as her mind continued to replay the events that had occurred only hours ago, or at least the events she could remember. Rome was the best thing that had ever happened to her. He was living up to an image she had only dreamed of, but in all reality, she had never seen herself being with a man in any capacity. Being a victim to Titan had ensured that within her mind, body, and soul. The only thing she'd ever wanted before was freedom. The freedom to live her life however she chose to, the freedom to use her powers and have the control she desperately wanted. The freedom to just be her. She had that now, along with a man she never thought she would need and a family that cared about her.

Alara jumped in the shower before dressing in a deep burgundy turtleneck with a pair of black wash jeans and her favorite combat boots. She stepped back into the bedroom and glanced at Rome once more before quietly making her way out into the hallway, where she descended the steps and made her way to her sister's bedroom door. She was tired of waiting to see her family and of Rome attempting to control every little aspect of her life. She knew he worried for her safety and that he wasn't entirely convinced that her brother and sister weren't still working for Titan in any capacity. She didn't believe they were. They wouldn't. She refused to believe in the possibility that they could.

She paused just outside Alondra's bedroom door and frowned when she saw a key in the door knob. So it was true. Rome really had been keeping them locked in their bedrooms during the day. He claimed it was a safety issue since the Guardians were forced to sleep, but all she saw was an act of war between them. He was treating her family poorly, and it ended now. With a glance to her right, she saw another key sticking out of Alaric's door knob and used the power she had received from Rome to unlock it telepathically. Satisfied, she turned the key in Alondra's door and pocketed them both so they couldn't be used again, and knocked gently before cracking the door open to peek inside.

Her sister was standing in front of the window with her back turned to her, but at the sound of the door opening, she spun around, and Alara was once again taken aback by the sight of her. It was like looking into a mirror, except dark circles surrounded Alondra's eyes, and she could practically see the exhaustion leaking from her pores.

"Is it okay if I come in?" Alara questioned with a soft smile.

"Of course," her sister responded as she tugged at the hem of her shirt. It was the same nervous tick Alara expressed on occasion.

"I've been hoping to see you but haven't had the best welcome since I arrived."

"You're right, and I'm sorry for that. I didn't know Rome was keeping you and Alaric confined to your rooms. It's bad enough that I never tried to seek you guys out after that first night. Rome isn't like the rest of them. He's stronger, so the sun doesn't make him sleep like it does for the rest of them, and he's been keeping me pretty occupied lately." Alara blushed with her confession. She wasn't used to this. Girl talk; if it even was that, or maybe she was getting ahead of herself. This probably wasn't that, and she found herself rambling because she was so nervous. And why wouldn't she be? She was standing in front of her spitting image, and a feeling of rightness was settling so profoundly within her bones that it was almost as if latches were clicking into place by the second. Realizing that she had a family, a brother, and a sister was unreal to her.

Alondra smirked. "It's okay, I haven't minded it much." Her eyes trailed back to the window to gaze out. "Besides, I'm used to being confined. I wouldn't even know what to do with myself if I was allowed to wander the halls. I have a view now, but before, I didn't, so it isn't too bad."

"Well, I'm here to break you out," Alara swung the door open and waited, "Everyone's asleep, even Rome, so what do you want to do?"

Guilt ate at Alara at the thought of her sister being stuck in this room daily. Alondra shouldn't be okay with confinement. She should have been fighting against it, and as her sister Alara should have been helping. She planned to make up for her neglect now that she could see what had been happening. She wasn't going to allow their mistreatment to continue. This moment wasn't about appeasing him but about helping her sister transition like she had once she'd been freed. It was her turn to help someone now.

———

ALARA LAUGHED at another cheesy line from the comedy movie on the TV in the living room. After Alaric had wandered his way downstairs, they had cooked breakfast and eaten like a family, but he'd headed upstairs shortly after to grant them time to bond. The murderous looks Alondra had directed at him were noticeable, but Alara couldn't for the life of her figure out why she hated him so much. It didn't make sense, but Alondra had asked to watch a movie before she could work up the courage to ask.

She threw several pieces of popcorn into her mouth just as her sister spoke up.

"Do you think we could go outside?"

Alara froze. Of all the questions she'd expected, that wasn't one of them. "What do you mean go outside?"

"I've been a prisoner my entire life, and the moment I was free, I was forced to run from the people that made me a prisoner in the first place, and now I'm a prisoner in a different manner. I've never been able to bask in the sun and feel the rays against my face. I never just listened to the breeze and smelled the flowers. I never got to feel true freedom. It's winter. There's snow covering the ground… real snow. I want to feel the coolness of the flakes against my skin. I just want to breathe without feeling like my every step is being monitored. If anyone could understand that, I thought it would be you." Alondra tugged nervously at the hem of her shirt once more as she stood up and approached the expansive windows that over-looked the front yard. She pressed her palms against the cool glass and smiled wistfully before she glanced over her shoulder. Her expression turned sour in an instant. "Was I wrong in that assumption?"

"No," Alara sighed heavily. "You're not wrong." She shifted the bowl of popcorn to the small glass coffee table and sat up straighter as she met her sister's gaze head-on. "But I can't just walk you outside. Titan is hunting us, and we don't know how close they could be or what they're planning. With Rome and his people resting for tonight's hunt, we can't risk walking out and something happening to either one of us. We're supposed to be flying under the radar, which means remaining unseen. They have eyes every-where, Alondra, so we don't want to risk them finding us and making it easy for them to get a hold of us."

"And how exactly will staying inside keep Titan from bursting down the doors while they sleep? That's as much of a possibility as anything else, isn't it? They could already know where we are, so what makes staying inside any safer during the day? Won't it actually leave us vulnerable since they sleep during the day?"

"Romulus has safeguards in place, and Titan doesn't know that Rome is hardly fazed by the sun. He can withstand it." She shrugged nonchalantly, "We'll be okay as long as we stay inside, but maybe later, I can convince Ami to take us for a walk in the backyard." She attempted to appease her but knew it fell on deaf ears when Alondra simply stared back. This wasn't going as she'd expected. They'd definitely been bonding, but now she could tell it had been ruined by her refusal to step outside.

"So I'm still a prisoner?" Alondra questioned with a raised brow and folded arms as if to protect herself from her harsh reality.

Alara shook her head vehemently. "Of course not; well, at least not anymore. I won't allow him to lock either you or Alaric up again, but for now, we need to stay off of Titan's radar, and the best way to do that is to remain inside until Rome handles the situation."

"I won't be trapped again, little sister."

Rome's sleep-filled voice came from the hallway, his clear blue gaze laser-focused on the woman who looked identical to his mate, yet smelled completely wrong. "Then leave." He pointed towards the doorway with a tilt of his head, "The door is just there if you really want out. I'll even give you money to make a hasty retreat but do not, and I mean do not tempt my woman away from the safety I can provide for her here. You won't like what I do or what lengths I'll go to to protect what I consider mine."

CHAPTER
TWENTY-FIVE

Rome attempted to keep his anger leashed as he glared daggers into the side of Alondra's head; all the while, he tried to penetrate her thoughts yet was met with a wall of ice that was just as impenetrable as her siblings. The few times he'd been granted admittance into Alara's thoughts was because she'd let her guard down. She felt safe and secure enough to occasionally leave her mind open to him, but her sister and brother were like walls of ice surrounded by steel. There was no give to their mental barriers, which raised the question of how. Alaric made sense because he was a telepath, but Alondra was a healer. She shouldn't have the strength to keep him out, yet her barriers matched her brothers. Barriers that could only be that strong after years of mental preparation and fortitude.

"Stop glaring at her like that!" Alara snarled as she moved to stand in front of him.

He glanced down, his glare instantly morphing into pleasure as he reached out to caress the side of her throat where he'd previously bitten her. He wished his mark would stay, but her ability to heal herself prevented it from remaining.

"I apologize, little flower, but I do not trust her intentions, and it doesn't help that I cannot read her." He replied honestly as his gaze flicked back to the person in question before returning to land on his mate.

"Don't apologize to me, Romulus. Apologize to my sister and stop trying to read her. It's rude, and unless you've been invited to enter someone's mind, you shouldn't."

He frowned and looked back to Alondra to find her glaring at him with her hands clenched at her sides. A fighter's response. There was no fear in her stare, just defiance and anger. It was anger he wanted to match with his own because she wasn't at all what she presented herself to be. She wasn't acting like someone who had been tortured and sheltered all her life. There was such a defiance in her that he found it hard to believe that Titan hadn't beaten it entirely out of her. After meeting Alara a few weeks ago, he'd seen the insecurity and fear within her, but with Alondra, there was none. Oh, he'd seen it when they hadn't known he'd entered the room, but now, that fear was gone. Had she been faking it for Alara's benefit?

"I apologize for my rudeness, Alondra," he lied even as he still attempted to breach her thoughts.

She nodded in acknowledgment and turned back to stare out the window. That allowed Rome to focus on his woman.

He wrapped his hand around her neck and pulled her against his bare chest as he leaned down to whisper into her ear. "You left before I could wake you the way I desired, preferably with my tongue between your thighs and my fangs in your femoral artery." He rubbed his lips against the sensitive point of her ear to ensure a whole-body shudder that brought a smile to his face.

"I needed to check on my family," she whispered back, "you haven't been treating them properly, and I need you to fix that. I refuse to laze around in bed with you every morning when my brother and sister can't even come down for breakfast alone. They aren't your prisoners, just like I wasn't when I first arrived. Treat them like family, or you'll have to let all of us go."

Rome stiffened. This was an ultimatum. He couldn't remember the last time someone attempted to throw one in his face, but he knew one when he heard one. Her face said that she was serious.

Alara would leave him if he didn't change how he treated her siblings. Indecision filled him. He wanted to protect her and the family he'd created for himself and his Eternals worldwide. He wanted to be a leader worth following and a man of his word, and he wanted to provide a safe space for the woman who was changing everything for him, but this wasn't something he'd been expecting. Not from her. She wanted him to trust virtual strangers with his other half and the lives of the men and women he protected. She wanted him to treat them as he treated her. That would never happen if they continued to be deceptive and secretive.

He shook his head and tightened his hand around the back of her throat, not to inflict pain or discomfort but enough to where she felt his annoyance. "I can't treat them as I treat you. You're my mate and queen, and they are nothing to me but a headache and the blood of your blood."

She gripped his wrist, and her expression hardened as a coldness entered her expressive eyes. "Then I'm leaving with them, and trust me...they will leave because I'll tell them to."

"And where would you go with Titan hunting you?" He snarled and wrapped his other arm around her waist to pin her to him. "You really think I'd allow my mate to be taken by them? No little flower, you'll stay where I can protect you, and you'll stay willingly, or I will make you a prisoner of your own making."

"You wouldn't!" She snapped.

"Try me," he whispered with a feral stare.

Silence stretched between them before Alondra spoke from her position near the window. "If you're both done staring daggers into each other, I'd like to know if I'm free to return to my prison and if the door will be left locked or unlocked for the duration of my stay."

"Leave us!" Rome snarled, "Your door will remain locked until I deem you aren't a threat to all I hold dear."

Alara dug smooth nails into his skin and glared as she spoke. "She won't be a prisoner, so no, you won't lock her up again."

She attempted to meet her sister's eyes but the tightly possessive hold he had on her throat prevented that and she froze when he growled low. The thin hairs that covered her body stood to attention as her eyes snapped back to Rome's feral expression. His lips were pulled back to reveal sharpened fangs, his eyes were lit up blue orbs that would seem eerie to a non-enhanced human, and the feeling of his erection against her lower stomach told her that he was angry, but he definitely wanted to punish her in a more intimate way then company allowed. She wanted to smile and test the clear challenge she saw within his eyes but she also needed to make it clear that she wouldn't be budging on how she felt about her family's mistreatment.

"Alara," her sister exclaimed as she moved forward as if to intervene.

Rome stilled her with a look and simply waited as his powers flared around him to cocoon him and the woman he held. He watched Alondra with a hard stare until she slowly left the room, yet there was still so much defiance in her eyes that he thought she'd refuse. Rome allowed the silence to stretch as Alara's body stiffened within his arms. He listened for the telltale sound of her sister's bedroom door closing softly behind her as she went in before he looked down at the woman in his arms.

"Why do you steadily go against me?" He questioned before releasing her from his hold to pace the room.

If he held her any longer, he wasn't sure what he'd do. He'd never hurt her, of course, but the need to make her submit to him in ways that were purely sexual ran rampant within him. When he was buried balls deep within her tight little body, that seemed to be the only time she listened, and as badly as he wanted that, he needed her to understand why he was so concerned for her safety.

"I go against you because you're being unreasonable, Romulus. They are my family, and I understand that that might not mean much to you, but it means a hell of a lot to me." Alara snapped angrily, "I never knew they existed. I never knew I had a family, to begin with. All this time, I was under the assumption that I was alone in this world. A fucking freak trapped with sadistic ass people that only used me and forced me to do things I never wanted to be a part of, and the whole time I had someone fighting to get me out, and I never knew it until it happened. I have them both in my life now, safe and away from the company we both despise, yet you insist on treating them like the enemy! How can they prove anything to you when you keep them at arm's length and treat them like less than nothing? And then you expect me to act like everything is fine. Well, I'm telling you once again I refuse to accept this. Change Romulus. Change this before you ruin what we're attempting to build between us."

"You want me to bend to your will and change how I treat your family, and yet you insist on withholding information, and they insist on withholding information! Information that I'm sure has the potential to help me protect you and your family as well as my own. Information that has the potential to possibly do harm. Do you think I take your safety lightly? The answer is no Alara. Just no."

The need to release the energy building within him was a power struggle as he continued to pace and avoid her gaze because if he looked at her now, he'd snap. He wanted to lash out, tame her, and make her understand why her safety was so important to him. He refused to bend on this. Something wasn't right with her siblings. For years, they'd been separated, them going through things and experiencing things she probably had yet to be exposed to. Her brother being a double agent meant he had the potential to still be a double agent for Titan in the hopes of weakening his people. Rome wouldn't put it past him, not after being attacked by those bastards moments after taking a phone call from him. He believed Alaric might have been working for the enemy, even unknowingly. On the other hand, Alondra was a mystery he needed to solve immediately. She was an anomaly that didn't make sense. She was a piece of the puzzle that just didn't have a place, or maybe he just couldn't see it, and not knowing where she stood was what made his protective instincts flare up. With her his hackles were raised, and the need to protect everything he cared for was at an all-time high. That sister of hers was hiding something. Something probably far worse than his mate was keeping from him.

"How can I convince you that they aren't out to hurt us?" Alara's voice pulled him from his thoughts.

"Ask them to drop the shields they have placed around their

minds and allow me access to their thoughts, and only then will I have no reason to doubt their intentions." He stopped his pacing and watched her, hoping to gain some ground, some form of trust on her part that he knew what he was doing. "If they can do that then how could I possibly continue to doubt them?"

"Isn't my word enough?" She whispered, a vulnerable expression taking her face captive as the spitfire that had razed against him only moments ago vanished.

Was this a manipulation tactic? Rome knew that women were excellent manipulators when it came to getting what they wanted. He'd experienced plenty of them over the years. He didn't want to place his mate within the category of other women and how they operated, but he knew their ploys. She had to know how weak she made him with the need to please her, but he'd never jeopardize her safety. She was the most important thing to him. Greater than his need to protect humanity. Without her he would be nothing. Tears gathered within her eyes, her hands tugged at the fabric of her turtleneck, and she bit down anxiously on her bottom lip. Her reactions seemed natural. He could feel her anxiety in the air.

Rome approached her, pushed back a few loose strands of curly hair from her face, and cupped her cheek gently. "My intentions aren't to harm you. Not your body, mind, or emotions, but sweetheart, you just met them, same as me. You didn't grow up with them. You don't know what they're capable of. As badly as you want to put all of your faith into them, you also have to realize that they could be playing us."

Silent tears trekked down her face in frustration as she spoke. "You keep saying that you're concerned about my safety and how you only want to protect me, but you almost hurt me, Romulus." Her eyes closed with her admission, "You made me fall for you when really all you see me as is property to do with as you wish, and you've robbed me of all sense of self. I can do nothing without your say-so; absolutely nothing."

"I've never 'almost' hurt you, and I never would. What the hell are you talking about?" He frowned and pushed on her chin until her head was tilted back and her eyes opened to stare back at him.

Her palms pressed into the flesh of his chest, ran down to the hem of his drawstring sweats, and clung to the fabric. "The first time you tasted my blood, you nearly went feral, but you had enough strength to pull away. What if you hadn't? You would have hurt me."

"But I didn't hurt you, and I never planned to. At the time, I only had a small suspicion that you were my mate. I never thought the needs you would evoke within me would tamper with the control I've learned to harness over the centuries." He cupped her cheek while his other hand slid beneath the fabric of her shirt to rub soothing circles into her lower back. His voice softened, and his eyes lost their hard edge, "Like I've told you before; we're the first to do this; to mate, and I don't intend to fuck this up. I was never going to hurt you, but I was damn sure going to take what I knew you weren't willing to give at the time. Needing you has become second nature to me. Pleasing you is all I want to do, but listen to me, little flower, something isn't right, and if you'd just take a step back and think objectively instead of emotionally, then you would understand where I'm coming from."

"I won't ask them to make themselves vulnerable to your mind games."

"Then the restrictions stay until I have my answers."

"You're a bastard for this."

He shrugged nonchalantly and smirked. "If it protects you, then I'll happily be a bastard, but know that that makes me your bastard." He swooped in for a kiss and captured her small gasp before he slid his tongue easily through her parted lips.

Her small moan made his hands tighten as he maneuvered them towards the couch before he took a seat and pulled her to sit atop his lap. Her hips cradled his own, their kiss deepened, and his senses wandered as he listened for any movement throughout the house. Silence greeted him, causing him to smile against her lips as his need to release his built-up stress increased. Alara's arms curled around his neck, her breasts crushed against his chest, and her hips rocked against him, rubbing against his swollen erection. Through the fabric of their clothing, he could feel her heat.

"Romulus," she whispered, "what are we doing?"

He nicked her lip with a sharpened fang and licked the drop of blood that welled up in the process. "If you have to ask, then I'm not doing something right, so let me remedy that."

Rome pulled her arms behind her back as he pictured her naked above him with her breasts pointed towards his mouth. His abilities flared up to envelop her lovingly before her clothing disappeared, and a shy expression crossed her face. He couldn't help but chuckle. His woman wasn't nervous. Sure, she was new to the sexual cravings that racked her body, but she was in no way shy, not after losing her virginity in one of the most carnal ways possible. He tilted his hips up and quickly slid his sweatpants down until his cock sprang out to slap against his lower stomach. Her eyes tracked the movement as her pink tongue peeked out to lick across her bottom lip. He snarled as his hand tightened around her wrist. With his other hand, he trailed it between her breasts before gripping each of her nipples, back and forth, back and forth until she was a squirming, moaning mess above him. He wanted to use both hands, but he needed her hands to stay put, and he refused to expel any more telekinetic energy that he might need for his hunt tonight.

He leaned forward to whisper into her ear, "Sit forward, little flower and put that pretty pussy right on my cock and swallow it whole," he moved back to relax against the pillows to wait and watch.

She didn't disappoint him. Alara sat forward until the heat of her cunt hovered over the mushroomed tip of his cock before she slowly sank down. His moan went deep as her warmth surrounded him like a glove, and his fingers continued to tease the tips of her breasts until she sank all the way to the base, earning herself a load of his precum. Her groan was thick and heavy, the sound drawing his balls up to his body as he shifted his legs wider. With the afternoon sun shining down upon them, he made out the slight perspiration that coated her skin, saw the strain within her legs, and watched as her beautiful eyes turned hazy with lust. Fuck, she was perfect. His perfect mate.

"Will you be a good girl and keep your hands right where they are so I can take what belongs to me?" He smiled softly, revealing fangs that had started to pulse to the beat of her heart.

She squirmed above him, her pussy fluttering around him as she moaned softly and nodded in agreement. "I'll do anything you want."

"That's my good girl," he crooned before wrapping a hand around her throat while the other rested on her hip before he thrust up and into her tightly clenched core. "Fuck yes," he groaned.

He was in heaven. Her pussy gripped him yet stretched to accommodate his large size as he drilled into her repeatedly. He wasn't gentle by any means as he watched her body for signs of discomfort. He found none, and instead watched the sway of her breasts, felt the cream from her cunt as it bathed his cock, and listened to the greedy moans that poured from her lips as she bounced above him. The closer he came to his orgasm, the more he felt his abilities flare up. He glanced down at where they were joined and snarled at the sight. He needed to see more. The hair that covered her mound obstructed some of his view. It kept him from seeing what he truly wanted to see, and that just wouldn't do. Rome tightened his grip around her throat, partially obstructing her airway, and watched as her eyes rolled into the back of her head with a breathless cry before her knees shook violently and an orgasm tore through her. He continued to pump into her, drawing out her orgasm as he slowed to a snail's pace until he forced himself to pull out before he could cum.

He moved quickly before she could question why he'd stopped and flipped them over until her back and arms were pressed into the couch's cushions. Her hair fanned out around her as he spread her legs and plunged back into the depth of her pussy with a brutally deep stroke.

"Romulus!" Alara screamed, her voice tinged with a hint of pain, yet her face was drawn up in ecstasy.

She attempted to close her legs and wiggle out from beneath him, but with her arms pinned beneath her back and the iron grip he had on her thighs, she had nowhere to go. He kept her legs spread wide and pinned, her knees nearly touching her ears as he folded her practically in half and split her open with his cock. His glowing eyes were glued to her pussy, watching as it opened and closed around him while her clit peeked at him beneath its hood. Her cream continually gushed from her center, her smell triggered his need as his fangs lengthened and his cock grew even harder. Her moans were cries now, lustful and loud, as he pounded into her mercilessly before he leaned forward to sink his fangs into the sensitive spot between her ear and shoulder. At the feel of his fangs piercing her flesh, Alara saw stars. Her orgasm slammed into her like a tidal wave reaching the shore as he pumped her full of his cum. He continued to sip at her blood long after his hips stilled in movement before he was licking at her throat and gently easing himself from her body. A gush of his cum leaked out from between her labia, and he smiled before he swiped a finger through the mess to push it back inside of her where it belonged. She moaned softly as her eyes slid shut, and her body slumped into blissful sleep.

"Let's get you back to bed, little flower," he chuckled as he lifted her into his arms to make his way back to his bedroom.

Rome's eyes snagged on the window as he went and sighed when he saw a considerable crack spindling through the glass. He would have to get that fixed, but behind the glass, he could see the snow had started to come down harder, nearly obstructing his view of the street before his eyes snagged and held onto a lone truck that hadn't been sitting there earlier. He searched with his senses and felt nothing, yet his alarm bells screamed that something was wrong. There was no way of telling if anyone sat inside due to the heavy tint surrounding the windows. X-ray vision wasn't one of his many gifts.

He searched for a heartbeat and found none. When he used telepathy to probe the surrounding area for someone unfamiliar or out of place, he also found nothing out of the ordinary. Whoever— if anyone— sat within would not be able to see inside his home, but the feeling of being watched hung over him. He clutched Alara tighter to his chest and forced himself to move for the stairs, hoping to get her comfortable before he would allow himself to investigate.

CHAPTER
TWENTY-SIX

I t was gone.

The vehicle that had occupied the street right outside of his home was now gone, and in its place was the snow that had fallen to cover the tire tracks, as well as any footprints that might have been left behind. The snow fell fast and steady, swirling around him as cold winds blew past him, chilling him to the bone—or at least it was supposed to if he had been human. Rome stood in the middle of the street, senses open and searching as he waited with bated breath for something to stand out to him, yet nothing did. The sun was just setting in the distance, and the need to hunt was pressing on him with an urgency he hadn't felt in centuries. He'd only felt this when he'd first been ordered by the Gods to protect humanity. Back when hunting was fresh and new, allowing him and his brethren to hone their fighting skills and make mistakes along the way Rome had always felt such an urgency to do as the Gods bid, but now…now he was stuck in a sort of limbo with Alara's safety and well being pressing heavily on his mind and heart.

The hair on the nape of his neck stood to attention just as Erick stepped outside and walked over with a solemn expression. His snow-white hair and skin complexion blended perfectly with the atmosphere, while his red eyes stood out starkly against the blanket of whiteness that surrounded them.

"Silas believes we should remain home for the night. He senses something bad enough to make his eyes take on that glassy look before he completely zoned out on me." He stated.

Rome glanced down the street, his senses still screaming that something was wrong before he spoke. "I'm guessing he didn't elaborate on why it was so important for us to remain inside for the evening?"

"Not a word. Just said we should stay close to home."

"We can't. I've already allowed too many days to pass where we've been sitting on the sidelines. They haven't said anything yet, but I'm sure the Gods aren't too happy with how lax I've been with our hunts. We can't continue to allow the Rogues to gain any type of ground within our area. I've allowed it too frequently these past few days, and as much as I'd love to stay home and hold my mate, we need to hunt and eradicate the vampires that have begun to take over my city."

"He'll want to remain behind."

"We have Amirishka for that."

Erick scoffed, "That won't make a difference. You know as well as I do that when he's stuck on a vision, he's simply stuck, so will you be ordering him? That may be the only way you'll get him out of the house for the night. Only a direct order might work."

Erick wasn't wrong. When Silas experienced his visions, he became one-track-minded and so stuck in the future that getting him to do anything else was nearly impossible unless ordered to do so. Rome was the only one capable of giving him orders he would actually listen to. He trusted heavily in Silas' ability to glance into the future, but sometimes, he had to be the bad guy and enforce things that had the potential to cause rifts between his people, and yet no one ever complained. Well, no one but Akio.

"How's the brother?" Rome questioned as he headed back towards the house, knowing full well that Erick would follow or risk being left behind.

"Whatever Alara did, it helped some, but the virus still spreads within him. What I don't understand is how it isn't weakening him in the slightest. According to him, he's only experiencing sharp pains where he was shot. Besides that, he appears to be functioning as if nothing is amiss. The other day, you say he claimed that he felt the virus slowly killing him, and now he hardly feels it."

"By the tone of your voice, I'm assuming you don't believe him."

Erick gripped him by the shoulder, stopping him before they could enter the home. "He's protecting his sister. I don't believe he wants her to heal him because he sees how much it weakens her. Part of me can understand his reasoning, but I don't understand how she's capable of marginally healing him in the first place. Have you figured that out yet? Has she told you what she sees when she heals him?"

"Not yet."

But he would. He would learn Alara's secrets even if it caused a rift between them because something wasn't right, and that feeling of uncertainty was spreading for him. Had he been wrong in assuming that she no longer sided with his enemy? Was she playing him just so he would weaken his guard and let her entirely into the fold? Was she attempting to learn their secrets before the trap was laid for Titan? Those thoughts ran through his mind as he entered the living room to find Maverick, Cairo, and Akio preparing for the night's hunt while Amirishka stood to the side, talking quietly with Silas. The fireplace blazed within the hearth. He could make out the sound of his mate moving around in the kitchen when she should have been upstairs and shook his head softly. He knew she couldn't help but be present when they left. She always felt the need to wish them well and help them with anything that they might possibly need last minute.

Rome headed straight for Silas and waited until his eerie hete-rochromia gaze landed on his face before he spoke. "Tell me exactly what you saw." It wasn't a question or a statement but a demand.

The room grew silent, yet they each heard the shower turn on upstairs as Alaric's heavier footsteps entered the bathroom within the hallway and the scent of pot roast cooked steadily within the slow cooker. Silas' expression was somewhat tortured, his gaze steadily jumping between everyone's faces as he searched for the right words. His voice was steady and sure.

"Someone is watching and waiting, and when the perfect opportunity arises, the enemy will gain the upper hand." His eyes locked onto Rome, "You'll yield for her. I see nothing once you drop to your knees in surrender."

Akio spoke up as he shoved a short sword into the sheath tied to his back. "What do you mean he yields for her? Yields what? The war?"

"It's unclear. All I know is that our king yields, and everything goes black. I don't see an ending, nor do I see how we get to that point. It's all flashes of events that have yet to occur, the future changing swiftly with each breath we take. Nothing set in stone yet set by fate."

"You're not making much sense once again, Si." Maverick snarled as he zipped up his black leather motorcycle jacket before swiping a hand across his face in annoyance.

"Does he ever?" Cairo quipped and plucked at the fabric of his black suit to remove the lint he could see within the material.

Rome pondered Silas's words. Was the mysterious vehicle a part of that vision? Is that who was waiting and watching for the perfect opportunity to arise? His gaze flew to the window where he'd first spotted the van and frowned, a part of him hating that he didn't have the sight as well. Maybe if he could see what Silas saw, he could better understand what Silas meant, but he knew it wasn't possible. The future was a fickle bitch, and Rome was nowhere close to accessing that power, no matter how hard he'd tried in the past. Having multiple abilities had its perks, but some of the gifts he had Rome would never be capable of accessing, although he'd tried for many years.

"When do they gain the upper hand, Silas?" Rome glanced toward the entrance into the kitchen as Alara came into view with a worried expression on her face. She had clearly overheard their conversation and wanted to know what was happening.

262

"Could be tonight, could be three nights from now, or maybe a month from now. It's unclear, sir."

"I see." He ran his thumb across his bottom lip, his gaze on Alara, "Tonight will still go as any other night. Hunt in twos and call for me the moment anything goes wrong that can't be handled. Silas, you'll be with Akio, and the rest of you pair up with whoever you'd like." His eyes shot to Maverick, "Mav, you'll fly solo tonight, but I'll pop in occasionally to make sure you're alright."

"My King," Amirishka spoke up and moved forward, yet he stopped her with a stern look and a slight shake of his head.

"No, Ami, you'll watch my mate and her family as I've ordered."

She stepped back immediately, her eyes dropping to the floor before she nodded. "Yes, my King."

"So formal." Akio chuckled and continued to strap blades to his body.

Rome shook his head in annoyance and tried not to let the sadness within Amirishka's expression and slouched shoulders affect him by focusing instead on the woman who currently ruled his every thought.

She was biting at her bottom lip nervously while tugging on the hem of her shirt, her gaze snapping nervously between him and Amirishka before she spoke softly. "I think we should talk, Romulus." She stepped back into the kitchen and began cleaning up the mess she'd made while cooking.

He headed for the kitchen without a second thought but made sure to push a single telepathic command into the minds of his guardians across the globe. *"Be vigilant tonight and allow no distractions."* Several acknowledgments came through to him—including from the warriors around the room—before they each headed out for the night. He would join them just as soon as he spoke to his nervous mate.

He approached her at the sink from behind and gently wrapped his arms around her shoulders and throat before placing a kiss on the back of her head. He inhaled slowly, taking in the light, airy scent of lilac that always seemed to cling to her. She always smelled of fresh flowers, primarily lilacs, and the smell always hardened him to the point of pain as he remembered the feeling of being inside her.

"From what I've learned over the years, women who usually utter the words' we need to talk' don't typically lead to a good conversation," He whispered.

"Ami should be going as well. You should have all of your warriors out there protecting the world from the atrocities of what Titan and the Rogues are capable of," she stated and scrubbed at the dish within her hands. "I don't need protection while I'm here. I can protect myself."

Those weren't the words he'd been expecting, and as shy and nervous as she got around them sometimes, he also knew she had a spine as hard as steel. "I know you can, little flower, but that doesn't mean you can't at least have backup."

"Backup for what exactly? You told me I was safe here, plus I'm sure Alaric would never let anything happen to me."

"It would simply be a precaution that would put my mind at ease. And what exactly would your sick brother do to protect you? He still needs you to heal him nearly every day. I won't leave anything to chance when it comes to you."

He quickly got frustrated with their position, removed the new dish she held in her hands, and placed it back into the sudsy water before he spun her around to gaze into her eyes. A slight frown tugged at the edge of her lips as her eyes constantly shifted away from him. He wouldn't have that. Rome took her chin in hand, pressed a delicate kiss to her lips, and groaned at their plushness.

"If anything should happen to you, I would burn the world to the ground and stop at nothing to kill whoever thought it wise to hurt you. I know you know that, so why not just indulge me?" He spoke against her lips and listened as Amirishka turned on the television to drown out their voices.

He knew she could still hear them. There was no way she couldn't with her supernatural hearing, but he knew it was her way of attempting not to eavesdrop and instead have a distraction from their conversation.

"I don't know anything about relationships, but I don't think this is normal, Romulus. You shouldn't put me before your duty. That came before I ever existed," she pressed her hands against the fabric of his leather peacoat right over his abs and felt the muscles clench beneath her palms. "But I can see you won't be swayed by my words, so fine…Ami can stay, but you need to go."

"As soon as you stop keeping things from me, we'll be getting a lot closer than we already are." He nipped at her bottom lip with his fang and smirked when she shuddered against him. "And I'll always put you before the rest of the world. You are my mate. Without you, everything would cease to matter for me but know that I won't be a man that gets led around by his dick little flower." He tightened his hand on her chin and snarled his next few words. "Don't underestimate the lengths to which I would go for you and because of you."

Her hands tightened within the fabric of his coat as he took her lips beneath his in a brutal kiss. He threaded his fingers through her hair and groaned when her body became pliant against his own. She practically melted for him. The need to take more and indulge in everything that was her sang through his blood before he forced himself to draw back.

"Be safe," she whispered, her lips brushing seductively against his chin.

With reluctance, he kissed her once more and left before the temptation to stay became too much.

VAN SCIVE, New Jersey, wasn't a large county, but it was large enough to allow the Guardians to hunt throughout different quadrants. Rome wanted to stick as close to home as possible, but he knew he needed to head more into the city where the Rogues would attempt to find their victims for the night. They didn't normally hunt in suburban areas. Not to say it wasn't possible, but it was definitely few and far between.

It was true that he'd been lax in his duty for the past few nights or even weeks. The fact that the Gods had yet to reprimand him for his negligence wasn't lost on him. He was failing himself, his people, and the humans he was responsible for protecting. He knew that, and still, he allowed Alara to muddle his mind, and make him forget his duties as he fell under the spell of her allure. She filled his thoughts daily. Sometimes now, all he could think of was fucking her into oblivion, nurturing her, and protecting her from all harm. At the same time, Rome wanted to learn every one of her secrets until she lay vulnerable and bare to him. She had become his everything and he refused to feel any type of remorse for that fact.

Without a thought, he dematerialized and appeared in the alley behind a liquor store in the busiest city within his county. It was many miles away from home, but he knew it was the prime area for hunting. The sound of a muffled scream several feet away was proof of that. Rome whipped around, his coat flaps flying open behind him as he shot through the alley towards the sound. He removed a dagger from one of the hidden pockets of his peacoat as his eyes took everything in. The path was dark, filled with the rank smell of an animal carcass that had probably been there for weeks and the overwhelming smell of body odor and trash. The scent that really captured and held his attention was the unmistakable smell of fresh human blood. It was tinged with fear. As he approached a dumpster in the far corner, that fear hung heavily within the area. Heavy slurping noises and crazed snarls could be heard over the ramble of cars coming and going a block away as he headed deeper into the darkness.

Huddled behind the metal bin was a large male wearing dark jeans and a short-sleeved shirt that showed off bulging muscles securely wrapped around a more diminutive form, his fangs buried so deeply within her neck that the possibility of screaming again was now lost to her. He hadn't yet noticed Rome's arrival, but the woman had when her bright green gaze landed on him and widened with hope. He pushed calming thoughts into her mind, instantly forcing her into a state of such relaxation that she'd no longer feel the pain of the bite or even realize what was happening to her. If things went well, he'd be able to erase the interaction entirely from her cerebral cortex before sending her on her way, but he had to handle the fiend that currently had a death grip on her.

With her taken care of, Rome focused on the man and penetrated the layers of his mind, but it wasn't easy. He was much stronger than anticipated. That seemed to be happening a lot lately. He didn't want the Rogue to realize that he was now inside his head, but when he saw a familiar face, his entire being locked up in shock. Why was this Rogue's thought process focused on his biggest enemy, Lukas fucking Titan? There was no way he could just kill him now. He needed information. Information he damn well couldn't get from a dead man.

Being not just the King of Eternals but the strongest and eldest of his kind, Rome had a range of powers that sometimes even he forgot just what he was capable of. There were abilities he had that he rarely used; for instance, his ability to coerce thoughts to fit his narrative. Telepathy was a potent ability he used daily, but it was just to read the thoughts of others as well as push thoughts into one's mind. What he had just done to the woman's mind, he now had to do to the Rogue, and that wouldn't be as easy to accomplish. Rogues had natural barriers that made it hard for telepaths to breach, and usually, they could feel it the moment someone else was walking through their thoughts. The one before him hadn't yet realized, and that's what gave Rome the advantage.

He pushed the thought of fullness into his jumbled mind and tried to accomplish the unthinkable. Rome needed the fiend to believe he was full and satisfied and that the woman beneath his fangs was now dead. It took precious seconds, but it happened. The Rogue retracted his fangs and allowed the woman to slump to the ground before Rome struck fast and hard. He reached out, snagging the bastard around the throat with one of his large hands as he pulled out his blade and held the silver tip against his jugular. The smell and sound of burning flesh was instant. Like Eternals, Rogues also had an aversion to the substance, but in a larger capacity. Rome could hear the slight beat of the woman's heart and knew that she still lived, so this meant the Rogue was a newborn not yet familiar with using the heightened senses he now had. If he had used his senses, he would have realized that the woman still lived, which also explained how Rome could sneak up on him during a feeding.

"What's your name?" Rome snarled directly into his ear and waited with bated breath.

The vamp shifted slightly beneath his hold, causing Rome to tense in preparation. It would have been easier to kill him outright, but he knew that would be a mistake. He was important. He knew things about his greatest enemy. Rome's instincts were screaming at him, telling him that this man had answers he needed. Answers that might give him a foothold within this war with Titan and the monsters they'd created.

"I won't ask again. Give me a name."

"It's Ethan. Ethan Jennings."

CHAPTER
TWENTY-SEVEN

He couldn't believe he'd been so stupid as to trust her, to let her worm her way into his heart and take over every little bit of his life. He'd allowed it, and now he knew the truth. Alara wasn't as innocent as she portrayed herself to be. He'd fallen for her beauty, fallen for her mind, and fallen for the ideal of the perfect mate. She wasn't perfect though was she? He was questioning everything he thought he knew now. The Gods had once told him that a mate was paired with an Eternal based on many things. Genetic compatibility was the main thing. He wasn't sure how it was done, but he knew powers affected the match, as well as scent, and taste. Alara matched everything he'd ever wanted in a mate, yet she chose to lie, mislead, and withhold information from him. She was beginning to remind him of his enemy. The more he learned the more his vision blurred with how he felt and what the truth revealed. And from a Rogue, no less.

He snarled, threw another dagger across the room, and watched as it sank into Ethan's broad shoulder and embedded into the wall behind him. A scream pierced the air of the abandoned building they'd found themselves in. After ensuring the human woman was cleaned up and found by the proper authorities, Rome flashed them into an abandoned warehouse that had seen better days. Evidently, no one had stepped inside the small space in years. Boards covered the windows and doors, dust covered every surface, and the air was staler than a loaf of bread that had been left out overnight, but here, no one would bother them. Unless, of course, they heard the screams.

"I've told you before, Ethan. I need silence to work; the quieter you are, the less pain I'll inflict." Rome stated as he pulled another blade from his jacket and twirled it around as he paced. "Let's start from the beginning again, shall we."

"Fuck man, I've told you everything I know." Ethan groaned, his body hanging from the multiple blades that had been impaled through his flesh and embedded into the wall. A pool of blood lay beneath him as the smell of burning flesh and fear filled the place.

"I don't feel like that's the truth, though, Ethan. You understand why I have trust issues now, don't you? So tell me why Titan wants my mate so badly…besides the fact that your boss wants to impregnate what I consider to be mine."

"It's not my fault that sneaky little cunt played you, but I'm telling you the truth. I've been telling you the truth since the beginning. I've worked for Lukas since I was eighteen years old before I became a part of his personal guard when I reached the age of twenty-one. I didn't learn about the siblings until I was in the inner circle. She was never supposed to be anything to him until that crazy bastard killed his own mother and took over the business. They were just supposed to be test subjects that could eventually help us in the war between humans and your kind, but Lukas wanted more. He wanted Subject One in a way that confused us all. He became obsessive and compulsive when it came to her. I don't know if she's got a magical pussy or what, but that asshole was hooked. Hooked to the point of self-destruction."

A blade flew through the air and pierced the bone of Ethan's kneecap, causing him to scream out again as Rome launched through the air and sank another blade deep into his side. He made sure not to nick any of the main organs. He didn't want him dying just yet. Rome's voice was eerily calm when he spoke. "Disrespect her again, and your life ends here and now."

"You'll be killing me anyway," Ethan gasped, "at least this way, it'll go quick instead of this slow torture you seem to be set on."

"You misunderstand," he stepped back with a frown, "nothing in the way you die will be quick if you continue to speak negatively about my woman. Yes, she has withheld certain things, but that is between her and I, not you. So no, you don't get to speak negatively about her unless, of course, you're beginning to love how I make you scream. You're running out of space for me to sink my blades, but trust me when I say I'll heal you over and over again until I'm satisfied, and only then will I end your miserable life and turn you into ash. Do you get it now? I can make this last however long I wish." Rome watched as the reality of the situation sank into his mind. His eyes widened in abject horror, and the smell of his fear intensified. Ethan was finally getting it. Yes, he would die here regardless, but the matter of how was entirely up to him.

"I understand."

"Good."

Rome turned his back and stepped away with a smile. As soon as he faced his enemy once again, he used his telekinesis to extract the seven blades that impaled his prey's body to the wall and sent them clattering to the floor.

Ethan fell, no longer being held up by the weapons, and groaned softly before he forced himself into a seated position with his back leaning heavily against the wall as blood continued to leak from his open wounds. "What else do you want to know?"

"This new drug. Explain it to me again."

"Lukas realized that we were losing the war and needed to devise a weapon to somehow slow you guys down because the vamps under his employ weren't doing their jobs well enough. They weren't doing anything that we hadn't already tried. Sure, they lent us strength, but in the long run, we were still losing people, and every time that bastard got disappointed in results, he killed them off. Not just Rogues but humans, too. No one was safe from his wrath. The virus didn't come into play until after subject one escaped. That pushed him to get that meek scientist to create it from her blood."

"So, from my understanding, my mate's blood fuels this virus?"

"Yes, along with a heavy sedative. We tested it on the vamps and learned that it had enough juice to instantly kill them, and when your female warrior was shot, we saw her go down. No one's seen her since. Did she die? Has he finally created a drug to rid the world of you and your people?"

Rome remained silent as his mind processed the information. It didn't sound like a lie; in fact, it made so much sense that he couldn't understand why he hadn't seen it before. God, he was so damn dense. His anger flared, energy pulsing from him in waves, yet he had no control over that. He didn't want control, not right now, anyway. He wanted retribution. She'd known. All this time, his mate had known precisely what drug was laced within the darts that harmed his people. All this time, she'd lied to him, acting as if she knew nothing when she was the reason it existed in the first place. She had become Titan's Trojan horse and she had known.

"Are you going to kill me now?"

Rome shook his head. "No, I have a few more questions. When were you supposed to report back to Titan, and are there more Kindred under his control?" He watched him, taking in the small movements and winces of pain that crossed his features before he had the nerve to actually smirk.

"Fuck Lukas and the damn company!" He gasped when the pain moved throughout his entire body before he focused on his words enough to push the rest of his statement out. "He turned me into this abomination after I failed to recapture subjects two and three. This was my punishment, so to hell with Titan and everything they stand for, along with the rest of those freaks trapped in cages!"

That explains the newborn status and his inability to use all of his senses, which could also explain his lack of healing cells. Just like Eternals, Rogues were capable of healing themselves, but only the older ones who had learned to use them properly.

"How many more does he have?"

"They weren't under my preview, but I know there were over a handful of them. Only the siblings were mine to worry about."

Rome filed the information away for a later date before a frown tightened his features. "How did he turn you, Ethan?"

He visibly shuddered. "He's got some poor sonofabitch shackled up in the lowest levels of the building where he forces him to change people. I was sent into his room, and when I came out, I was nearly dead. A few hours passed, and before I knew it, I was this freak show that couldn't go a day without draining someone dry, and the sun was now my worst enemy. Sometimes, the ones that go in never come out breathing again. I wish that would have been the case for me, but I could never be that lucky, could I?"

"I don't feel sorry for the hand you were dealt. Maybe that's just karma for you."

Without using too much of his telekinetic power, Rome slashed his hand through the air, sent a burst of pure energy straight into Ethan's throat, and watched as his head tumbled to the floor as it severed from his body. Only seconds went by before the body slowly began to disintegrate until only the clothing that had covered him, along with the blood he had already lost, remained.

He glanced towards the boarded windows and knew he had only a few hours left until the sun would breach the horizon and send the Rogues slinking back to whatever hellhole they'd climbed out of for the night. If he played his cards right, he had time to kill a few dozen more. He collected his daggers from the cement ground and dematerialized before landing in a darkened corner of the local college campus where they hadn't yet fixed a few of their lights. The college was several blocks from where he'd found Ethan, and it was a prime hunting area for vamps to find unsuspecting humans. College kids were easy prey thanks to the long studying hours and late nights of drinking until drunkenness. A human with impaired judgment was far easier to control than one who was not.

Rome flashed onto the roof to scan the grounds below and listened for any disturbance within the area. The campus wasn't overly large, but it was large enough to need several Guardians to monitor it. This was usually Akio and Maverick's favorite place to hunt because of the slew of vamps that would walk the grounds. Normally, Rome stayed clear of the area to give his warriors more of a chance to hone their skills. Each of them was formidable in their own right, but it didn't mean they couldn't use the practice as well.

A noise to his left drew his attention as he focused on the slight form of a woman rushing for the library steps as she pulled her jacket tighter to her body. Four men followed closely behind her but far enough away to not be much of a concern if she happened to look back. Which she didn't, but Rome knew better. They were Rogues, and they were hunting her. He could make out the slight hue of their red eyes as they watched her, smell the scent of old blood attached to their clothing, and barely made out the peek of fangs when one of them smiled softly. The snow crunched beneath their feet as their gait sped up. Any moment now, one of them would put on a burst of speed, sweep her off her feet before anyone could take notice, and rush off with her to feed for the night. They'd most likely share her since they were hunting together. Rome had to prevent that from happening. He pushed a thought into her mind to keep walking no matter what she might hear as he dropped from the building and pulled his soto swords from the scabbard hanging from his back. The four Rogues froze before their lips peeled back from their fangs to snarl aggressively. Rome smiled, glad for the fight, and launched towards them with his blades raised and ready.

This was precisely what he needed to rid his thoughts of Alara's deception. He needed the anger and blows that would indeed land in the scuffle. He needed to beat someone within an inch of their life and do it repeatedly until the aggression left his body. The distraction from his thoughts was a blessing he hoped would last him throughout the night because the anger he still felt about the situation would do him no good if he returned without expelling some of the excess energy that ran through him. He needed calm before approaching his woman, even if it took him all night.

Alara sipped her French vanilla coffee; the TV droning on from the living room could be heard as she stared out into the backyard through a window over the kitchen sink. The snow had stopped falling at some point through the night, yet blankets of it covered the ground. At least three inches of the white substance. She would never tire of the sight; it was beautiful, but worry filled her. Rome hadn't returned from last night's hunt. She knew because she'd checked every room and found him nowhere within the house, and with the rest of the Guardians sleeping through the sun, it wasn't as if she could ask one of them. Alara had tried several times to reach out to him telepathically and had heard nothing back. She just knew something wasn't right. He would never leave her to worry. He always came home to her.

Always.

She turned at the sound of footsteps approaching and smiled when Alondra and Alaric came into view, yet her smile quickly vanished as concern filled her expression. Her brother wasn't looking too good. Dark circles framed his eyes, his lips were pinched, and pain practically radiated from his skin. She could feel the virus feeding off of him from across the room. It called to her and made her stomach turn in disgust. She hated what Titan had created because of her tainted blood.

She quickly placed her cup on the counter and crossed the kitchen when Alaric sat at the large island countertop and put his head atop the cool surface. "When did the pain return?" She questioned with a frown as she placed her hands on either side of his head.

"It doesn't matter," He groaned as he clutched his side.

"It matters, dammit. You have to tell me when this gets bad so I can stop the virus before it spreads to your heart. Do you want to die!?"

"Of course not, but we also know there's no cure, Alara, and I don't want to weaken you and cause you pain by healing me."

She wanted to slap him. She was furious and tried not to let it show as she focused all her attention on attempting to heal the parts of him that were infected with the virus. It was a slow-moving

277

process. Alara knew she couldn't heal every infected cell, but as soon as she was sure she'd healed as much as she could, she dropped her hands and swayed backward when she felt exhaustion pulling at her. She felt her sister supporting her weight but frowned when she felt something hard pressed up against her spine. She stilled the moment Alondra whispered into her ear.

"If you do anything besides what I tell you to do, I'll shoot you and leave you bleeding out before I kill everyone else as they sleep. Nod if you understand me, little sister."

Alara nodded stiffly as the urge to fight roared through her like an open flame, but Alaric's bent-over form kept her in line. She couldn't risk him or anyone else being hurt because of her inability to follow directions. She would never forgive herself. She tried to reach out to Rome telepathically and felt nothing, so she focused on her brother to get him to sense the danger.

That was a mistake.

Alondra dug the gun into her back and tsked softly. "We're on the same wavelength, little sis. I can sense it anytime you two talk telepathically, so I suggest you cut that shit out now and put your hands back where they were. I need you to knock big brother out but don't kill him, just put him to sleep, and then we'll be taking a ride somewhere."

She did as she was told and gently placed her hand on the back of his neck before she started slowly siphoning his energy. She wasn't sure what taking his energy would do to him since he was already weakened from the virus. With him already bent over the counter with his head resting on his arms, it was easy to tell when he fell unconscious beneath her touch. His body slumped harder within the chair as his breathing turned deeper. She checked his vitals, afraid that she'd siphoned too much, but found his heart beating steadily before she pulled away reluctantly. The weakness she'd experienced moments ago evaporated as his energy filled her before a cold band encircled her throat and clicked into place. The power disappeared, cutting off abruptly as if it had never happened. Alara gasped in shock as her hands flew to her throat and encountered the familiar feel of the golden collar that had graced her neck for most of her life. A sick ball of dread settled within the pit of her stomach as the implications of what was happening finally sunk in.

Her sister worked for Titan. Rome had been right. Her sister was a mole.

Tears gathered in her eyes, but she pushed them back as Alondra gripped her arm and pushed her towards the front door. She stumbled slightly and gasped in pain when the gun pressed into her back more forcefully. She tried to drag her feet and failed miserably when her head was jerked up roughly by her hair, and she was forced onto the balls of her feet from the tension.

Her sister snarled into her ear. "If you don't get moving, I'll shoot our dear brother instead of leaving him there for them to find. Your choice, Alara! Get moving now, or watch Alaric bleed out."

The tears fell freely this time as she moved with new purpose towards the door. She opened it and instantly shivered from the cold wind that blew inside. The thin black leggings and blue long-sleeved sweater did little to protect her from the elements, but what made it worse was the thin socks that covered her feet. She was essentially barefoot without the ability to even draw on her own energy to conserve body heat.

She shivered and wrapped her arms around her body in a sore attempt to stay warm. "Where are we going?"

"See that black truck parked down the street?" Alondra indicated towards the lone vehicle idling by the curb, "We're going to walk over there and climb into the back."

The cold and fear fought within her the closer they got to the blacked-out vehicle. The tears came harder now as she attempted to turn her head and get one more look at the house that had become her home but cried out when Alondra stabbed the gun into her back even harder. This wasn't her sister, at least not the one she'd imagined for herself. No, this woman was the enemy. Now that her rose-colored glasses were no longer affecting her, Alara could feel the malice that leaked from her. She was exactly what Rome had warned her about. A wolf in sheep's clothing. Okay, maybe he hadn't expressed it in exactly that way, but he'd tried to warn her about trusting the family she hardly knew.

The moment she approached the truck, the back door swung open, and Lukas Titan's cold green eyes met hers. A smirk pulled at his thin lips as she was pushed into the vehicle until she practically sat atop his lap before she slid to the floor at his feet. Alondra climbed in behind her and closed the door. Tinted windows and heat surrounded her as she stared into his fathomless gaze. Her fear morphed into terror, but Alara dared not speak. She didn't even dare to move when all she really wanted to do was fight him, the two soldiers who took up the front seats, and her backstabbing sister. She wanted to lash out. She wanted to show them that they'd messed with the wrong Kindred, but staring into his gaze chilled her to the bone more effectively than the weather ever could, and the collar around her throat reminded her that she was just as powerless as she had been before.

His voice was sickly sweet when he spoke, making the ball of dread in her stomach burst to spread throughout her entire body. "When subject three told me she could reacquire you, I wasn't convinced, but color me surprised. It worked out perfectly, didn't it." He caressed her chin and chuckled when she shrank away from him. "Let's see if you can be better behaved this time around. Shall we?"

She shook her head and opened her mouth to speak when his gaze hardened, and pain spread throughout her entire body. Currents of electricity slammed into her as he pressed the button of a remote. Her hands pulled frantically at the collar around her throat as her body jerked and spots danced within her gaze. Darkness enveloped her, her heart stuttered within her chest, and her body slumped into unconsciousness.

No more fear, pain, or thoughts were running rampant within her mind. Alara now understood that she would never be truly free, not as long as Titan existed.

CHAPTER
TWENTY-EIGHT

Her entire body ached. That was the first thing she noticed when she came to. The second thing was the feel of something cool wrapped around her ankle and the feel of something rough like sandpaper against her skin. Alara's eyes flew open, and bright lights pierced her pupils as she took in her surroundings and felt the moment her stomach dropped out from under her. She was in a room that was more like a box with pale white walls. There was a bucket in one corner that smelled like piss and despair, and when she glanced down at her ankle, it was to find a steel manacle wrapped around it along with a length of chain connected to the post of the bed she found herself laying across. The mattress was stiff beneath her as she plucked at the generic hospital garb that covered her body before she froze and zeroed in on the lone woman who sat in a chair near the door. It returned to her then, having to siphon Alaric's energy, leaving Rome's home, and being taken against her will by Titan. Worst of all, she remembered the betrayal from her sister, who was watching her as if she were a bug under a microscope.

"Why?" Alara questioned as she rubbed at her dry throat. "Why would you do this?"

How long had she been out, and why did it feel like glass was serrating her esophagus? She felt the collar around her throat and still tried to access her power, but she felt nothing. No, it was worse than that. She felt empty. The feeling of incompleteness resonated within her, but most of all, she hated what Rome might think when he returned to find her gone. He would be devastated. He'd probably rain fire down upon the earth until he found her, or at least that's what she hoped would happen. She needed to have hope that he would find her brother and know that she had been taken. She held onto that hope, knowing that if she didn't, her mind would go to dark places better left forgotten.

Alondra cleared her throat, uncrossed her legs to lean forward, and braced her elbows on her knees. "You want to know why I betrayed you and brought you back to Titan? You want to know why I lied and deceived the people who supposedly 'saved me'?" She scoffed, "Well, the answer is simple. I picked the lesser evil. I chose the enemy I knew instead of the enemy I didn't."

"But the Eternals aren't evil! They pro-"

"You know nothing!" Alondra snapped as she came to her feet. Her eyes were narrowed in anger, her hands clenched at her sides as she began to pace the small confines of the room. "They're liars, Alara. They're deceitful, evil creatures that think they're protecting humanity from Titan when it's really the other way around; being with you these past few days has proven as much. You hated how he treated us, yet he never stopped and continued painting me as the enemy. Why? Because I refused to be vulnerable and let my walls down? Well, I'm sure he's regretting how he treated me now, huh?"

Alara glared back, not understanding where her anger came from and why she was so against Rome and his people. Sure, she'd essentially been a prisoner, but Rome and his people had never hurt her. Not once. "I guess I should have listened to him instead of wanting that familial connection, but since you seem to have all the answers, why don't you explain it to me then? If Titan is so great, why'd you bring me back to the man who plans to rape and impregnate me just to get a hold of any children I might bear? If Titan is the lesser evil, why did Alaric get us out?

Why did he return for you and risk his life again just to get you out?"

Alondra frowned and paused in her pacing. "No, that's not right. Lukas told me he had no intentions of hurting you; he promised me that if I brought you back, he'd keep us safe and show you your true potential. And our dear brother only came back for me out of guilt. To me, getting you out was all that mattered to him, and he came back because if you ever did find out about me you might not have forgiven him for leaving me behind. That's what Lukas told me."

"Alaric wouldn't do that. And you believed Lukas's lies? You actually believe him after being a prisoner to him and this corporation for the entirety of our lives? You believe the man who forced me to kill and then hurt me when I didn't comply? I can't even imagine what he did to you or what he forced you to do. When did he tell you this? When did he promise you anything?"

It didn't make sense. Alondra had to be brainwashed or suffering from some type of Stockholm syndrome. That was the only thing that would make sense as to why her sister was so dead set on being with Titan.

"I won't lie and say that Lukas hasn't done terrible things; he has. I know he has, but those creatures that call themselves Guardians have done worse. Did you know they are responsible for some of the wars throughout the years?"

"What are you talking about? I don't know anything about any wars besides the one we're currently in with Titan and the Rogues they created."

"Titan didn't create Rogues. Rome did."

Alara frowned. "No, there's no way he'd ever do that." She climbed from the bed and came to a stand with the chain scraping loudly against the cold tiled floor.

Her sister chuckled harshly and moved a step closer. Her eyes were glassy, movements shifty, and sweat beaded her brow and upper lip. Something was going on with her. Alara tried to make sense of her crazed expression and short temper. This wasn't the woman she'd started to get to know in recent days. "I'm guessing he never told you that little tidbit of information, did he? You see, that's the thing about the Eternals. They're stronger than us, faster than us, and exceptionally resilient, and they know it, but ultimately, they're all liars who profit off of our ignorance as the lesser species. As long as humans are unaware of them, they have free reign to feed off of us and kill us. We're nothing but entertainment and food to them."

"You're not making any sense." She swung her arm out, indicating the space around them. "You did all of this for what, Alondra? Some misguided information that these bastards put into your head? Rome had nothing to do with the creation of those savages; that's all on Titan. You have to believe me and get us out of here before something happens that can't be undone." She attempted to soften her words, hoping to get through to her. "Lukas will hurt you the moment you fail him, and he'll hurt me too; I can promise you that. You saw what he did to me in the truck. He could have killed me. Is that what you want? My death?"

"He wouldn't have killed you. He just needed to teach you a lesson. He needs you."

"Teach me a lesson? Alondra, he nearly killed me! What could he possibly need me for when he has your loyalty?"

She shrugged. "I wasn't given that information, but I do know he doesn't plan on harming you."

"He's already done that. What did you think electrocuting me did? This isn't a game and I don't want to be his captive again, don't you understand that?"

She tried to keep the panic out of her voice to avoid letting her true feelings show. She wanted to be brave, or at least she tried to present an image of bravery. She found herself tugging at the scratchy fabric of her shirt and forced her hands to her sides as the sound of a lock disengaging came from the door before it opened to reveal the man that starred in her every nightmare. Lukas smiled as he entered the room, leaving the door open to an equally bare hallway. He was leaning heavily against his cane, a three-piece gray suit covering his body, and a pair of black Ferragamo shoes that brought the look together. His green gaze stroked over her body like a lover's caress as he ambled close enough to touch her. Alara forced herself not to retreat, although every part of her told her to move back and away from the dangerous man before her.

"Back home at last," he chuckled, his voice sliding over her skin like hot grease from a frying pan. "Your sister tells me you've been sharing a bed with my enemy. Is this true? Did you give him what I know belongs to me?"

She didn't answer. The fear racing through her made her blood run cold with dread as she pictured all of the things Lukas would do to punish her for what he saw as an infraction. For years, he'd drilled into her head that they were meant to be and that she was his and would be his until she died, yet she had never believed him. She'd never fallen under the guise of his delusions, although she'd pretended to play the part of the listening ear and submissive woman. Alara had never been the submissive woman for him, just cautious. Cautious enough to realize that he would and could inflict and enjoy the pain he would ultimately cause her.

He always did.

Lukas gripped her by the chin and yanked her close, ensuring she felt the ridge in his pants from the hard-on he sported. His voice was a snarl when he spoke, "Answer me, Alara; did that bastard touch what belongs to me, and did you allow it?"

She risked a glance at her sister to see if she took notice of what was happening but found Alondra's gaze riveted to the floor in complete and utter submission. It was as if she'd been trained to simply obey even if words had never been spoken. She was like a robot, yet Alara could see the fear within her and knew that it matched her own. Her sister was just as trapped as she was, but another chain shackled her. A shackle of the mind.

His hand tightened on her chin, making her face ache in tandem with her pounding heart. "Would you like to feel the electricity pulsing through you again? Is that it? You miss the bite of pain it grants you?" He smiled and ran a finger over her plush bottom lip with a wicked smirk that turned her stomach. "Let me remedy that."

He stepped back and slipped his hand into his pocket. Alara

knew what would happen next and simply braced herself as a powerful electric current snapped throughout her body and sent her to her knees. She cried out from the pain. This was worse than all the times before. She felt it in her marrow as every joint within her locked up, and her teeth sank into her tongue and drew blood. She wanted to cry out and scream from the pain that tore through her, but just as quickly as it started, it ended, and she found herself lying on the floor with drool and blood leaking from her parted lips. Her lungs heaved as she struggled to catch her breath, and her eyes closed to force back the flood of tears that followed. He always did love her tears. Her hand reached up to grip the collar around her throat as the need to kill him slammed through her with a vengeance. She would kill him before she escaped again because, this time, she'd fight harder to free herself. She wouldn't lie down and take whatever he dished out this time. This time, she would fight for her freedom and earn it.

Alara carefully shifted onto her hands and knees, yet she couldn't climb to her feet or even push herself up. She was too unsteady, too confident in her knowledge that if she attempted to stand, she'd probably fall face-first into the ground because of how sluggish and weak her body now felt. She wouldn't give him the satisfaction.

Lukas stepped forward, his black Ferragamo shoes coming into focus as he stepped on her hands and forced a small cry from her lips. "We're going to head upstairs where you will contact Romulus and get him here. He is to come alone and unarmed, or I will kill you where you stand. Is that understood?"

She nodded meekly before he walked away without once looking back to see if they were following. At least for now, she would obey him to avoid his anger. Alondra dropped down beside her as she pulled a small key from the pocket of her jeans and released her from the chain that kept her shackled to the bed. "Get up and follow me, or I can't help you," Her sister whispered so softly that she almost didn't catch her words before she stood and moved for the door.

Alara struggled to her feet, her breath laboring with every move she made until she felt she could walk without feeling her bones scrap together in agony. She opened her mouth to speak when her sister cut her a look from the corner of her eye and quickly left the room as if her heels were on fire. She wasn't sure what that had been or what she'd meant, but with no choice left but to follow, she headed out into the empty hallway. No other people were wandering about, and there were no windows to see out of. The hallway seemed to stretch forever, with multiple doors along the corridor. It was leading upwards as if they were underground.

She silently followed behind them until they reached an elevator. That foreboding feeling she felt intensified. She didn't want to join them. She wanted to get as far away from them as possible because even though her sister had whispered words like she meant to help, she didn't believe them. She'd believed in her lies before, and look where that had gotten her. No, she'd do things with a clearer head this time around. Lukas had mentioned something about going upstairs.

Alara stepped into the elevator and paid attention to the button he pushed before they headed up, but she also noticed the finger-print scanner. Something scratched at the back of her mind, something she couldn't help but question. "How are you expecting me to get in touch with him?"

Lukas smirked. "Because of their weakness to silver, I was able to build this base from the ground up. I installed a few fail-safes to ensure their senses could never fully detect what was happening inside if they happened to find it, so once we reach the upper levels, I'll turn off that power dampener of yours, and you'll get out a message to him. With the silver-lined walls your powers are useless in the lower levels."

"How do you know I can communicate with him?"

"Don't insult my intelligence, Alara. Your dear sister has already made me privy to your ability to telepathically speak with him, so that's what you'll do, and he'll come if he truly does care for you like she says he does."

She seethed on the inside as she pressed her back against the cool elevator wall. Tears threatened to fall at the betrayal that continued to come from all sides. How much had Alondra told him, and when was she able to do so? Questions zipped through her mind at warp speed as she tried to figure her way out of this. If she called Rome here, there was no telling what would happen to him. He couldn't be hurt because of her. His people needed him; humanity needed him, and she was unimportant. Irrelevant. She could die, and the world would never even notice.

Alara circled her arms around her waist and jerked when the elevator stopped and the doors opened up into an expansive room the size of an auditorium. Dim lights shined in from the skylights, showing her that the sun was slowly beginning to fall and that the snow had finally stopped, but rain now poured. The large ware-house held a metal examination table with silver shackles and a large computer connected to it. Three doctors manned the station but did not look up from their work as they exited the elevator and crossed the room. Her sister trailed off to the right and stood as she had before, with eyes cast down and her hands laying limply at her sides. Alara focused on Lukas as he placed his cane against the table before approaching her. Although it took effort, she stood still and stiffened further when he limped behind her and pressed himself against her back. A sick feeling settled within her as his arms banned around her body. He made sure not to touch her skin even as he pressed the tip of a blade not so gently against her throat.

His voice was a purr when he spoke. "Deactivate her power dampener, but the second it looks as if she plans to touch me, you send a shock so strong into her body that she may not survive it." Lukas pressed his lips against her throat before he shifted back slightly, "Call for him, Alara, and make sure to warn him that I will slit your throat the moment he tries to make a move against me."

She felt it the moment her collar was turned off. Her power flared through her like the starving beast that it was and warmed her in ways that brought a small smile to her face. It would be so easy to kill him now if she could just get access to his skin. If she could just touch him all of her fears would evaporate. Lukas must have felt a shift in the air because his arms tightened around her, and a new sound reached her before her gaze zeroed in on the soldier standing behind her sister with a gun pressed against her temple.

"I see I've got your attention now, so do what I've asked; Alara or your sister suffers the consequences instead of you."

There was laughter in his voice; she heard it, yet she knew this was no joke. He would kill Alondra without feeling an inch of remorse, and she'd be forced to watch her die. She couldn't live with that. She was still her sister even if she had betrayed her. Alara closed her eyes and focused on the man she yearned for as her heart fragmented into several million pieces and her mind filled with words she never thought she'd say to another living being. She needed to get them out in case she never had the opportunity to. He had to know how she felt.

"Romulus, I love you!"

CHAPTER
TWENTY-NINE

As soon as he knew the sun was descending from the sky to begin a new night within his city, Rome flashed into his bedroom and froze. He reached out with his senses to pinpoint the disturbance he felt in the air. He inhaled, the scent of his mate faint enough to send a sliver of shock through him as he flashed into the kitchen to find Alaric knocked out cold. He was slumped within a chair in front of the kitchen island, his body at an awkward angle yet still somehow staying in place without falling from his position to the floor. Rome looked him over for injuries and found none. He pushed healing energy into him and waited until Alaric's eyes snapped open. He leaped up from the seat, eyes wide with fear as he glanced around before landing on Rome.

"She took her. Dammit, I heard her whisper something, but I reacted too slowly." He ran a hand down his face and sighed heavily as his voice edged towards pain. "She took her Romulus."

Rome's blood ran cold at the words he had hoped to never hear. He wanted to ask questions, but he already knew the answer. He knew exactly who *she* was. He snarled and stepped away as he projected an energy shield around his body, and his powers lit up like beacons in the dark. The urge to lash out and destroy his enemies tugged at him like a dog with a bone. He should have come straight home. He should have given up on his need to keep hunting and returned to his mate, yet he hadn't. He could have protected her if he had been here, but he'd still been angry even after the sun had lifted into the sky and cast the demons away. He'd still been so full of mistrust and hurt that he'd flashed to the other side of the world where night had just begun so he could fight more of them.

One hundred and three.

That's how many rogues he'd killed within a fifteen hour period, and still, he'd wanted more bloodshed but instead had forced himself to return to his edge of the world and face his problems like a true male. He should have returned sooner. If he had, this would have never happened. Alara would still be with him, and her traitorous sister would still be under a watchful eye. He'd known it. All this time, he'd known that something was off about her. The way she held herself apart from everyone else, the look in her gaze when she thought no one was watching her. He'd seen it all, and still, he'd let her stay. He'd let her get close enough to his mate to take her away from him. A savage growl escaped him as he grabbed the nearest chair and tossed it across the room, but before it could shatter from the impact of hitting the wall, Erick was there, snatching it out of thin air before placing it back on the floor.

"What's happened?" He questioned with a frown as his red eyes scanned the room to locate the problem.

"My sister has taken Alara," Alaric stated.

Rome snarled again, dark thoughts pounding through his mind of all the things that could be happening to her before he forced a calm he didn't feel. He moved for the front door and simply stood there, head pressed against the wood as he lowered the shields around his mind in an attempt to locate her. She wasn't dead. He knew that with every fiber of his being, but he felt nothing. No sign of her mental signature hung around, and her scent had long since dissipated. His throat tightened, his nerves climbing higher as his fangs lengthened with a vengeance before the pressure of Erick's hand on his shoulder registered.

"My king, what would you have us do?"

What would he have them do? He didn't know. He didn't even know where to start, and that was tearing a hole through him that he wasn't sure he'd ever be able to fill. If they didn't find her before something happened to her, he'd end his life right then and there. At the thought of losing her to the inevitable death that all humans faced, a raw sound was ripped from him as his telekinetic energy built and crackled around him like a whip. Erick stepped back hesitantly as several other presences made themselves known, along with their voices.

"Sir," Cairo, always the person of reason, spoke up, "we can search the immediate area. They couldn't have gone too far."

"I do not sense her dammit! Something is blocking me." His voice was barely recognizable through the rumbling growls that refused to cease.

"This has to be the work of Titan." Amirishka stated, "That's the only thing that makes sense, and we had a feeling the sister wasn't what she seemed."

"Who else would it fucking be? They had to have gotten to her somehow!" Alaric paced around the room, his mind searching endlessly for even a small trace of his sister's mental presence.

Akio chuckled, "You're lucky Ami's currently on Rome's shit list, or she'd be cutting you from balls to sternum without a second thought, but since you fall under the category of untouchable, you're safe. For now."

"Would you shut the fuck up? This is serious!" Maverick glared as the power of his animal forms pushed and writhed against his frame as he fought for control.

Yes, Alara had hurt him. She'd lied and manipulated him in ways that made Rome question if what they'd been building between them had even been real, but when he thought of how she would look at him, he knew. He knew without a doubt that she was his, and he was hers. Maybe he could go far enough and say she loved him, but he needed to know why she would do any of this. Why would she keep the truth from him? He would find out just as soon as he located her, and then he would kill the people responsible for her disappearance. Even if that meant killing her sister.

Rome locked his gaze on Maverick's gold-glowing eyes. "Shift and find her, Mav. You contact me as soon as you can get a lock on her scent."

Maverick nodded and headed for the back door. He stepped out into the rain and shifted into a large Belgian Malinois with sleek fur before he took off like a bullet from a gun chamber. If anyone could pick up her scent, it would be him. He had the best sense of smell within the group, especially when he shifted.

"The rest of you, head out and find my mate by any means necessary," Rome ordered before he stalked into the kitchen to grab a glass of brandy he didn't actually need, but he needed to keep his hands busy before he did something reckless.

Each of his warriors left after strapping more weapons onto their bodies before he was once again alone with Alaric. In the back of his mind, a question thrived and spread through him before his eyes narrowed, and he found himself stalking Alaric until he had him pressed up against the wall with his hand wrapped around his throat. This seemed to be a familiar position for them. A position that could become very permanent if he didn't get the answers he desired.

"Are you in on it!?" He glowered as his eyes brightened further before he forced himself past the first layer of defense within Alaric's mind.

Alaric winced in pain as blood slowly dripped from his nose before he lowered his shields and allowed Rome complete and utter access. Rome wasted no time searching through every little crevice within his memories and thoughts before he pulled back and stared at him with a new respect. He knew he'd never truly like Alara's brother, but he could at least respect him, especially after learning everything Alaric had done to get them to this point. If not for him, he never would have met his mate, and for that, he was thankful beyond measure, but he'd been lying to them about something else. Something Alara would probably never forgive him for.

Alaric wiped at his nose as he spoke. "Did you find what you were looking for?"

"How have you been keeping it from her?"

"The same way you've been keeping things from her. Besides, she doesn't need to know how bad it really is. She'll have you in the end."

Rome simply stared back at him without uttering a single word. What could he say? Her brother was dying faster than they'd anticipated, and he was hiding it somehow, covering up the actual pain he was feeling daily. Alara's healing sessions only kept the virus from reaching his heart and other major organs, but each day she healed him, she only prolonged the pain in another sense. It appeared she had missed a vital organ, and Rome wouldn't be the one to tell her. He couldn't. It was Alaric's story to tell unless he chose a path that Rome wouldn't recommend.

He opened his mouth to give his opinion but stilled when Alara's voice whispered through his mind like a feather and wrapped around him like a cocoon. *"Romulus, I love you."*

He immediately jumped on the opportunity to speak with her and learn her whereabouts. *"Little flower, where are you? Show me."*

"You have to listen, please... he's threatened my sister. If not for that, I would have just allowed him to wipe me from the face of the earth, but I can't watch her die. I can't be the reason for any more deaths if I can help it, so please just come with no backup or weapons and surrender yourself."

"Show me where you are! Now, Alara." His order was met with silence, yet he knew she hadn't pulled away. *"Please, my love, show me."*

"Promise me first. Promise me you'll save Alondra. She's still my sister, no matter what she's done. She's just as much a victim as I am."

He couldn't promise her. No, that wasn't true. It wasn't that he couldn't. Rome wouldn't promise her something he couldn't deliver on. He had no inclination to save the woman who had betrayed his mate in ways he would never forgive. He wouldn't give her those words and mean them, but he would lie to get her back.

"I promise."

"Thank you."

Her voice in his mind was full of relief as the image of a barren warehouse filtered through his mind as he seemed to look through her eyes, when in fact he perused her memories. He wanted to inform Alaric of the new development, but he knew he'd insist on coming, and he couldn't risk him tagging along. He wouldn't lose her brother to Titan or anyone else, so he sent a mental broadcast to reach his warriors worldwide.

"I've located my mate. If anything should happen to me, my mantle falls to whomever the Gods deem worthy of the position. It has been an honor and a privilege to serve with you all."

He severed the connection to his people before anyone could get a word off. He didn't need the cavalry racing in to save him. He needed his people safe and as far away from Titan as possible. They would never survive what Titan would put them through; Lincoln almost hadn't. He wouldn't risk them when he still had to save the woman who had captured his heart.

Alaric's expression screwed up into a frown, and he stepped forward as if to grab him before Rome flashed away and out of reach. He must have picked up on the telepathic message as well without realizing it. With the picture of the warehouse within his mind, he forced his body to materialize before his enemy after hastily ridding himself of each of his weapons along the way. There was no telling where they would end up, and Rome cared little. The moment he appeared before Alara and the man who had forced his hand, he felt the presence of harmful silver all around him. He wanted to glance around and locate where it was coming from, but the sight of blood slowly trailing from his mate's neck ensured his vision never strayed, although he felt others within the room.

"Move an inch out of line, and I kill her here and now, Romulus. What do you say? Will you willing surrender?" Lukas chuckled as the blade pressed deeper, causing Alara to wince in pain as several more drops of her blood trickled down her throat.

Rome wanted to react and use his gift to wrap around the bastard's throat or heart and kill him slowly, but he knew that the moment Lukas sensed any type of influence over his body, he would slit Alara's throat. He would never survive losing her. He needed her to walk out of here alive, so he stood as still as he could and pushed all of his protective instincts into the back of his mind. His eyes lost their inhuman glow, and his fangs retracted before he could speak without a snarl.

"What do you want from me?"

"What I've always fucking wanted, Romulus. I want your life and your power. I want everything I damn well deserve, and you are going to give it to me." His expression morphed into a glare, "You are going to tell me how to make more Eternals, and you are also going to help me do it."

"And why would I do that?"

"Because a little birdie told me that Alara is much more to you than a simple bed partner. She's your mate, right? Your other half? Well, how would you like to see me slit her open from ear to ear if you don't give me what I desire?"

Rome tensed as his eyes burrowed into green, emotionless eyes. He would do it. He would slit her throat without a second thought, and there was no telling if he could save her from such a wound. He was already weakened from his hunt and healing Alaric from his sisters' siphon. There was no telling how much healing energy he would need to push into her for her to survive a severe wound, especially with that power dampening collar around her throat and he would never risk her.

"If you kill her you lose your bargaining tool. Just let her go and I'll do whatever you desire."

"You'll do whatever I want regardless because if I kill her here and now I won't regret my decision but I'm damn sure you will. You have no leverage or power here, Romulus. Now kneel and allow one of my doctors to administer a sedative so that we may begin."

Silas' premonition came to Rome almost instantly. *You'll yield for her, and it goes black. I see nothing once you drop to your knees in surrender.* This is what Silas had spoken of, and he'd been right. He would surrender because he couldn't lose her. Rome had been searching for her for centuries, not actively, yet a part of him had known he would meet his match one day. Now that he had, he would do everything to save her, even surrender to his enemy and give him what he desired. He would be a lab rat. He would be a victim. He would be anything he needed to be to get her free.

"Please," Alara cried out. "Don't"

His eyes locked onto hers to see the fresh tears that had started to pour before he slowly knelt and placed his hands behind his head. He never looked away. Not even when he felt someone moving in from behind him and not even when he felt the prick of the needle piercing his neck. He felt it the second the virus hit his bloodstream. He tried to keep himself from reacting because he knew it wouldn't work, or at least he thought it wouldn't, but this time it was different. The dosage was larger. It was more potent, and he felt it the second it took hold of him. His eyes grew heavy, his ears began to ring, and his heart rate slowed to dangerous levels before he found himself falling face-first into the hard concrete and promptly passing out.

Who would save them now?

CHAPTER
THIRTY

lara couldn't stop her tears from falling as she sat in a chair several feet away from Rome's unconscious body. They'd strapped him to the silver examination table, silver manacles were clamped around his wrists and ankles, and a silver collar had been placed around his throat. She could smell his flesh burning, could see the red welts spreading across his body, and she absolutely hated it. If not for her, he wouldn't be here at the mercy of their enemy. Lukas hadn't stopped smiling since the moment Rome fell unconscious, and that smile had only gotten wider when Rome was strapped to the table. Multiple men and women in lab coats had converged to run a million and one tests on him, and she could do nothing but sit and watch. She was strapped to a chair with her arms pulled behind her back and her ankles trapped against the legs of the wooden seat. A guard stood only a few feet behind her while her sister stood silently beside the man who, only moments ago, had held a gun to her head. She knew because she couldn't help but look back and glare every few moments. She'd been played. She should have known that Lukas would never hurt her sister because then he'd have no leverage. She'd been stupid and worried, and now she was afraid and forced to watch as the man she loved was put through test after test.

She wasn't sure when it had happened but Alara knew without a doubt that she loved him. She loved this man that had bulldozed into her life and taken over everything.

"Why the hell isn't he waking up?" Lukas questioned one of the doctors manning the computers as he paced with his cane.

A man with wide-rimmed glasses and coiffed blonde hair spoke from his position at the monitor. "Sir, he should be awake soon. His vitals are strong and steady; it's just taking a moment for the tranquilizer to wear off."

"And the virus? How is that affecting his genetic makeup? Will it affect the cells we need?"

"No, sir. Not to our knowledge."

"Good. Call me the moment he awakens, and you'll keep her," he stabbed a finger in Alara's direction, "watching until the moment he takes his last breath. If she dozes off, you shock her to within an inch of her life until she opens her eyes. She will bear witness to everything that happens to him, or each of you will suffer along with her." He headed for the elevator and paused before glancing over his shoulder at Alba, "Subject 3, I expect you to make sure your lovely sister behaves herself."

Her head snapped up before she nodded quickly. "Of course, sir."

He left them then, cane tapping lightly against the ground as he headed into the elevator and began descending to the lower levels of the building. Alara breathed a little bit easier as her eyes scanned the warehouse. Everyone seemed to have a job to maintain as three people manned the computer attached to the examination table. Six guards stood along the inside perimeter of the building with their bodies ramrod straight and their eyes constantly scanning the room. The only one who seemed lax in their duties was the soldier standing marginally behind her as the clack of his fingers on a screen reached her ears. Was he texting? She peeked over her shoulder, and sure enough, he was, and her sister's gaze was fixed firmly on her.

"Still think you're choosing the right side of this?" Alara questioned, her voice full of annoyance and anger even as her body protested her now uncomfortable position as her fingers slowly began to numb up.

"Of course." Her sister replied, yet her eyes said differently. Her eyes said she wasn't too sure of her decision to back Lukas and his mission.

"Have you been paying attention to anything that's been happening? You're a prisoner just like me, just in a different way, and you're okay with this? You're okay being a mindless soldier to a man that could care less about you?"

"Why wouldn't I be sure?" Alondra pointed at Rome's prone figure, "he and his people want to make us cattle. They want to drain us dry and eradicate us from this world. I'm on the winning side of this war, and this is where I'll stay."

"So what were those words you whispered to me about helping? Were those just words to get me moving? Were you giving me a false sense of security so I would do whatever you wanted? Is that it? Were you using my love for you to manipulate me? Just tell me the fucking truth for once, Alondra!" Her voice rose with every question, her anger getting the best of her as she cursed herself for being so easily manipulated once again.

Alondra stepped away from the guard, although he failed to notice as he steadily tapped away on his phone, or maybe he just didn't care what she did. She glared, her eyes shifting around the room before coming back to her with a different emotion now present. It looked like remorse, but that couldn't be right, could it? Alara watched her a little bit closely now, although her arms screamed in protest from the position she was in.

"You don't know me well enough to love me," Alondra stated, her eyes shifting nervously around the room once more.

"You're right. I don't know you, but since the moment I knew you existed, I've always treated you like my sister because that's what you are, and I do love you. I love you enough to tell you that you're fighting for the wrong team and that when this blows up in your face, and it will, I tried to save you from that end." She turned to face Rome when a soft groan came from him.

He shifted slightly as she leaned forward in her seat and waited with bated breath for him to say something. She didn't have to wait long. "Little flower?"

She jerked within her bonds and slowly fumed when he didn't do the same. Was he truly just going to surrender? Would he seriously not even try to get free? He had to have some type of plan, like waiting for the others to show up and get them free, or maybe he was plotting something out within his mind, and he just needed time to think because they couldn't just give up and allow Titan to win. They needed to find a way out of this.

Alara spoke so softly that she was sure only Rome could hear her. "Do you have a way of getting us out of here alive?"

His voice was raspy when he spoke, similar to how she'd sounded when she'd first awoken several hours earlier. "I don't want you hurt, so you'll stand by and allow Lukas to do as he pleases with me. Do you understand?"

No, she didn't understand, and quite frankly, she didn't want to, but Alara was sure that everyone within the room had heard his words. She could feel their eyes on them and even heard one of the men draped in a white coat speaking softly over the phone. He was contacting Lukas. There was no doubt in her mind, but what would happen once he returned? They'd already drawn Rome's blood and poked and prodded him nearly to death. What else was left? What more could Titan want with him other than his death?

She didn't bother whispering this time, and she couldn't keep the nervousness from her voice. "What do they plan to do to you?"

"Whatever they wish, I suppose."

Her anger rose. "But why? Why would you lie down and allow this? I thought you said if anything should happen to me, you would raze the earth for me. Well, something's happened, Romulus. We've been captured by our enemy, and you mean to tell me that you have no intention of getting us out of this? I'm powerless, I can't save myself, or I would have already."

He snarled and spoke softly, yet his words were like a dagger to the heart. "Did you plan on telling me about your blood and this new virus? Did you plan on telling me how you're the reason that my people may become ill and die if hit with one of these tranquilizer darts?"

What was she to say to that? How had he learned the truth? She thought she would have time to tell him or at least find a way for him and his people to not be susceptible to the drug. Being the reason for his people's demise wasn't something she wanted to be blamed for. She hadn't agreed to be a part of the drug, and she damn sure hadn't given Titan free rein to use her blood as they desired, but they'd done it anyway. She was an accomplice without meaning to be, and now he would condemn her for it. Maybe he'd even take back everything he'd ever said about protecting and fighting for her. His actions at the moment seemed to be proof of that.

Alara couldn't keep the fear of abandonment from surfacing as she stared at Rome's profile. "I was going to tell you," she sniffled and cursed Lukas for having her tied up without any way to wipe away the snot attempting to roll from her nose and the tears from descending down her cheeks.

"When? When did you plan on telling me? I'm sure you knew about it the moment you healed Ami, and yet you said nothing, so how about you sit here and say nothing for the duration of our stay. I'll try to keep his focus on me for as long as I need to."

She opened her mouth to respond. She wanted Rome to understand that she hadn't meant to hurt him or his people; she had just been scared. She would have told him the truth, eventually. Eventually just never came, and now someone else had told him before she could get a chance to. It looked terrible on her part, making her look even more untrustworthy than before, and maybe that hurt her chances even more at forgiveness. He had to forgive her, though, right? They were mates, after all. Wasn't there something within that bond that made it impossible for your other half to completely write you off or would he be done with her?

The sound of Lukas returning could be heard over the beeping of the machines as he slowly walked into her peripheral vision and approached the side of the table until he stared down into Rome's eyes. "So you are awake." A smile stretched his lips, giving him a macabre look. "It seems we have some catching up to do, old friend."

"It seems we do."

ROME STARED at the man above him and barely kept a vicious snarl from emitting from his throat. He hated the bastard. Lukas looked just like his father, his father before him, and so on. Shit, he looked so much like that bastard Theolonius Titan that anger coursed through him like a tornado. Rome wanted to vault up from his prone position and tear his fangs right through his jugular just to watch as the life left his body and reduced him to nothing. He'd known the Titan family since he was five hundred and thirty years old, between 1492 and 1553, when he'd been avoiding capture from the man that had created the Titan corporation. It was because of Rome's mistake that Titan had learned about the existence of Eternals. During World War 2, they'd fought almost to the death, back when silver affected Rome on a deeper level, and capture had nearly been eminent. Now, after almost a thousand years of life, the things that had once weakened him before no longer had their potent effect. Did the sun and silver still cause pain and burning? Of course, but not nearly as much as they should nor as much as Lukas had prepared for. Titan's files on Rome and his people were outdated as far as Rome was concerned. His restraints were proof of that.

Rome shifted slightly beneath the metal that held him down as it sizzled against his skin, but it stood no chance against the rapid healing cells that powered through his body. He suppressed them just enough to look like he was entirely under this bastard's control and despised it. To show weakness to his enemy was like a lion exposing its belly to another lion. He wasn't weaker than Lukas by any stretch of the imagination- even in his current position- but to get intel and make sure he got his mate out of this situation, he needed to play ball. He needed to expose his belly and allow his enemy to have the upper hand. He needed to play a part in this sick, twisted game and hopefully come out unscathed on the other side because he needed information.

Lukas smirked and glanced towards Alara before he spoke again. "Does she know our family's history? Have you told her the truth about what you created and brought unto this earth? You and your people are the true monsters here, and Titan was created to protect humanity from your kind."

"Telling her that would have been a blatant lie." He responded with a glare. "She knows as much as she needs to know."

"So you haven't told her about the Rogues and your plan to enslave the human race to make us your personal blood bank?"

"If that's what you choose to believe, then that is your own perspective." Rome shifted marginally beneath the manacles against his skin and groaned when the silver burned through healed flesh once more. "My warriors and I know the truth. For centuries, your family has hunted my kind in the most gruesome of ways, and we've fought back and won on several occasions. I've been made aware of the Kindred you've been locking up in the hopes of aiding your side of the war. It's a war they know nothing about; if they did, they would free themselves from the shackles in which I'm sure you've dressed them in. Each side has lost people in a bid to protect what we individually believe to be right, but you know the truth of the matter. You just refuse to yield, so we must war because the power you seek will never be granted to you."

"Well, we see who's winning the war now, don't we, Romulus?"

"What are you talking about?" Alara frowned as she attempted to ease the ache within her arms. "Are there more people like me and my siblings?" Alara glanced over her shoulder to see that her sister had also stiffened at the news. If they were, in fact, keeping other Kindred hostage, what did that mean for them? Would they be trying to save them as well, or would they leave them to their fate if they ever did escape?

Rome could sense heavy layers of silver all around him, not just the silver that shackled his body and realized that Titan had definitely stepped up its game within this war between them. As the drug ran its course through his body, the more his abilities began to make themselves known once more. Soon, nothing would hold him back from unleashing hell on Titan and every individual who played a part in the destruction of his people and the kidnapping of his mate, but first he needed answers.

"I have it under good authority that you have more Kindred, so where are they, Lukas?" Rome inquired and tested the strength of his bonds once more as more of his power began to flow through him. Red lights began to flash and flicker as an alarm blared loudly throughout the building. Soldiers tensed and drew their weapons as the doctors scrambled over the readings printing out from the computer. Oh, they'd definitely stepped up their game if they now had sensors for when they used their abilities.

"What's happening?" Lukas questioned and quickly approached the monitors. "Have his warriors arrived to attempt a rescue?"

"No, that can't be it." The lead doctor stated nervously as he pushed his wide-rimmed glasses farther up on his nose. "A powerful surge disrupted our equipment. We've lost connection of the cameras, microphones, and his vitals."

The guard standing behind Alara spoke up as he moved forward and placed a gun at the back of her skull. "Sir, communications are down; I can't reach central." He tapped the cool metal against her, making sure to dig into the sensitive tissue. "I know it's him. Stop now, Romulus, or I'll blow a nice little hole into the back of her pretty little head. She'll have a hard time healing from such a wound. Would you like to chance it?" He cocked back the chamber and smiled.

Rome grew still and suppressed his gifts. The alarms quieted, and silence once more reigned.

"Try that again, and I'll be forced to turn my attention to Alara, and we both know you don't want that," Lukas commented as he approached the table again. His gaze was intent and malicious as he stared down into Rome's blazing gaze. "Now tell me how you knocked out my electronics. You should be so doped up with the virus that your abilities are unattainable. The cognizance you usually obtain should be non-existent. Have your abilities become more heightened? Are you even more powerful than before?"

Rome's eyes cut over to the man behind his mate and narrowed dangerously. "You know that if you hurt her, you get nothing from me, so I suggest you order your man to step down before I show him what I can really do without ever lifting a finger."

"Blakely, step back and return to your position." Lukas stated with a jerk of his head before his gaze returned to Rome, "So, her people are Kindred. What does it mean, and how many of them are there?"

Rome stared back with a blank expression. How the hell was he going to get them out of this without risking his mate? He'd agreed to answer the questions Lukas provided. He'd promised to give him anything he wanted, but now that he was here, he wasn't sure what to say or if these stupid monitors could detect a lie. If it could sense the use of his abilities, then what else could it do? He wouldn't endanger his mate anymore then she already was. He hadn't accounted for this. Titan had gotten smarter. They were learning new ways to take him and his people out and for once he was unsure how to proceed. Lukas was several steps ahead and adamant on blocking him at every turn.

THIRTY-ONE

Alara didn't want to cry anymore. She'd cried enough to last her a lifetime, so she forced her tears back and kept her eyes locked on Rome as he jerked beneath his bonds. Current after current of electricity slammed through him until Lukas turned the dial down and approached the table with a furious expression. He'd been torturing him for hours now, barely pausing to let him catch a breath long enough to answer, and with each electrocution, his skin paled further. Rome was barely healing; the red marks were more prominent on his skin, and his eyes were dull and almost lifeless.

"Romulus, I need answers, and I need them now. We've been at this for hours. Aren't you tired of the torture? Don't you want relief? Just tell me how to create more of you." Lukas snarled in annoyance.

Alara jerked within the chair, her arms and shoulders protesting against the uncomfortable position she had been left in for hours. "They can't be created dammit, he's already told you this!" She screamed.

Her voice was raw from voicing her anger, sweat covered her body from her feeble attempts to get free, and the need to protect

Rome swam through her at a dizzying speed. This wasn't supposed to happen. If she'd denied calling him here, he wouldn't be here now in this situation. His life wouldn't be in danger, and he would have forgotten about her over time. Alara was sure of that, but with the threat of her sister's life, she'd done the only thing she thought would save them.

Lukas turned to her as his green eyes narrowed. He moved until he stood before her, his face twisted into an unsatisfied grimace as he glared at her. "Did you happen to grow a spine while you were with him and his people, my little Alara? If so, we'll have to break that defiance I see within your gaze. That just won't do."

"I'm not your little anything, and I never will be. I'm telling you that I've already asked him this, and I doubt he would lie to me. They can't create more Eternals, and they can't reproduce; it's not within their genetics to do so. You're wasting your time! Just let him go."

She didn't know if she was speaking the truth. It wasn't something they'd gotten in depth with when Rome had told her about Rogues and Eternals, but she knew that Rogues could not procreate. They weren't creatures that had been born but instead created. There was no telling what they were capable of doing regarding the next generation of them as a species. That went for Eternals as well, but in regards to creating more....Alara wasn't sure. That was something Rome had never spoken of.

"Then I have no use for him. You, on the other hand, can give me what I desire." Lukas commented with a smirk as he gripped her beneath the chin and leaned into her space.

She attempted to jerk away from him, yet his hold held her steady, his overpowering cologne clogging her nose as his lips brushed softly against her cheek. Her stomach curled in disgust as another rush of sweat dripped from her pores. He was too close to her lips for comfort and too close to taking what she never intended to give. She struggled within his hold when Rome snarled with aggression. The sound of bending metal pierced the air as he fought his restraints, his energy filling the room around them as he fought to free himself. Even as weak as he undoubtedly was, he still attempted to protect her from harm. Relief poured through her at the thought of him breaking free and finally getting them the hell out of there, but her relief was short-lived when Lukas spoke.

"Inject him again with the highest dose possible. Once he's knocked out, I expect a full dissection of his body after draining him of every drop of blood he holds. We'll need it for the reproduction of my army. If he dies, I suggest you work quickly to retrieve what I'll need to further my work. It doesn't look like I'll be getting the answers I seek." He gripped her arm, unlocked her from the chair and yanked her up onto her feet as his man—Blakely— followed closely behind them. He tugged her towards the elevator, his breath whispering against her ear and sending nervous chills down her back, "I think it's about time we finish what we started all those years ago, don't you think?

"Why would you need his blood to reproduce your army?"

"Of course, he didn't tell you." Lukas chuckled harshly. "Well, my sweet Alara, the Rogues would have never come to exist without Rome. When my family first discovered him and drew blood in battle, we took the few droplets we found and created more before injecting that blood into test subjects. That's how we gained our army and our leg up in this war."

Horror filled her at the thought, even as she fought to keep her eyes on Rome. The doctors moved to push a larger dose of the virus they'd created into his body. The moment it was administered, Rome's body began to jerk violently within his manacles. She screamed and fought, working her way away from Lukas's hold just before his goon lifted her into his arms into a fireman's carry and followed his boss into the elevator. Her arms were handcuffed behind her back, making it practically impossible to fight against his hold, and yet she still tried even as her eyes stayed glued to the man who had captured her heart.

Had it really been days ago that she'd fallen for this man? He'd become someone she could genuinely sacrifice herself for. When she looked at him, she saw forever. She saw a future that once had been closed off to her. She saw love, understanding, and utter devotion. Even after everything, Alara saw a man worth going to war for. She couldn't let Titan do this to them. She wouldn't be a victim to them again, and she couldn't see Rome perish for her mistakes. She wouldn't survive it if Lukas did, in fact, get what he wanted and end his long life. She wasn't strong enough to survive what he had in store for her. She wasn't strong enough to survive without the man who had given her true freedom. Rome had given her everything when she thought she'd had nothing left.

"Alara!" Rome cried out seconds before his body jerked once more before falling limp.

She screamed. Not caring what anyone might think or what anyone might do as monitors blared throughout the building. Was it to signify his death? Was he really dead? What else could it be? She saw the flat-lining of his heart even as Blakely entered the elevator, and the doors closed softly behind him. As the four walls closed in around her, she felt the presence of the two men as something within her slowly began to shrivel up and die. She couldn't shield herself from the hurt that slammed into her heart and mind. Wet tears slid down her cheeks as she was placed onto her feet and pressed into the furthest corner of the elevator. The need to crumple to the ground and give up was strong, yet she remained standing even as her entire body trembled with anger and fear. She wouldn't give them the satisfaction of seeing her on her knees. The collar felt heavy against her throat as the reality of her situation edged in on her thoughts.

Lukas spoke, his voice breaking through her thoughts, sending her stomach churning as acid scratched at her throat with the need to vomit. "Once we reach the lower levels, I wish not to be disturbed. Alara and I have a lot of catching up to do."

"I'll never give you what you want," she snapped as her gaze stared vacantly at the walls surrounding her, "I'd rather die than be anything to you, especially a victim again."

"You'll give me whatever the hell I want, and trust me, you'll enjoy it." He chuckled darkly.

She tuned him out as her mind took her to better times. She disassociated quickly and effectively. Whatever he had in store for her, she would ensure he never broke her mind like before. She would never be that weak again, never subject herself to the abuse of a narcissistic prick, and never again forget how powerful she was. She had to wait for her moment, wait for the perfect opportunity to strike and get out of there, but she wouldn't just free herself. She'd be taking Rome with her because he couldn't be dead. There was no her without him. She would save him even if it took all of her power to heal him.

IT WAS STILL and silent around him. Rome's muscles were relaxed, his senses were back, and yet something felt off. Something was wrong. His eyes were shut, and no amount of trying would get them to open. No sound reached his ears, but when he inhaled, the smell of roses and sex filled his lungs. He went stiff. He knew that smell, and he knew it well. He was locked within his mind where his meeting with the Gods and Goddesses would occur. Within the mental world they'd created for him centuries ago, many things were possible that even he wasn't entirely sure of, and this was one of them. He'd never dug this deeply into his mind to the point of not feeling his body. So yes, something was definitely wrong with this picture.

"Hera, why can I not open my eyes?" He questioned as he forced his body into a fighter's stance and summoned two long swords to fill his hands.

The thought of this being his punishment for neglecting his duties for as long as he had caused his stomach to turn with a vengeance. Is this where the torture and dismemberment would take place? Where was Alara, and what had happened? The last thing he remembered was that virus slamming through his body as he was injecting once more and his mate was carried away from him. He needed to be with her, protecting her from the atrocities he was sure Lukas had prepared for her. He had to stop whatever was about to happen before she was exposed to Titan's evil. Being here meant he couldn't protect her, and that just wouldn't do.

"Send me back now, Hera, you witch!" He snarled as his fangs burst through his gums.

Her voice was soothing yet rippling with power when she spoke. "I did not bring you here, Romulus, but I will gladly keep you for your blatant disrespect if you curse my name again. Or would you prefer to meet my brother Hades in the afterlife over returning to your new mate?"

Her threat made him freeze up. He could feel her all around him. The goddess Hera wasn't just any goddess. She had been the one responsible for the war within the heavens that had changed him and the rest of his Eternals. Hera had thrown a fit to rival any war, and battle had ensued. Although she wasn't their sole creator, she was definitely the one who pulled the strings of God and men whenever she chose. Her jealousy was legendary, her cruelness unmatched, and her beauty only spoken about in whispers.

He scoffed lightly. *"Are you telling me that I'm dead? Did that bastard truly kill me?"*

"No. It would take more than that to kill your body, but your mind, on the other hand, has fractured. You forced yourself into a coma like state and came here seeking safety within the temple of the Gods. I am unsure how you were capable of doing so. You are the first of your kind, Romulus. The strongest, fittest, fastest, and most durable in every way. Things that affect your brethren no longer affect you. You've changed, adapted, and grown stronger than we ever anticipated, and now we cannot risk you being lost to us."

"Where is my mate?"

"Within the clutches of your enemy, of course."

"Then why the fuck am I here? Is this to be my punishment?"

He slashed out with his blades and met air as his senses attempted to locate her. Anger was pulsing through him, along with an emotion he hadn't felt in centuries.

Fear.

He feared for his mate, feared for the things that would happen to her if he didn't return, and feared for the person she'd become if he didn't get to her before the damage was already done. He shouldn't have played his games with Lukas. He should have killed him on the spot and gotten her home. Instead, he'd forced himself to play victim to learn more about his enemy, and now he was here, trapped in some mental vault with no idea how to get free.

Hera sighed heavily as the feel of her presence within his mind grew larger. *"As I've told you before, your mind has fractured Romulus. It has shut down and closed itself off to protect and preserve your body. You are giving the illusion of death to the mortals that surround you. If we aren't quick about this, you may yet just die, warrior."*

"Can you help me return?"

"For a price, of course."

Rome stiffened when the feel of something warm brushed against him, but he didn't jerk back. He stood his ground and simply waited. He had to. He needed to get out of here. Whatever she wanted, he would give her with no questions asked. All that mattered was getting back to his mate and making sure this never happened to him again.

"Tell me what you want."

"I want her siblings to survive. Which means I'm enlisting the strength and cunning of you and each of your warriors to defend them until I deem otherwise."

He growled low, but what other choice did he have? He nodded solemnly as his weapons vanished and his fangs retracted before two more entities filled his mind—the goddess's Nemesis and Athena. Although he couldn't see them either, he could feel them surrounding him. He wasn't often visited by the goddess of retribution, but over the centuries, he had learned that she favored him above all Eternals, and Athena came and left when she chose. On occasion, it was just to pick fights with Hera.

"Romulus." Nemesis' voice wrapped around him along with a sense of danger just before a swift pain stabbed through his shoulder blades and robbed him of breath. *"I give you the gift of flight to help you as they have helped me. Exact your vengeance and save the future of your kind."* Her words slammed into him, along with a searing pain that ripped through him, causing him to cry out in agony as he knelt on the ground. A pair of black translucent wings sprouted from his back and draped around him like a lover's hold.

Athena spoke next, not giving him time to comment as the other goddess vanished. *"Warrior, I shall heal your mind, but you must be the one to fight your way back to consciousness. You've stayed long enough."*

He felt it the moment healing waves were pushed into the tears within his mind. The need to get back to his mate pulsed through him, along with the reality of what had just occurred. He hadn't just been touched by goddesses; he'd been blessed by them. They'd bestowed upon him an honor he wasn't sure he deserved, but he wouldn't waste it. No, he would fight because no mere mortal or otherwise had ever had divine intervention such as this. The wings along his back melted into his skin as he pushed himself ruthlessly through the darkness of his mind and back to reality as healing wave after healing wave pulsed through him.

. . .

Rome's eyes shot open when he returned to consciousness to find several doctors surrounding him, along with needles and equipment. They'd moved fast. He could feel just how much blood they'd taken, and he was much weaker than he'd been before, but that didn't matter. They would take no more from him, and everyone responsible for helping Titan restrain his mate would perish before he left here tonight.

Without much thought, he used his telekinesis to snap the silver manacles holding him in place and grabbed the closest human to his right before he sank his fangs deep into their carotid artery. He could only take a few sips of their blood before nausea began to creep in, and he was forced to push the long-nosed bastard away from him as he snarled with rage. His blood had been foul. It wasn't what he needed. He needed Alara's. He needed his mate.

As the alarms blared, the guards came to attention, and bullets began to fly as the doctors dropped to the ground to avoid the crossfire. He erected an energy field around himself before using his telekinetic gift to propel the bullets back towards the men who had shot them. Several groans of pain licked at his ears as blood poured from several gushing wounds. He could smell the taint of their blood and knew that there was no saving them from the corruption that had already begun to embed within their minds. He didn't have time for this. He couldn't save them from themselves and all the atrocities they'd taken part in throughout the years. With a wave of his hand, everyone but Alara's traitorous sister fell to the floor unconscious. Once his people arrived, he would allow them full reign to do as they pleased with their enemies.

Alondra didn't run or cower from him, but she didn't meet his eyes either. He saw the tear tracks that had dried on her cheeks as he approached her. Rome wanted to kill her where she stood but instead he would send her back to his home and leave her within the cells of his basement to rot. He recalled Hera's words. He was to protect her even as every cell within his soul screamed at him to end her miserable existence.

He gripped her by the chin and forced her to meet his burning gaze before he spoke, his voice low and cutting. "Where has he taken her? I cannot sense her through all of the silver that's embedded within the structure of this building, but I know she is here. He would want to visit me as soon as he is done with her, so where would he take her?"

"Back to her room within the lowest level of the building." She replied as a fresh set of tears began to run down her face. A new vulnerability shone in her eyes before she reached up to clasp his hand between her own. "I swear to you, I didn't think he planned to hurt her; he promised me he wouldn't. I thought I was doing the right thing. I thought you and your people were the enemy. I didn't mean for any of this to happen. You have to believe me."

"Don't apologize to me. Once I get my mate back, you'll apologize to the woman you were supposed to protect, apologize to the woman you betrayed, and stay the hell out of my way." He bared his fangs and gripped her chin tighter. "I'm supposed to protect you, but trust and believe me, Alondra, I can make your life a living hell and still keep you safe! Do you understand?"

Her nod was the only confirmation he needed before he released her. He wasn't one to hurt a woman, and he would never want to harm his mate's sister, but that didn't mean he wouldn't sic Amirishka on her to teach her a valuable lesson about loyalty to one's own.

He stormed for the elevator even as he attempted to use his gift of teleportation, but nothing happened. Was it the silver keeping him grounded? He frowned and entered the enclosed space to find a handprint scanner. It seemed to be the only way to control the elevator, so he placed his hand on the sensor and forced himself to focus on the electrical signals and cords that filled the building before literally tearing a hole within the structure with his mind. It left Titan blind as cameras, intercoms, and communication devices died abruptly and swiftly. It wasn't too wise to keep everything on the same electrical grid on their end. The sound of a blaring alarm pierced the air as red lights began to flash rapidly, and the elevator began a slow descent into the hard-packed earth. He still couldn't sense his mate, but he knew without a doubt she was below, possibly fighting for her life to get away. He couldn't figure out why only a few of his gifts were accessible to him but he needed to get a warning out to his Guardians so they would know what they were walking into.

Rome lowered the barriers within his mind to send out a telepathic message to his warriors. *"I've found Alara within an abandoned building on the west side. Come prepared to kill and be mindful of the silver. The building is packed with it so it'll affect your abilities, as well as weaken you. Do not be caught unawares."*

A chorus of yes sirs filled his mind before he forced himself to focus as he summoned his long swords when the scent of his mate began to tickle at his nostrils. He snarled deeply when Lukas's scent greeted him as well. He planned to kill the bastard nice, slow, and without mercy. There would be no leniency for him; no amount of pleading would stop Rome from tearing his head from his body, but first, he needed to ensure his mate's safety.

He was coming for her.

THIRTY-TWO

Alara's face felt like it had been run through a meat grinder after receiving another punch across her right cheek. She tasted blood from the split within her lip, but that wasn't what gave her pause. No, the man glaring down at her as she scrambled backward across the floor is what gave her pause. From the moment they'd entered the bedroom she'd been released from her chains and he'd lashed out, hitting her repeatedly until landing that final punch to her face. He was livid. His green eyes pulsing with anger in a way she had never witnessed before. After years of living under his thumb, she had gotten used to the constant look of displeasure that came from him, but this anger was different. He'd never physically hit her before, but electrocuting her almost to death was his favorite form of torture. To actually put the energy and effort into actually laying his hands on her with aggression was something entirely new for her. For them both.

"Remove your clothes and get on the bed." He tugged at the tie around his throat and placed his cane against the wall before he pulled a small device from his pocket. "Do it or suffer the consequences, Alara. I won't be made to wait long."

She recognized the small black device for what it was. It had been the bane of her existence for most of her life. Her hand clutched at the gold that encircled her throat and cringed at the thought of being electrocuted again, but what would she rather suffer? Lukas atop her as he forced himself inside of her, or jolts of electricity frying her brain cells? There was only one option. One answer.

"I'm not just going to lay back and let you do whatever you want to me." She glared as her voice shook with fear and anger, "If you somehow manage to get on top of me and take what you want, it'll be because you raped me. I won't just lie still, so prepare yourself for a fight because that's exactly what you'll be getting. I'm not going down easy, Lukas!" She climbed to her feet and retreated until her back was pressed firmly against the wall.

She was trapped in a corner now, the bed to her left and the door placed perfectly behind him. She needed to get to that door, but first, she needed that small black device that he held in the palm of his hand. She needed to get him closer, preferably without the object in his hand, so that she could escape. A plan was forming in her mind, something that had the potential to fail if she didn't get it just right, and she needed to get it right.

The smirk covering his face sent chills down her spine, which got even worse when he spoke. "What do you think will happen here? Do you think you'll get free? That you have a chance of getting away? Well, I'm here to tell you that that will never happen again. You are stuck with me, Alara, so get used to that reality and welcome the pain. Besides, you're supposed savior will be dead soon anyway, and anyone who could have helped you will be eradicated from this earth as well to join that bastard Romulus in hell."

He pressed that godforsaken button, sending electric pulses through her, forcing her to her knees in agony as her muscles spasmed uncontrollably. A scream got lodged in her throat as the feel of her heart trying to burst from her chest registered through her consciousness just as the pulses stopped and the pain began to slowly bleed away. It took her a moment to realize that he'd advanced on her, but by the time she realized, his hand was buried in her thick hair as he dragged her to her feet. Her pain morphed and centered in on her scalp that now burned from the aggression practically leaking from him as he crowded her into the wall. His other hand wrapped around her throat, cutting off the oxygen she couldn't bear to lose.

"I want you to fight me," Lukas whispered only inches from her face, "I want you to fight me, Alara, because when you finally yield, it will be the most beautiful sight I'll ever get to see in this lifetime. You'll surrender to me, and when you do, you will love it!"

Before she could jerk away, his lips were covering her own. The feel of him against her turned her stomach, but the oxygen he was depriving her of left Alara with no room to fight as her nails dug into the skin of his wrists and her legs flailed loosely beneath her. He surrounded her. His presence was everywhere as he slowly snuffed out the hope and light she had seen for herself, but she refused to give up even as stars winked in and out of her vision. She could feel herself getting lightheaded as his cold, thin lips brushed against her skin as he made his way to the side of her throat. She tried to fight the pull of lightheadedness as her nails dug deeper into his skin, drawing blood that caused him to wince before he drew back cautiously.

"Release me, or I shall have Blakely come in to hold you down as I take you in every way I possibly can before I fill you with my seed." He growled through clenched teeth as he loosened his hold on her throat.

She gasped in a startled breath and dropped her hands to her sides. She didn't want to, but she needed to. She needed to lure him into a sense of false safety, even if that meant allowing him to have a small piece of her. She could get free. She had to.

"Good girl. Now grab your pants and push them down for me."

Her eyes widened as she shook her head marginally and stared into his terrifying gaze. Allowing him to press his sick lips against her skin was one thing, but removing her clothing for him was another matter entirely. She couldn't do it. No matter how badly she wanted to get away and survive this, she would never grant him more access to her body than this. Even now, with his hands pressed firmly against her skin, she wanted to die from that alone. She couldn't imagine baring her lower half to him and leaving herself so exposed. She needed a way out of this.

Where had that remote gone?

Alara glanced down to take in his form and saw a slight bulge in his front pocket before his hand tightened against her throat to cut off her air supply once more. Her gasp caused a smile to stretch his lips wide as he pressed his lower body against hers. The urge to vomit was strong as the smell of his cologne filled her lungs, along with the smell of spearmint gum.

"Drop them, Alara, or I'll rip them from your body myself."

"Please," she gasped.

Lukas wasn't weak by any means. His grip was sure and tight, causing black spots to dance in her vision as she fought to bring in more air. Her lungs protested, and her hands flew up to grip his wrist once more before the sound of him chuckling filtered through her ears. Dread consumed her along with her fear as his hand left her tangled hair to grip the fabric of her pants. It was thin and scratchy against her skin, but it was the only safety net she had before he ripped them from her body and exposed her to the coldness of the air. She fought him harder now. Desperation bleeding through her as she fought to get free. He hardly reacted, and yet his hand tightened further against her jugular. Black spots turned to complete darkness as she fought to remain conscious. The sound of his hum of approval filled the air, followed by a blaring alarm that caused him to jerk away from her abruptly. She sagged to the floor and struggled to catch her breath as Lukas walked away to retrieve his cane before he swung the door open wide.

"What the fuck is going on?" He questioned the moment his eyes locked onto his guard.

Their backs were turned to her as they watched a red light pulse as the sound of the alarm filtered through the hallway and blocked out all other sounds, even her ragged breathing. Her time to escape was now, and she couldn't waste it, but the soreness within her throat shattered her focus. Dizziness still held her within its web as she climbed to her feet and dragged the sheet from the bed to wrap around her waist. Her pants were a ripped mess on the floor, and her window of opportunity was closing. God, her body ached all over, and the swollenness within her face was starting to give her a massive migraine, yet she moved as quickly as she could for the door. Her hands clenched into fists as she readied herself for the fight ahead, and yet the moment she was an arm's length away from Lukas and what she needed, an electric current coursed through her and immediately brought her to her knees once more.

The voltage was higher, pulling her under a sea of blackness that terrified her more than she already was. She couldn't lose consciousness now, and she couldn't let him win, yet her body slumped to the floor, and the coolness of the ground bled into her skin as the current finally stopped. Her body continued to jerk long after the fact. She couldn't control the twitching or the clenching of her teeth. It was unavoidable as she watched them enter the room before closing and locking the door behind them.

Lukas's voice penetrated the dark haze that was her mind. "Grab her and hold her down."

Alara couldn't move to fight him off as Blakely yanked her up by the arms and carried her to the bed. She couldn't use her gifts to heal herself or suck his energy dry. All she could do was lie there as his guard tore the sheet from her body before trapping her arms above her head. The very pressure of his hold on her wrists caused her to lose feeling in her hands as the blood was cut off. She cried out weakly and attempted to kick and buck as Lukas's taller form pinned the lower half of her body to the bed. The scrape of fabric and male hardness between her legs caused her to scream as tears began to leak from the corners of her eyes, and her legs were forced wider apart. God, this was really about to happen. He would rape her, and there was nothing she could do to stop him.

"I told you she would scream." Lukas chuckled.

The rasp of his zipper lowering filtered through as a stillness she'd never expected to feel flowed through her. She forced herself to curl into a ball within her mind and drift away from reality. If this was happening, she wanted to be as far away mentally as she could get. She wouldn't survive otherwise, and as badly as she didn't want this to happen, she also realized that there might be no saving her now. They were here. They'd reached a moment in time where escape for her was improbable, and worst of all, she was incapable of saving herself.

That hole within her mind opened wide and swallowed her whole, and she let it. She closed her eyes, forced her body to relax, and allowed her tears to flow freely. She would be broken otherwise. He would take her body, but she couldn't allow him to take everything. She wouldn't allow him to take her mind as well.

Lukas brushed his fingers along her hairline before his hand grabbed a rough fistful of her hair and pulled. The burn was excruciating, yet she remained silent. She wouldn't give him any more ammo even as her body protested from the pain.

He spoke roughly, his voice cutting through her just as surely as a sharpened blade would. "I see you're getting it now. You're mine, Alara, and that's all you'll ever be. I'll fuck you and use you until I tire of you, and even then, I will never release you. Everything you are is because of me, and everything you'll ever be is because of my say-so. You are Mine! Mine!" His lips claimed her own in a clash of teeth warped with possession, but she forced herself to disassociate even further.

She couldn't let him win.

Rome.

Alara thought of Rome and sank further into the mattress and the dark recesses of her mind as Lukas loomed over her. She would survive for him and the happiness that they could have. He would come for her. He had to, because thinking he died would only cause her to rush to meet him in that afterlife. He would come for her.

ROME decapitated yet another Rogue with the brutality of a seasoned warrior gone berserk. His fangs dripped blood along with his swords, his eyes pulsed with the violence that sang through his body, and power careened through his veins in stronger waves than he knew how to handle. All around him was chaos. Dead bodies littered the floor, fires burned in various rooms up and down the hallway from spilled beakers and flammable objects while his warriors continued to fight off the remaining Rogues and humans that continued to attack. The enemy refused to yield. His men had arrived only moments ago but had immediately jumped into action, and still, he had yet to find his mate. He scented her everywhere, and yet there was no sign of her, and his mind was going haywire with the possibilities of what she could be experiencing.

He was stalking down the hallway that seemed to have no end when a man in a gray jumpsuit ran from a room and directly into his chest. Rome yanked him up by the collar of his shirt and snarled menacingly as he looked him over. Why did almost every single man here seem scrawny and nerdy with wire-rimmed glasses pushed over their noses? And why was the man in his arms currently pissing his pants? The smell of urine caused his nose to twitch in distaste as he pulled him closer to speak through bared fangs that refused to retract.

"Where is Lukas Titan!?"

The weasel of a man pointed a finger down the long hallway. His voice came out small and tinged with utter fear. "L-last door b-back. T-t-the d-door has a h-handprint sensor. It's t-t-the only way in."

"And what do you do here," he glanced down at the name tag dangling from his left breast pocket, "Louis?"

"I w-watch the s-s-subjects."

His stutter was annoying, and the smell of his urine even more so. Rome forced himself into the man's mind, rearranged his memories, and created new ones to make him forget the last few years of working for Titan before he dropped him unceremoniously to the ground in an unconscious heap. He gave himself only a second to see that his Guardians were handling the rest of Titan's employees before he headed for the last door at the end of the hall.

Alara's scent was more pungent here, along with her fear and desperation. It caused his stomach to cramp violently before he threw his entire body into the door that was clearly lined with silver. It flew inward. His eyes immediately locked onto the men restraining his mate between them as Lukas rutted between her legs.

The sight caused a rage like nothing he'd ever experienced to flow through him as he launched his swords across the space between them. Lukas received a blade through his spine while his guard was thrown backward by the velocity of the sword as it embedded into his chest before Rome sent Lukas flying through the hair with a flick of his wrist. A sickening crunch shattered the room's silence before Lukas fell limp. Rome shot across the room until he was standing above his mate.

Her right eye was swollen shut, bruises and marks covered her flesh, and the unmistakable scent of another man's cum filled her. Her eyes were unseeing as she stared at the ceiling, no signs of life residing within her gaze. He gently grasped the offending metal around her throat and snapped it in half before cradling her in his arms and pushing healing waves into her body. The pull of her gift was strong as she began to siphon from him almost immediately. He allowed it and watched as her wounds healed before his eyes. Something cool and wet slid across his cheeks as he pulled the sheet from the bed to drape across her lower half before stepping from the room. The wetness that fell from his eyes to splash against her skin was a sight he hadn't seen in several years. He was crying. Tears that seemed foreign and unnatural poured down his face in rivulets, but what shocked him even more was the feeling of utter helplessness as he headed for the nearest exit. Getting her as far away as possible was his main objective. He cared for nothing else. He'd failed her. He hadn't been quick enough, and the guilt was eating him alive.

He sent a telekinetic message to Silas and Erick as he boarded the elevator. *"I found her. I want you to burn the establishment to the ground. No one gets left behind."*

Silas responded in record time. *"What about the innocents?"*

"Save the Kindred. Fuck everyone else; let them burn." He cut off the connections before either of them could voice another question or opinion as he entered the elevator and began his ascent to the top. The Gods could punish him later for killing off the humans who weren't fully corrupted yet.

He wished his gift of teleportation could get them out of there faster, yet each time he tried, he was met with a barrier while his other gifts worked perfectly fine. Something powerful was blocking him, but none of that mattered now as he stared into Alara's unseeing gaze.

"Little flower," he whispered and ran a gentle hand along the soft skin of her face.

She didn't respond except to blink. She remained still and stiff against his body as he pulled her closer in an attempt to warm her. Her power continued pulling at him, giving her face a brighter color, yet her eyes remained dim. She even refused to look at him. He attempted to breach her mind and met a stronger mental barrier than she'd ever had before. A sickening fear filled him as he stared down at the woman who had come to mean everything to him. Something had been taken from her. That light that seemed to glow out and into him was now diminished, put out like a flame that had never existed. He couldn't feel her within him or scent the happiness and passion that usually flowed through her blood. The scent of cool water and jasmine had been erased and replaced with an emptiness he didn't know how to fill.

"I'll get you home. I can help you heal." He brushed his lips against her forehead and snarled harshly, "I'll bathe in the blood of the ones you have hurt you and get your revenge. For you, I'll burn the world."

CHAPTER
THIRTY-THREE

Alara stared out at the rushing waves of the shore, her shirt and pants clinging to her skin as the wind beat against her. The urge to walk into the water and never come up tore at her mind and filled her thoughts with the possibility of finally lifting the weight that seemed to press against her chest. It had been weeks, three to be exact, since Rome had carried her from the Titan warehouse, and still, the actions of that day attacked her very being like a scorned lover on a rampage. Her skin felt forever dirty, her insides felt like they belonged to another, and the man who insisted on shadowing her every move felt like a shackle she didn't want. He feared for her mentality, worried about what she would do now that she thought she was forever broken, but there was nothing he could do about it. There was no way he could help her; there was nothing she wanted done, and in fact, she just wanted to be left alone. She wanted to drift away like the waves in the sea and find herself sinking beneath the layers of the ocean to forever stay trapped in the darkness. At least there, she wouldn't have to relive what had happened to her, she wouldn't have to think, and she could just be.

She pulled at the fabric of her shirt as she continued to stare out at the waves. Rome had brought them to a private island where he owned a home large enough for him and his warriors, yet they all had stayed behind in Van Scive to continue their duties. He occasionally left and brought a few of them by to visit, or Erick would ride over on a boat and dock it at their pier, but for the most part, it was just them unless he brought her brother over for a few days at a time. Alaric was here now, sitting silently beside her as he gave her her moment. He never pushed or tried to get her to talk; he simply stayed beside her in mutual silence. Since the attack, she hadn't spoken to anyone. It wasn't that she couldn't. Oh no, she could speak, but what would she say? She damn sure didn't want to talk about what had happened. Alara just wanted to forget, and she wanted everyone else to forget as well, especially Rome.

Rome was angry every second of every day with eyes that constantly watched her. She could feel the guilt that radiated from his pores whenever he was near. She could hear the caution in his voice when he spoke, his tone practically pleading for her to talk to him. Rome wanted her to express herself and tell him what had happened that day and what he could do to fight her demons. Little did he know that there was absolutely nothing he could do. He'd already tried and failed. Her demons had escaped and were now in the wind, and there was no telling when that demon would be back to cart her away again.

After getting her far away from the Titan warehouse, the rest of the Guardians scoured the building and hunted down everyone involved in the capture and torture of the Kindred and Eternals. Silas had been tasked with locating Lukas and making sure the bastard was dead, yet he and his guard Blakely had been long gone before they burnt the building to the ground. The only good thing to come out of it all was the release of several Kindred men and women. Cairo had been ordered to place them in different homes under the guardianship of several immortals across the world to better protect them, while Akio was ordered to search and locate where Titan had moved their home base. Alara kept up with everything happening around her, even when Rome tried to shield her from the dirtier parts of what they did to gain the upper hand in the war against Titan. The only hard part to hear was that Lukas was in the wind, and no one had a bead on his location. She thought she could handle this. She thought she could live another day to fight again, but instead, Alara found herself wishing that she had died in that fire as well.

Was this what depression felt like?

Had she fallen so far that death seemed like the better option?

"It won't help," Alaric commented as his fingers dug into the softness of the sand before he cupped a handful, only to watch it slide through his fingertips in a haphazard waterfall. "I won't lie to you and say it gets easier because I can't even begin to understand how you feel. What I do know is that it isn't easy getting past trauma and fighting those thoughts that tell you to just give up. I've been there, but the answer isn't your death. The answer is to fight harder than you've ever fought in your life to prove to yourself as well as your enemy that you won't let them win. You can't let them win, Angel."

She strengthened the barriers of her mind when she realized that the only way he could possibly know what she was thinking was if he had read her thoughts. God damn him if he did because if he was capable of reading her, then so was Rome, and although he was halfway across the world hunting down Titan Rogues in an effort to get answers, she knew that it was still very possible for him to read her thoughts from a distance. Their mating had made that possible. Since the night he'd carried her from the warehouse, Rome had changed. He had become stronger, faster, and more brutal than before. He was on a mission, and it was a mission he refused to let anyone thwart him in. With newfound strength and power, there was no telling just what he was capable of, but everyone knew he was out for blood.

Alaric broke the silence again as she dug her toes deeper into the sand as the sun slowly descended from the sky. "Rome is taking me back to Van Scive to check on Alondra." She flinched at the mention of their sister's name even as he pressed on, "I'll return in a day or so, but when I do, I'm going to need something from you. I need something that tells me you won't really just give up and try to end it all because you can't keep going through life like this. It isn't healthy. You need to talk and express yourself, even if that expression is anger. I can introduce you to one of the Kindred they saved if you want. Her name is Brianna, and she went through something similar to you. Maybe if no one else understands, then she can."

For the first time in weeks, Alara turned to her brother, parted her lips, and spoke, her voice sounding just as broken as she felt. "So she was pinned down, stripped, and raped by a man she absolutely loathed? She was beaten and nearly electrocuted to death just so this man could impregnate her with his child and tie her to him for the rest of her life? Did she have to force herself to dissociate just so she could escape the pain and humiliation of having someone take what she wasn't willing to give?" Her voice grew in strength with each word she spoke. "If she wasn't beaten, raped and nearly impregnated by a savage monster, then no, I don't think we have much to relate on, so I think I'll pass. And in the future, can we just stick to silence because I don't want to talk, so just leave me be okay?"

Alaric stared back at her with a devastated expression on his face before he reached out to gently wipe away the tears that had begun to trail down her cheek, yet she flinched away from his touch. He opened his mouth to probably feed her more words of encouragement when, instead, a darker, more compelling voice spoke from behind them and sent Alara's heart rate soaring.

"Not likely, little flower." Rome stalked towards them from the large beach home with his dreads dripping wet from the shower. His chest was bare while black cotton sweatpants clung to a narrow waistline. His eyes shot to Alaric, "Leave us, brother."

Alaric stood and left her to deal with Rome alone without another word. Normally, her brother would fight to protect her, even from the man striding towards them, but in recent weeks, the two had begun to bond in a way she hadn't anticipated. Now, they were working together to get her out of her slump. She watched as Rome took his place beside her on the blanket while his eyes ran over her in a slow perusal, and the slight tick within his jaw told her that whatever he was about to say wouldn't be something she wanted to hear. In fact, everything he said lately wasn't something she wanted to hear. She knew that, in some ways, Rome blamed her for what had happened. There was no way he didn't because even she blamed herself. She shouldn't have been so trusting, shouldn't have called him to save her, and she should have fought harder. All of those thoughts battered at her mind like a ram against a gate as she stared into his furious blue gaze.

Rome reached out and stroked his finger casually against her exposed throat, where her pulse beat vigorously. She tensed beside him, yet she didn't pull away as she had with Alaric. His gaze hardened and softened just as quickly, but he didn't move back. "Tell me, little flower, would you lessen what happened to her because she didn't go through the exact trauma as you? Is her pain and suffering meant to mean less?"

She shook her head solemnly. That woman's pain wasn't less than her own; she knew that, and yet the only way for anyone to understand her would be to go through what she had gone through. How else would anyone know her pain and what she struggled with? It wasn't something she could see anyone else understanding unless they had stood in her shoes.

"I've met Brianna, and although her story is not yours, she did experience trauma that changed her. She was scarred and broken in more ways than one, but her story isn't mine to tell, so if or when you feel up to it, maybe you can speak with her and see what I see. For now, I'm simply happy to hear your beautiful voice again." He continued to caress her throat and watched her slowly relax beneath his touch, "good girl," he whispered.

Alara gasped when her core tightened in remembrance of what they shared. A part of her missing that connection and wanting it back, but the thought of penetration caused her stomach to turn violently, along with the remembrance of Lukas calling her a good girl as well.

"No," he snapped and grasped her chin in a crushing hold, "what was that look for? Where did your mind go?"

"It was nothing," she lied.

"That wasn't nothing. What was that look of disgust for? What have I done? Is my touch now repulsive to you?"

Alara gripped his wrist when his hold on her chin tightened

marginally. She knew he would never hurt her, but her fear wasn't hers anymore. She didn't know how to voice how she felt or how to tell him what the actions of another had done to her or how it had reshaped what she saw in the world and what she saw in men and how they would now look at her. It didn't matter to her that Rome would never hurt her. It was the fact that he was that much larger, that much bigger, and that much stronger than her in every way that simply drove a stake through her heart. If he wanted to take anything from her, he could, and what could she possibly do? How would she stop him?

His voice softened along with his grip. "Little flower, I can't help you if you don't tell me what's going on. What is it? What have I done wrong?"

"You've done nothing," she whispered, her voice sounding much smaller than she'd anticipated. "Everything you've ever done was to protect me. Romulus, you've never failed me. I failed myself, and now I have to live with that. I have to live with the fact that I trusted too easily and a man we both hate has now ruined me for the man I didn't know I needed. I'm broken. I'm so broken that I can't even see all of the pieces that have fractured."

"Why do you think you're broken? You're still healing from a trauma that should have never happened. Tell me what I did to trigger you. Was it my touch?" He released her slowly, although the need to keep that connection was vital for him. If he could never stop touching her, he would.

"Your touch and praise made me remember what we shared and how fierce our connection was, but it also scared me because I don't think I'll ever be able to have that again without feeling sick to my stomach or…thinking of him. He said those same words to me that day. He called me his good girl."

Her eyes strayed back to the waves rolling and batting at the shore. It was safer watching the waves tumble and crash than meeting his gaze and seeing the disappointment that was sure to follow her statement. She didn't want to be a disappointment for him. She didn't want to be something he regretted or pitied. Alara didn't think she had it in her to be what they once were. She didn't know how to overcome that fear and uncertainty or the disgust that would rise if they attempted to push past the boundaries she now had. She felt tears streaking down her cheeks at the thought of leaving a relationship she desperately wanted with the man beside her. What else could she do? Alara refused to hold him in place or be the shackle that left him unfulfilled and neglected within their relationship. If she could even call it much of one now.

"Was? Have your feelings changed towards me? Do I remind you of him somehow or was it just the words?"

Her gaze whipped back to him as shock covered her features. "Of course it's not you," she snapped.

"Then maybe what we need is to create new memories to rid ourselves of the old." He stated. "If you want, I can erase the memories you have and replace them with new ones. I can make you forget entirely; maybe that would help you heal. As for me telling you you're a good girl, that won't change. He won't take the pleasure you find in those words away."

She thought about it, but it didn't take her long to see the issue. "My body will remember even if my mind doesn't, and why would I want to forget that moment? What if I'm pregnant, Romulus? What if he was successful in getting what he wanted?"

"I can assure you that you are not pregnant, little flower." He reached out as if to caress her cheek yet decided against it and simply let his hand drop back to the blanket. "I've known for several days now that your menstrual cycle will be starting soon, and each night, as you sleep, I do a health scan on your body before I leave for the night. And as far as your body goes…well, I'm sure we can make new memories for you if you truly wish for it. I can't process another life for us. If you're thinking of walking away from us I don't think I'm strong enough to let you, but I'll respect your need to not be intimate."

Relief filled her at the news. It was an emotion she hadn't felt in a while, but the feeling of it swept through her like a tsunami, and she found herself launching forward before she could think better of her actions. Her arms wrapped around Rome's throat as her body came flush against his in a fierce hug. The fear she thought would grab hold of her didn't, and the thoughts that usually ran rampant within her mind finally settled. She could breathe a little easier, and what she smelled was heavenly. She inhaled Rome's clean fragrance and took in the scent that first captured her attention when they'd met. He smelled like warmth and safety. He smelled like hers.

His arms wrapped gently around her waist before pulling her until she straddled his lap. She tensed at first but quickly relaxed when she realized he wasn't holding her tightly or keeping her hostage. She was free to pull away if she wanted to, and when she glanced into his eyes, they told her as much. With every look and breath, he told her without words that she was safe with him even after everything she'd done.

"You really would never hurt me, would you?" She whispered.

Rome cupped her cheek as his blue gaze brightened further. "I would die before I ever hurt you, Alara. Haven't I proven myself already?" His thumb tracked along the fullness of her bottom lip before his eyes fell shut. "Even with everything that's happened between us, I would never harm you. From the lies, deceit, and dishonesty, I have never wanted to hurt or cause you pain. Question you? Yes, but hurt you? Never! All I want in this world is to keep you safe as I protect the rest of the world from my enemies. To have you by my side as I do would be my greatest accomplishment. You are everything, little flower; everything and more. Even if you don't see it. I don't know what to do to prove that to you."

Alara simply stared back at him. Since coming into his life, she had upended it, but he'd taken it in stride. He protected her even when she withheld information or blatantly lied to protect herself and her family. He became her shield and sword whenever she needed him. Rome had become her everything. She could trust him. He'd proven that to her over and over again.

She cupped his cheeks within the palm of her hands and watched as his eyes flickered open when she spoke with a hushed voice. "Just love me." She pressed her lips against his softly at first until the remembrance of him triggered her mating response and caused all of her erogenous zones to spark to life. Maybe she wasn't as broken as she'd thought.

THIRTY-FOUR

Rome gripped Alara's hips in a gentle hold, although every part of him screamed with the need to conquer and dominate the woman who was currently grinding softly against him. He could smell her hunger and desperation, yet he held back. He'd be damned if he triggered her in any way. He never wanted to be the reason why her mind traveled back to that awful day. He would only be her light in the darkness. He would only be her joy.

He stilled her movements and slowly pulled away from her tempting lips. "What are you doing love?"

As badly as he wanted her to continue, he also knew that she'd been extremely hesitant of his touch only seconds ago and downright terrified. Whatever this was, he needed it to be authentic and not just a knee-jerk reaction to finding out the news of not being pregnant. He refused to be another bad memory or even a mistake to her. She needed to be sure that this was what she wanted.

"You want me to love you," he stated, "but you need to tell me what that means for us. I'll follow your lead and let you control whatever this is, but I need to know what you want."

Her expression turned sheepish, almost embarrassed. She bit

her lip as her fingers tugged softly on the ends of his dreads. "I want to fix us. I want to fix me."

"There's nothing to fix, little flower, because there's nothing wrong with you. How does this feel with you being on top of me like this? Is this triggering you in any way?"

"No, I like this." Her small fingers kneaded the back of his neck like a newborn kitten as she smiled shyly. "This is the most normal I've felt since that night. Whatever this is, I want to keep going. Romulus, he didn't win."

Rome settled her lower half against his own, lining his erection up directly with her wanton center. He would leave nothing to chance. He was hard and ready but refused to pressure or push her into something she might not want. He needed her to know what moving forward meant for him. If it meant the same for her, then he would stop at nothing to make this moment as memorable as possible for them both. He would stop at nothing to put her fears to rest and erase the actions of the last sexual encounter she'd had.

"You'll tell me if you become uncomfortable?" He questioned.

At her soft nod, the restraint he'd held onto snapped in half. He curled a hand around her throat and dragged her face down until their lips met in a feverish kiss that stole the breath from his lungs. He'd missed this. Missed her. Her scent enveloped him as she fell deeper into his embrace, and her softness melted against his hard body. Her tongue licked hesitantly against his bottom lip and caused his fangs to descend. He smiled and groaned hoarsely when her petite body rubbed against him. Alara's palms trailed along his skin as their kiss deepened, and his hand on her hip snuck beneath the fabric of her shirt to caress her lower back and urge her to rock into him. Her small moan was swallowed up by his tongue thrusting into her mouth. Her nails dug into his shoulder when he slipped a hand beneath the waistband of her pants and gripped the globes of her ass. His other hand tightened around her throat seconds before he moved like lightning and had her splayed out beneath him.

Alara tensed up the second her back touched the blanket, and his body pressed against hers. The scent of her fear turned his blood to ice as he slowly drew back to gauge her reaction. A paleness he'd only seen once before was written clear across her face, and her eyes were glued to the sky. She was trembling now, and it wasn't from pleasure. She was terrified. It bled from her skin like an open wound that refused to scab over and heal.

Rome quickly launched away from her before he spoke softly, hoping to pull her mind away from the dark corner it had crawled into. "Alara, sweetheart, I need you to talk to me and tell me you're okay."

She didn't respond at first, and he was half tempted to approach her and shake her out of her dark memories, but he knew that, ultimately, that wouldn't be good for her. He didn't need to be the cause of any more of her trauma. Dammit, he hated this. He cautiously tried to penetrate the layers of her mind and was surprised when he met no resistance. Her walls were down, and the actions of that night from several weeks ago were playing on repeat within her mind. He heard her silent screams, felt the disgust that she felt for herself, and watched as every part of her soul began to fracture and break from the pressure of her memories. He wanted desperately to erase them and fill her mind with better ones, but he knew that wasn't what she wanted, so he had to find a way to pull her out of this. He needed to bring her back to reality and somehow teach her that what had happened to her was not her defining moment. He had to teach her that she was not broken nor tainted or unwanted. To him, she was everything and more.

Rome was done going easy on her. He refused to let her become a shell of herself or allow that bastard Lukas to continue to reside within her mind when he deserved nothing. He moved beside her to lay on his back and forced her body to spread atop his own before he gripped her chin and forced her eyes to connect with his. Her hands were pressed against his chest, her knees lay on either side of his waist, and her core was once again aligned with his cock; although his erection had long since lost its hardness. At first, Alara didn't respond, but the longer he stared into her eyes and whispered her name into her mind, the more he saw reality creep into her stare. Finally, she blinked only to glance down in embarrassment at his chest, where her small nails had dug into his pectorals.

347

"I'm sorry," she whispered.

"Don't be sorry. Just tell me what we can do to fix this. Was it being on your back that triggered you? Would you rather be on top?" He questioned and forced her to meet his eyes once more. "I need transparency, little flower because I intend to get you through this. Not just for you but for myself as well. I can't watch you curl into yourself and lose all the joy I saw you building since the moment we met. I can't bear seeing you this way."

"Y-yes. I don't want to be on my back. That's how he had me."

Rome wasn't used to bending to the whim of another. He wasn't used to bending at all for anyone but the Gods he followed, but for his mate, he would do anything. He couldn't believe he had forgotten how he found her. "Okay. No back." He ran his hand up the front of her body and paused at the pulse that beat frantically within her throat.

His eyes fastened onto that erratic beat as his fangs began to lengthen in hunger. It had been weeks since he'd adequately fed, and his body was starting to feel the effects of that hunger, but no amount of blood he attempted to ingest would do him justice. It wasn't Alara's blood, and since their mating, his body had changed and morphed into something he hardly recognized. Her blood was the only kind that sustained him for longer than a day. It wasn't just the mating that had changed him. The blessings Athena and Nemesis had bestowed upon him also affected him. His shadow wings didn't just grant him the ability to fly or exact vengeance on his enemies, but they awarded him the ability to withstand the sun completely. They also changed how he tele-ported. That had taken some getting used to, and while others couldn't see them unless he willed it, they were always visible to him. With the healing of his mind, he'd mastered a tranquility he'd never known was possible. He could breach even the toughest of mental shields if he tried, yet somehow, Alaric was still impene-trable unless he lowered his. All in all, he was a fiercer warrior who wielded the strength and power of a God, but with Alara, he was weak.

She watched him with a furrowed brow as he continued to stare at the pounding rhythm of her heart. She swallowed harshly, "When was the last time you fed?"

His hands had moved to her waist, where he ran lazy circles against her exposed skin as his gaze slowly trailed back to her face. "Since our mating, I've only been capable of feeding off of you without becoming sick to my stomach, but while I've been giving you space I've had small sips here and there. If I happen to keep that blood down, it doesn't sustain me for long."

Her expression turned thoughtful before she frowned. "Over a month, then?"

"Yes."

"You need to feed Romulus. Why haven't you said anything? I can clearly see how hungry you are. How are you not weak right now?"

He smirked, making her core pulse and tighten in anticipation. "Little flower, are you offering? Can I sink my fangs into your delectable throat and take what rightfully belongs to me?" His cock hardened at the thought of finally receiving her blood after weeks of going without before he trailed his hands farther up her body to cup her bare breasts beneath her shirt.

His snarl was unrestrained, his eyes beginning to pulse as his power thrummed through his bloodstream and his need pulled at him like a starving beast. Alara's gray-blue gaze lightened, and a small smile tugged at the corners of her lips before she slowly tilted her head to the side to expose her throat to him. Need slammed through him, yet he held back. God, the strength it took not to pounce on her was academy award-winning strength, but his hands never paused, and his gaze never wandered from her face. He had to be sure. Rome knew without a doubt that the second her blood touched his tongue, he would strip them both bare and take her in any way he could have her. He needed her to be okay. He needed to know that when he lost all sense of self, she would be there to catch him when he fell, just as he would be there for her. Most importantly, he needed to know that doing this wouldn't cause any new nightmares to crowd her mind.

"You know what will happen once I drink from you?" He tugged at the hard points of her nipples and watched her squirm atop him with a soft moan as her eyes slid shut.

She nodded, but that wasn't enough for him.

"I'll strip you and fuck you. Do you understand?" His hands paused as he silently waited for her eyes to open and focus on him. "Once my fangs sink in, my essence will slide into your bloodstream and cause an instant orgasm that will trigger your need to mate as well. After that, it'll take me less than a second to be inside of your tight wet cunt. Are you ready for that?"

"Can I stay on top?"

He growled low and nodded before he jerked into a sitting position and poised his sharpened fangs right over her jugular. Her scent curled around him, her hands threaded through his dreads as he slowly erected a shield around them. It would give off a hazy view of them—making it nearly impossible for anyone to see them—and protect them from any possible danger. The moment he knew no one could possibly see them, his fangs sank through her skin and into her vein until a drop of her blood touched his tongue and sent his senses spiraling. Her moan of pleasure scoured his balls and sent his fangs deeper as the smell of her sex grew stronger from her instantaneous orgasm. With a single thought, their clothes dissolved, leaving them bare to the wind and sky as he slowly impaled her onto his throbbing erection. Her moan turned into a groan, her nails dug into his scalp as he forced her hips to rise and fall above him as he steadily sucked at the wound on her throat.

He never wanted it to end. Alara's cunt sucked him in and bathed him in her wetness. Her moans constantly vibrated against his tongue as he continued to take in the nectar of her blood, and her hands gripped him tightly as she rode him without restraint. His energy flared and pulsed around them as her power began to pull at him in a demand for sustenance. He extracted his fangs the moment he was satisfied and groaned harshly when her pussy spasmed and her scream echoed around him.

"Good girl," he grunted and shifted them until he was flat on his back, and she was forced onto the balls of her feet. Rome gripped her hip in one hand and her throat in another as he fucked her deeply and snarled at the tight feel of her pulsing and flexing around him. "Take your pleasure, little flower. Don't you dare stop."

She screamed in ecstasy when he bottomed out inside of her, and his balls slapped consistently against the curves of her ass. He hammered into her from below and watched the bounce and sway of her breasts as his hand tightened around her throat and restricted her airway. Her pussy continued to tighten around him, signaling her incoming orgasm before her eyes rolled into the back of her head, and her scream nearly shattered his eardrums.

"Fuck," she whimpered, her blunt nails dug into his chest as her legs trembled beneath her. "Romulus, please." She cried out when he angled his hips until he tapped against her G-spot, triggering another orgasm as her eyes fluttered closed.

"Please, what? Please fill your pussy with cum?" He continued to guide her above him and smirked when her core continued to flutter around him. "Tell me your mine, and I'll give you what you want, little flower. Just say the words." He snarled.

"Romulus…I'm yours."

Those softly spoken words triggered an orgasm so intense that his balls spasmed and stars burst behind his eyelids before his cum filled her to the brim. It leaked from her and began to run slowly down his balls, but he refused to pull out. No, he had every intention of remaining inside of her until well into the night. The visceral need to own her in all ways took hold of him and held him hostage, but he didn't mind it. Alara was his, and she would never know differently.

Her soft body fell limp against him, her eyes slid shut, and her breath evened out as it brushed against the nape of his neck. He chuckled and rubbed circles into her back as euphoria filled him along with the feeling of contentedness he hadn't felt in a while, yet in the back of his mind, he knew he still had things to handle. Before he forgot, Rome lowered the barriers of his mind and searched for Erick's signature until he sensed him rousing from his slumber.

"Sir?" Erick questioned, *surprise and caution evident in his tone.*

"I'm expecting an update on the doctor that created the virus using my mate's

blood, and I need the location of that bastard Lukas. I need answers, Erick. You'll have three hours to get it if you haven't already. Gather the others to assist, and I'll be seeing you soon."

"Of course, sir."

Rome slowly replaced the barriers around his mind as he continued to rub circles into Alara's back. He chuckled softly when she moaned and shifted above him to get into a more comfortable position before his eyes drifted shut. He had three hours to bask in the afterglow of sex before his duties took over, and he wouldn't waste a minute of it thinking about anything but her.

CHAPTER
THIRTY-FIVE

Alara sat comfortably curled up on the couch with a throw blanket covering her lap as she patiently waited for the rest of the warriors to return from their nightly hunt. Shortly after waking on the beach to find Rome sleeping peacefully beneath her, she discovered him still hard as a rock within her. Attempting to climb from his lap had caused him to awaken and take her once more before he'd teleported them back to his home in Van Scive to allow her more rest before this apparent meeting. She'd been happy for the reprieve, glad to be alone for the first time in weeks as he'd left her to sleep, yet she hadn't slept. Instead, her mind had raced, and her heart had continued to pound in her chest at the remembrance of him inside of her, claiming her and running away all of the dark memories that had overtaken her mind. Falling under the seductive power of Rome had shifted something within her. He had brought her back to the woman that had been growing since her first successful escape from Titan. A new light had filtered in and found a place, banishing the darkness that had consumed her every thought. That light gave her a sense of peace and calm that she hadn't felt in the past three weeks, let alone the entirety of her life trapped within Titan's walls. She wasn't completely over what had happened to her but this was a start.

Rome abandoned his position in front of the fireplace and approached her. His thick dreads were pushed back and twisted into a severely tight bun atop his head. He was decked out in his all-black garb with a long-sleeved v-neck and slim-fitting jeans that hugged every muscle he owned, including the massive erection he was sporting beneath the zipper. His clear blue eyes were brighter than they'd been hours ago, and his full lips were quirked up into a warm smile as he gazed at her with heat before crouching in front of her. One of his hands easily slid beneath the cover and rested on her knee before he moved it up higher and rubbed soothing circles into her thigh. He curled his other hand around the nape of her neck and dragged her closer until he kissed her and stole her breath from her lungs.

"Are you okay, little flower?" He whispered against her lips.

Alara smiled against his lips and kissed him back before she replied. "I'm better than I've been in awhile, thank you for checking on me."

"Of course."

"I didn't know it would be this type of meeting," Akio chuckled as he walked into the living room. He must have come from the lower levels where the control room and monitors were since he carried his laptop loosely at his side. "Will you two need a minute?"

Rome smirked against her lips and stood swiftly before approaching Akio and pulling him into a brotherly hug. "You're early. That's a first. Normally, I'd have to pry you from those monitors to get you to do anything except maybe hunt."

"True, but this…this is a meeting I'll happily attend since I have good news. News everyone I'm sure would love to hear."

"We'll wait for the rest to arrive before you tell me what you've found."

Akio nodded in agreement just as Cairo, Maverick, and Silas stepped into the house wearing equally grim expressions. It told Rome all he needed to know about their night. They hadn't successfully found the needed information, but Rome would still be asking to make sure. He wouldn't just assume that they had failed, but their expressions didn't give him much room for hope. They needed the scientist and the man who'd inherited a disgraced legacy meant to destroy his people. They needed Lukas Titan.

Amirishka and Erick trailed in from the direction of the lower levels, with Alaric walking silently behind them as he approached his sister and took a seat beside her. His arm dragged her into his side before Alara tucked her head into his chest in a tight hug. They'd just been together a few hours ago, but this was the first time she reciprocated his affection in three weeks. Their interaction on the beach must have given her enough comfort to feel okay with someone else's touch, but he would be watching his mate closely to ensure she stayed that way.

Rome started the meeting, his voice rumbling throughout the large space, garnering everyone's attention even as they spread throughout the room to sit, stand, or lean against the wall. "Did you locate Lukas?" He spoke to no one in particular since they each had been tasked with finding him or the doctor. He hoped for nothing but good news.

Cairo spoke up first as he stood stoically against the wall. "Lukas is in the wind, and we can't get a lock on him, but we believe he has siblings. We've picked up chatter about a charter plane coming into town carrying several people who are supposedly related to him by blood. We believe they are coming in for a meeting, but we haven't been able to pinpoint where and when it would happen or when and where the plane would be landing."

"We've failed you," Maverick commented from his position on the floor beside Alara. This had quickly become one of Maverick's favorite spots to sit whenever she was around. After their interaction in the woods weeks ago, they'd quickly become close friends, and since then, he seemed to never leave her side unless ordered to do so. At first, it had bothered Rome because, at a point in time, he knew that his Guardian had cared for his female in a way that wasn't strictly platonic. Now, he viewed it as another Eternal capable of protecting his mate if, for some reason, he could not.

"You haven't failed me yet; besides, Akio says he has information we'd all love to hear."

"Wait," Amirishka frowned in annoyance. "So we're just going to ignore the fact that Cairo just said it's very likely that more Titan scum would be entering our territory, and we have no idea when and where?"

Alara spoke up from her relaxed position and gripped her brother's hand tightly in the process. "He has three siblings. Two younger brothers, Evan and Ezekiel, and a sister, Tori, but I've never met them. On occasions, he would speak of them when he would force me to dine with him, but I don't know much about them."

"I was part of Lukas's inner circle and knew of Ezekiel. He's just as sadistic as his older brother, probably even more so." Alaric commented. "I never knew they had other siblings."

"Interesting." Cairo approached Alara from his still position against the wall as his turquoise-purple eyes flickered with uncertainty. "Maybe if we knew why he was so obsessed with you, we could figure out his next move and where he would be. It's obvious that his family is only coming into town because he needs assistance of some kind." His gaze flittered to Rome, "Or maybe there's another reason. Didn't you say you hurt him during the rescue? That you pierced his spine with a blade? There's no way he could have survived that."

"But I know what I scented when I checked the room after they left," Maverick snarled. "He was gone, and so was that damn guard of his, and I scented no other within the room. The only scent I picked up was of their blood, which led me to a hidden door I couldn't access to follow after them, but by that time, you were already setting the place ablaze with your flames."

"But how did they just get up and walk away? Someone had to have helped them, but how? And where was this hidden door?" Erick interceded even as his gaze remained steadily out the front window. "Someone was waiting for an opportunity to get them out…someone who clearly valued their lives enough to save them."

Silas froze, his eyes gaining a faraway look before his voice went eerie with the weight of his vision. *"Deception she is, wrapped and warped in beauty. She will be the catalyst, the one to complete his soul, but first, he must die. Break down her walls and win her heart, or watch your brethren fall."*

They each watched as Silas seemed to come back to himself. His expression remained sheltered, and his body remained tense before he glanced around the room with a frown as he rubbed at the back of his neck. His nervousness was evident. Visions for him were always accurate, but at times, they weren't something he even realized he was doing. Rome believed that the Greek Goddess of sight and vision, Theia, was the reason for it. It was true that the Gods only spoke to him, but that didn't mean they wouldn't or couldn't talk 'through' another.

"What did any of that mean?" Alaric questioned as his relaxed position turned tense.

"No one ever knows what his visions mean," Amirishka scoffed as she pulled one of her hidden blades out to twirl between her fingers. "What do we do about this family reunion? Clearly, Lukas is alive somehow after surviving Rome's blade, and he's summoned them here, but how do we find out what for?"

Akio raised his hand from his seated position on the other end of the oversized couch. "I think I know the answer to that." He opened his laptop, his fingers flying recklessly over the keyboard as he scanned the files he'd compiled within the last few hours. "Now, I couldn't get anything on this elusive doctor, and although Cairo fried all of the systems and burnt the warehouse as well as the lower levels to ash, I was able to find footage of a black nondescript van on the traffic cams a few blocks away. The issue is that you never see where it came from. It just simply appeared."

"Lucas." Alara shuddered.

"That was my guess, so I followed the van until the driver stopped at a gas station several miles away, and I got this."

He rotated the laptop until the whole room could see the still photo of a small form climbing out of a van. Their face was covered with a blue ball cap, and a sweatsuit covered their body. Akio flicked to the next image, where their back was facing the camera after closing the door to the van. He had zoomed in on the back of their neck where a small waning crescent moon sat starkly against pale skin.

Alara gasped as Alaric tensed beside her. "They're Kindred." She whispered in awe, "We all have the same mark."

Rome frowned. "Play the rest of the tape."

Akio hit play, and they watched as the Kindred ran into the gas station before running back out with multiple bags loaded with God only knew what. Their movements were sure and decisive. They moved like someone who knew what they were doing, and at no point did the cameras catch sight of their face. The only thing that stood out was the mark on their neck. It was the only identifying feature, and as the video shifted between traffic cameras, they watched the van progress through the streets of Van Scive until they finally lost sight of it due to the blind spots along the roads.

"That's all I've got, but at least now we have somewhat of a head start," Akio commented as he closed the laptop with a smile. "We just have to find them. They disappeared somewhere along the upper west side of the city."

"Then I suggest you all head out into the upper west side and find them before the sun has time to rise in the sky," Rome stated as his eyes drifted to his mate's closed-off expression.

Amirishka paused in her knife play. "Am I free to hunt as well, or will I be watching the prisoner down below?"

Alara flinched at the reminder of her sister remaining locked up within a cell in the lower levels. Since their escape, that's where Alondra had been placed and where she would stay. There was no telling when or if she would ever have the freedom to walk around as she had once done before, and quite frankly, Alara didn't think she could ever trust her again enough to allow that. Not after what she had done, not after her betrayal.

"I'll remain behind with my mate for tonight." Rome held out his hand for Alara to grab before he pulled her up from the couch and into his waiting arms. His lips pressed firmly against her forehead before he pushed a thought into her mind. *"I'd like us to continue where we left off, little flower."*

She smiled and tightened her arms around his waist when Alaric

360

spoke from his position. His voice was solid and sure, while his eyes depicted a man fighting a losing battle. "Allow me to go out as well. I'm steady with a gun, I never miss my mark, and my hand-to-hand combat excels any Titan operative they could ever pit against me."

"Even the Rogue vamps?" Maverick smirked as he climbed to his feet, "I find that very hard to believe."

"You're still affected by the virus." Alara turned within Rome's arms to pin her brother with a glare, "What happens if you're out there and something happens? You've been experiencing dizziness, nausea, and headaches that sometimes even my healing can't combat against. What you need is rest."

"No, angel, what I need is the doctor who created this damn thing so that we can come up with a cure before it's too late. If we can get to them through this person in the video, then that's what we should do, and I should be allowed to help. It's my life in jeopardy. It's my life that's hanging in the balance. I should have a hand in the downfall of my enemy."

"But-"

"He's right, little flower." Rome tugged her closer to his chest as he met her brother's stare, "You'll pair up with Silas tonight. He'll be the easiest one to reach me if anything should happen while you're out in the field. Make sure you're dressed in our garb, and you wear a bulletproof vest; we have a few on standby. I figured you might want to join our ranks one day, so I altered a few things for you. Silas will show you where."

The silence in the room was deafening, yet no one went against Rome's statement. Each of his warriors nodded in understanding before they headed out for the night while Silas and Alaric trailed toward the bedrooms. Rome waited with bated breath before he slowly released his mate. He could feel her anger. It radiated from her, and when she spun around, the emotion was clear and evident within her gaze. She was furious.

"If you think for one second we're finishing what we started earlier, then you are sadly mistaken." She snapped as her hand slapped against his chest, "How could you be okay with him going out there?"

He tilted his head to the side, his eyes eating her up as he envisioned all of the ways of getting her undressed and inside of her before he focused on the argument she clearly wanted to have. "Would you rather he sneak out like a thief in the night? Because I promise you, mate, he would have done exactly that. At least now we have someone we trust watching his back."

"He wouldn't have snuck out if I had asked him to stay."

"Would you like to chance that?"

She glared at him, misty gray-blue eyes narrowed in annoyance before her expression softened. "I just want him safe."

"And he will be. With Silas." He pulled her back into his arms and smiled, "Two telepaths working together might be beneficial. They won't need to speak at all while they're out, and if anything should happen, then either one of them could reach me a lot faster than if I had paired him with one of the others."

"Okay, that may be true. So what do we do now?"

"I was waiting for you to ask that."

His eyes flashed with hunger, his fangs dropped, and his lips captured hers in a brutal kiss. He teleported them to their bedroom as his power sizzled around them, enveloping them in a cocoon of sexual energy and telekinetic power that sent their clothes falling from their body with a single thought. Alara sucked at his lip and licked at the sharpness of his fangs. The need within them soared to higher heights as Rome pressed her body up against the nearest wall and pulled her legs around his waist. The heat of her core was warm against him, tempting him to simply slide into her depth. He knew she was wet enough to take him and wanted him just as he wanted her, but he needed to hear the words she'd only whispered into his mind.

Rome gripped her around her throat and pulled back just enough to look into her lust-filled gaze. "I need you to repeat it?"

"Repeat what?"

She gasped when the tip of his erection brushed the wet folds of her cunt, and his hand tightened fractionally around her throat. It was never in anger, and it was never something that made her feel uncertain or afraid; instead, it lent her strength. It was a strength that allowed her to see just how much she affected this powerful man who led an Immortal group of beings. The fact that he felt such a loss of control when it came to her wasn't lost to her. The knowledge that she meant so much to him warmed her in ways she had never experienced until coming into his life. He had quickly become a large piece of her just as she had become one for him. They were two halves of one whole.

"Back when you were a captive, you told me something when you thought it might be the last time we ever spoke." He loosened his hold and gently massaged the fullness of her bottom lip. "Do you remember what those words were?"

Alara nodded hesitantly, unsure if she could usher those words again. "You want me to repeat what I said?"

"Only if you mean it, little flower." He shifted them, making sure to apply pressure as he slowly sank into her warmth. "Say it if you mean it, and I'll give us what we both need."

She chuckled softly, cupped his cheeks, and whispered the words she never thought she would get to say in person. "I love you, Romulus. Through everything, I love you."

"Good," he snarled and sank the last few inches of his cock into her. He watched her face morph into pleasure as a mini orgasm ran through her and forced her warm core to strangle him in a tighter hold. "Give me three more."

Rome knew he wasn't asking for much as he lifted and dropped her onto his straining erection, his hips cocking back and forth as he pounded into her and took her like a starved man. His fangs glistened under the room's lighting, his eyes zeroed in on her jugular, and he struck, sinking deep into her carotid as another orgasm washed through her. It was too soon, yet the grip of her center forced his own release as he sucked at the base of her throat and groaned when she moaned around him and climaxed again.

He released her throat, licked at the wound, and watched it heal beneath his gaze before he looked into her eyes. "I love you too, my little flower," he whispered, capturing her lips in a slow, drugging kiss.

EPILOGUE

Six Months later

Alara stood at the threshold that led into the lower levels of the house she now considered home and debated whether she should descend or hold off for another day. It was early, and Rome had yet to return from his nightly hunt, yet every other Eternal was already in bed for the day. This was the perfect time for her to confront her sister. She needed to know why she had done what she'd done and why it had taken her so long to realize the truth. She'd chosen the wrong side within this war, and the trust she had once had in her was possibly broken beyond repair. Now that things were somewhat settled and her mental health was better than it had once been, Alara felt like this was another hurdle to be jumped, so she would jump.

Gripping the rail tightly, she descended the steps, passed through the infirmary, and approached the cells where her sister sat unmoving on a cot in the center of hers. Alara hadn't seen her sister in months, yet she looked exactly the same, and it looked as if Rome had wanted her to at least be comfortable down here. A small night-stand and dresser had been placed within the cell, along with several books on a small bookshelf. There wasn't much room to move around inside due to the items they'd given her, but she didn't seem to mind.

Alondra glanced up the moment Alara approached the bars. Her expression became sheltered as she looked her up and down before a soft smile graced her lips. "I'm glad to see you looking better."

"Yeah, no thanks to you." Alara couldn't keep the anger from her voice when she spoke, "Can you tell me why you did it? Why did you give me up? Did I really mean that little to you?"

"Is that really what you think? My choice wasn't easy by any means. I did it for us. I did it to escape the people I thought were our enemies. I did it to protect you. It may not have seemed like that then, but I didn't know Lukas was the monster he turned out to be."

Alara began to pace as thoughts filled her mind, pushing her following questions forth. "So you were never forced to do things while we were captives before Alaric got you out? Did you truly never know his cruelty and how dark it could get? If so, I'm glad you never had to endure torture at his hand, but if you did, it begs the question of how you could turn on your flesh and blood after I had finally found happiness."

Alondra stood and approached the bars cautiously. "Lukas told me we were at war and that I had to build endurance in case I was ever captured. I needed to be able to withstand any form of torture if I was ever taken by the enemy. He needed me to be capable of handling anything, and so I withstood it. Everything he threw at me I overcame and then some. I refused to be a disappointment to him like I was to his mother. At least with him, I wasn't overlooked and seen as less than nothing." She sighed heavily, "I was seen, Alara. He made me feel important. Cherished even, and so when he told me I needed to retrieve an operative that had been taken, I jumped at the opportunity to please him. I didn't know it was my own flesh and blood, but by then, it was too late to go back on what I had promised him. It was just too late."

"It's never too late to do the right thing. According to Romulus, you proved that in the end. You showed remorse for what you'd done and told him where he could find me. Even before that, you tried to help me in the smallest of ways, but where does that leave us now? How can we ever trust you not to deceive us again? How do you propose we move past this? You've been down here for months yet you seem okay with that. Don't you want to get out of this cell?"

"Is that even possible?"

Alara didn't pause even as she tugged recklessly at the hem of her shirt. Was this something she could get past? She wasn't entirely sure, but she had to try. She hadn't yet moved past the events of that day and what Lukas had taken from her, but she had grown from it. She no longer saw herself as a victim; instead, she saw a survivor whenever she looked at her reflection. She trained with Amirishka and Maverick daily until she was sweating buckets and panting for breath. Every day, she learned a new technique so that in the future, if she was ever retaken, she could fight harder and keep herself safe if her powers were ever neutralized again. At first, Rome had been hesitant to let her get thrown around by his warriors, but he had quickly learned that training her to fight was something she would never budge on. No matter how many times he'd attempted to persuade her with orgasms, Alara had stood firm against his unique brand of torture until he finally relented. Still, everyone had under-stood that Rome could be nowhere within the vicinity while she practiced. The first time he'd witnessed Maverick with his hands around her throat, he'd attacked and almost killed one of his closest friends. They'd learned from that mistake.

"I think if you prove yourself, we can get on a better page with each other." Alara finally responded, "We'll never be what we were, but maybe we can be better than that. Maybe we can actually be sisters."

Alondra clutched at the bars of her cell and smiled softly. "I'd really like that."

Alara finally stopped pacing and turned to face her sister with a similar smile on the edge of her lips. "Then I'll talk to Romulus about letting you out of there. He'll be home soon, so we shouldn't have long to wait. Once I speak with him, I'm sure he'll let you return to your room on the upper levels with the rest of us. He'll want to see into your mind."

"It's okay, I understand."

Alara moved to speak again but instead thought better of it and simply reached out to place her hand against the back of her sister's knuckles before she turned and headed up the stairs. She wanted to stay and talk longer, maybe get to the heart of why Alondra had truly deceived her because there had to be more to it, but she knew for a fact her mate would be returning home soon, and she wanted to be waiting in bed when that happened. She smiled wider at the thought of what he would do once he got home yet paused the moment she stepped into the living room to find her mate standing patiently beside the couch with a closed-off expression on his face.

———

ROME STOOD STOICALLY beside the couch as his gaze raked over Alara with a feral look. She shouldn't have been downstairs visiting her sister, but there was nothing he could do about it now. He'd heard the tail end of their conversation and wasn't yet sure how to digest it. He didn't think her sister deserved an opportunity to redeem herself, but he wanted his mate comfortable, and if that meant letting her sister free from her cell, he could make that happen. Would a guard be on her ass constantly? Of course. There was no other way he would have it until she could prove her loyalty, but he had other matters to discuss with his wayward mate.

"You lost, little flower?" He questioned with a smirk, "Shouldn't you be upstairs waiting with my breakfast?"

"I figured it was time to tear down another wall and speak with my sister. I'm sure you heard the tail end of our conversation, so, don't you think it's about time we allow Alondra to come up and integrate herself into the family?" She responded quietly and crossed the room until she stood before him with only a breath separating them.

"I'll see what we can do about that once I speak with her alone. Would that please you?"

"As long as you're actually going to give her a chance to get into your good graces." She smiled softly. "Now, if you'd like breakfast,

I'm sure I could remedy that for you." She cocked her head to the side, exposing her throat to his gaze.

He reached up to run his fingers over her pulsing vein and chuckled. "I'm sure you could mate, but we have much to discuss. We'll talk in our bedroom." He pulled her into his arms without another word and dematerialized, only to end up at the foot of their bed with Alara now staring up at him with a frown.

"What's wrong? You never turn down my blood, especially when you've just returned from a hunt."

He stared down into her loving face, unsure if he wanted to disturb the peace they had built over the last few months. What he was about to reveal had the potential to fracture the foundation of what they had built so far, and being the reason for that fracture caused fear to stir within his heart. She might never look at him the same. She might even go so far as to leave him where he stood. Numerous avenues were possible.

"There are things you don't know about Eternals that even my Guardians are unaware of. Secrets that could tear us apart or bind us together." He cupped her cheek and ran his thumb lightly over the plushness of her lips as her much smaller hands reached up to clutch his wrist. "I need you to know that I never said anything because I was forbidden to, but now...well, now I can't see you hurt, even if it may cause the Gods to rain down hell upon me."

"Then you shouldn't say anything," she whispered, her eyes looking back at him in earnest before his gaze locked on the large diamond ring that sat on her ring finger. She'd agreed to marry him only days ago and he never got tired of seeing another symbol of his connection to her.

"It's about Alaric."

Her face screwed up into a frown. "What about my brother? Is he okay? I just healed him last night before you all went out? Was he hurt? He never came to me when he returned with Silas."

Rome caressed her lip lightly as a war took place within his mind. He had to tell her the truth. "He wasn't hurt, but back in the warehouse, when I was being tortured, you told Lukas that Eternals couldn't be made. Do you remember that?"

"Of course I do, why?"

"Because we can. We can be made, and I think I can heal your brother entirely, but in doing so, he'll become like me...an Eternal. This is a closely guarded secret for good reason, but once I heal him, my warriors won't be too happy with what I've kept from them."

"You're telling me he'll no longer be sick? That he won't die?" He nodded and watched as tears gathered in his mates eyes before she hugged him tightly and whispered. "Heal him. Whatever you have to do, you heal him."

Rome hugged her back as his mind wandered. There was no guarantee that Alaric would agree, and he might have been bringing another war to their doorstep. This time, with the very beings that had created him and his people in the first place. It was possible that even within the ranks of his Guardians, there would be dissent once they learned the truth. His hands tangled into Alara's hair before he kissed her forehead. The fight was over for them, but the war was just beginning.

ACKNOWLEDGMENTS

To have a support system that's there for you and believes in you enough to push you for the things you want to achieve in life is honestly one of the best feelings in the world. When it came to writing this book, I wasn't sure if I would even finish it or what trajectory it would have with every chapter I wrote, but along the way, I did have people who pushed me to finish and urged me to do the one thing I love to do. And that is to write.

So, I want to thank the people who have stood by me during this entire process. To my sisters, Toya, Mica, Brii-Ann & Diviniti, and my brothers, Ronald & Al'Zander. You guys have pushed me my whole life, and I love you each individually in my own way. The strength you guys have given me through everything is more than I could ever put into words, and I appreciate each of you sincerely. I love you guys to the end of time.

To my best friends Rohmel, Melissa & Ronita, words couldn't express the gratitude I feel for each of you. Rohmel, you've been my closest and longest friend and the person who has stood by me through everything. You're the rock I never knew I needed and a bit of an inspiration for my MMC, so thank you, truly. Melissa, I want to say thank you for coming into my life and becoming one of my closest friends. You are indeed an exceptional being, and I love you to the ends of the earth for loving me as a sister and my best friend in the only way you can. Ronita, you beautiful soul, I love and appreciate you for being there through everything with me. Your patience with my shenanigans needs to be rewarded.

If you weren't mentioned personally, know that you played a part in helping me finish this book and pushed me to never give up on my baby. Thank you to the people who have always believed in me, and I hope you keep pushing me to create the magic I do when I type.

ABOUT THE AUTHOR

Tasha Taylor is a full-time Telemetry technician who enjoys writing as a hobby but wants to make it into a career. She's been writing since the age of seven; whether it be poetry, short stories, or novels, writing has always captured and held her interest, as well as reading a well-thought-out book. She enjoys spending time with her Mainecoon Eros and her friends and family in her free time. With this book, Ms. Taylor hopes to reach those who want fantasy, love, and everything in between.

www.ingramcontent.com/pod-product-compliance
Lightning Source LLC
Chambersburg PA
CBHW051445260626
47162CB00001B/255